"I must find my enemy and kill him."

Morgan patted the rifle, the cutlass, and brace of pistols he'd brought from Astoria. Whatever else happened, he had a debt to repay. Lone Walker, though a stranger, had risked his life for him.

"I shall stand with you," Morgan told him.

"There are many of the enemy."

"I shall stand with you."

"And White Buffalo has stolen a sacred power. His magic is strong. It is said no man can destroy him."

"I shall stand with you," Morgan repeated.

"Why?" the Blackfoot asked, still puzzled.

"Because you are my friend."

"Friend?" said the Blackfoot brave. He stood and clasped the forearm—wrist to wrist—of his companion, the white man, Morgan Penmerry. "Let it be so."

SCALPDANCERS

Kerry Newcomb

BANTAM BOOKS
NEW YORK · TORONTO · LONDON · SYDNEY · AUCKLAND

SCALPDANCERS
A Bantam Book / August 1990

ISBN 0-553-28560-2

Published simultaneously in the United States and Canada

Bantam Books are published by Bantam Books, a division of
Bantam Doubleday Dell Publishing Group, Inc. Its trademark,
consisting of the words "Bantam Books" and the portrayal of a
rooster, is Registered in U.S. Patent and Trademark Office and
in other countries. Marca Registrada. Bantam Books, 666 Fifth
Avenue, New York, New York 10103.

PRINTED IN THE UNITED STATES OF AMERICA

RAD   0 9 8 7 6 5 4 3 2

For Patty, Amy Rose, and P.J.

Elkhorn Creek

PROLOGUE

1814
In the Time of the Muddy Face Moon

What do you want of me? Why don't you speak? Above Ones, send me my dreams, give me my vision. I will follow my dream quest wherever it may lead.

I cannot bear the silence. The stillness in my heart, the shadows on the wall of the sweat lodge mock this poor one.

I hear the chanting in the village. I hear the water's song as the ice cracks and life returns to Elkhorn Creek. And still, Cold Maker, you imprison my spirit. Morning will soon come to the world beyond the sacred circle of this spirit fire. Four days have I fasted. And four times this night I have crawled on hands and knees into the sweat lodge and brought wood to the sacred fire. I have sprinkled the flames with cedar. I have made offerings to the four horizons and prayed and sweat. My limbs shine with moisture; the breath burns in my chest.

Just five mornings past I was in another place where the earth trembled beneath the hooves of a buffalo. I raced the wind and the smell of blood was in the air and I rejoiced to know there would be glad songs in the lodges of a hungry people, my people.

Maiyun, *do not abandon me. All-Father, my spirit follows the path of the sacred smoke. Find me worthy, Great One, give me my vision.*

A man could get killed . . .

Sixteen hundred pounds of buffalo bull broke through an ice-crusted barricade of Russian thistle and took the first horse on the tip of its short curved horns. A brown mare neighed in anguish and its rider, Waiting Horse, kicked free. The bull raked horseflesh, disemboweled the mare, and veered toward a second tormentor, a Blackfoot brave who raised his short bow and loosed an arrow at the enraged animal. The shaft bit deep into the bison's tender hide just behind the shoulder, yet the bull never lost a stride. *Iniskim* was hurt and knew who had done the hurting. The animal bellowed and charged straight for the brave on the mountain-bred gray.

Lost Eyes notched another arrow. The gray mare responded to the pressure of his knees and cut to the left to avoid the buffalo's charge. Without warning, the plucky little gray went down, its forelegs buckling; the ground underfoot gave way as a prairie dog burrow caved in on itself.

Lost Eyes jumped free of his mount and tossed his bow aside. The last of his arrows spilled from his otter hide quiver. He landed shoulder down in a patch of snow, plowed a furrow in the white-mantled grass, and rolled to a stop a few yards from where he had landed.

He felt the earth tremble against his cheek and willed the world to cease its dizzying spin. Gathering his strength, the brave waited until the last possible second and then shoved himself out of the bull's path. The buffalo rushed past, an unstoppable avalanche of fury, as Lost Eyes slipped over the edge of the draw and slid to the bottom of an eight-foot drop in a shower of pink shale and loosened earth.

Two days of sunlight had scoured much of the meadow of snow, but here in the shadows of the draw Lost Eyes sank midway to his calves in a crusted drift. Shaking the grit from his long braided hair, he clawed his way back up the slope and reached the meadow in time to see Waiting Horse, the young man afoot, attempting to limp out of the path of the buffalo. But the great shaggy beast would not be denied this day and bore down on the helpless youth.

"Ho-hey-a, Iniskim!" Lost Eyes shouted and waved his hand, hoping to distract the buffalo.

The animal stumbled and lost a stride, then continued its attack. Waiting Horse glanced over his shoulder and cried out to the All-Father. He tried to run, but his leg had been injured by the falling horse. His ankle wouldn't support his weight.

Lost Eyes ran to his bow and searched wildly for one of the arrows he had lost. He found one hidden beneath some trampled grass, fitted the feathered shaft to his sinew string . . . Too late. He looked up just as the bull caught Waiting Horse on the tip of its horns and tossed him high in the air. The young man flopped to the earth and disappeared beneath the cruel black hooves of the beast not a hundred feet from Lost Eyes.

The Blackfoot sighted and launched a second arrow, but at that distance the arrow was only a nuisance to the bull. The first arrow, through the lungs, should have been a killing shot. However, the beast refused to die. *Iniskim* altered its course yet again but quickly lost strength and labored for breath as blood filled its lungs. Lost Eyes, enraged over the fate of his companion, welcomed another attack. He gathered another couple of arrows and hurried to catch the reins of the gray mare as it struggled to its feet. Lost Eyes swung up onto the gray and spied a trio of horsemen coming from the far end of the valley: the other members of the hunting party. They rode at a gallop across the snow-checkered meadow, anxious to be in on the kill. They must hurry, thought Lost Eyes.

The bull, though dying, lowered its head and charged. Its reflexes were dulled now and its speed diminished, but *Iniskim* was still dangerous at close quarters.

Lost Eyes leaned forward on the neck of his mount and rode straight toward the buffalo.

"*Ha-hayiia, Iniskim!* Horned killer, this day your flesh will nourish my people!"

Lost Eyes was a young man in his seventeenth winter, built strong and lithe, and he sat his horse as if he were one with the galloping mare. The horse's breath mingled with his own, clouding on the cold high-country air. Waiting Horse lay broken and lifeless in the buffalo grass, but Lost Eyes forced himself to concentrate only on the deadly beast bearing down on him.

Horse and rider rapidly closed the gap. Lost Eyes' pulse quickened. The young bull bellowed and plunged toward the gray mare. But the horse quickly danced aside, and the bull viciously swiped empty air. Lost Eyes twisted; the bowstring snapped his left wrist on release; the arrow flew straight and true. Its hardened-sinew warhead passed a rib and pierced the bull's fighting heart.

The beast staggered another twenty yards from the sheer momentum of its charge. Then its legs gave way and the animal collapsed and rolled on its side. The buffalo kicked fitfully for a moment, then settled into death.

Lost Eyes rode around his kill and hurried to the side of his fallen friend. He dismounted and knelt by Waiting Horse. The young brave was still alive, but the light was fading fast, and Waiting Horse, seeing the steam rise from his ravaged belly, began his death chant.

"All-Father,
I have run with the horses,
I have stalked the blackhorn antelope
And stolen the feathers of the hawk.
But today *Iniskim* has killed me.
I am young, not old. A young man should die
In battle—an old man in his lodge surrounded
By his children.
I am in neither place.
Find me, All-Father.
Let me not wander in search of you.
Let me—"

Waiting Horse grimaced. His features were deeply etched in pain. The dying man's eyes opened and for a moment he recognized the brave at his side. Lost Eyes' hair was unadorned with eagle feathers. His buckskin shirt and leggings were simple and bore no markings or designs. No spirit symbols linked him to animal or element or to the power of the Above Ones. These were things received in visions. And he was Lost Eyes. He had yet to walk in his soul. He had yet to see what was beyond seeing.

Waiting Horse knew him even through his pain-clouded vision. He reached up and touched Lost Eyes' features, smearing the man's cheek with blood.

"Now you are marked," Waiting Horse said in a dry, rasping voice. He lowered his gaze to his own ripped belly, a curious expression on his face. After all, it wasn't every day a man saw himself with his insides torn out. Suddenly he arched his back. Lost Eyes struggled to hold him down. Then Waiting Horse relaxed and fought no more and entered the Great Mystery.

Lost Eyes looked to the ice-glazed ridges lying golden in the sun and the gleaming snowcapped peaks of the Big Belt Mountains stretching across the western horizon. These were barrier ridges of bald-faced granite rising above the tree line, a veritable wall of mountains broken by a gap several miles to the south where a high-country meadow threaded its way across the Continental Divide, the Backbone of the World.

In this meadow the Scalpdancers had settled along the banks of Elkhorn Creek. It was a place of beauty—one that Waiting Horse would never see again. But the mountains in their sun-bright mantle of gold were places of power where a man's spirit might ride with the Above Ones forever. So Lost Eyes looked to the mountains as he waited at his friend's side. The other hunters would be there soon.

The camp fire made a beacon in the night and led the last four stragglers out of the darkness of ponderosa pines and barren-limbed aspens. Two travois, one bearing a

buffalo carcass, the other the blanket-wrapped form of
Waiting Horse, entered the circle of light.

The arrival of the four caused quite a commotion among
the half-dozen Blackfeet huddled near the flames, especially when the one travois's tragic burden was revealed.
Waiting Horse had been a popular youth, well liked by
young and old. Lost Eyes dismounted and ground-tethered
his horse while the other braves clustered around the slain
man. Only Wolf Lance, who had hunted alone this day
and returned to camp empty-handed, made the effort to
approach his friend. Wolf Lance was a year older than Lost
Eyes and carried an extra twenty pounds on his chunky
frame. His moccasins padded across the hard-packed earth.
Joy and sorrow mingled in his expression.

He asked only one question, how? and listened without
recrimination as Lost Eyes recounted the events of the
hunt. The rest of the Scalpdancers who had ridden with
Lost Eyes lost no time in embellishing the tragic death of
Waiting Horse and shifting the blame onto Lost Eyes.
Many of the Blackfeet standing by the travois had grudgingly
joined this hunt. Men had died on other hunts, but they
believed nothing good could come of keeping company
with the man called Lost Eyes. The Above Ones had
turned away from him. Why tempt disaster by riding with
him? In the end they had listened to Wolf Lance and
Waiting Horse and joined the hunting party. And now,
after five days, they had nothing to show for their efforts
but one buffalo and one corpse.

Their voices carried on the still night air.

"He counseled us and called us women because we
feared," Black Fox said. "See what has happened." He was
a burly man of twenty-three, the oldest of the party and a
natural leader by strength of arms and cunning.

"Waiting Horse is dead. We warned him," Tall Bull
added. A man of average height, he was quick in battle
and two Crow scalps decorated his buckskin shirt.

Another brave, Broken Hand, whose deformed left hand
had only two fingers and a thumb, carefully tucked the
blanket beneath the corpse. He had been closest of all to

Waiting Horse, and when he lifted his gaze, it was to focus blame on Lost Eyes. He stepped around the travois and started across the clearing as Lost Eyes moved toward the camp fire. Broken Hand blocked the other brave's path.

Broken Hand's braided hair adorned with two eagle feathers and the beadwork patterns on his buckskin coat revealed he had fulfilled his vision quest and could be called by a man's name. He was a proud man.

"No," Broken Hand said to Lost Eyes. "You will not share our fire. You have done enough. We will finish the hunt without you."

Lost Eyes tried to step around the man only to be shoved backward. Lost Eyes batted the brave's hand aside. Broken Hand grabbed for the war club dangling from a rawhide tie at his side. He jerked the weapon free and raised it threateningly.

Lost Eyes made no move toward a weapon of his own. He merely stood his ground, his brown eyes gentle and filled with remorse. Yet there was no weakness in his stance. Though he grieved as much as any of the others, he would not accept blame for the death of Waiting Horse.

"Now will you slay me, Broken Hand, and take my scalp to hang upon your coup stick?"

Broken Hand glanced at the weapon in his hand. Slowly, reason returned to his expression, dimmed the fire in his gaze, dulled the urge to exact a vengeance that wasn't his to seek.

"Strike him!" Black Fox shouted.

"I will not." Broken Hand lowered his war club and shoved the wooden shaft back through the rawhide loop at his waist.

"Strike him. Are you a woman to fear him so?" Black Fox snapped, his hand upon the travois. "He killed your friend."

"*Iniskim* killed my friend," Broken Hand answered.

"Your words, Black Fox, do not fly straight. They are crooked with the jealousy that wishes to keep Lost Eyes from calling your sister to his blanket," Wolf Lance said, seeking to distract the hunt leader.

Two braves by the travois nodded in agreement, and as hunger overcame their sorrow, they fell to butchering the buffalo carcass. The animal's organs were quickly sliced away and carried to the camp fire.

Black Fox stood silently apart from the others for a while, then followed the aroma of roasting meat back to the fire and sat near Tall Bull.

Lost Eyes squatted near the flames and let their warmth leach the chill from his limbs. He took comfort in Wolf Lance's faithful presence.

"Someone must bring Waiting Horse back to our village," Broken Hand said.

"I will do it," Lost Eyes said and looked up into the faces of the hunters. "Then you may continue the hunt without me and perhaps find good fortune."

No one offered a different suggestion. Lost Eyes didn't expect them to. By virtue of their silence, they assented. In the morning Lost Eyes would depart, taking his ill omens and misfortune with him, riding a lonely trail southwest, with naught for company but dark thoughts and a dead man.

This is a cold trail. I will follow it no longer. It is toward a vision I began. But the path is as fleeting as a shadow and I am the shadow walker, waiting to be made whole, to walk among my people as a man.

Show me my spirit sign. All I see is what has been.

Lost Eyes entered the village at midafternoon. The same cold breeze that tugged at the newly budded aspen limbs ruffled the fringe of his buckskin shirt and leggings. Clouds scudded across the cobalt sky and cast their churning shadows on the valley floor.

The spring that fed Elkhorn Creek flowed from the side of a craggy ridge at the north end of the valley. Icy water seeped from a gaping wound in the slope, wore a furrow in the topsoil, and broadened into a creek about as wide as a young man could leap. The creek followed a course parallel to the bordering hills and meandered out into a meadow of yellow buffalo grass before it petered out a few miles from its source.

The Scalpdancers, a Blackfoot tribe numbering about one hundred seventy families, had settled their village against the northern ridge close to the spring. Under attack, the men, women, and children could flee upslope to the safety of the pine forest and higher still to the natural battlements of weathered granite ranging the length of the ridge like the exposed spine of some massive primordial beast.

Sometimes it is the sound rather than the sight of home one remembers most, the wonderful country longed for in the solitude of lonely odysseys. For Lost Eyes, home meant the bubbling of the spring that nourished Elkhorn Creek and the noises of children among the circle of tepees in the Blackfoot village.

Horses, grazing along the creek, whickered as the hunter approached on his gray. Boys afield laughed and challenged one another and fired their small bows at an escaping ground squirrel. Women sang as they gathered roots, carried water from the creek, or cooked. The faint rasp of scraping knives on drying deer hides lingered in the air, mingled with the creek's own rippling music and a chorus of barking dogs announcing the arrival of Lost Eyes as he paused on the edge of the village.

For a moment the scene held, one of those brief fractions of a second when the sun seemed to pause in its westward trek, and a wondrous sense of peace filled Lost Eyes' heart.

Then the reality of his world intruded upon his thoughts: He was a man without a vision, and homecoming was not always a time of joy.

Several braves rode out from the village at a gallop, renting the stillness with their wild cries. They would have made a threatening sight to an enemy. Lost Eyes only smiled; he knew them all by name. They were youths on the verge of manhood, their heads already full of glorious deeds and daring days to come. Their enthusiasm faded as they saw Lost Eyes not only led a packhorse laden with meat but a second horse bearing a dead man. Three of the Blackfeet immediately took up a position behind the travois, forming a makeshift guard of honor for the dead man.

As old men and women, girls and boys, paused to watch, Lost Eyes rode straight toward the cluster of tepees adorned with the arrow markings of the Bowstring Clan.

Fool Deer, the father of Waiting Horse, saw the travois and recognized his son's horse. He stood; a shaft of wood and a stone tool used for straightening the shaft fell from his grasp. His wife, Many Walks Woman, rounded the lodge. She had been bathing with her sisters, and her shiny black hair was plastered to her skull. She entered laughing at some tidbit of gossip her sisters had just revealed, but the merriment ended abruptly and her brown eyes widened with astonishment.

Lost Eyes dropped the reins of the packhorse and then reverently handed the reins of the travois horse to Fool Deer. He was a good-natured man, but in this hour his demeanor was as formidable as a thunderhead.

Many Walks Woman ran to the travois; a stifled cry escaped her as she sank alongside the blanket-wrapped remains of her son. Her sisters, Berry and Dancing Creek, had already begun a lilting wail, a chant soon picked up by other wives of the Bowstring men.

"The meat is yours," Lost Eyes told Fool Deer in a gentle voice. "Your son has given his life that our people might have food."

Fool Deer glanced silently at the packhorse and then back at the man who had brought his son home. Fool Deer's expression revealed his black thoughts: A man without vision brings misfortune. It had happened before; it would happen again.

"My son rides with the Above Ones," Fool Deer said in a hollow voice. "But who, Lost Eyes, will ride with you?"

* * *

Beat the drums for me. Play softly the ceremonial drums and face the four winds. And sing for me, Sparrow. Keep within me, and keep me in your heart. I will play upon my flute. I will call you out into the night. I will open my blanket to you, that we might stand together in the night, beneath the glimmering camp fires of the Above Ones.

Breathe the warmth. It flows around me, through me. Sweat stings my eyes and I am blind. No matter. What I seek lies within. Like dreams. Like Sparrow.

Lost Eyes rested on his bulrush bedding, his spine against a willow backrest, and watched Moon Shadow, his aunt, move her ungainly form about the lodge. Lost Eyes' mother had died in childbirth; his father had fallen to a Crow lance three years ago during a retaliatory raid against the traditional enemies of the Blackfeet. Moon Shadow was the only mother Lost Eyes had ever known. It was said that she had been taken to wife once long ago, and that her husband had been a cruel, ill-tempered man who had whipped her unmercifully. The people of the village had little tolerance for such behavior. The husband was eventually driven out, but Moon Shadow chose to live in the lodge of her deceased sister and care for the motherless boy.

Moon Shadow sang softly to herself as she brought Lost Eyes a rawhide bowl of boiled venison. Rolls of fat hung from her arms, and perspiration streaked her round, flat face. Her hair, streaked with silver, hung in two thick braids that rested on her immense bosom.

"Eat," she said as if to a little boy. "I will bring you more."

"There is only one of me," Lost Eyes chided gently. "This will do."

"A scrawny one at that," Moon Shadow observed dryly. "Even the village mongrels do a better job of hiding their ribs." She handed him a spoon carved from bone.

Lost Eyes scooped out a morsel of meat and dropped it into the small sacred fire that burned in the center of the tepee. By such an offering he hoped to please the All-

Father. He took a pinch of cedar and elkmint and crushed bitterroot and sprinkled it onto the flames, completing the customary ritual. Then, with stomach growling, he devoured his meal while Moon Shadow, from her bedding across the lodge, looked on with pleasure. She was as sorry as anyone for the death of Waiting Horse. But she had seen enough of life to accept the inevitable. She was grateful that her son, Lost Eyes, had returned safely.

Sunset painted granite peaks crimson, gold, and deep purple, and left a flourish of clouds that lingered until the first stars glimmered on dusk's dark canvas.

Lost Eyes brushed aside the entrance flap and stepped out into the dying light. He watched the colors fade into night and felt the air grow chill as the earth released what little warmth it had harbored throughout the day. Moon Shadow came out and sat near the remains of the cook fire, banking the coals, then moving a tanning rack nearer to the embers, where the deerskin on the frame might dry a little more quickly. She took a stone scraper and worked the hide one more time. She would repeat the process come morning.

"That will make a good quiver for my arrows," Lost Eyes said.

"*Saaa-vaa*," Moon Shadow retorted. "Moccasins for my feet, selfish one."

A shadow detached itself from a nearby tepee and moved toward the sound of their conversation. The mongrel approached, head down, ready for the first stone hurled in its direction. Moon Shadow tossed a strip of dried meat toward the dog. The animal quickly gobbled up her gift and came forward, tail wagging and licking its shaggy chops.

"You always have some gift to offer us homeless pups," Lost Eyes remarked affectionately. The dog took a second tidbit and then happily scampered away.

"Always the same thanks. You take what I have and abandon me." There was self-pity in her voice. Moon Shadow knew very well where he was bound in the night.

"I always return, my mother." Lost Eyes pulled his pelt

blanket around his shoulders and in so doing dropped a small reed flute he'd hidden inside his shirt. It was a slim little instrument, only six inches long, that he had carved himself. He sheepishly retrieved the flute. Taking care to avoid Moon Shadow's omniscient stare, he hurried from the lodge and walked out to the perimeter of the village.

He circled the encampment and entered from the north, passing among the tepees of the Kit Fox Society, whose members were always first in battle. Black Fox's tepee was near the center of the circle, for he had risen in prominence over the past few years and it was said he would one day sit in council as a chief of the Kit Fox Society.

But tonight, Black Fox was elsewhere. The proud warrior had a beautiful sister named Sparrow whom Lost Eyes was determined to visit. It was dark when he reached her lodge. Across the village, ceremonial drums had begun to sound a low, steady throb, and voices, in unison, sang the song of the dead. Yet Lost Eyes had chosen to stand in the night and play upon his flute for life and love.

Inside the tepee, Yellow Stalk, the woman of Black Fox, placed a restraining hand upon her sister-in-law's arm. "Sparrow, you mustn't." The music of the flute drifted through the hide walls. A series of trilling notes came as rapidly as a bee darting among bitterroot blossoms, then slowed and became more lyrical and enticing.

Sparrow, at sixteen, was ripe like a wild plum, ready to be picked and savored. She was small boned but strong and quick, as strong willed and stubborn as her brother, and like a small bird she endured by being deft and observant. Sparrow wore her hair braided and adorned with clay beads and braid holders of brushed buckskin and porcupine quills. She wore a deerskin dress and calf-high moccasins, a gift from Yellow Stalk.

The wife of Black Fox was older by three years. Yellow Stalk had plain, square features that a smile transformed into a countenance of genuine beauty. She wore a buckskin smock that snugly covered her swollen abdomen, revealing her fourth month of pregnancy.

In truth, Black Fox's wife had been nothing but kind

since Sparrow had joined her brother last autumn. The Blackfoot villages scattered among the northern Rockies gathered once a year, during the time of the Leaves Falling Moon, to renew ties, to tell stories, and to sing the sacred songs. Black Fox had met his wife at such a gathering several years ago and, finding Elkhorn Creek to his liking, had remained among Yellow Stalk's people. Sparrow had merely intended to visit her brother but prolonged her stay throughout the hard wintry months. The village of the Buffalo Grass People, where she had lived, lay farther east, out on the plains. Sparrow preferred the natural windbreak offered by the surrounding mountains. To the north and west lay Ever Shadow, where the terrain became even more upthrust and crisscrossed with rugged glacier-scoured passes: There the *Maiyun,* the Spirit Ones, sang in the lost wind and wandered the high lonesome. The flute song beckoned Sparrow like the voices of the *Maiyun.*

"He is a man without a vision," Yellow Stalk said. "Your brother would not allow it."

"My brother is not here," Sparrow replied.

"But he sees through my eyes." Yellow Stalk wasn't smiling now, and her square features turned severe, her eyes full of admonition. "Wait. Other men will stand in the dark and play upon their reed flutes, and their songs will sound the same."

"No. I will know the difference." Sparrow gently tugged free of Yellow Stalk's grasp and started toward the entrance flap. Flames danced in a circle of stone; shadows played upon the conical walls of the tepee. The fire, the bedding near the blaze, the warmth within—all seemed so safe and comfortable.

Outside, uncertainty reigned. Cries of mourning lingered on the air at sunset. Waiting Horse had been placed upon a burial scaffold on a hillside to the west, a hidden place ringed by aspens, where breezes played and birds sang in the sunlight in the time of the Breeding Moon. Sparrow could sense the safety here in the lodge.

The flute called. There was nothing to stop her now,

save her own misgivings. Sparrow ducked through the opening and abandoned the lodge's familiar warmth for the uncertainty of night and a song that called her by name.

Lost Eyes opened his blanket as Sparrow approached, her face downcast, a timid smile upon her lips. His arm trembled as he settled the blanket around her shoulders. Now that she was finally here with him he didn't know what to say.

So he led her away from the lodges, down toward the creek where the mooncast waters bubbled merrily. Other flutes sounded in the night, adding an eerie counterpoint to the keening wail drifting down from the hill of the dead.

Lost Eyes paused to listen to the lament. Sparrow studied the young man beside her and read the tight-lipped resolve in his expression. He appeared unaffected by the songs of sorrow floating on the currents of night.

"Many Walks Woman will keep her vigil throughout the night," Sparrow said.

"It is night for her." Lost Eyes held his emotions in check, no easy task, for he trembled at the very nearness of the young woman walking at his side. He tensed, expecting her to blame him for the death of Waiting Horse. He said, "Some say it was my doing."

"What do you say?"

"That I loved Waiting Horse like a brother. But he rode too close to *Iniskim* and his arrows did not find their mark. *Iniskim* killed him. Not I."

There was an urgency in his voice, as if he were trying to convince himself more than Sparrow. No matter, she believed him.

He held a branch for her, then ducked as the two of them emerged from a willow grove lining the creek bank. They made no effort to conceal their progress and crunched noisily through the underbrush only to startle a woman kneeling on the creek bank. Owl Bead, the rotund wife of Tall Bull, clambered to her feet, clutched a water bag to her bosom, and beat a hasty retreat, leaving in her wake a trail of water from the unstoppered bag. The formless shadow stalking toward her out of the brush could have been anything. She wasn't taking any chances. Lost Eyes and Sparrow laughed and walked along the creek in the moonlight.

"Poor Owl Bead, now she will alert the camp, crying that a bear has entered the village," Sparrow said.

"Perhaps the men will come for us with spears and arrows."

"And hang our hides upon the tanning racks when they are done." Sparrow stopped and stared down at a patch of ice that had yet to succumb to the spring sun.

Something a couple of yards upcreek had caught her attention, a patch of darkness beneath the translucent barrier of ice, just off the creek bank in the silvery light. Lost Eyes saw it too and drew close to the silhouette. He knelt, as did Sparrow, both of them anxious to discover what was trapped beneath the ice. She found a fist-sized chunk of granite, worn smooth by water, and handed the stone to her suitor.

"What is it?" she asked, leaning forward to peer over his shoulder.

"We will see," Lost Eyes told her and struck the surface a mighty blow that sent slivers of ice exploding up into his face. The river splintered and icy water swelled upward through the wintry wreckage, and up from the silvery shallows a doll floated to the surface, like a corpse rising from its grave. Lost Eyes drew back despite himself, for the doll was no child's toy. It was a medicine doll, the figure of a man carved out of a ten-inch-long chunk of pine. The doll bore a series of markings, Blackfoot by design, but it was the doll's face that caused Lost Eyes to shudder. Some knife had rendered an all too familiar countenance in the wood and placed two white beads like sightless orbs in the carving's haunted facade.

Clouds scudded across the moon, obliterating the light as the now black waters recaptured the doll and bore it into the center of the creek and away.

"What did you see?" Sparrow whispered in a tight, nervous voice.

"Myself," Lost Eyes said.

* * *

The medicine fire is nothing but embers. I could breathe them into life once more. But what is the use? The night is ended. And all I have seen is what has been . . . a death and Iniskim, a woman and a medicine doll. My spirit too is imprisoned. Who will set me free? Even if my vision is black water and mystery, I will bear it. I am weak; my limbs shudder like stalks of buffalo grass before an approaching storm. The sweat has ended and there is nothing to do but live. Sparrow waits without, Wolf Lance too. What shall I tell them? Shall I lie and claim that which I have not seen and earn the wrath of the All-Father? Surely, the Above Ones would curse my deeds and all whom I touched, and the prophecy of the medicine doll would come true.

No. My words will fly straight. It is all I can do. They will ask, who are you now? And I will say, I am a seeker of visions. . . . I am Lost Eyes.

PART I

Macao

1

March 1814

Captain Morgan Penmerry bet everything he had on his cock. It was an Asil, that plucky breed of rooster with plumage the color of day-old blood. The gamecock weighed over five pounds and every ounce full of fight and fire. Its body was compact and powerful, hard as whalebone to the touch. The Asil's beak was short and as nasty-looking as a dirk; its natural spurs had been trimmed to half an inch and a set of silver spurs—looking for all the world like miniature bayonets—were secured on its shanks. Morgan kept the gamecock hooded and his hand never ceased stroking its scimitarlike feathers.

Morgan Penmerry was a broad-shouldered, barrel-chested Cornishman, who at the age of eleven had stolen away on an American merchant vessel out from Bristol bound for Cape Cod. In twenty years he had risen from stowaway to captain of his own three-masted bark. A fur trader, he plied the waters of the Pacific and ranged from the west coast of the Americas to the trade ports of the Far East. Only a couple of weeks ago he had arrived in the Portu-

guese colony of Macao with a boatload of furs and a crew
of rogues ready to unleash themselves upon the crowded
thoroughfares, the gambling parlors, brothels, and rum
houses in the city and in the surrounding emerald hills.
Macao was a place to satiate every vice: There were more
ways to hell than to heaven in the city at the mouth of the
Pearl River. Whore cribs flourished in the cathedral shadows. Brawlers ranged the alleyways a stone's throw from
carefully tended Chinese gardens.

Morgan brushed a strand of his chestnut-colored hair
back from his brow and strode purposefully to the center
of the dirt ring. The air in the fighting house was thick
with the stench of blood and tobacco smoke, the pungent
aroma of brewed tea and salted fish. Here men of means
wagered on a blood sport and fondled their concubines
and drowned themselves in rice wine.

"Captain, you gotta be crazy. You ain't gonna put the
Hotspur on the line?" Temperance Rawlins groaned. He
was a lean, lanky New Englander, a Connecticut-born
graybeard who had known Morgan since the captain's
stowaway days. Temp Rawlins's bushy eyebrows arched up
his broad, blank forehead. Only a few silvery wisps of hair
clung to his skull.

Despite Temp Rawlins's towering presence and advanced
years, it was Morgan Penmerry who carried the aura of
command. He ran a hand through his bushy mane and
swaggered past the crowd of Chinese, Portuguese, Spanish,
English, Americans, and Russians who enjoyed the
Cornishman's showmanship. They greeted Morgan's arrival in the ring with a chorus of epithets and good-natured
challenges.

Derision turned to cheers as he ordered Temp to place a
sack on the ground; the *Hotspur*'s first mate dutifully
obeyed.

The fighting pit was a circular depression dug out of the
earth. Its sides were graded and wooden benches surrounded
the hard-packed earth of the pit itself. The three-foot-high
stone wall circling the arena had been inlaid with shells

and pictographs symbolizing bravery, stamina, and good fortune.

Morgan winked at Temp and nodded to Chiang Lu, a silken-voiced middle-aged man, whose enthusiasm for the sport had prompted him to build the cock pit behind his personal residence on a hillside overlooking the Pearl River above the opulence and squalor that was Macao.

Chiang Lu was particular about who climbed the steps to his hillside villa. Only aficionados of the fighting cocks and only men of wealth were invited to the pit. For now, Morgan Penmerry was a man of wealth. Should he lose, Chiang Lu's servants would summarily escort him to the garden gate. At Chiang Lu's a man's fortunes rose and fell more swiftly than the tides.

"A pretty sack, my honorable friend," Chiang Lu said. He bent down, retrieved the pouch, and opened it. "Curious," he purred as he removed a large brass key. He was immaculately trimmed, and his graceful hands deposited the gold pouch in the folds of his cobalt-blue silk coat. The gold-stitched dragons adorning his sleeves seemed to wink as he tucked the key away. The Chinaman loved to gamble and loved a mystery even more.

"The key unlocks the warehouse at Tung Wan Pier. You will find a shipload of furs and fine pelts within," Morgan said.

His wager was immediately repeated in several different languages.

"A most interesting wager," Chiang Lu replied, eyeing Morgan's fighting cock. "I am told your pelts are always of the finest quality."

"Then match their worth in gold and bring your best gamecock," Morgan challenged.

Temp Rawlins sighed in relief. The wagering hadn't gotten out of hand—yet. He anxiously eyed the bill of ownership jutting from the wide black leather belt circling the captain's solid waist. Morgan had held the bark as a last resort if his bluff hadn't worked. But Chiang Lu had accepted and now Temp could only groan to think of the consequences if Morgan lost. There'd be hell to pay if

Chiang Lu tried to collect his winnings. A fire in the hold of the *Hotspur* had damaged most of the cargo during a squall in the South China Sea. But Morgan Penmerry wasn't a man to take a loss lying down—not while his good-natured, larcenous self could formulate a plan to transform disaster into a tidy profit.

Morgan Penmerry was young and brash and too damn confident for his own good. True, his shoulders were broad enough and, yes, he was as quick and agile as a dolphin at play. But Temp felt the young captain lacked the cool, calm head that a man in his profession needed.

Chiang Lu was as shrewd and dangerous as any man Temp Rawlins had ever known. And this crowd, of every nationality, was armed to the teeth with knives and pistols, and there were several rifle-bearing bodyguards. Chiang Lu's own private entourage, the Blue Wing Dragons, were black-clothed henchmen armed with kris—wavy-bladed daggers of Malaysian origin—and handguns. Their heads were shaved, their impassive faces devoid of pity.

"We cling to life. Even when every breath is agony," Chiang Lu remarked and called for a servant. The servant bowed to his master, Chiang Lu whispered in his ear. The servant nodded and hurried back up the steps to the place Chiang Lu had reserved for himself among the spectators. There upon a dais carved of stone a teakwood chest had been set alongside a thronelike chair. The servant touched a hidden latch and a panel in the chest swung open. The servant retrieved a white silk pouch embroidered with brightly colored blossoms and green lily pads.

"It is a mystery, do you not agree?" Chiang Lu continued.

"What are you getting at, Chiang Lu?" asked Morgan.

"But what is life without mystery?" the Chinese warlord said. He lifted a delicate hand and indicated a couple standing at the entrance to the arena. Morgan lifted his gaze and saw an older man, garbed in black frock coat, black trousers, and cleric's collar. He was a portly middle-aged man.

The young woman standing alongside the reverend was a nubile lass of about twenty—if that old. Comely as a

well-trimmed clipper, Morgan thought. Even better looking—
for what ship could boast of auburn tresses and cream-
colored skin and such an appealingly well-rounded bosom
and derriere?

Her dress was buttoned to the throat. She wore a
charcoal-gray shawl about her shoulders in an attempt to
conceal what nature had endowed her with. Such an
attempt was doomed to failure with a girl like this cleric's
daughter, if indeed that was her relationship to the older
man.

"That is the Christian Missionary Emile Emerson and
his daughter, Julia. I have ordered them to leave Macao;
yet they come to seek terms, hoping I will permit them to
remain. I have refused once before, still they persist.
Why?" Chiang Lu shrugged. "You see, Captain Penmerry,
another mystery. Ah . . . my servant."

The man Chiang Lu had dispatched returned with the
silk purse. Its contents jingled as Chiang Lu tossed it from
one hand to the other. He issued another order to his
servant and the man hurried off.

"Gold sovereigns, the amount of which shall remain
unknown, like the wealth of your furs. I wager one mystery against another. What say you?" His almond-shaped
eyes flashed.

Morgan made a show of trying to decide, when in truth
any amount in Chiang Lu's purse would be more than
what his ruined cargo might bring. The captain glanced in
Temp's direction, winked, then faced Chiang Lu. "Agreed!"

His answer was translated and passed among the surrounding throng. But Chiang Lu was not finished. He had
been carefully appraising the gamecock Morgan Penmerry
held.

"A fine bird. This honorable one hopes he may find a
suitable opponent." Chiang Lu smiled. Morgan's blood ran
cold, for despite the Chinese warlord's civility, there was
not a trace of warmth in his eyes. "I find," Chiang Lu
continued, "I must avail myself of an esteemed associate's
assistance."

"Oh, shit," Temp muttered from behind the captain.

Morgan turned and allowed his gaze to sweep across the audience. Chiang Lu's servant had passed among them and stopped alongside another ship's captain, a man Morgan immediately recognized.

"Demetrius Vlad," Morgan said.

Captain Demetrius Vlad was a known criminal, an exile who, it was rumored, plied the seas not only as an "honest" merchant but kept a pirate's colors as well, ready to fly at will. Of course, such dark tales remained unsubstantiated, for no one had ever lived to offer proof.

Vlad was a man of average height, with finely chiseled, almost feminine features. His brown hair was concealed beneath a purple scarf tied close to his skull and draped down his back. A close-cropped beard followed his jawline and added substance to a slightly receding chin. Vlad carried a bamboo cage under his arm as he descended to the floor of the arena. He wore high-topped boots, as were the fashion, and tight linen trousers and a scarlet waistcoat adorned with brass buttons and gold braid.

His foppish manner did not fool Morgan Penmerry, who knew the exiled Russian to be a skilled swordsman. Vlad bowed to the Cornishman and his host, Chiang Lu.

"I believe you know my esteemed associate," Chiang Lu said to the fur trader.

Morgan's interest was aroused. The Chinese warlord obviously implied a closer relationship with the Russian than Morgan had been aware of. Considering Vlad's reputation, it made sense.

"Captain Vlad has supplied me with innumerable services. He is a most resourceful . . . uh . . . partner," Chiang Lu explained without revealing anything of substance.

Macao was a chaotic port over which Chiang Lu cast a long shadow. However, there were any number of noblemen eager to take Chiang Lu's place in the sun. An unscrupulous renegade like Vlad no doubt came in handy in controlling any serious competition. Morgan wondered if Chiang Lu's home guard, the ominously impassive Blue Wing Dragons, were strictly for defense of Chiang Lu's hillside estate. Might they not be dispatched through the night-lit city to swoop down like birds of prey on some hapless merchant who had encroached on Chiang Lu's economic domain?

"Captain Morgan Penmerry is it? We're old friends," the Russian said in perfect English.

"You'd better rethink that term, Demetrius. It hardly applies to you and me," Morgan said.

Vlad frowned for a second, then chuckled softly. "'By Tre, Pol, and Pen, you shall know the Cornish men,'" the Russian quoted. "And I know you, Penmerry. Rogue, scoundrel, trickster."

"At your service." Morgan bowed grandly with a sweep of an imaginary hat.

"No, at yours." Vlad reached into the cage and withdrew an enormous black Asil, the same breed as Morgan's, but half again as large. The bird had been hooded to keep it docile.

A murmur of disbelief and approval filtered through the crowd, and betting was renewed at a furious pace. Odds were changed at the sight of the big black, and Morgan's Asil became the immediate underdog. Still, there were a few shrewd men who saw past the difference in size and noted in Morgan Penmerry's blood-red bird a quickness and quality of breeding worth risking their gold on.

"Do I detect antagonism in your voice? My, my. How uncharitable. After all, we are so much alike in nature." Vlad added as he stroked the black. "We are both men of the sea. We do not mind bending the rules of a game so long as we win."

"Maybe you're right, Demetrius. However, there are some games I will not play. And in that, we differ."

"Such as..."

"Well— Let's just say the *Hotspur* flies only one flag, that of a free trader, and has no use for the skull and crossbones."

Vlad flushed. The affront left him speechless. Under different circumstances he would have put his glove in Morgan's face. "Out of deference to our host I shall allow that remark to pass," Vlad said, tight lipped and seething from Morgan's insult.

"Then return to your seat. My wager is with Chiang Lu," Morgan said, warily eyeing the black Asil.

"He is my esteemed associate," Chiang Lu interjected, enjoying the confrontation he had instigated. A servant had brought him a plate of *dim sum*—succulently prepared appetizers of shrimp dumplings, morsels of fried taro, and steamed beef balls covered with lotus leaf. Chiang Lu sampled one of the dumplings, then returned the saucer to his servant. He washed down the food with a few sips of chrysanthemum tea. "You will fight the black," the Chinese lord concluded, wiping his fingers on the servant's shirt sleeves.

Morgan shrugged and said, "As you wish." He took his place on one side of the arena. Temp Rawlins followed him, a look of complete exasperation on the old seaman's weatherworn visage.

"Captain, I'm thinking the old brig lizard that raised you oughta be keelhauled 'cause he did a piss-poor job," Temp growled.

"He was a salty dog, but I wouldn't trade a king's ransom for the times we shared." Morgan winked at Temp. "He taught me the love of ships and how to tell a squall from a hurricane."

Temp was not easily swayed by the compliment. "Too bad I didn't learn you when a bluff's gone too far. We'll wind up throat-slit and hanging from a meat stall on the Rue de Lorchas."

"Bah. You're seeing only one side of the coin." Morgan glanced toward the rim of the cock pit in hopes of spying the reverend's daughter, and sure enough, Julia Emerson was still there—watching him, or so it seemed. Morgan bowed. The girl looked startled, caught off guard, and she pointedly turned her attention elsewhere.

"We got enough troubles. A parson's daughter's about as lucky as a dead albatross. You better keep your mind on the troubles at hand," Temp warned.

"Troubles? What troubles? Little Red here is prime."

Morgan's Asil sensed the hour was at hand and the bird uttered a guttural trill.

Across the pit Vlad removed the hood from the black and stepped to the center of the arena. The Russian exile looked bold and confident—and why not? Who faced him but a craggy, crooked-nosed Cornishman with more brawn than brains?

Morgan turned his back to the Russian and nodded to Temp, who wearily held the gamecock while Morgan drew a small amber flask from the sash circling his waist. The slender bottle contained a mouthful of whiskey blended with a fiery curry. Morgan drained the bottle, retrieved the gamecock, and spewed the contents of the flask onto the gamecock's anus. The Asil's brassy caw rose an octave and turned positively shrill. The bird struggled violently to free itself from Morgan's grasp. The fur trader hurried to the center of the arena and held the pain-crazed gamecock inches above the ground. Vlad and Morgan nodded to Chiang Lu, who retreated to the dais. The feathered combatants pecked at each other, eager to battle.

At Chiang Lu's signal a servant crashed two tiny cymbals together. Morgan and the Russian, on cue, released their gamecocks and darted out of harm's way. The Asils hit the ground and attacked.

The Russian's black was obviously accustomed to intimidating lesser gamecocks by virtue of its size. Little Red had no quit in it. And size meant nothing. Pain blinded it. Pain drove it into such a furious state, the gamecock would have lunged for a lion if the beast had been dropped into the pit.

The cocks closed with a flurry of flapping wings, jabbing beaks, and raking spurs. Nothing suited them like combat. They were bred for war like gladiators of old.

The Asils fluttered into the air a few feet, then dropped to the hard-packed earth and rose again, thrusting down with the metal spurs.

The black gave a good account of itself. By rights, Morgan's gamecock should have retreated and perhaps even surrendered, brought down by the wounds streaking its muscled frame, but the curry and whiskey that had blistered the inside of Morgan's mouth drove the smaller gamecock mad—and the madness saved its life.

The black was a vicious fighter, but it had never learned cunning. It was used to having its adversaries crumble before its onslaught. Not this time. Morgan's ploy had left the red berserk. The gamecock felt none of its wounds; it knew only rage.

Little Red was unstoppable; the smaller bird's ferocity overpowered the black for all the latter's size and strength. Slowly, for the first time in any contest, the black gave ground, confused by the savagery that confronted it. And in retreating, off balance, the Russian's gamecock began to miss with its flashing spurs. Blood spewed from a dozen wounds and matted the bird's once sleek black feathers. Suddenly, to the utter astonishment of Demetrius Vlad and his cohorts, the black collapsed, its throat slashed. The gamecock flapped its wings in a fitful, piteous gesture of defeat while its conqueror continued to jab and slash with all the mercy of a Hun.

Morgan gingerly stepped up behind his Asil and caught up the bird. He kept a firm grip on the wings and kept his own lower anatomy clear of those crimson spurs until he'd returned the gamecock to its bamboo cage. Captain Morgan Penmerry turned then to accept the enthusiastic applause of the few men shrewd enough to wager on his success. The rest of the crowd grimaced in disgust as they paid their debts.

Morgan swung around and faced Chiang Lu upon his dais and held the valiant red Asil before him in a ritualistic salute to the owner of the pit.

"I believe you owe me a sack of gold!" Morgan shouted above the crowd.

A gunshot reverberated off the walls of the arena and the cage flew from Morgan's grasp as a .50-caliber lead ball shattered the bamboo and destroyed the battle-scarred gamecock within. The room fell silent and those men with bodyguards darted behind their hired henchmen as the shattered cage bearing the gamecock's bloody remains skidded across the earthen floor.

"I saw what you did." Demetrius Vlad lowered his flintlock. Black smoke curled from the pistol barrel. "That flask was illegal. In this pit you must win your gold fairly."

"Son of a bitch," Temp growled and reached beneath his coat. Morgan stayed the old seaman. The Cornishman had counted three of Vlad's crew seated among the spectators. And then there were the Blue Wing Dragons. True, these henchmen were in Chiang Lu's employ. Then again, so was Demetrius Vlad. So Captain Morgan Penmerry swallowed his anger and kept Temp Rawlins from getting them both killed.

"I have no other gamecock to contest with," Morgan said.

"Neither do I," Vlad replied.

"Then what do you have in mind?" Morgan Penmerry did not like the way Vlad was grinning.

For an answer the Russian exile tossed the pistol aside and held out his hand. His second in command, a beefy Moroccan known as Abdul, handed Vlad a cossack's saber.

"So that's it," Morgan said under his breath. He glanced down at the remains at his feet and recited:

> "Behold a generous train of cocks repair,
> To die for glory in the toils of war.
> Each hero burns to conquer or to die;
> What mighty hearts in little bosoms lie."

It was all he remembered of a poem he'd once discovered in a faded little journal. The words seemed a fitting epitaph.

Morgan Penmerry fixed the Russian in a steel-eyed stare. Vlad, uncowed by his opponent's gaze, advanced to the center of the pit. Morgan glanced up at Chiang Lu. The Chinese warlord seemed unmoved by the turn of events. As for the spectators, they immediately began to wager among themselves as if another two gamecocks had been brought into the pit.

Vlad unfastened his waistcoat to free his sword arm. Morgan, in blousy shirt and tight nankeen pants, was unarmed save for a throwing dagger hidden inside one of his high-topped black boots. But Temp Rawlins carried a cutlass. . . .

"No, sir. This is plumb crazy," Temp moaned as Morgan slid the old seaman's blade from his belt.

The basket hilt fit easily in Morgan's grip. He took a couple of swipes at the empty air to accustom himself to the weight of the blade. It was a common weapon, un-adorned in contrast to the gold-filigreed hilt of the cossack saber Vlad brandished. The cutlass was no work of art, simply a tool—thirty inches of curved, heavy, steel blade jutting from a utilitarian brass hilt and sharpened to a point for thrusting, with a razor-sharp edge for slash and parry. Yes, it was a tool right enough, made for only one purpose: killing.

Gold and notes of credit changed hands at a furious pace as Morgan cautiously stepped within the reach of Vlad's saber. The crowd chattered among themselves as tension grew. "The Russian seems so confident and just look at that saber." "Such a fine weapon and several inches longer than Penmerry's humble blade." "Wager on Vlad, look at his bearing, study his poise." "How can we lose? Vlad is a prancing stallion. And Penmerry, look at him, slouched, thick bodied like an ox."

The two men faced each other and within seconds the silence between them quieted the crowd circling the pit. Here was the ultimate sport. And like ancient Romans, these revelers of Macao grew still in wicked anticipation of what was to come.

Demetrius Vlad was the first to move. He lunged forward and brought the cossack saber slashing down in a vicious attack designed to cleave his troublesome foe from nose to navel.

It didn't happen. Cossack steel crashed against Morgan's blade and rang out with a resounding clang. And Morgan, with surprising quickness, stepped inside the Russian's reach and delivered a vicious kick to Vlad's right leg, at the side of the knee. The Russian lost his balance as his leg buckled. He toppled backward, unable to avoid Morgan's attack. The cutlass glanced off the saber and swept down and across, catching Vlad along the left side of his cheek and forehead. The Russian shrieked, dropped his saber, and covered his face in his hands. The contest had lasted all of fifteen seconds.

"An eye for an eye," Morgan said as Vlad groaned and tried to stanch the blood seeping through his clenched fingers. No one cheered now. Vlad's men hurried to their captain. Abdul, his black features gnarled with anger, reached for the gun he carried. Chiang Lu's purse of gold landed with a resounding "ker-plop" on the ground between Morgan and Vlad.

"Enough," Chiang Lu called out. "Captain Penmerry is victorious. He entered under my protection. He will leave the same way."

The Moroccan dropped his hand away from his gun and moved to help his compatriots carry Vlad from the arena.

"Son of a bitch! Jackal!" the Russian shouted. "You'll wish you had killed me. I swear it."

"He's right." Morgan retrieved his pouch of gold. He chanced a peek up at the rim of the arena, but the girl and her father had vanished. Too bad, Morgan thought. Still, he had the gold.

"How much?" Temp Rawlins asked. He and the captain climbed the stairs leading out of the arena.

"We'll count it at the warehouse," Morgan told him, keeping his voice low as Chiang Lu left his dais to block their path. The Chinese warlord smiled and played the part of a gracious loser.

"You have taught me a valuable lesson today, Captain Penmerry."

"I try my best," Morgan said. "A man should always be open to new ideas."

"Yes," Chiang Lu purred. He folded his hands across his chest. "I hope tomorrow you will allow me to inspect the furs you have stored in Don Rodrigo's warehouse."

Morgan blanched. "The furs?"

"Why, yes," Chiang Lu said. "Since I did not win them, I shall have to buy them. I will come at noon."

"Uh...that might be a little too soon," Morgan stammered. "I mean—I have to arrange them. Some are still aboard ship."

Chiang Lu nodded. "Very well. The day after. I merely wish to assist you in a speedy departure from port. Captain Vlad is—Well, I am certain you can foresee what will happen should you overstay your welcome. Until the day after then." Chiang Lu bowed and returned to his dais. Another two men had entered the cock pit to try their birds.

Temp Rawlins leaned toward Morgan. "Things'll get kind of dull once we leave," Temp said.

Indeed they would, Captain Morgan Penmerry reflected. But just about the time Chiang Lu arrived at the warehouse and found he'd been tricked into wagering a sack of gold against a shipment of prime pelts that didn't exist— there might just be some more excitement in Macao. More than the captain and crew of the *Hotspur* had bargained for.

2

Tung Wan Pier was nigh deserted in the slate-gray light as the late-afternoon mist became steady rainfall, turning the narrow alleyways to quagmires. Morgan could only be grateful that the main thoroughfare wore a layer of crushed rock and seashell. The wheels of the carriage dug deep into the surface and rolled on, leaving miniature canals in their wake. It had been an uneventful journey from Chiang Lu's hillside villa down to dockside. While Temp counted their winnings, Morgan busied himself in silent observation of the city. He never ceased to marvel at the various nationalities rubbing shoulders in the crowded streets.

Vendors hawked their wares in Chinese, Portuguese, and English. Women unfurled yards of fine silk in every conceivable shade: Bolts of brilliant green and crimson, satin blue, shimmering opal, and royal purple caught Morgan's fancy. They passed wine merchants and meat shops offering everything from pork loins to skinned rabbits and rack of dog. There were tailors and artisans, stalls of fortune-tellers and mah-jong parlors, and enclaves where fishermen hawked fresh-caught fish, squid, sea snails, and sole. As the carriage entered the Rue de Lorchas, the shops gave way to rum houses and gambling casinos and luridly lanterned, centuries-old Portuguese villas that had been turned into brothels in which any fantasy could be arranged for a profit.

"Forty-five hundred dollars in silver coins," Temp declared, oblivious to the rain that splashed in under the roof of the carriage. The driver, a wizened Spaniard with an ugly pockmarked face, fared even worse. His seat was open to the elements. Still, he was luckier than the ricksha boys afoot. The Spaniard at least had a horse to curse as he whipped the poor beast to a brisk trot.

Morgan had no use for such cruelty, but he held his tongue. It didn't concern him. He made a point of not involving himself in another's problems be they man or beast.

"Why, that cheap bastard," Temp continued. "Chiang Lu only wagered . . . hell . . . not even half what our pelts usually bring. An honest man would have wagered a chest of gold sovereigns."

"In this case the amount is a handsome profit," Morgan said. "Damn!" He eased back in the carriage. "She wasn't on any of the streets we passed. Maybe she hadn't left Chiang Lu's?"

"Who?" Temp asked—then realized just exactly who the captain was talking about. He scratched his grizzled chin and sighed. "Tell me, Captain, just when was the last time you had your teeth kicked in by a pretty face? Seems there was that Chinese girl in Canton. And the little Chinook squaw in Astoria."

"I can handle myself," Morgan said.

The carriage skidded in the road as the Spaniard hastily applied the kick brake and gave the reins a savage tug. Across the street at dockside the *Hotspur* loomed shadowy and silent as it rode out the downpour tethered to the pier by a pair of thick coiled ropes. The warehouse, a two-story structure, had been built opposite the pier. A pair of heavy oak doors could be thrown wide to accept wagonloads of goods from the boats. Lantern light glimmered in the window of a smaller door near the corner of the building. Here Don Rodrigo kept his office. The Portuguese merchant lived in a loft above his office, all the better to keep watch over his holdings. He considered himself a nobleman and required his associates to refer to him as a don, as would a titled Spaniard.

Tung Wan Pier was located in a deserted stretch of the Rue de Lorchas. The rum pots and brothels were congregated a few blocks away. Still, the criminal elements were known to drift west along the avenue and from time to time spill over into the warehouse district. So none but a fool went unarmed.

Like a forest of starkly limbed trees, other masts from other ships revealed themselves in the slate-gray light. Brigs and barks, junks and schooners lined the piers further along the avenue. But the downpour had chased the dockworkers from the street and provided an excuse for men to drift away in search of fleshly pleasures. As the first droplets of rain slid beneath the collar of his greatcoat, Morgan envied the absent workers. He paid the Spaniard ten patacas and followed Temp as the older man darted for the lamp-lit door.

"Twenty coins of silver is my fare," the ugly little Spaniard called to Morgan.

"Ten was your price up on the hill," Morgan reminded him.

"Twenty or I shall have the constable set his guards on you," the driver insisted.

"You'll summon them with your dying breath," Morgan cautioned. He thrust a hand into the pocket of his greatcoat as if reaching for a weapon. The Spaniard considered his options and decided against risking his life for a mere ten coins. He spat in the street and lowered his head to the rain, cursed aloud and vented his anger on the hapless mare at the end of the reins. The carriage rolled away as thunder followed the crack of the Spaniard's whip.

Morgan hurried to the warehouse and darted through the open doorway into Rodrigo's sparsely furnished office.

The room measured nine by eighteen feet, with a mahogany desk, a rack of files, and several ladder-backed chairs, three of which were occupied by men warming themselves near a Franklin stove.

"Trouble?" Temp asked, stepping aside to permit his captain to enter the room.

"A difference of opinion," Morgan replied and shucked his coat. Water dripped from the hem and soon formed a puddle on the floor beneath the ornate brass rack in the corner.

The men by the fire exchanged glances and welcomed their captain with halfhearted enthusiasm. The largest of the three, a shipwright by the name of Ansel Arvidson, waved a hand toward an enameled teapot resting on the burner of the cast-iron stove.

"Take some tea, Captain. It'll cut the mud from your gullet." The big Swede hoisted a steaming mug of the black brew to his lips.

The other two men, Jocko Britchetto and his younger brother, Tim, raised their mugs in salute. The brothers were dark-skinned, strapping lads with windburned features and rock-hard torsos. Life at sea had agreed with them. These were simple men, not given to pretense or deception. Their faces were an open book to Morgan Penmerry, and he could read at a glance something was amiss.

He walked through the office and entered the warehouse through a side door. The interior of the building was a dark, low-ceilinged room running two hundred feet deep and a hundred feet wide. It boasted a loft of similar dimensions. A broad lamp-lit stairway at the far end of the building led to the storage room above. It was an old building, showing its age in the splintered rafters and the roof that leaked in several spots. Morgan could peer up into the loft overhead through any number of holes in its flooring.

Don Rodrigo, the owner of the warehouse, stood amid twin mounds of blackened crates. He held a storm lantern to light his way through the shipment the crew of the

Hotspur had unloaded under cover of night. The merchant held what once had been a prime otter pelt. But the fur was singed in several places and the skin was no more than a worthless rag.

Except for Don Rodrigo and a pair of water rats scurrying across the rafters, the warehouse was empty. It should have been crowded with the crewmen of the *Hotspur* waiting impatiently for Morgan to return with whatever loot he had managed to con from Chiang Lu.

"These pelts... ruined. Who would buy such as these? They are nothing. And no doubt I am storing them for free. Eh?"

Morgan held out his arms in an attitude of vulnerability. "How can you harbor such terrible thoughts about me? Don Rodrigo, have I ever cheated you?"

"Whenever you get the chance," Don Rodrigo flatly replied. "I have not forgotten the last time you stayed here. I remember how you promised me an evening in the company of a young virgin from Madrid. Fair as a flower, you said, and skin as smooth to the touch as silk. Only you did not tell me there was so much of this skin. She weighed three hundred pounds!"

"I'd hardly call that cheating. I admit I forgot to mention her size."

"Forgot? I needed a ladder to climb atop her. And if she was a virgin, I'm a Jesuit." The diminutive merchant shrugged. "With nothing to sell, you are as destitute as I." He was resigned to being a poor man.

"Get your money from Rawlins," Morgan said.

Don Rodrigo glanced up in surprise. "Chiang Lu gave you money for these hides?"

"In a matter of speaking. Now all I need to do is get out of port before he finds out their condition."

Don Rodrigo blanched. His eyes grew wide as saucers. "Are you mad? Chiang Lu will send the Blue Wing Dragons after your head. Mine too. You must leave. Leave immediately. Dump the hides off the pier and go." Don Rodrigo began to pace; his thick-bellied frame seemed an ungainly mass upon his spindly legs. "Doomed," Don Rodrigo moaned.

"Belay that," Morgan said, sick of such talk. "Come and take the money that's due you. We'll soon be gone, and none the wiser."

"And sail without a crew?" Don Rodrigo held the oil lamp overhead to better illuminate the empty interior of the warehouse.

"Aye," Temp Rawlins said, walking into the warehouse. "Ansel Arvidson has taken the wind from my sails with the news, my lad." Temp held out a bottle of brandy pilfered from Don Rodrigo's private stock. The merchant was too upset to notice.

"Where's my crew?" Morgan asked, suspecting the worst.

"Scattered to the rum houses and down dockside looking to hire on with the first ship that will have them. No one figured you would return with a full purse." Don Rodrigo rounded Morgan and edged toward his office.

"Let's hope they ride anchor on their tongues," Morgan replied angrily. "At least until we round them up again." He brushed Don Rodrigo aside and headed into the warehouseman's office with Temp at his heels. "Ansel, Jocko, Tim, roust yourselves from that stove!"

Arvidson and the Britchetto brothers bolted from their chairs as Morgan Penmerry returned to the office. They grabbed coats and caps. Morgan barked his instructions. He was in no mood to be trifled with.

"You scour every wharf crib and alley if need be, but find our lads and bring them back." Morgan took the money pouch from Temp and gave it a shake. The coins inside jingled merrily, a sweet silver tune to a seaman's ear. Arvidson wet his lips and his eyes sparkled. The brothers grinned at each other. "Tell the lads we sail tomorrow night. And there's double shares for one and all, but we must make ready come sunup."

Morgan turned to Temp, who took a swallow of brandy and read his captain's mind. He handed the depleted bottle back to a much dismayed Don Rodrigo, who glared at the bottle's diminished contents.

"Don't ask," Temp sighed. "I'll join the search. I'd sooner be keelhauled than stand around waiting for Chiang Lu to discover how you tricked him." He tugged a cap from his belt and covered the wisps of hair on his head. He tucked a brace of pistols in his belt and donned his rain-spattered coat once again.

The other men armed themselves and followed Temp out into the downpour.

Silver coins in payment for my life's blood, Don Rodrigo thought as he watched the men leave. And in his mind he saw the nails being driven into his own coffin, heard the hammer strike with a resounding bang-bang-bang. The diminutive merchant gasped and covered his mouth to stifle a shriek. The hammering came not from his thoughts, it filled the whole office. "No," he gasped as Morgan started to unlatch the front door.

"Chiang Lu wouldn't knock," Morgan replied. He opened the door and stepped back; his right hand brushed the flintlock pistol at his waist in a precautionary gesture that betrayed his own nervousness. His hand quickly fell away as Emile Emerson and his daughter entered the office.

Don Rodrigo, seeing a young woman and the reverend, sighed in relief.

"May we speak to you, Captain Penmerry?" the reverend asked, stepping in out of the rain. Water dripped from the hem of his greatcoat and the brim of his sodden black hat.

Julia Emerson flipped the cowl back from her features and met Morgan's frank appraisal with a demure smile.

"I knew it," Morgan said, speaking directly to the missionary's daughter.

"Sir?"

"I knew you'd have green eyes," he said.

Julia blushed and lowered her gaze from the brash, rugged-looking captain.

"I am Dr. Emile Emerson," said the girl's father, attempting to divert the captain's scrutiny. "And my daughter, Julia Ruth Emerson." The reverend planted himself between the captain and the girl. He was as round as a

Virginia ham. His eyes were green like his daughter's, though bloodshot from lack of sleep, the trademark of a worried man. From the way Emerson carried himself, Morgan had the distinct impression that this Bible thumper could spew fire and brimstone with the best of them.

"I must apologize for intruding at such an hour."

"It isn't late," Morgan said. "The storm only makes it seem so." He turned and walked toward the cast-iron stove. Don Rodrigo, the soul of politeness, poured two more cups of tea.

"Here, Miss. Warm yourself." He indicated an empty seat by the stove. Ever the gentleman, he helped the young woman out of her hooded cape.

"Thank you," Emerson said, speaking for the both of them, a habit that annoyed his daughter but seemed perfectly natural to him.

Emerson grunted in satisfaction as he removed his greatcoat by the stove and held his hands out to the warmth. Then he reached inside his vest and produced a flask of brandy and added a dollop to his tea. Don Rodrigo emptied the contents of his cup into a nearby corner and took his measure of brandy straight.

"Many thanks," the merchant said.

Morgan was intrigued by the visit. He usually had as little to do as possible with men of religion. Morgan's truth was a fair wind, calm seas, and the strength of fire and steel. Gold, guns, and a woman... these were things worth living for and all of heaven that he needed to know.

"There are other fires to warm yourself by in Macao, Dr. Emerson," Morgan said. "And teahouses that serve a better brew than the twice-boiled pitch Don Rodrigo can offer."

Emerson studied the younger man a moment and smiled despite himself. He appreciated directness.

"I have come to ask you a question," the reverend said, momentarily setting the teacup aside. He folded his hands across his well-rounded belly. Sweat beaded his forehead and glistened in his snowy side-whiskers and the ruff of white hair that circled his pinkish skull like a wreath. "Tell me, Captain Penmerry, do you believe in God?"

"If you mean do I give anything away, the answer is no. As for God, save your preaching. I believe in what I can see, what I can hold with these two hands, or buy or fight, or... make love to."

He glanced in the girl's direction and saw the color creeping up her throat.

"Sir. There is a lady present," Emerson scolded.

"There are no ladies in Macao," Morgan said. "Only women."

"And few gentlemen," Julia spoke up in a silken tone.

Morgan smiled. He liked the show of sparks.

"So, she speaks," the captain observed wryly. He crossed the room and cleared a space for himself amid the charts and record books strewn upon a wide table set against the wall. Morgan perched between a pair of hurricane lamps.

"Well now, I doubt you've come to convert me, Dr. Emerson."

"No," Emerson replied. He wiped a forearm across his forehead, he patted his pocket but could find no scarf. The lamplight played on his hands. His were work hands. They might have been soft once, but twenty years of missionary work in the far-flung places of the world had left his hands as rough and calloused as any shipwright's. "I don't prose-lytize. I attest to the presence of God through my actions and let the Almighty win souls Himself." The missionary finished his tea and looked at Don Rodrigo. "That will be all, my good fellow. Now permit us the use of your office and may heaven smile on you."

Don Rodrigo rose from his chair and, grabbing up his tools, muttered that he had more leaks to repair in the bedroom above. The merchant sauntered off with tools in one hand and a bucket and extra shingles in the other. If there were to be conspiracies, he wanted no part of them.

When they were alone, the reverend felt freer to speak his mind. He helped himself to another cup of tea. Julia declined any more; she continued to meet the captain's gaze. Indeed, she took girlish pride in the way Morgan's eyes seemed drawn to her. Her curved lips and ample bosom did wonders for the somber-colored garments she wore.

"A most impressive performance today, Captain Penmerry," Emerson said. "I must say, anything that causes Chiang Lu displeasure, I applaud, though generally I abhor violence."

"Chiang Lu has opposed my father's ministry ever since we helped one of his servant girls escape to Canton. She was a pathetic child and he had cruelly mistreated her." Julia Emerson brushed an errant auburn strand from her cheek and tucked it behind an ear. "For that he has driven us out of Macao."

"I'm hardly in his good graces. There's nothing I can say to convince him to allow you to stay," Morgan replied.

"On the contrary, I want you to help us leave," Emerson explained. "I bought a ship with the last of my inheritance. A bark. Smaller than you're accustomed to but a seaworthy vessel nonetheless." Emerson stood and reached inside his vest for a sealskin packet of papers and approached Morgan.

"My mission might have ended, but not my duty. I intend to establish a church at Astoria, on the mouth of the Columbia. However, I shall need a pilot to guide us to our destination. I've brought a list of what we've taken aboard." He handed the packet to the captain.

Morgan stared in open-mouthed amazement at the reverend. Had the man taken leave of his senses? Not that crossing the Pacific with the missionary's comely daughter didn't have possibilities. Morgan laughed aloud and passed the unopened sealskin-wrapped papers back to Emile Emerson.

"I am master of my own ship," Morgan said. "Do you think I would give that up?"

"It was our understanding that you already had. After losing your cargo . . ."

Morgan erupted from the table and caught the reverend by his wide white collar, tearing the material. Emerson's revelation had ignited Morgan's short fuse. Julia bolted from her chair and moved to defend her father.

"Hold it!" the captain growled with such ferocity the girl stopped in her tracks. Morgan, seeing the defiance etched in her features, relented. He eased his hold on the reverend and halfheartedly patted the wrinkles from Emerson's collar. "How did you know?"

"Why, a man asked to join my crew not four hours ago. He was most disgruntled and told me of your troubles. He wanted to ship out as soon as possible. Unfortunately, we were unable to take him aboard," the missionary said.

"Leave my father alone!" Julia snapped angrily. Her admonition was after the fact, however. Morgan's anger was already directed elsewhere. He left them both and slowly walked to the front of the office and peered through the window at the downpour.

"Damn," Morgan said under his breath. If Emerson had heard, then it was only a matter of time before rumors climbed the hill to Chiang Lu's villa.

"Perhaps this is not an appropriate time to discuss an arrangement," Emerson said. "If you wish to join us, we leave the day after tomorrow. I shall do the best I can—with or without you."

Emerson pulled on his greatcoat and helped Julia into her hooded cape. Their carriage was just outside the door. It would only take a few steps into the deepening night to reach the hitching post and untether the horse. Morgan had become uncommunicative.

Still, Julia chanced another outburst and gingerly approached the captain. Morgan towered over her, but she didn't back down. She placed her hand on his forearm.

"I'm sorry if we brought you bad news," she said, then followed her father out into the night. And the gloom that mirrored Morgan's own dark mood was almost made bearable by the warmth that lingered where she had touched him.

3

Emile Emerson stared across the breakfast table at his recalcitrant daughter. The arrangement of plates, teapot, and cups was like some battlefield separating two camps engaged in a war of unspoken hurts. The motion of the bark riding the subtle currents of the bay left the parson off balance and dreading the ocean voyage to come.

"Stubborn, stubborn, stubborn child. This is our last day in China. Tomorrow morning we set sail. Can't these final hours see peace between us?" Emerson unclasped his hands and reached toward his daughter, who was still in her dressing gown. She drew back. The reverend was worried. This strange behavior had begun soon after the death of his wife, Julia's mother. But he had tried to help Julia through the grief while intensely suffering his own.

Julia stood and walked to the cabin window at the stern of the ship. The captain's cabin was the only comfortable quarters on the bark. Emerson had partitioned the cabin in such a way that a small area was screened off for the young woman's privacy. She used the captain's bed while her father had a pallet on the port side of the room for himself. A shelf crammed with books would help him endure the long voyage to come.

Emerson waited for her to respond. When she remained silent, he merely sighed aloud and muttered a litany of "Stubborn-stubborn-stubborn" yet again. He stared down at the rice cakes and salted fish and preserved eggs he had purchased from a vendor on the pier. It was his last breakfast in China. He was about to open a new chapter in his life. He was leaving behind the only home Julia had ever known.

"Perhaps my sister was right. I should have sent you to live with her family in London," Emerson declared with a hint of finality in his voice.

"Indeed!" Julia snapped, turning on him, her arms folded across her bosom. "At least then I would not have been present to see you give up everything you've built and run like a frightened rabbit from that scoundrel Chiang Lu." She blinked her moistened eyes and dabbed at them with the sleeve of her dressing gown.

"So that's it," Emerson said. "At last . . ." He shoved breakfast aside. "Scoundrel is hardly the word for the likes of Chiang Lu." Emerson felt his pulse quicken at the mention of the man. Had Chiang Lu not wished to keep his public reputation above reproach, the missionary would have been killed for interfering in Chiang Lu's affairs. The hatchets of the Blue Wing dragons were razor sharp and killed quickly, without mercy, in the dark of night. Emerson had seen men with their skulls cleaved.

He had his doubts that the Almighty would somehow intercede on the missionary's behalf and save him. History was full of martyrs. To his own shame Emerson dreaded the consequences of openly defying Chiang Lu. It made far better sense to begin anew, somewhere far from an adversary like the warlord.

"Dear daughter, do you want me to end up like the others who have gone against Chiang Lu? Will that make you happy?" He reached out to her, but she drew away. "I am a man of peace. A man of God."

"A man of nothing," she blurted. "If God cared so much about us, He wouldn't have taken Mother. He wouldn't allow the destruction of everything we had or for us to be driven from our home!" Her cheeks flushed; her hands knotted into fists. The role of dutiful parson's daughter had become too wearisome to continue. "I'll show God! And I'll show you! To the devil with this pretense!"

"Daughter, you blaspheme."

"To the devil, I say," she repeated venomously.

Emerson slapped her across the mouth. He had acted on reflex, without thought. Julia staggered back, astonished for a moment; then her smarting cheek crinkled as she coldly smiled.

"Thank you, Papa."

"I didn't want—I didn't mean to . . ." Emerson began, his voice strained. "Julia, you've always been my good right arm."

"I'm more than that, Papa. I will be a whole person, my own self. Not God's and not yours."

Emerson searched her expression and felt uneasy at what he saw. He mustered all his dignity, every iota of authority. "You will not leave this ship. Do you understand? I forbid it. I have business ashore. I expect to find you here upon my return."

He did not wait for a reply but gathered his frock coat and flat-brimmed black hat and strode from the ship's cabin. The oak door slammed shut with a ponderous finality.

Demetrius Vlad backhanded the servant, spilling the breakfast the poor man had carried as a peace offering from Chiang Lu's own kitchen. No matter the hapless man had brought the platter of covered dishes all the way from Lu's hillside villa to the sun-washed hacienda off Peacock Alley that served as the Russian's base of operations.

Vlad was in agony. The left half of his face, concealed beneath a layer of bandages, burned with the fire of hell, or so it seemed. The servant, blood trickling from the corner of his mouth, tried to bow and back away as he scrambled to his feet. Vlad, driven mad by the pain, descended on the cringing servant, who darted for the doorway and received a boot to the backside for his trouble. He caromed off the balustrade and tumbled down the stairs to the courtyard below. Vlad grabbed a pistol from a nearby bedstand and reached the balcony just as the servant dashed through the gates and into the crowded thoroughfare of the street beyond.

"Run!" Vlad shouted. "Run, you whore's son! Tell your master I'll break my fast on Penmerry's vitals and nothing else!"

"He meant no harm, Captain," Abdul said, entering from the hallway. Vlad spun around and leveled the pistol at his black lieutenant. Abdul took little note of the weapon pointed at his solid midriff. He calmly patted dust from his white blouse and black satin pantaloons and picked his path among the eggs, diced pork, smoked eel, and rice cakes littering the floor. The Moroccan shook his head in dismay. He'd known hunger in his day and hated the waste of food.

"Shoot me, Captain, and you'll never hear the news I bring. Good news to make your heart light as the summer breeze." He nudged a rice cake with the toe of his boot, knelt and picked it up, brushed away the dirt, and sampled the morsel. The texture was chewy and flavored with almond, honey, and orange, almost imperceptible, that lingered on the palate.

Vlad cursed and walked out onto the balcony overlooking the walled courtyard with its untended gardens and lichen-covered fountain crowned by a marble goddess whose head had been shot away by some drunken brigand. Several of Vlad's crewmen were taking their siesta in the shade of the vine-covered walls or beneath domed porticoes, where small gray birds flitted among the slanting shadows.

The clouds above quickly sealed the fissure through which the sunlight had reached the earth and became

once more a solid charcoal-colored barrier blocking those
warming rays. Shadows dissolved and the moist still air
awaited yet another downpour. It was just past noon, Vlad
noted with regret. Beyond Peacock Alley the whores that
frequented the Avenue of Innocents would have yet to
arrive. The Russian exile wanted a woman. He could send
for one of Chiang Lu's courtesans—but in truth, Demetrius
Vlad wanted no more to do with Chiang Lu since the
merchant had failed to back the Russian and allowed
Morgan Penmerry to depart to the safety of his ship and
crew. Yes, a woman would help. He conjured a pleasant
image and enjoyed his fantasy for a single sweet moment.
Then reality intruded in the sound of the Moroccan's
deep, gravelly voice.

"What did you say? What news?" Vlad asked.

Abdul swaggered across the room, retrieving a couple
more rice cakes as he moved to join his captain on the
balcony.

"There is a seaman named Boller. Whiskey loosened his
tongue and my dagger kept it wagging. He used to be
cook aboard the *Hotspur*, but he quit because Penmerry
had no money to pay his wages." Abdul's eyes twinkled
and a grin revealed a ragged row of teeth. "Why not wait
till Penmerry sells his hides, you be asking, and I answer,
'cause there are none. All his prime pelts damaged in a
fire, blackened, burned, or tainted by smoke."

"No pelts at all? Everything ruined?" By the blood of
the Almighty, this was even better than a whore's dalliance!

"Just about."

"Then Chiang Lu wagered against nothing, a key to an
empty warehouse."

"Now you're full sail onto the truth of it, my captain,"
Abdul said.

Vlad laughed, then winced for the effort. He had to
subdue his delight or writhe in misery. As much as he
hated Morgan Penmerry, he respected the fur trader's
ploy. He had plucked a silk purse of coins right from the
warlord's own belt. It was sheer thievery, a calling Demetrius

Vlad had ample experience in. Morgan Penmerry, a common high seas robber after all!

If only Chiang Lu knew. To see the diminutive merchant puff himself up in outrage, to watch him sputter and fume—now that would be amusing.

"That Captain Morgan, he's a sly one right enough." Abdul cocked his head to one side. "But if you pull a whisker from a tiger, you better hope he does not waken, eh?"

Vlad read his lieutenant's intentions. The Russian touched his bandaged face, fingers toying at a strand of gauze as his thoughts worked out a scenario in which he might have his revenge on Morgan Penmerry and Chiang Lu both, and turn a tidy profit in the bargain. Set the dogs upon each other and while they're at each other's throats, raid their masters' villas.

"Send word to Chiang Lu of Penmerry's deception," he ordered. Vlad glanced over his shoulder and studied his reflection in a mirror hung inside the room. He could easily recognize the brawny Moroccan outlined against the backdrop of gray light. But Vlad's own finely sculpted face was ruined forever. Morgan Penmerry was to blame for that, and now he would pay.

Demetrius Vlad whirled and fired, startling Abdul. The gunshot reverberated off the walls of the courtyard and brought several of the Russian's crew staggering out from their quarters, muskets in hand.

The lead ball thudded into the figure atop the fountain, blasting away the goddess's left breast. The crewmen below milled about in confusion, realization slowly dawning that they were not under attack and that the echoing gunshot was but a product of Demetrius Vlad's rage. The guards plodded back to their station at the gate. The remainder of the men lowered their muskets and returned, grumbling, to their women and rum and makeshift beds.

Vlad lowered his gaze to the balustrade, where a small brown beetle worked its way along the top of the stone.

"Tomorrow, that bug will still be alive and whole, but I'll wear Morgan Penmerry's mark forever."

Captain Morgan Penmerry didn't wait for permission to board the *Magdalene*, Emile Emerson's ship. He walked up the gangplank to the deck and no one moved to stop him. It was obvious he was in a foul mood and his temper as easily triggered as the brace of flintlocks tucked in his belt. No one wanted to end up like Demetrius Vlad. In truth, the duel at the cockfight had become the talk of the waterfront. Although most men applauded Morgan Penmerry's victory, they kept their delight to themselves, for Vlad's enemies too often disappeared. The combined fear of Vlad and a healthy respect for Penmerry enabled the fur trader to reach the deck of the *Magdalene* unchallenged.

It wasn't a large ship. Morgan estimated it to be about one hundred twenty feet from bow to stern and about one hundred forty tons. He judged that the seventeen men who readied the ship were all the crew she needed.

Morgan glanced around and caught the nearest man by the arm. The seaman stepped back and raised a knuckle to his forehead. He was a mulatto and sweat beaded his coffee-colored features.

"Where's the reverend?" Morgan asked.

"Reverend Cap'n Emerson ain't about," the seaman said, hefting a fifty-pound sack of rice flour to his shoulder. He started to elaborate, but a shadow fell between them and he hurried off toward the stairwell amidships leading to the hold.

Julia Emerson had emerged from the captain's cabin and advanced toward Morgan. The reverend's daughter was as sternly clad as before, in a high-necked dress with a gray bodice and charcoal skirt, but the otherwise somber effect was offset by a gaily patterned apron depicting an elegant flotilla of brightly stitched swans.

"Captain Penmerry, indeed have you had a change of heart? Do you intend to pilot us to the northwest coast of the Americas after all?"

"I'm looking for Drexel Reilly, one of my crew. I was told he hired on with you yesterday."

"Then he is the *Magdalene*'s carpenter now," Julia stated flatly. She folded her hands upon her apron and studied this brash, bold-talking sea captain.

He wasn't a pretty man; there was certainly no trace of the dandy in his rough features and brawny physique. He'd founder on the floor of a ballroom, to be sure. If the cloth he was cut from was coarse, it was also strong and resilient: It might never dress a prince, but it fit a man. Her eyes dropped to the thatch of black curly hair matting his chest where his shirt had come untied. Then she lifted her sparkling emerald gaze to meet Morgan's dark eyes. She remained uncowed by his stern visage, and Morgan Penmerry could only sigh and allow his scowl to melt away.

"I thought parsons' daughters were a weak-kneed, trembling lot." Morgan ran a hand through his hair.

"On the contrary, Captain Penmerry," Julia replied, fastening a bonnet in place and tying the ribbon beneath her chin. "A minister and his family must be able to endure even the most austere hardships. We may turn the other cheek, but we don't back down. So you see, there is a great deal you have to learn about ministers and their daughters."

"When is school in session?" Morgan asked. "I just might sign on, if the right teacher is about." He stepped back and flashed her a daring grin. He was becoming more and more intrigued by this woman. He liked her spirit as much as her well-curved figure.

"As this is my last day in Macao, I should like to visit someone special. It is a long walk, but as you have a carriage . . ." She looked down the gangplank to the carriage and mare tethered to a post alongside the walkway. "I assume it is yours."

"Don Rodrigo's. You might say I borrowed it." Morgan chuckled, adding, "And he might say I stole it."

"Good. Then I'll allow you to drive me. And in return, I will tell you all about daughters of ministers."

She held out her arm, waiting for him to escort her down the gangplank. Morgan looked at her in disbelief. His own ship, the *Hotspur*, was undergoing feverish preparations so that she could sail away under cover of night and escape Chiang Lu's wrath. He had no business following some missionary around the port city no matter how appealing her auburn tresses and delicate high-boned features or the way her abundant bosom swelled with each breath, rose and fell like the billowing tides of the sea.

"Agreed." Morgan bowed gallantly and took her arm in his. "On one condition. This someone special had better not be a wealthy nobleman or his arrogant young offspring in heat."

Julia's expression changed. Morgan sensed he had touched a nerve and he wondered if she was going to back out. But her reaction lasted a moment, then vanished, though when she spoke, a note of hidden sorrow colored her tone of voice.

"Don't worry, it's a woman," she explained. "My mother."

AGNES MARIE EMERSON

BORN APRIL 11, 1774
DIED OCTOBER 5, 1813

FAITHFUL SERVANT
OF THE LORD

The marker was carved of native stone, the letters scratched in an irregular, though legible, style. The Christian cemetery was atop a hillside north of town. A wheel-rutted path led from the cluster of villas beyond the city and wound through the lush green countryside until it reached the top of the hill. A Portuguese priest had erected a statue of the crucified Christ near the wooden gate. The cemetery itself was surrounded by a wall of stones piled two and a half feet high. A path of crushed shells led from the gate to the mission church and school approximately fifty yards from the cemetery. A small wood-frame house for the missionary's use stood to the side of the school. In stark silence, still as the grave at Morgan's feet, the Cornishman kept a sympathetic vigil with the girl.

"I prayed to God not to take her," Julia sighed. "I made a pact with God. I'd give up everything if only she would live. It was a cough that just wouldn't leave. It grew worse and worse, and then one morning she died. Early . . . before sunrise, I was sitting beside her. She reached out and touched my hand and asked me who I was—then she died."

Morgan was no stranger to death; he had faced the grim reaper on several occasions. But this was different. He watched a rivulet of tears spill down Julia's cheek and envied the young woman's courage. Captain Morgan Penmerry did not fear death. But he dreaded being so close to someone that he could not endure a final farewell. He lacked her courage to be brokenhearted.

"God . . ." was all he muttered.

"Don't you pray?" Julia asked.

"Did it do you any good?" Morgan replied with a question of his own.

Julia had no answer, for in truth the captain had touched upon a grievous doubt she was loath to share. The loss of her mother had shaken Julia's own faith. She reached into an apron pocket and drew forth a wooden and cloth doll her mother had made for her long ago, a lifetime it seemed. Flowers were not enough to leave on this last visit to the grave site. She looked around at the other graves and markers—some with Portuguese names, some with Chinese, others with English names—joining the dead of different nations by a common faith and a common fate. They had all perished in a foreign land, far from home.

The missionary's daughter knelt by her mother's headstone and placed the doll against it. On this last day she must leave something of herself, a part of the innocent past when everything was sure and good and bright. Maybe it would be again someday. Or, perhaps, sensing the shadows on the edge of the brightness was all a part of growing up. She rose and faced the man at her side.

"Why did you want me to come along?" Morgan's question hung softly on the stillness.

Julia turned and started toward the gate. Morgan dutifully followed. When they reached the carriage, Julia Emerson suddenly spun about and wrapped her arms around Morgan's neck and kissed him full upon the lips in a bruising and passionate display that caught the captain totally off guard. By the time he managed to respond, she broke away and backed toward the wheel of the carriage. Her bonnet had come off and hung down her back. Her chest rose and fell with each breath.

"Today I visited my mother for the last time. Today I kissed a man for the first time," she said, attempting to regain her composure. "Everything is changing. Everything I knew and trusted and counted on. Nothing will ever be the same again. And neither will I." She unbound her hair, letting the auburn tresses fall, and her eyes flashed with defiance. She laughed aloud, a brittle sound, and turned to climb into the carriage. She glanced toward the church to find her father standing in the doorway, watching her. There was no doubt he had witnessed her behavior. She held out her hand and allowed Morgan to help her up, then scooted over, making room for him beside her.

Julia grabbed the whip and applied it to the mare, and the carriage lurched forward. Morgan had to grab the edge of the seat to keep from being dislodged as they sped away from the hillside and the watcher in the doorway. Once they were out of sight beyond a granite outcrop, Morgan managed to wrest the lines from the woman's grasp and rein the carriage to an awkward stop. Julia tried to regain control, but he caught her arms and drew her close, to take a kiss of his own.

"No," she halfheartedly protested. "We sail at first light. And I shall never see you again."

"All the better," Morgan said and took his kiss, over-powering her token resistance. She was fire in his arms.

"I know a place . . ." he began.

"Take me there," she said.

4

Temperance Rawlins bellowed for the trio of men unloading the barrels of salt pork to cease their efforts and wait for him by their wagon. Then Temp trotted up the gangplank and with a nod to young Tim Britchetto forced the younger man to stand aside. Tim set down the barrel of provisions he'd just carried aboard.

"When it comes to my salt pork, I like to inspect the wares," Temp said with a wink. "Now I've eaten more'n my share of stale bread, but I'll not be goin' to sea with wormy meat." The first mate drew his cutlass and worked the tip of the blade under the barrel lid and pried the covering loose. He lifted the lid. The odor would have bowled over a buzzard. "Now that'll steal the wind from your sails," Temp gasped. "Tainted. Look at them maggots wiggle." He sliced a chunk with the cutlass and lifted the tip of the blade to hold the rancid morsel beneath Tim's nose. The chunk was riddled with maggots feasting on the rotted flesh.

Tim grimaced, almost gagged, and tried to look innocent, but Temp wasn't buying his act.

"How many times have I told you to inspect these supplies before they come aboard?"

"But they come from Don Rodrigo. He's a friend, ain't he?" Tim protested.

"The only friend a sailor has is common sense," Temp retorted and he rapped a knuckle against the youth's skull. "Let it sink in, lad; listen to old Temp Rawlins and maybe one day you'll captain your own ship like Morgan Penmerry. Why, if it weren't for me takin' him under my wing so to speak when he was but a young pup and learnin' him the ways of the sea, he'd have wound up danglin' from a yardarm or tossed into the sea for shark bait, mark me well." Temp glanced about the deck. His eyebrows arched. "Speak of the devil, the captain hasn't showed yet?"

There was little activity on the deck, though Ansel Arvidson and a half-dozen men labored below deck, repairing the burned-out timbers in the ship's hold.

"Not that I've seen," Tim replied, eager to shift attention from the salt pork. "And we've a dozen men gone again. They figured once we outfitted the ship there'd be nothing left to warm their palms but blisters. They want their wages in advance."

"Damn their black hearts," Temp cursed. Then he cocked an eye and stroked his stubbled chin and studied the youth across from him. "What say you, Tim Britchetto? Do you and Jocko plan to cut your losses and jump ship?"

Anger flashed like distant lightning in the young man's eyes. He drew himself up, hooked his thumbs in his belt, and assumed a defiant stance, planting his feet firmly on the deck as if daring any man to try and move him.

"I'm Penmerry's man. So is my brother," he stated.

To Tim's surprise, Temp laughed in his face and clapped him on the shoulder.

"Good lad," Temp said. "My doubts was all pretend. You might not know salt pork from saltpeter, but you'll do." He waved toward the wagon at the foot of the gangplank. "Now get this barrel back where it come from and I'll see Don Rodrigo."

Temp started down the gangplank as Tim refitted the lid to the pork barrel and hoisted it to his shoulders. The afternoon was drawing on. Though the captain's business was none of his concern, Tim voiced the question anyway.

"Mr. Rawlins, just where is Captain Penmerry?"

Temp turned sharply as if to admonish the youth. Instead, he shrugged. The question was plaguing him as well.

Not that there was anything for the captain to do. It was Temp Rawlins's job to see that the *Hotspur* was ready to take to sea. The first mate had an uneasy feeling that Morgan had gotten into trouble—not with Chiang Lu though. Worse. Morgan had left that morning to look over the crew of the reverend's bark in hopes of finding some of the *Hotspur*'s crew. If he had found the missionary's daughter instead . . .

"You worry about your duties and don't be frettin' over the welfare of Captain Penmerry. He can take care of himself and you and me as well." Temp tugged a wool cap onto his almost hairless skull and continued down the walkway and onto shore.

A burly seaman named Gude and Jocko Britchetto, under the watchful gaze of the wagon driver, a slim, sullen-faced Chinese in the employ of Don Rodrigo, had begun to inspect the pork barrels, pronouncing the contents of one spoiled and another just beginning to turn.

The *Hotspur*'s first mate strode toward the warehouse. A mongrel hound nipped at the man's heels. Temp sent the animal baying with a well-placed kick to the side. A local merchant named Chi Do spied Temp from a nearby stall and managed to intercept him.

"Out of my way," Temp growled at the Oriental man.

"Indeed. As you wish. But I have prepared three baskets of smoked fish, my honorable friend," the merchant declared. "I refused to sell them to any other ship until I visit my good friend Captain Penmerry and my good friend Mr. Rawlins." Chi Do had to hurry to keep abreast of the long-legged old seaman.

"Name your price, Chi," Temp said without breaking stride.

"One thousand patacas will lift me from poverty," Chi Do proposed. Today he wore a threadbare brown silk coat, but Temp had seen him in finery and parading among the rum houses and taverns with an entourage of courtesans.

"Two hundred and fifty," Temp countered without pity. "If you wish to rise high, why not climb the Thousand Buddha Cliffs?"

"Seven hundred and I will still be able to marry off my daughters with handsome dowry," Chi Do appealed. "And may Buddha bless you."

"Five hundred," Temp said. "I know your daughters. One of them is already married. As for the other, there's not enough gold in Macao to see her wedded or bedded."

"Agreed." Chi Do shrugged and bowed. "I fear you have spoken the truth. My eldest is an arguesome child with all the appeal of a goat. But all is not lost. I know a blind farmer just beyond the China gate. . . ." Chi Do bowed again as Temp paid him; then the merchant hurried back to his stall to attend to the baskets, the smallest of which stood five feet tall and was heavy with a load of smoked and salted fish.

Temp continued on to the warehouse. He glanced anxiously at the ominous sky. If the weather worsened and they couldn't slip away at sunup, there would be hell to pay. Damn Penmerry, would he never take things seriously?

Temp hauled the double doors to the warehouse open; they banged against the back wall as the irate seaman barged into the storage area. Gray light streamed in behind him and illuminated a pyramid of pork barrels and crates. "Don Rodrigo, you scheming blackguard. Show yourself. Those new barrels fooled us, but my nose found you out. I'll have decent salt pork or by heaven it will be your hide in the barrel." Temp's voice carried throughout the warehouse and returned unacknowledged, for the

Portuguese merchant was either hiding or had business away from the pier.

"He doesn't seem to be here," a mild-mannered voice said from the doorway leading into Don Rodrigo's office.

Temp, startled, swung around and recognized the missionary, Emile Emerson. "You looking for the tricky little bastard too?" the first mate asked.

"No. I thought I might find Captain Penmerry here," Emerson replied, trying to keep himself under control. His hands firmly clasped his Bible. He feared to loosen his hold upon the Holy Scripture for fear of picking up a gun. "Is Captain Penmerry aboard ship?"

"Here? That young rake? Hardly," Temp scoffed. "If I know the captain, he's probably found him a properly disposed gal and enticed her to mischief." Temp started to laugh, then realized to whom he spoke. He gulped and tried to fumble his way out of the hole he had dug for himself and the captain of the *Hotspur*. "What I mean is these Chinese gals can be mighty willing—uh, I mean for the right price . . . the ones that work in the Banyan Gardens or House of Heaven. That's what I mean."

Emerson's fingers tightened on the Bible, the knuckles bloodless. "I see. . . ." the missionary managed to say. Without another word he turned and walked from the office, his shoulders sagging as he made his way past the first mate and out into the street.

"Temp Rawlins," the first mate muttered to himself, "sometimes you talk too damn much." He followed Emerson out of the warehouse and watched as the black-clad figure made his way along the pier. How bright the man's tight white collar seemed, even from a distance, even in feeble light.

What few rooms the Jade Willow Tavern could offer were airy, lushly appointed accommodations that belied the inn's austere, brown-washed facade. Julia took note of the way Madame De Builliard, the tavern's proprietress, fussed over Morgan Penmerry. Though Madame wore too much powder and rouge, and her attire was suggestive, to say the least—her bosom all but exposed beneath a bodice of lace frills—she had aged with grace. Her body was trim and desirable; her eyes sparkled and her appetite for life was infectious. She appraised Julia frankly and glanced knowingly at Morgan as she gave them a key to the last of her available rooms. Julia knew that her own high-necked and purposely drab dress had roused Madame De Builliard's curiosity, and she had the distinct feeling her presence in the company of Captain Morgan Penmerry would be the subject of gossip throughout the Jade Willow Tavern.

Once in the room and alone with Morgan Penmerry, alone with and for the first time in close proximity to a man other than her father, she tried to conceal her misgivings as she crossed to a velvet-draped window and peered out at the street below—a noisy thoroughfare with what seemed an unending parade of humanity. There were children at play, fish merchants, silk peddlers, a silk-clad hawker hauling a two-wheeled cart piled high with caged birds. A girl sold preserved eggs from a makeshift stall.

Where were they all going? Where was anyone going? Julia shifted wearily. She sensed Morgan studying her and drew her shoulders back. Julia noticed a set of toylike brass figurines on a metal base. Her first impression was one of innocent admiration for the piece until closer examination showed one of the figures to be a goat standing on its hind legs, its phallus erect. Julia touched the base of the figurine. At the slightest jostling, the animal plunged its organ between the open legs of a plump, elfin lass, who eagerly accepted the animal's sex. In and out, the goat merrily plunged home. Julia blushed and lowered the brass work to the table.

She needed a drink. No, several drinks. The reverend's daughter averted her gaze from the frolicsome goat. The room's main article of furniture was an elaborate four-poster bed whose carved headboard displayed a magnificent array of naked maidens erotically entangled with a host of willing and obviously aroused lads.

Morgan Penmerry kicked off his high-topped boots and sank into the down mattress and clasped his hands behind his head. He grinned, amused by the young woman's discomfort, for every furnishing—from the japanned bed table to the needlework on the curtains, from the design on the paper screen masking the dressing area to the ink-on-rice-paper drawings adorning the walls—displayed acts of foreplay and intercourse. Though by no means were the renderings crude or tasteless. Each depiction was the work of an anonymous but highly skilled artist.

"Oh, God," Julia muttered under her breath. Spying a bottle of rice wine and glasses on a table near the door, She made her way across the room and helped herself to the strong, bitter drink. Actually being here, alone with the captain of the *Hotspur,* had taken some of the wind out of her sails. She gulped her drink and poured another, emptied it into her gullet and poured yet a third.

"Better go easy on that," Morgan said. "Madame De Builliard brews her own drink. It starts off civilized but turns into an ogre by and by."

"I can handle myself, thank you," Julia reminded him. She finished her drink and helped herself to a fourth. Sweat beaded her upper lip. The room seemed terribly warm. She walked back to the window and tried to figure out how to open it. The latch resisted her efforts.

"Your father saw us," Morgan said.

"Does that frighten you?" Julia said, facing him. The room shifted unsteadily like the deck of a ship. "He might call the wrath of God down on you. Don't worry. He can call all day and night, and there'll be nothing. Nothing."

Morgan couldn't miss the resentment in her voice. "Last night you were prepared to scratch my eyes out when I braced him in Don Rodrigo's office. Now you hate his guts. I'm curious. Why?"

"I don't hate him!" Julia snapped, protesting too vociferously to be believed. She softened her tone. "I do—and I love him. Both, you see. No, how could you? What do you know of love?" Julia drained the contents of the wineglass. The warmth in the pit of her stomach was seeping up to her chest.

"All these years, teaching children of the Christian God,

the one God who hears the cry of the poor. My mother gave up everything to follow my father. She thought him a saint. But she was the saint. Always dutiful and quiet and caring. Always able to laugh at hardship."

Julia Emerson filled her glass yet again. She spilled some down the front of her dress and didn't care. "And then she took sick and never got better. I prayed and prayed, but she died anyway. My father told me to have faith. In what? I say." She sat on the edge of the bed and as Morgan reached for her, Julia realized what she had done and stood again, out of his grasp.

Morgan sighed and leaned against the headboard and wriggled his toes while Julia paced back and forth at the foot of the bed.

"My father, the saint," Julia sneered and raised her glass in salute to an invisible guest, her own father. "But what kind of saint lacks the courage of his convictions, gives up everything he has ever worked for, everything he has built, and runs from the likes of Chiang Lu?"

Morgan shrugged, uneasy at her description. "No saint. Just a man. And a man grows weary, a man knows fear, a man can crumble under the burden of having to be a saint."

Julia gave him a sharp glance, swallowed her drink, and set the drained glass on the end table near a stick of incense, its tip aglow.

"A reverend's daughter has to be prim and proper. As saintly as the one she calls father," the young woman observed. Her voice was low and thick, and she had to concentrate on each word. The room was so terribly warm. What was she trying to say? Oh yes. "And if the father is but an ordinary man, then isn't she just an ordinary woman?"

"I wouldn't call you ordinary," Morgan said as her fingers fumbled with the buttons at her neck. She ran her hands down across her chest and cupped her breasts, then returned to her throat and unfastened another two black glass buttons.

"What would you call me?" Julia said, rounding the

bedpost at the foot of the bed. Her hands closed around the teakwood post and caressed its lacquered length, enjoying the sensation of its delicately carved surface as her fingers stroked from tip to mattress.

"I don't think I'd call you. I couldn't wait that long." Morgan gulped. The suggestive manner in which she handled the bedpost had aroused him. "I'd find you and carry you away." He sat upright and reached for her.

"If my father can sin, so can I," Julia said, pursing her lips.

"My sentiments exactly." Morgan pulled her onto the mattress.

"And when it comes to sin, who better to deal with than a devil like yourself," she added.

"Well, I wouldn't go that far," Morgan stammered. A rogue perhaps, but he reserved "devil" status for the likes of Demetrius Vlad.

"Surely you are too modest," Julia said and kissed him.

Her mouth bruised him as her tongue sought his and her arms clung savagely to him. Morgan closed his eyes and lowered the woman onto her back and matched her passion. A trail of jasmine incense drifted like some diaphanous serpent upon the ether and mingled with the rosewater-and-lilac scent of Julia's cream-colored flesh. She tasted of wine. And the fiery warmth of her body emanated from her clothes.

She released her embrace and her arms fell open as if to give herself completely to him. Morgan rose up, kneeling, to tug his shirt off over his head. He'd never wanted a woman so badly, never sensed so much restrained desire just waiting to be unleashed.

Julia was warm.

Julia was ripe and willing.

Julia was . . . *snoring?*

Morgan froze and peeked through the neck opening of his shirt. She inhaled, then snored softly as she exhaled. Her eyelids fluttered a moment, then there was nothing but the rising swell and fall of her ripe breasts as she drifted on the tides of sleep.

Morgan Penmerry glared at the nearly half empty bottle of rice wine. He leaned across the unconscious woman and snatched the bottle and raised it high overhead as if to crash it against the wall. He paused, then lowered the bottle.

"*Salude*," he said to Julia Emerson and with a sigh of good-natured resignation drank a toast to the somnolent object of his desire.

She was drowning in a dream, flashing hot and cold, first ice, then ignited gunpowder, and all the while submerged, caught in an invisible undertow of memory.

Julia heard her name called and saw her mother's smiling face and reached for and through the image. It disappeared and gave way to a row of sweet little children, neatly arranged and seated on a wooden bench while Julia taught them numbers and read to them and played with them. How they laughed at her antics. *My, the Christian Miss Emerson can be very silly. But she feeds us when we are hungry. She clothes us when we are naked.*

The children faded into the blackness and another image formed, a rough-hewn man, certainly no Christian from the look of him. He stood in the center of an arena, surrounded by men clamoring for blood. His name was Morgan Penmerry; his reputation was checkered at best. He was called a rake and a brawler, a dangerous man—yet she saw dignity in him. She felt drawn to him in a way that left her guilt-ridden and confused.

Like some reflection upon the surface of a pond, Morgan Penmerry shimmered and dissolved and re-formed as a dragon mask, whirling and dipping while firecrackers exploded in the street and pinpricks of fire filled her mind's eye as she surfaced from sleep. But she had not completely freed herself, for one last memory blossomed into fruition: a goat rising up to plunge its phallus between the open, yielding thighs of a brass maiden. She was not quite human nor was her partner totally animal. The figurines, at the slightest touch of the brass base, joined and parted, joined and parted, mimicking the union of a man and woman, mirroring the desires Julia Ruth Emerson had once struggled to suppress.

Julia awoke, opened her eyes, and perused her surroundings, momentarily disoriented; there was a pressure on her chest. She glanced down. A man's arm! She turned her head and wound up nose to nose with Morgan Penmerry. His arm was draped across her bosom. He was asleep alongside her in bed. In bed!

"Oh!" She bolted upright in the night-darkened room and tumbled off the bed to land in a tousled heap with her skirt and underclothes over her head. A bottle crashed to the floor. Morgan awoke with a start, bolted out of bed, and promptly entangled himself in Julia's legs and fell to the floor on top of the startled girl.

"Unhand me, sir. How dare you!" Julia frantically crawled out from under the captain of the *Hotspur*.

"What the hell?" Morgan sputtered and pawed his way past underclothes and legs.

He managed to stand as Julia pulled herself back onto the bed. Realizing she was back where she started, the reverend's daughter leapt from the bed as if from a hot plate. She reacted too quickly and the blood rushed to her head as the aftereffects of the rice wine took hold. She toppled forward. Morgan caught her by the shoulders and helped her to sit on the edge of the mattress. She stiffened in his grasp.

Morgan sensed her reserve. "Don't worry. I'll light the lamp by the window." He started around the bed. "Ouch. Christ in heaven." He'd found the remains of the broken bottle. The captain yelped and gingerly limped to the cane-backed chair near the window. A single candle cast its feeble glow, scarcely illuminating the room. Morgan used it to light an oil lamp on a table close at hand. He turned the wick up until black smoke coiled out the flue, then lowered the flame to a comfortable glow.

He checked his foot, removed a glass splinter from his big toe, and then retrieved his boots and stockings, taking care to avoid the shattered bottle. Julia's fearful gaze followed his every movement. Her head throbbed and her stomach turned flip-flops. Reality flooded in. She knew where she was now.

"What have you done to me?" she gasped.

Morgan looked at her, astonished. He chuckled and rubbed the sleep from his eyes. "I'll tell you," he muttered. Well, Temp had warned him. He contorted his features into a bestial caricature. "Everything!" he growled. "First I kidnaped you; then I dragged you upstairs to this room. You fought, oh how you fought, but I slapped you to the floor and poured rice wine down your throat, and when you were no longer able to defend yourself, I ravaged you. Captain Morgan Penmerry had his way with the missionary's daughter. And why not? He's the devil, ain't it so?"

Morgan ended his fabrication by looming above the girl, his eyes wide and his lips drawn back. He bristled with menace. Then he shrugged.

"After that we fell asleep and dreamed of sugarplums," he concluded.

"I dreamed of my mother," the woman replied.

In the beginning Julia had been cowed by his performance. As he ranted on, the truth of the evening rushed back to her; it was like opening a book to a previously read page. She had to admit it was rather a sordid little chapter, one she already regretted—not that she harbored any less grief or felt any less betrayed.

She watched Morgan retrace his steps to the window and peer out at the night. He hadn't planned on consuming a whole afternoon with this dalliance. No doubt Temp was fit to be tied by now.

The Jade Willow Tavern had been built on a low hill six blocks from the waterfront, close enough to attract seamen with money but far enough from the docks to avoid the riffraff. The moon was a baleful smear behind the clouds, yet even in its feeble glare Morgan could make out the masts and crosstrees of the *Hotspur*, arranged like crucifixes afloat by the pier.

Julia buttoned her bodice and managed to stand. She brought a hand to her forehead and groaned. "Ohhh..." she moaned.

Downstairs Madame De Builliard, playing a harp, began to serenade the few remaining patrons of the tavern, who took their rum, smoked their clay pipes, and dreamed of home. The Frenchwoman's voice was throaty and a touch flat. Yet the sincerity in her voice carried the song and it drifted up from below, wistful, nostalgic.

"She sings of better days and truer loves," Morgan interpreted.

"You speak French?" Julia asked, surprised.

"No, but I know Madame De Builliard." He gestured toward the door.

"Come, little sinner, I will take you home to your father's ship. Your virtue unblemished."

Julia blushed and lowered her gaze and followed him to the door. She paused, looked up at him. He was strong and ruthlessly single-minded. For all her bravado, Julia knew she had been at his mercy. And he desired her; he'd made that abundantly clear.

"Why?" She wanted to understand. "Just why is my virtue unblemished? Am I not as comely as the others you've bedded—beneath this same roof no doubt?"

Morgan, exasperated, raised his eyes to heaven, grabbed his gunbelt and cutlass from a chest by the door and vanished into the hall.

"Wait!" Julia called and hurried after him.

They moved quietly along the musty narrow hallway, quickening their pace as they neared the top of the stairs and the sepia-colored glare radiating from the tavern below. A door close by creaked open and a young Chinese woman peered at Julia. The Chinese woman stood naked in the doorway, her hair tousled from lovemaking. Perspiration traced a glistening trail between her small brown-tipped breasts. She appeared to recognize Julia Emerson and commented on her discovery to another person in the bedroom. A man's laughter carried from within.

"Missy Julia," the young woman said, struggling with her English. "You look for Christian God here?" The Chinese woman licked a finger, then drew a circle around each breast. "You find him, tell him to see me. I make him very happy."

Julia stopped in her tracks and stared. "I remember you," Julia said. The young woman's name was Mai Ling. "You came to the mission school. I taught you to read and write." But Mai Ling had left after a year.

Mai Ling shifted her gaze to the floor. "Life teach me more than you," she replied and closed the door.

Julia's eyes grew moist and the color drained from her face. Morgan touched the young woman's arm.

"That one made her choice. You can't take the blame for it," Morgan said.

"What do you know? You're as much a heathen as any of them," Julia snapped at him out of her own anger. *Or as much as I,* she added within, for she wasn't certain of anything anymore.

"On the contrary," Morgan said. "No man who has ridden a quarterdeck beneath a full moon round as a sovereign above the waves and turning the black sea to molten gold . . . no man could help but believe in God. I never yet met a seafarer who hasn't called on God when the sky darkens and the wind sets to blow and the air boils green as witches' bile." Morgan shook his head. His craggy features split with a smile. He brushed his dark hair back from his brow, winked, and added, "A heathen? Not hardly. I believe in God, lass. I just don't take Him as seriously as you."

5

Downstairs Madame De Builliard stopped in the middle
of her song, something she usually never did, for melan-
choly French ballads were her personal favorite and the
source, Morgan suspected, of her vitality. Madame had
spied her favorite fur trader on the stairway, and the
proprietress of the Jade Willow was loath to let him escape
without speaking to him. She had news that might save his
life. The streets of Macao weren't safe this night.

The lower floor of the Jade Willow Tavern had little in
common with the rum houses nestled cheek to jowl along
the waterfront. Madame De Builliard's establishment re-
sembled a French château with handsomely appointed
sitting rooms insuring privacy and a minimum of commotion for the discreet visitor. The main parlor fronted the
house and was furnished with lushly cushioned divans and
chairs spacious enough for royalty, covered in stitchery
depicting herons and butterflies and flowers of every conceivable hue.

Nubile young maidens in silk dressing gowns moved

among the few remaining guests, bringing them glasses of
mulled wine, thick clay mugs of hot tea laced with rum,
and platters of roast lamb and fresh bread. Madame De
Builliard settled her harp on its rest and left the comforting
glow of the fireplace for the drafty shadows of the foyer,
excusing herself to her patrons, three of whom were
Chinese and the others traders from Barcelona.

Julia unbolted the front door and tried to hurry outside,
fearing some new insult or innuendo from the Frenchwoman.
Morgan restrained her. The captain sensed something
amiss. He glanced toward the Seth Thomas clock on the
mantel and saw the hour was a quarter past midnight. The
parlor of the Jade Willow should have been crowded by
now, for Madame De Builliard was popular with all the
wealthier elements of Macao, from landholders to merchants, from Portuguese military officers to Chinese warlords.

Morgan stepped through the doorway and peered out at
the cobblestone thoroughfare winding off toward the waterfront. The air was damp, thick with moisture. A chill
mist had descended, diminishing the already feeble glare
of the street lanterns and muting the few remaining
sounds of an ominously quiet city.

He heard no vendors, no sound of carriage or ricksha,
no drunken revelers, no beggars, nothing save the distant
angry clamor of a stray dog and the scuffling of a rat along
the bamboo awning of an apothecary shop across the
narrow street. Morgan retreated into the foyer, frowning,
unsettled by the stillness.

"Maybe I do not need to warn you, eh, my little
cauliflower?" Madame De Builliard said as she approached
the couple. The Frenchwoman inspected Julia. The proprietress of the Jade Willow obviously assumed the couple's liaison had proved more romantic. "The night is
young. Stay here. This is a house of love. Be with one
another. I am not so old that I cannot see what is meant to
be." She pulled a silk kerchief from the sleeve of her
gown, which was a swirling concoction of amber-and-pink
silk.

Julia blushed at Madame De Builliard's observation.

Morgan coughed and cleared his throat, momentarily at a loss for words. For a brief second he considered the idea of luring Julia back upstairs. But he'd already committed one foolish act. He'd spent a day and half a night with the young woman with nothing to show for it but an ache in his loins and chaos in his heart.

"We'll go," he said.

Madame De Builliard shrugged. All men were stubborn. Yes, they thought the same of women, but she knew the truth. Leave them to their own devices—that was her creed. Charm them, take their money, and then *au revoir.* And yet, Morgan Penmerry had helped her once and defended her somewhat-tarnished honor against a drunken pair of Portuguese sailors. Their rum-soaked boldness had bought the two scoundrels cracked skulls and a dunking in the Pearl.

The Frenchwoman blocked the doorway and in a low voice said, "A moment more and hear my rhyme."

Madame De Builliard fancied herself a poet and often recited her verses while accompanying herself on the harp. Morgan had decided that the woman's couplets usually sounded better the more rice wine or rum a man consumed. But he humored Madame this night.

"As you wish, but be brief," Morgan said. "My lady has her reputation to uphold."

Julia bit her lower lip as her cheeks reddened. Whatever reputation she had was certainly a shambles after this night. Of course, she was leaving Macao, so what did it matter?

Madame De Builliard cleared her throat and said:

> "Do not go forth into road or park
> If evil would escape your sight.
> Beware the shadows, watch the dark,
> For winged dragons fly this night."

The Frenchwoman finished her recitation, touched a finger to her lips and then to Morgan's. She seemed to be honestly concerned for their welfare, and Julia was forced to reevaluate her opinion of the infamous Madame De Builliard.

Morgan caught the Madame's hand and, bowing, kissed it. He tried to hide his misgivings behind a gallant display. Chiang Lu must have discovered Morgan's deception. Word had somehow traveled up the docks to Chiang Lu's hillside villa and he'd loosed his henchmen with only one purpose in mind, the death of the one man who had played Chiang Lu for a fool.

"Better lock your shutters and keep a musket by the bedside," Morgan warned the proprietress of the Jade Willow. "Someone is sure to have seen us arrive."

"Then they'll see you leave," Madame replied, hardness in her voice. The Jade Willow was her domain and though she dreaded trouble with the likes of Chiang Lu, she wasn't about to run from him either. "I can take care of myself."

Morgan led the way into the night-shrouded street. Don Rodrigo's horse and carriage were where the captain had left them, tethered near a water trough alongside the tavern. Julia crossed behind Morgan and started to climb onto the leather-covered bench seat. Morgan appeared at her side to help her take her place. He continued to hold her longer than was necessary, yet she did not pull away.

"I have behaved poorly," Julia said.

Being with Julia was like running naked through the woods, Morgan mused. You never knew if it was going to blow hot or cold.

"Are you laughing at me?" Julia asked pointedly, noticing the wry smile on his face.

"No, ma'am," he replied. "I just took a notion, is all."

"Well then," Julia said, patting out the wrinkles on her dress. "Perhaps we should start for the Rue de Lorchas before you take another." She sounded ever so proper again, and struggled to maintain the facade despite the fact that half an hour earlier she had awakened in bed with Morgan Penmerry. She sagged back against the seat and sighed.

Morgan climbed in beside her and handed her the

lines, a gesture that caught Julia by surprise. She wrapped a blanket around her shoulders and looked questioningly into his rugged features. Strange, she didn't fear him now, even as he tugged a pistol from his belt and checked the load and added a trickle of black powder to the flash pan. He cradled the weapon and glanced at Julia.

"You know your way?" he asked.

"Yes," she replied, certain she could manage these narrow, gloomy streets.

"Then hurry. And if anyone blocks our way, run them down," Morgan grimly told her.

The hairs rose on the back of Julia's neck; tension slithered up her spine. Morgan expected trouble. Julia began to realize the gravity of her situation.

The captain briefly considered leaving Julia and making his way afoot. But Macao was no place for a woman to be riding alone in the wee hours of the night. The port was teeming with riffraff eager for a chance at such an attractive young fair-skinned woman. No, he resolved, Julia was better off with him. At least he could afford her some protection.

Before Morgan had time to reconsider, Julia cracked the carriage whip, and the mare bolted into the street. Morgan steadied himself and searched the shadows skimming past for Chiang Lu's assassins. He suspected the greatest peril lay ahead, where the dark ships rode at silent anchorage waiting for the morn. If there was to be trouble, it would no doubt begin there.

The *Hotspur* lit the night. Flames fed hungrily on the main deck and fo'c'sle and lapped the length of the foremast, leaping to the mainmast and mizzenmast in quick succession, consuming the wood and canvas and the rigging that stretched from the spars to the main deck like a spider's web. Chiang Lu's henchmen, in two johnboats outlined against the glare of the burning ship, cast loose the cables they had used to tow the *Hotspur* out into the estuary away from the dock and the merchant ships riding easy at port. Chiang Lu wasn't about to gut the entire waterfront for vengeance' sake.

Four blocks away a carriage rolled up to the pier where the *Magdalene* was anchored. Men lined its main deck, watching the attack and making no move to involve themselves. As Julia reined in the mare, Morgan, dumbfounded, stared at the floating fireship—once his own sturdy brig, now a funeral pyre for his hopes and dreams.

Chiang Lu hadn't wasted any time. Morgan wondered who had carried word to the warlord. The orange glow illuminated a stretch of the pier and dockside where the *Hotspur* had been anchored. All that remained were three coils of rope, a quantity of timber stacked like a pyramid, and a pair of abandoned freight wagons. A number of hooded figures darted among the shadows, ventured into the lurid light only to disappear once more.

A musket roared; gunfire blossomed in the doorway of Don Rodrigo's warehouse. A fusillade of gunshots echoed from around the docks. Morgan shifted his gaze from the melee to the *Hotspur,* now engulfed in flames.

An unearthly shriek carried across the water from the unfortunate vessel. One of Morgan's crewmen had escaped from below deck only to find himself trapped, his clothes trailing fire. The poor soul's voice rose an octave as his flesh blistered and burned. He blindly staggered to portside and pitched headfirst over the rail and fell like a comet into the estuary. The flames sizzled, winked out, leaving the seaman to bob lifelessly upon the Pearl's mirrored surface.

Morgan's features darkened; his mouth was an almost invisible slash lost in the stubbled set of his jaw. He seemed totally devoid of emotion and had the look of a man who suddenly no longer cared if he lived or died so long as he let his share of blood. Julia shivered and drew back from him as he spoke without facing her, his eyes riveted on Chiang Lu's hooded assassins as they inexorably closed in on Don Rodrigo's warehouse.

"Get out of the carriage," he ordered.

Julia started to argue with him, then thought better of

the idea. Morgan's voice had all the warmth of a drawn cutlass. She couldn't blame him, not with his ship lighting the harbor. She knew what it meant to lose everything. Save for whoever had barricaded themselves in the warehouse, the Rue de Lorchas—for a hundred yards in either direction—was devoid of life, mute testimony to Macao's unwritten law not to become embroiled in another man's troubles.

"Get out," Morgan repeated, grabbing the reins from the woman. He glanced past her and noticed Emile Emerson, lantern in hand, striding down the gangplank of the *Magdalene*. The reverend was coatless. His rumpled shirt had been hastily tucked inside his pants, and his sleeves were rolled up past his elbows. He headed straight for the carriage. Morgan could sense the man's anger, but he had no time for a confrontation with Emerson.

Morgan's own private war lay ahead, with the men who had destroyed his ship, Chiang Lu's own Blue Wing Dragons.

"Where are you going?" Julia whispered.

"To hell, looks like."

"Be careful," she said and climbed out of the carriage.

"Sure," Morgan replied and taking the whip, brought its wicked length snapping down across the mare's rump. The animal bolted forward. Morgan lay the whip aside and transferring the lines to his left hand, dragged a pistol from his belt. The carriage careened along the uneven surface of the Rue de Lorchas. It pitched to and fro like a shallow-draft schooner in a squall.

He guided the charging mare right toward a cluster of hooded figures advancing across the street toward the warehouse. So intent were these assassins on the men within, the rapidly approaching carriage went unnoticed. Ninety yards became seventy then fifty then thirty.

"C'mon!" Morgan said through clenched teeth. "C'mon!" Thirty yards—twenty—ten—suddenly the ground shook. The wharf was bathed in brilliant light. Out in the estuary, the *Hotspur* exploded as the flames reached the powder magazine below deck. A blinding flash preceded a deep-throated roar; a ball of fire shot upward and became a column of fire and blasted timbers. The debris trailed a shower of embers like a swarm of fireflies caught in a billowing mass of black smoke.

The blast startled Chiang Lu's henchmen and they turned their backs on the warehouse to gape in awe at the *Hotspur*'s death throes. Then, sensing danger, eight men whirled as one—too late—for suddenly the driverless carriage plunged into their midst. Scattering, the Blue Wing Dragons loosed a volley of pistol fire and riddled the leather sides and back of the carriage. One man shrieked and fell beneath the mare's flashing hooves. The iron-rimmed wheels clipped another assassin, fracturing his collarbone, cracking a couple of ribs, and causing him to drop the wavy-bladed kris and the pistol he'd so boldly brandished. The man staggered back and shouted to his cohorts that the carriage was empty. However, Morgan Penmerry appeared in its wake. His greatcoat flared like the wings of an enormous black bat as he charged the hooded killers who had fired his ship.

An assassin closed in on the left. The big-bore pistol bucked in Morgan's left fist, spewed fire and powder smoke. The lead slug caved-in the hooded henchman's face and slammed the man to earth. Morgan parried a sword thrust, spied another flash of steel out of the corner of his eye, and spun and caught another short sword's vicious jab on the hilt of his cutlass. Morgan lunged forward, feinted, then swung the cutlass in an overhanded hack that mortally wounded a black-clad figure sneaking up behind him, kris in hand. Chiang Lu's henchman, caught by surprise, sank to his knees, his throat spurting blood.

Morgan allowed momentum to spin him full circle so that he faced the opponent he had knocked off balance with the feint. Chiang Lu's guard wasn't alone. Another three of his sinister companions had joined him. They were dressed alike, all in black with only their cold, passionless eyes visible beneath their masked features.

One of the new arrivals leveled a pistol at Morgan. The

other three closed in to finish what was left after the first man had emptied his gun.

"Stop!" a woman gasped.

Morgan recognized the voice. With sheer horror he saw Julia Emerson stumble breathlessly forward. The assassin with the gun panicked and turned toward this latest intruder. His finger tightened on the trigger.

"No!" Morgan shouted and threw his cutlass like a spear. The blade entered just below the hooded man's rib cage, sank deep into his vitals. The assassin gasped, fired his weapon, and blew a hole in the street, spattering Julia with shell and mud. The henchman somehow found the strength to stagger off among the shadows—to live or die, Morgan never knew.

The captain placed himself between Julia Emerson and the shadowy figures positioning themselves for one final attack. The Blue Wing Dragons had regrouped from the carnage. The uninjured assassins, Morgan counted seven, soundlessly advanced, short swords and kris or keen-edged hatchets reflecting firelight.

"Are you unharmed?" Julia asked in a hoarse voice.

"Yeah, but not for long." Morgan grabbed her lantern. It certainly wasn't his weapon of choice, but it would have to suffice. "What the devil are you doing here?"

"I came to help," Julia said.

"Thanks."

"I did keep that man from shooting you."

"Thanks."

"Well, of all the ungrateful . . ."

"Oh, Christ, what do you want me to say?"

"You can just try to mean it, is all."

"When I throw this lantern, pick up your dress and run like hell," Morgan said. Seven of Chiang Lu's killers closing in and Miss Julia Emerson was worried about sincerity.

"What will you do?" Julia asked, retreating a step as the assassins started forward.

"Probably pass you," Morgan said. "Now run!" He shoved Julia in the direction of her father's ship, hurled the lantern, and took off after her. The lantern exploded at the feet of the hooded men and doused several of Chiang Lu's private guard with flaming oil. Morgan's attackers leapt about in a mad dance as they slapped at their smoldering calves and thighs and cursed the fleeing couple.

Gunfire erupted in the night yet again. Morgan winced, ducked on reflex, and steeled himself against the shock of a wound. Nothing? He glanced over his shoulder and to his heartfelt relief saw Temp Rawlins, Tim Britchetto, and another of the *Hotspur*'s crew, a swarthy gunner named Hoyt, rush from the warehouse, their flintlocks blazing as they caught the Blue Wing Dragons by surprise, dropping two of the killers.

Chiang Lu's men tried to regroup in the face of Temp's attack, but a second volley came from the muskets of Macao's *polizia*—down the Rue de Lorchas. The Portuguese constabulary had entered the fray.

Outnumbered and outgunned, Chiang Lu's men melted like phantoms into the night.

"Come back," Tim Britchetto shouted. "You bastards killed my brother. I'm not done with you!" But the fleeing killers paid him no mind. Tim would never forget the sight of Jocko lying dead on the burning deck of the *Hotspur*.

Temp Rawlins ran over to Morgan. The old man's features were powderburned. Blood seeped from a flesh wound on his right arm. He was too angry to notice his injury.

"They were all over the *Hotspur*. Never even seen or heard 'em till they towed her away from the pier. Don Rodrigo went for the police. Tim and Hoyt and me had to fort up in the warehouse." The old seaman spat and wiped his mouth on his forearm. "I told you chasin' a dress would be your ruin. You should have been here, Captain. Not playing 'bushy park' with the parson's daughter."

Morgan flushed and looked away. He had no defense. Temp's admonition cut him as deep as the bite of any lash.

"Nothing happened."

"Don't tell me," Temp said. "Tell him." He looked past the young captain without a ship.

Morgan turned and saw the Reverend Emile Emerson marching toward him. Julia was matching her father step for step.

"Oh no," Morgan sighed. His pulse raced, adrenaline pumping, the blood lust slow to dissolve. He shifted his attention to the *Hotspur*. Blackened remains, ravaged timbers, he watched the remnants of a shattered hull slip beneath the surface of the water, dragging with it a broken spar that trailed a swath of canvas sail like a shroud. What more could happen this night?

"Signore Penmerry," a man called out from the *polizia* as they arrived on the scene led by Don Rodrigo. One of their number, a handsome aristocrat in rumpled military attire, his scarlet short coat festooned with soiled gold braid, a plumed helmet tucked beneath his arm, stepped forward to introduce himself. The rest of his command kept their muskets pointed ominously at Morgan. "I am Capitano Jorge Rossi. And it is my unpleasant duty to place you under arrest for the robbery and murder of the merchant Chiang Lu."

6

The last of the fires flickered out and the street would have been plunged into darkness but for the lanterns carried by the *polizia* and Don Rodrigo. It was to this diminutive merchant that Morgan turned.

Capitano Jorge Rossi had repeated the one phrase he could say in English, Russian, French, Chinese, Spanish, and even Arabic. Beyond his statement of arrest he could converse only in Portuguese and French. Rossi would have cut a dashing figure with his narrow face and heavy black eyebrows except for the look of resignation in his red-rimmed eyes. Lamplight did little to hide the veins that crisscrossed his prominent cheekbones and the unhealthy pallor of a man given to excess drink. Morgan had heard rumors that the *capitano* was the errant offspring of nobility, banished to a posting in Macao as punishment for bedding his own sister. Morgan didn't relish the idea of placing himself in the custody of a man totally without scruples. A streak of larceny was one thing, total decadence quite another.

The *polizia* had arranged themselves into a single rank, a couple of feet apart. To Morgan's right stood the *Hotspur*'s three remaining crewmen, watching first their captain then the *polizia*. Julia Emerson stood just behind Morgan, as astonished as he at the news of Chiang Lu's demise.

Emile Emerson, quite out of breath from his exertions, covered the remaining few yards at a trot, brushed past his daughter, and confronted Morgan. He was relieved Julia was unharmed and furious at the man who had taken her God-knew-where, done God-knew-what, and carried her into a melee in which she might have been killed.

"By heaven, sir, I will have a word with you!" he proclaimed, his round features livid with rage. Before the portly missionary could vent his spleen at the brigand who had "kidnapped" his daughter, the *polizia* once again intruded.

"Signore Emerson," Rossi began. "It is my unpleasant duty to also arrest you for the murder of Chiang Lu."

The reverend was all set to unleash his righteous anger. He sputtered several unintelligible words, his face aghast.

"Is this what you call going for help, Don Rodrigo?" Morgan growled, his rugged features streaked with perspiration.

Don Rodrigo shifted his weight on his spindly legs and tried to make the best of an embarrassing situation. "My friend, it is none of my doing. Chiang Lu's body was found in his garden, his throat slashed. The Portuguese position in Macao is fragile at best. Despite Chiang Lu's many rivals, there will be a hue and cry over his murder." The bullet-headed little man shrugged and kicked the red mud from his boots of Spanish leather. "The guilty parties need to be brought to justice. Quickly. You understand."

"Yeah, we're elected," Morgan said.

"There will be a tribunal, of course. You may declare your innocence . . ."

"And then be handed over to the Chinese for execution," Emerson interrupted, his quarrel with Morgan momentarily set aside. He had lived in Macao long enough to know that justice was the casualty of expediency. Even as despair settled on him like a cloak, Emerson found in this blackest hour a kernel of hope, of faith unextinguishable. He had not been abandoned. *Trust in the Lord*, Emerson told himself as he stared into the guns of the *polizia*. *Lord, send all thy angelic host to rescue your poor servant, that all may know the goodness and the glory and the power of God*. The reverend silently prayed and closed his eyes.

Salvation came not in the form of some celestial servant dispatched from the throne of the Almighty but in two hundred thirty-five pounds of whipcord and whalebone, of muscle and guts, of foxlike cunning and never-say-die bravado. Salvation came in the form of a man.

During his interchange with Don Rodrigo, Morgan Penmerry had gradually edged closer to the warehouse owner until at last the smaller man was in reach. Don Rodrigo kept a small-caliber flintlock tucked in his belt. Morgan swallowed, and rehearsed in his mind what must happen. He'd only have one chance and he'd have to make it count.

Capitano Jorge Rossi turned to his command and barked an order. The *polizia* moved to separate Morgan and Emerson from the others on the pier. While Julia, Temp, and the rest were trying to think of something to do, Morgan acted. He snared Don Rodrigo's belly gun, cocked the weapon, and placed the cold steel muzzle against Rossi's throat to keep him from bolting. The *polizia* turned their muskets on Morgan.

"Don Rodrigo, tell the *capitano* here that unless Rossi's men back off, it will be my unpleasant duty to blow his brains out," Morgan said. He expected at least some hesitation on Rossi's part, to save face at least. Instead, Rossi frantically ordered his men to retreat and lower their weapons.

"Appears the *capitano* here has a guilty conscience," Morgan observed dryly. He turned to Emerson.

"Rouse your crew and lower the johnny boats," Morgan said. "We'll tow the *Magdalene* away from the pier till we catch a breeze."

"We?" Emerson coldly questioned.

"Sure," Morgan replied. "You need a pilot and I'm captain of nothing but wreckage. I'll bring you to Astoria, but the *Magdalene* is mine when I've seen you through."

"See here—" the reverend blurted. The scoundrel had absconded with his daughter and now had the audacity to assume a kind of partnership. "Of, of all the impossible . . . nerve. Do you think I would take you on after what has transpired, after you—with my daughter—the very gall."

"Have it your way," Morgan said with a shrug. "Stand over there with Rossi's men. Temp, you take the lads to the *Magdalene*. We leave tonight. Tell Emerson's crew the reverend has been arrested and it's every man for himself."

"You can't be serious!" Julia exclaimed, hurrying over to confront Morgan. Her eyes reflected firelight through her mud-streaked features.

"Your father made his choice," Morgan told her.

"I won't allow it," she snapped.

"You're in no position . . ."

"Wait!" the reverend said. He took a moment to compose himself. "I agree to your arrangements. Pilot us to Astoria." He glared at Morgan. "And when we reach our destination, you and I will settle what is between us. But I expect your conduct to be above reproach."

"You have my word," Morgan said. He then turned back to Don Rodrigo. "Tell the *capitano* he will be my guest until we are out in the estuary. Then we'll give him a boat and point him to shore."

Don Rodrigo translated. The *capitano* retorted, rapid-fire, the merchant replied, and so the two went back and forth. In the end Don Rodrigo prevailed, his argument given credence by the gun at Rossi's skull.

"He says you are the son of a pig," the little merchant said. "And many other things not so nice. But he will do as you tell him."

As a sign of good faith the *capitano* cracked an order and his guard followed by placing their muskets on the ground. Morgan took his prisoner by the arm and started down the Rue de Lorchas, and the rest fell into step around him. Morgan kept the gun visibly pressed to

Rossi's head to keep any of his men from trying anything. Emerson, walking abreast of Morgan, stared at him as they hurried toward the waiting bark.

"What is it?" Morgan finally asked, made curious by the man's scrutiny.

"You weren't what I expected," replied the man of God. "No gold sword, no shining wings, certainly no halo."

"Don't lose heart, Dr. Emerson." Morgan flashed a wicked grin. "The Lord works in mysterious ways."

Demetrius Vlad could have had Jorge Rossi killed, but there might come a day when Vlad would have need of the Rossi family's influence. Better to take the incompetent officer under his wing and use him—or dispose of him—later.

The Russian dug his boot heels into the mud at the edge of the shore where the mouth of the Pearl emptied into the sea. Islands like humpback whales rose out of a morning mist made golden as the newly risen sun broke through the overcast sky. A wind gust tugged at the hem of Vlad's dark green greatcoat and curled the rolling waves a frothy white.

Rossi, arms weary from having to row to shore after being set adrift from the *Magdalene*, chattered incessantly, explaining for the third time that Morgan had tricked him, Don Rodrigo had tricked him, fate itself had tricked him. It wasn't his fault. None of it was his fault and he washed his hands of any blame.

"Which doesn't change the fact that the Chinese will have your head for allowing Chiang Lu's murderers to escape," Vlad chuckled, tucking his hands in his greatcoat as he watched a lonely gull spiral over the rolling tide.

Rossi started to counter, but caught himself. He was finished in Macao. The sooner he abandoned the post, the better.

"What will I do?" Rossi pleaded. Looking past the Russian, he saw Abdul dismount near the sulky that had brought Vlad and the *capitano* out onto this narrow, treeless peninsula. The Moroccan tethered his mount to the broken, battered bow of a johnboat jutting from the mud. Abdul headed for the two men at land's end, his purposeful strides carrying him along the length of the narrow peninsula. He wore loose-fitting undyed nankeen trousers, a cotton shirt, and a waistcoat of black broadcloth. He'd tucked a brace of pistols in the wide leather belt circling his waist. Moisture streaked his ebony features as he approached.

Demetrius Vlad stepped back to take Abdul's report. Vlad folded his arms across his chest and stroked his close-cropped beard. A recently changed gauze bandage covered the terrible wound that was Morgan Penmerry's legacy.

"I have arranged for the water, dried fruit, and a supply of salted fish. Our men will begin loading as soon as it arrives at the pier," Abdul explained. "There is a rice farmer named Lao who would be willing to butcher his hogs for the right price."

Vlad nodded. "Meet his price and see about powder and shot. And Madame De Builliard no doubt can supply us with rum. She has done so in the past. But none of that swill she calls wine; I'd sooner drink your stallion's water."

Abdul chuckled, the sound of his voice deep and resonant like far-off thunder. Vlad turned toward Rossi, who avoided the black man's gaze.

"You're leaving?" the *capitano* observed. "Take me with you."

"And leave your command? Your posting?" Vlad asked with false incredulity. Like a cat toying with its prey, Vlad smiled and stroked his moustache as he once again faced the gray expanse of water lapping at the shore. "Come aboard at night. Allow no one to see you. Remain below deck until we leave Macao. You may use my cabin."

Vlad's brig was a sturdy, deep-draft ship, larger than the *Hotspur* had been and carrying a crew of thirty men. Thirty-one now, Vlad figured, for he would indeed put Jorge Rossi to work. His fine soft hands would be rope burned and calloused within a week.

Rossi almost wept for gratitude. He reached out to shake the Russian's hand, but Vlad ignored him.

"Take my horse back into town," Abdul offered. "Then wait for sunset. Ride."

"Yes . . . yes, thank you," the *capitano* gasped, bowing toward Vlad. The wayward son of Portuguese nobility hurried back toward the horses. When he was well out of earshot, Abdul spoke.

"Do you think he suspects, Captain Vlad?"

"Once we're at sea, it won't matter," Vlad replied. "Take care, though, that you spend none of Chiang Lu's gold. Some of the coins bear his name."

"As you wish," Abdul said. He waited on his captain, devoted in his loyalty to the exiled Russian. Vlad was a curious mixture of aesthete and bloodthirsty brigand. He had not batted an eye while slicing Chiang Lu's throat from ear to ear. Now he stood in abject appreciation of the lonely horizon and seemed at peace.

Miles from Macao Morgan Penmerry stood on the quarterdeck and braced himself against the rail while the *Magdalene* rode the swell and trough of the choppy sea. He was alone on the quarterdeck, his hands on the ship's wheel, getting the feel of the craft. He breathed deeply and felt his entire being restored with each lungful of the cool, briny air. He wanted to roar, to sing, to bellow to the men scurrying around the deck below or climbing the rigging to check the sails. Alone with his thoughts and grateful for the solitude, he allowed the past to peel away like curling paint. It was useless baggage. He was in the middle of picturing such an image when Julia Emerson made her way up from the main deck. She carried a cup of steaming black tea brewed strong and bitter, the better to cut the fog in a tired man's brain. But Morgan wasn't tired. Not yet. He's escaped the *polizia*, imprisonment, and a probable execution.

"I brought you drink," she said as she stood beside him. She had changed her clothes and now wore a simple brown tunic and knee-length trousers, stockings, and black buckled shoes. Her long auburn hair was gathered by a strand of leather and hung down her back. Her well-rounded figure filled her new attire in ways Morgan found positively delectable. Things were looking up already.

"Well, if you must gape at me like a half-wit, I shall retire below." Julia turned to go.

"Wait, lass. Allow a man his moment to appreciate beauty where he finds it."

Julia paused, turned toward him, and mirrored his appraisal. His good humor left her all the more puzzled. "I don't trust you," she said.

"Wisdom and beauty."

"And you with naught but the clothes on your back and those soon worn thin, no doubt."

"Aye."

His attitude was infectious. Julia had to struggle to hold on to her gloom. She attempted to overpower him with the truth.

"You lost your ship."

"Aye."

"And all your money."

"That's a fact."

"Everything!"

"And then some." Morgan's craggy, rough-hewn frame could no longer contain his emotions. He tilted his head back and began to laugh. His body shook, his features turned red, his eyes grew teary as the laughter coursed through his veins, and he had to struggle to keep the brig on course.

The crew below halted in their work. Temp Rawlins peered around the mainmast and forgot to bellow at the slackers nearby. Tim Britchetto dropped to the deck from the rigging and stared with the rest at Morgan Penmerry.

"Is he mad?" someone asked in a gruff low voice.

"No matter," said Temp, and he squinted at the men around him. The leathery old seafarer wondered if there was one among them who could understand. "He's free."

PART II

Backbone of the World

7

May 1814

"I sing that the world will not die.
I am the wind's daughter;
I am the fire's bride."

The old woman outstretched her hand, keeping her wrinkled
flesh just above the lapping flames. She unclenched her
fist and dusted the blaze with sacred meal—a mixture
of pounded roots, dried berries, powdered ram's horn,
and a pinch of the soil in which she had been born so
many winters past she no longer cared to count. She
added a leathery morsel, brown as a button, a piece of
what had once been her own umbilical cord saved for her
by her shaman father, whose bones lay in Ever Shadow,
the mountain ranges to the north.

As the sacred mixture disappeared into the heart of the
fire, the flames took on a rose-colored glow. The old
woman's eyes rolled back in her head and she loosed a
wild, soul-wrenching cry that rose in pitch and volume
like an onrushing torrent, a flash flood of unearthly sound.

Her cry coursed through her frail-looking frame until it seemed she must split apart from the effort. Then the outburst faded, her endurance flagged, and she leaned against a willow backrest and listened to dying echoes of herself. The long, thin tufts of her snow-white hair spilled over her shoulders and the willow frame supporting her.

She placed a hand on her wrinkled breast and tried to remember when it had once been full of milk. She made soft cooing sounds, as a mother might make in the stillness of night as she nurses her young. The old woman pretended to nurse and watched the shadows on the walls of her dwelling shift and dance until at last, to her way of seeing, the shadows coalesced and a stygian shape hunched forward, coaxed out of the darkness by the flames and the old woman's song.

> "I am the wind's daughter.
> I am the fire's bride."

Her eyes brightened in her hungry face, whose beauty had long since faded like wild strawberries in winter. Her lips had grown dry as leather. As a maiden she had sung for the green, unquenchable fire of spring coursing through her veins. Now she sang a different song, for the flame in her heart was wisdom, not desire. All that remained of youth were the eyes, fierce and unblinking as she peered from the world of her dwelling into the spirit realm, where the *Maiyun* danced and dreamed in timeless sleep.

"I see," she said. "Tell me. Do the flames speak straight as a hawk plummets to his kill? Tell me. For I am she who was born to know. I am the song giver. Is it time?"

Embers cracked. Coals red as blood, bitter bright as vengeance, pulsed with a life of their own, as love and hate live on beyond one's final breath. A fire does not die with its maker, but lingers to warm or wound whoever comes to the circle of flame.

The old woman closed her eyes and listened to a voice another might say was merely the sighing wind or the singing creek—but she knew different. If her body lingered in one world, her heart and soul walked another.

She listened, and her parched lips whispered, "It is so," to the revelation of the Above Ones—a truth she had sensed for days. The beginning had brought her to the end and the end was but the first step of another beginning. One lives, loves, dies along the path of the Great Circle. *She must be ready.* The hour was at hand.

It was good to know what had to be done. The old woman was afraid, yes, but it was good to know.

Lost Eyes stood upon the summit of the world—or so it seemed. It was always that way, vista after vista, whenever he found a break in the forest, whenever he followed a deer trail through the slanted sunlight in the high country. Here in the lost places there was peace. The *Maiyun* lived here, spirits of the green earth and purple crags, of the golden sunlight and black storms.

Today Lost Eyes did not stand alone in the sighing wind. Sparrow was with him, though she should not have been. Black Fox would be angry and punish her. How like her namesake was this girl, Lost Eyes thought as he watched her on horseback, hair streaming like the long mane of the brown mare she sat. She was slight and quick like a sparrow, though her fawn-colored eyes were full of daring and subtle promises.

It was the time of the New Grass Moon. And here upon the swollen hills that lapped at the Backbone of the World, spring was never more evident. Across the pass and another hour's hard ride for Lost Eyes and Sparrow, a cascade of icy blue water plummeted a thousand feet down the granite face of Singing Woman Ridge into a thirty-yard-wide pool. A perpetual rainbow formed in the spray that hovered above the sacred pond.

Spring lived in this pass; the world's rebirth seemed to begin right here in the towering stalks of Indian poke and corn lilies, some as tall as a man, crowned with yellow-green starlike flowers and bordering a yard-wide ribbon of water left by the thaw and runoff from the pond formed beneath the cataract. Here were the fragile stalks of glacier lilies, whose brilliant yellow upswept petals had attracted a swarm of bees from a hive in a nearby storm-shattered pine. Pink-and-white bitterroot blossoms added their pastel hues to nature's canvas.

Lost Eyes watched as Sparrow guided her mount around a cluster of orange mountain dandelion. She led her suitor's own sturdy gray, for he had walked the deer trail on foot, filling a pouch with mountain mint as he searched for an appropriate spot to rig a snare and catch one of the red squirrels so busily announcing his intrusion. Their strident piping had pierced the stillness as they fled from the forest path to the safety of the nearby pines. Lost Eyes sighed and tucked away his snare as Sparrow approached. The horses startled a pair of rosy red grosbeaks who shot skyward and raced toward the comparative safety of the tree line; they dipped and darted effortlessly against an azure sky.

Lost Eyes knelt and scooped a handful of dirt in the palm of his hand, then held his arm outstretched, allowing the rich earth to sift through his fingers.

"Truly this is ground-of-many-gifts," he said.

"There is more for you to see—a mystery," said Sparrow.

Being alone with her stirred something deep within Lost Eyes. He felt flashes of fire and ice from his toes to his testicles. "A woman is all the mystery a man ever needs," the young brave said.

"It is one you will never understand." Sparrow laughed. She struck Lost Eyes a gentle blow upon the shoulder with a willow rod. "Now I have counted coup on a Scalpdancer!" She galloped away, her merry challenge ringing on the wind.

Where was she leading? Lost Eyes shrugged and leapt astride the gray and rode off down the path Sparrow had blazed through the buffalo grass.

Woman and man rode at a breakneck pace that took them from the hillside to the sun-drenched floor of the pass. The brown mare was swift, but the long-legged gray soon pulled abreast. Yet every time Lost Eyes tried to count coup on the young woman with his bow, she would alter her course just enough to elude the warrior's grasp. And, oh, her good-natured laughter taunted him unmercifully. But Lost Eyes continued his pursuit, determined to catch her and return the strike and recapture his dignity. The chase lasted the length of the valley. It ended when Sparrow halted her mare near where the waters of the cataract plunged into the spring-fed pond beneath Singing Woman Ridge.

The rippled surface of the pond reflected the blue sky and the glacier-carved granite cliffs. The brown mare had come to a halt so suddenly that Lost Eyes momentarily lost control of the gray. He tugged on the rawhide reins and clamped his legs around the gray's belly, caught a fistful of mane, and just managed to stop himself from vaulting forward over the horse's head. The gray pranced at the edge of the pool in the spray of the cataract. A rainbow hovered above the pool, lending a magical aura to the place.

Lost Eyes had never ventured so far into the pass. Like the other men of the village, he kept to the ridges, for this was a sacred place and only a few shamans of the tribe had ever approached the waterfall. He dismounted only because Sparrow did. Man and woman ambled to the pool's edge. She knelt in the moist grass and cupped water to her lips.

Lost Eyes gasped and pulled the woman to her feet. Sparrow glared at him, caught off guard by his action. Too late, she had already drunk from the sacred pool.

"Do you not fear the water demons? They will pull you under!" Lost Eyes exclaimed. "Here is living water left by the Ones-Who-Came-Before, the Forgotten People. Now the *Maiyun* claim this place. Foolish girl, do you not know the truth of it?"

"Do you?" Sparrow said, hands on hips. She was not about to be scolded by him as if she were a child. "Old tales for old women and their men to whisper about on lonely nights when Cold Maker comes. But I am young

and warm, and it would seem I have more courage than a
Pikuni brave." She faced him squarely, awaiting his reply.

"Bold talk for a girl of sixteen winters," Lost Eyes
scoffed. "I am not afraid."

"Prove it. Drink from the pool," Sparrow retorted, her
lithe frame poised as if to dart away.

Lost Eyes studied her teasing smile, then glanced with
some trepidation toward the pool of icy water. He dreaded
the deed. It wasn't bad enough the Above Ones came
down from the Backbone of the World to drink beneath
the Bow-of-Many-Colors. Ghosts lingered here as well.
Shamans told stories of hearing a woman singing the spirit
songs, a woman unseen whose voice, it was said, drifted
through the granite walls of the ridge itself. Some claimed
it was the voice of Woodberry, a medicine woman who had
defied the Above Ones and been carried away by water
demons, pulled to her death beneath the glassy surface of
the pool.

Lost Eyes gingerly made his way through corn lilies.
The ground softened underfoot, and his moccasins left
deep impressions in the soil. He moved slowly as if
stalking game; in truth, it was his own deep misgivings
that gave him pause. At last pride overrode fear and
superstition, and he sank to his knees by the pond and
hunkered forward to drink.

He broke the cold mirrorlike surface, dunked himself
face first, and emerged with his hair streaming as he
gasped for breath. He cupped a mouthful of icy water,
then paused to study his own image as it reassembled on
the surface. He saw a young man with far too serious
features, a guarded young man, dark eyed and quick,
intelligent. He liked to think he saw courage there and a
chance at maturity and wisdom.

No demons rose to attack him, so to prove himself as
courageous as Sparrow he chanced another drink and
splashed water over his face, neck, and head. He eased
back on his haunches and again watched his reflection.
For a single brief second, he saw himself covered with
blood, his eyes staring through a mask of crimson. Lost

Eyes sucked in his breath and straightened. But the moment had passed and he saw only what he truly was . . . a young Blackfoot brave who had yet to accompany his first raiding party or ride to battle much less suffer such a grievous wound. Maybe it had been a demon come to the surface to warn him away. He shivered and stared at the water. A hand touched his and he whirled about, only to find Sparrow at his side.

The girl retreated a step, startled by his quickness and the look of raw fear in his eyes. She moved past him to the edge of the pond and, standing in the imprint of his knees, looked down. She saw only herself, a girl of sixteen, her lustrous black hair adorned with doeskin braid holders. She wore a beaded dress of brushed elkskin and calf-high moccasins that she herself had decorated with tiny glass beads Black Fox had brought from a raid down on the Tongue River, many days' ride to the south in the land of the Crow. She saw herself and none other in the ripples at her feet.

"What did you see?" she asked, regretting her decision to enter the pass. She had wanted to show him the cliff paintings she had discovered beneath a granite ledge just a stone's throw from the falls. These crude drawings of a large tusked animal being slaughtered by a handful of hunters armed with spears and firebrands had been left by the Forgotten People.

"What did you see?" she repeated. Still he did not answer. Sparrow came to him, crushing the lilies of spring in her path.

His arms opened to receive her. She stood in his embrace. Lost Eyes breathed her in; she smelled of wood smoke and chokecherries. Her warmth leached the sudden chill from his limbs. He stroked her hair as he held her in his arms. Sunlight glimmered on the surface of the pond and refracted onto the granite cliff where the ancient hunters had left the story of their lives upon the walls of the pass.

Lost Eyes had heard of such depictions. Great power resided in the age-old drawings. He could see clearly now in the rarefied air of the high country. Who were those forgotten ones and what mystical beast had they attacked? Perhaps it was some kind of shaggy buffalo, a demon creature of terrible strength. His gaze dropped from the pictographs to the waters noisily plunging into the pool. Yes, there was power here. He had glimpsed a fraction of it, and it had shown him his own death.

"What have I seen... nothing." He laughed bitterly. "Remember who I am. I have no vision."

"I know who you are," Sparrow replied, growing warmer in his arms. The fear had left him, she sensed. It was good. But she knew better than to try and coerce him into explaining what had spooked him there by the pond.

Lost Eyes looked down at the woman in his arms. The ground behind her was inviting, the new grass would make a perfect bed. In his mind's eye he saw them both entwined upon the silken blades of spring growth.

As if reading his thoughts, Sparrow pressed herself against him and a throaty purr sounded deep in her throat. She did not care about custom or tradition or what was right or wrong. All that had been swept aside in the face of her own deep feelings and the longing to give herself to this young man. She was perplexed that he held back.

"I cannot," he explained as he dropped his arms to his side. He loved Sparrow. But she should have a man, a whole man to care for her and be with her. And he was not whole. The All-Father had turned from him.

"Why?" Sparrow asked, wanting the young man as much as he wanted her.

"Because I am Lost Eyes." The young brave walked away from her and headed away from the pool and the woman, turning his back on mystery and love.

He never reached the gray mare grazing a few yards from the pool. Sparrow never called to him, never cried to him in anger or remorse, never told him the truth: that they were bound each to the other and that for all his pride, her love could make him whole. None of it was said, for quite suddenly they were no longer alone in the shadow of Singing Woman Ridge.

A stranger in the mist, a Blackfoot like no other, a brooding, powerfully built, solitary figure had materialized west of the pass. He rode slumped forward over the neck of his blaze-faced stallion. The horse, smelling water, increased its pace. As the stranger neared, Lost Eyes recognized the buffalo horn symbol painted in white clay paste on the stallion's shoulder. The symbol stirred in Lost Eyes' memory a story told among the Scalpdancers, a tale passed to their children of a legendary warrior and shaman, a man of great courage and prowess who had been banished from the village along Elkhorn Creek for committing a most terrible, dark deed.

Lost Eyes had been a child of six winters and unconcerned with the problems of adults. His had been a world of rough play, pretend battles, and learning the skills of the hunt. And yet, even such a headstrong youth had heard of the man called White Buffalo, slayer of the sacred beast, taker of the animal's name and the animal's power.

The Blackfoot brave watched the horseman loom larger still. Now the stallion's hoofbeat echoed along the cliff. The man appeared to be at least a head taller than Lost Eyes, maybe more. But this trail-worn figure seemed hardly the stuff of legend, drooping forward as he was onto the neck of the stallion. The man's long hair was streaked with silver and hid his features. A slight breeze tugged at an eagle feather braided into a lock of his hair. The feather had been notched and edged with red war paint, indicating the wearer had slit an enemy's throat and taken his scalp. The stranger's buckskin tunic hung in tatters about his muscular torso, and blood had coagulated in the cuts that streaked his coppery flesh. A flintlock rifle was slung over his shoulder, and his right hand firmly gripped the hardwood shaft of a long-handled war club, its length wrapped with rawhide and inlaid with silver beads. The weapon's stone head was encrusted with dried blood.

The stallion paused and raised its nostrils to catch the

scent of the man and woman and the mares by the pool. Finding no threat, the stallion continued its course unbidden by its rider. Lost Eyes wondered if the warrior was dead. Just to be on the safe side he drew the knife at his waist.

The stallion bore the rider to the sacred pool and when it reached the water, the weary animal eagerly drank its fill. Lost Eyes hesitated and then, when the stranger made no move to dismount, the young brave sheathed his knife and began to circle the pool warily.

"White Buffalo," Sparrow said in an awed whisper.

"I don't know. Perhaps."

"Is he dead?"

Lost Eyes glared at her and left unspoken his admonition that she asked too many questions.

"It is White Buffalo," Sparrow flatly pronounced. She fell in with Lost Eyes. However, the woman wasn't as cautious and stepped on a dry twig that broke beneath her moccasins with a muffled snap just loud enough to spook the stallion away from the sacred pool and dislodge the rider and the elkskin packs draped across the stallion's rump.

The fallen man groaned but made no move to help himself. Lost Eyes hurried to his side, freed the rifle, and then turned the man face up. The warrior's pain-drawn features were hidden behind war paint, a streak of white that covered the upper part of the man's face, from the bridge of his nose to his forehead. On close examination Lost Eyes also noted ragged wounds in the warrior's left shoulder and right thigh. Arrows had pierced the brave's limbs, but from the torn, bloody flesh and the way the wounds were made, it was clear the brave had broken the arrows off at the flesh and forced the pointed shafts out. Blood had caked both the entry and exit wounds.

"Is he dead?" Sparrow repeated, drawing close and peering over Lost Eyes' shoulder at the fallen warrior.

Even in repose the brave possessed an aura of menace, of great strength and latent violence. How could such a

man be killed? And yet he lay so still and his wounds were
so grievous.

Lost Eyes didn't know, but it seemed as if the man were
surely dying if not already dead, and the young Blackfoot
started to say as much when he heard the voice of the
wind—the voice of a woman singing. The sound was
almost imperceptible at first and Lost Eyes suspected his
own senses had deceived him—except that Sparrow heard
it too. Her hand tightened on his arm.

"*Saaa-vaa-hey*," Lost Eyes muttered. What was this?
He turned toward the granite cliff rising above them, its
weathered facade cracked and scoured from rain and snow.
Nothing moved save the plunging ribbon of water.

The voice carried above the merry burbling of the
stream as it threaded its way out across the pass. The song
seemed to come from all directions at once, from the very
ground—no the ridge—everywhere at once.

As if the ghost woman's song wasn't unnerving enough,
suddenly the fallen warrior reached out and caught Lost
Eyes by the front of his buckskin shirt. "Crow dog," the
wounded man rasped and bolted upright.

Sparrow gasped and fell back, but Lost Eyes was caught.
Indeed, he was frozen in place as the wounded man stared
at him and through him. "You are among your own
people," Lost Eyes gasped. "I am one."

"I am White Buffalo," the stranger hoarsely replied. "I
have no people."

Lost Eyes grabbed the shaman's wrist and tried to pull
free, but the fallen man had a grip of iron and he raised
himself up and brought his face inches from Lost Eyes.
His breath smelled of pipe smoke and blood and pemmican. White Buffalo's puzzled expression faded and gradually
became one of recognition. He eased his hold and sank
back upon the ground. He turned his granitelike features
toward Sparrow and his eyes flickered with renewed interest.

Sparrow shifted uncomfortably, feeling naked before his
steady scrutiny.

"I'll cut wood. You lash the travois together," Lost Eyes

said, stepping between the two. "I will help you as soon as I backtrack him."

"Why?" Sparrow thought him too cautious.

"Because the Crow are our enemy also." Lost Eyes led her away from the pond and over to a stand of young saplings suitable for a litter for the wounded man.

"It will be slow going. Black Fox will be furious," Sparrow chided gently. Actually, she was certain she could defuse her brother no matter how angry he became.

The soft green branches of the willow saplings brushed her cheek as Lost Eyes hacked through the tender trunks with his hand ax, leaving Sparrow to bend and break them and trim away the branches with his tomahawk. When she had enough wood for a crude travois, the young woman lashed the saplings together with rawhide strips torn from the fringed sleeves of her knee-length dress. All the time she could sense White Buffalo studying her. Sparrow worked uneasily and tried to keep her mind on the task at hand, but the tightness between her shoulder blades distracted her. She glanced up as Lost Eyes galloped away to the west to retrace White Buffalo's trail. She twisted around to see if the wounded man had lost consciousness. He was staring at her, though his arms trembled from supporting himself.

Sparrow licked her dry lips and wiped the moisture from her brow and shifted her point of view to the plunging falls. She considered a break from her labors, wondering if she could ever drink enough to slake the thirst she felt. Save for the gray mare receding in the distance, nothing disturbed the silence.

Silence? And what of the singing woman—had they both dreamed the voice? No, impossible. Sparrow had heard it with her own ears. Then she heard another voice.

"What are you called?" White Buffalo asked.

"Sparrow," she replied timidly, unable to lower her guard in his presence.

"Sparrow, come to my side." His strength appeared to be ebbing, for he sank back upon the earth.

The girl of sixteen winters left the travois and haltingly

crossed to the wounded man's side. His arm rose slowly. She sank into the blackness of his eyes and became transfixed as his hand cupped the back of her neck and then turned to iron as it forced her down to him. She tried to resist, but his power overwhelmed her. She was helpless to stop him from forcing her face to his wound, her mouth to his ragged, bloody flesh. He laughed and whispered, "I take your spirit into me. Drink of my blood, little one. Is it not living water? Now I claim you. Now we are joined. My blood has claimed you."

A woman's voice drifted on the wind, faint, tremulous, yet in its own way powerful, for the Above Ones worked their wiles in the world of men. The voice came from everywhere and nowhere, but in its wake White Buffalo released the girl. She shoved against him with such force, she toppled over on her backside and crabbed on her hands and heels away from his side.

"Too late!" White Buffalo roared and his voice reverberated through the pass. He was joined to her by blood. The girl was his. He listened to the yellow silence; the strange unearthly voice had grown still in the pulsing sunlight. See, there was no spirit song borne on the spring air. He did not fear the Above Ones. He was White Buffalo. He had stolen the power of the sacred beast.

As the shaman lost consciousness and succumbed to his wounds, his last thought was that he would live . . . forever.

Sparrow kicked at the unfinished travois and saplings. Sobbing, she wiped her mouth on the sleeve of her deerskin dress but could not rid herself of the taste of him. And what did the shaman warrior mean, "too late"?

There was blood upon the buffalo grass.

Lost Eyes counted the dead. Two Crows were sprawled at arm's length, one with a broken spear shaft jutting from his chest, the other with the lower half of his jaw blown away. A third brave lay thirty feet from his fallen companions. He had hidden in the rocks and loosed his arrows at White Buffalo; he probably accounted for both of the shaman's wounds. Brains and blood congealed on the

warrior's skull where White Buffalo's war hammer had
caved in his forehead. The vultures had already begun to
feed when Lost Eyes entered the box canyon. These great
ashen-gray scavengers seemed reluctant to abandon their
dinners, and Lost Eyes made no real effort to disturb
them. Shadows circled the canyon, gliding soundlessly
over the rims and the granite cliffs cutting the narrow
canyon off from the pass.

A brief violent struggle had been waged here with no
mercy shown the vanquished. Even the horses were dead,
sprawled pitifully where they had fallen, caught in the
middle of White Buffalo's berserk attack. Broken bows,
spears, and war shields littered the canyon floor. Three
men, stout warriors all, had been killed in a matter of
seconds by the one they had ambushed. Their torsos were
streaked with war paint, their mounts wore spirit signs,
but White Buffalo's medicine had been stronger.

The scavengers were gathered for their feast. Lost Eyes
turned his gray about and rode at a gallop out of the box
canyon. A few vultures flapped their wings and scolded
the retreating figure; others remained aloft until the man
thing was well out of the canyon.

Lost Eyes, oblivious to the carrion birds, noted instead a
faint set of unshod pony tracks that led out of the canyon and
immediately angled away from the course White Buffalo had
chosen. It could well mean that there had been four braves
hidden in the canyon and one had escaped to report White
Buffalo's whereabouts. Lost Eyes considered himself as courageous as the next man, but he held no illusions about his
ability to fight off an entire Crow war party. The sooner he
and Sparrow left Singing Woman Ridge the better.

He touched his heels to the gray mare's flanks and the
sturdy mount rode down the pass and quickly distanced
itself from that place of death.

By the time he returned to the spring, Lost Eyes had
expected the travois to be nearly completed. What he
found were scattered poles and a truculent young woman
already mounted and waiting for him.

Sparrow sat impatiently astride her mountain-bred pony

as Lost Eyes pulled alongside her. She did not wait for his questions as he glanced from the woman to the unconscious White Buffalo.

"I am returning to our village." Sparrow cast a quick glance in the direction of the wounded man. "Come with me."

"Speak straight. What are you saying?" Lost Eyes could tell the shaman still lived. White Buffalo's chest rose and fell with every breath. "We cannot leave one of the People for the Crow dogs to hunt and kill."

"White Buffalo has no people. He has said this," Sparrow snapped at him.

Lost Eyes reached for her arm, tried to hold her back and reason with her. Had the lost spirits of this place driven her mad? Her conduct angered him. Whatever else, the wounded man was a Piegan, a Blackfoot warrior, and a man of the Scalpdancers. But these were arguments and he had no time to quarrel.

"Help me."

"No. Leave him!" She pulled free. "I have spoken."

"No." Lost Eyes stubbornly refused.

"Then save him yourself." Sparrow started to leave him, yet held back. What could she say to make him change his mind? That she had tasted his blood—that she feared White Buffalo for the desperate darkness she had glimpsed behind his flashing eyes? Words failed her. There was evil here, and despite the love in her heart and her yearning for this man without a vision, she turned from him and rode away.

Lost Eyes made no move to stop her, puzzled though he was at her abrupt shift in temperament. She had dared him and teased him and brought him to the spring, wholly unafraid and heedless of his warning.

"Yet I remain," he whispered to himself. He knew that he must stay, that he must carry White Buffalo to safety. He thought he knew why. But a man cannot glimpse all of the journey, only the path at hand, the few steps before and those few behind. Had he glimpsed the truth, had he been able to peer into the heart of the mystery, Lost Eyes might never have taken that first step.

8

The banks of Elkhorn Creek were ablaze. Camp fires burned throughout the village but none more brightly than the great council fire in the center of the circled lodges. The north end of the valley was filled with sight and sound. Tonight, a man's fate would be decided. It was a dark and bloody business, but it had to be done.

Distant drums summoned the elders to council to decide whether a man must live or die. The drumbeat continued steadily; it never varied, neither swelled nor faded but stayed the same, monotonous and insistent, like a beating heart. An eagle, disturbed by the sound, surged for freedom.

The council drums beat on as the elders made their way through the village, moving with one mind toward the ceremonial lodge. Here came the leaders of the clans or warrior societies: the Kit Foxes and Crazy Dogs, the Bear and the Bowstring clans too, for the council was open to all men unafraid to die—men who had counted coup and proved their bravery in battle. Such a man was Black Fox.

Sparrow's brother kicked at a mongrel pup as it gingerly approached, looking for food. The little scavenger whimpered as the brave's moccasined foot connected with its backside. The pup fled. Black Fox immediately regretted the action. He was not by nature cruel. Among the Kit Fox Society he was considered brave and generous to a fault. There were few to match his skill with the elkhorn bow. He seldom returned from a hunt empty-handed. And those of his clan who were less fortunate were free to share in his bounty. So with regret, he watched the pup scurry past his wife, who maneuvered her child-swollen frame out of the frightened animal's path.

It was the twilight hour. As the sun lay beyond the mountains, the western horizon donned luminous robes of wine and purple and pink. But the onset of night brought no peace to the Blackfoot village nor to the lodge of Black Fox. It galled him still how Sparrow had finally returned in midafternoon on a well-lathered mount. She had ignored her angry brother's interrogation other than to admit she had been with Lost Eyes. Such lack of respect for one's older brother was intolerable.

Yellow Stalk watched her husband a moment as if considering whether or not to approach him. He was displeased with her as well, for she had interceded on Sparrow's behalf and placed herself in the path of his anger. Before long, word reached him of Lost Eyes' arrival and the wounded man who had returned to the village of the Scalpdancers—White Buffalo.

Even Black Fox was too young to have known the shaman, but the stories were as familiar to him as to anyone. He would attend the council this night and listen to the tribal chiefs, men like Kills The Bear and Dog Chases The Hawk and Fool Deer and Crow Striker. These elders spoke with wisdom. They would know what must be done.

Sparrow emerged from the tepee and, pretending not to notice her brother, started down to the creek, bearing a pair of empty water bags over her shoulder. Yellow Stalk resisted the urge to delay her husband from the council. She saw Tall Bull hurrying toward her husband. Yellow

Stalk wrinkled her nose with distaste as he approached.
She was not impressed by his courage or feats of bravery.
She knew only that Tall Bull kept a stout willow branch to
beat his wife, Owl Bead, whenever the mood touched
him. Yellow Stalk was by no means the only one who
resented the brave's behavior. There had been talk among
the elders of the Kit Fox Society to expel Tall Bull from
the circle if he did not mend his ways.

Yellow Stalk tried to catch her husband's eye, to reassure herself that everything was all right between them.
But he still blamed her for defending Sparrow's disobedi-
ence. Black Fox retained his sullen expression and pointedly
avoided eye contact. Yellow Stalk muttered a meaning-
less sound that expressed her feeling of exasperation.
Warriors, for all their deeds of glory, were so much like
children, at times tamed by love and at other times as wild
and unpredictable as the coyote, the great trickster. Yellow
Stalk winced as the child within her moved, and she
mentally told her baby, *Yes, that is your stubborn father.
Be like him. But not in all things.*

Her child-to-be was ample compensation for the discomfort of the moment. She would give birth in the
Season of the Sun.

The music of the drums carried to the creek where
Sparrow knelt to fill the water bags and reflect, there in
the sweet green rushes, amid the shadows. The council
would decide whether or not there would be peace. What
if Black Fox had his way and Lost Eyes was sent away,
banished like White Buffalo? What would she do then?
Abandon all and follow him? Foolish. She had warned
him. She had pleaded with him to leave the wounded
shaman behind. He was a cursed one. Now Lost Eyes
might well be cursed with him and suffer a fate similar to
the wounded man's.

Sparrow submerged her hands in the icy creek and
cupped water to her face and sucked in her breath,
gasping at the cold bath. She rocked back on her haunches,
her flesh tingling.

"*Saaa-vaa,*" she muttered and dried her features on the sleeve of her dress. She glanced up, taking comfort in the first stars twinkling against the cobalt horizon to the east and enjoying the last few lingering rays of sunshine reaching up from the other side of the Backbone of the World.

Sparrow found a fragile peace in this solitude. What else was there but to sit alone and wait for the council to decide White Buffalo's and Lost Eyes' fate—and, indeed, her own.

Lost Eyes circled his lodge yet again, checking on his spear and war shield and the rack of smoked meat. He stopped by the gray mare, ground-tethered close at hand. All the while he listened to the tap-tap-tapping of the council drums. His father would have spoken for him, had he lived. But Lost Eyes was alone and had no place at the council of elders. He hated having to stand apart and allow others to decide his fate. It went against his grain, but there was nothing to be done. He secured the gray mare for the third time that evening and paused to study the faces of the women circling his lodge. They kept their distance, fearful of the wounded man within. Lost Eyes ducked into the tepee, where Moon Shadow waited with living water to slake his thirst and a bowl of venison stew to take the edge off his hunger. But the hunger he felt could only be appeased by knowledge, not food. He wanted to know what the elders had in store for him and he did not relish his prospects, not if men like Black Fox had their say. Sparrow's brother could be very persuasive. Lost Eyes tried to hide his misgivings from his aunt as he reclined upon his pallet and willow backrest and accepted the food she placed before him.

He sacrificed a morsel of venison to the All-Father by placing the food directly into the flames. The meat sizzled and turned black.

"A waste of food," White Buffalo remarked gruffly, watching the young man.

The lodge smelled of wood smoke and sage. Firelight bathed the walls with a comfortable glow. Everything was as it should be within the tepee. Against the walls were parfleches of herbs and medicine pouches containing roots and seeds. A bow and otter skin quiver of arrows hung from one of the lodge poles. And nearby lay a deerskin bag of White Buffalo's belongings that had not been examined despite Moon Shadow's natural curiosity.

If the rotund old woman held any ill will toward her wounded guest, she did not express it other than in her concern for Lost Eyes, which was plainly evident in her features. Worry lines etched her brown face, flared out from beneath her eyelids, creased her forehead where her black and silvery hair spilled forward to frame her round cheeks.

White Buffalo watched in bemused silence as Lost Eyes finished his prayer offering and managed a tentative sip of meat broth. He dabbed his fingers in the wooden bowl and scooped a chunk of venison into his mouth. He wasn't truly hungry. Eating was only a pretext to please Moon Shadow, a sham he couldn't continue for long.

Lost Eyes set the bowl aside. White Buffalo reached across and took the bowl and greedily devoured its contents, shoveling meat and broth into his mouth with his fingertips. He tossed the bowl at the feet of Moon Shadow, who dutifully set it with the other bowls in a stack near the door.

Lost Eyes panicked for a few brief seconds—just long enough for the gravity of the situation to sink in. What had compelled him to bring White Buffalo back to the village that had banished him? He shivered as ice seemed to fill his veins. The shaman warrior was grinning at him. And Lost Eyes sensed something of the power in the man and shuddered, no longer feeling in control of his own actions. He told himself that he would have brought any wounded Blackfoot to the village.

"Do not fear the drums," White Buffalo said. "What are they but stretched hide and willow sticks."

"I do not fear them," Lost Eyes retorted, not wishing to be thought a coward. "But in council men will decide your fate and mine."

"They are mere men," the shaman said contemptuously. "Does Bear Cloud still live?"

"He died two winters ago."

White Buffalo seemed pleased. "And Red Hat?"

"Killed on the Bear River by the Shoshoni," Lost Eyes told him. "But there are other elders. Fool Deer has no liking for me. Kills The Bear and Crow Striker will also decide."

"No," White Buffalo said. "I will decide. You have saved my life. It is a debt I will repay, young warrior. But tell me, why are you called Lost Eyes?"

"Because I have received no vision." He stared into the embers of the fire in the center of the lodge.

"Now I understand." White Buffalo leaned against the backrest and stared up at the smoke coruscating through the vent at the top of the lodge. "Now I know why you heard when I called."

Lost Eyes stared at the man as if he were mad. *I heard nothing. What does he mean?*

White Buffalo winced as he repositioned himself, then sighed contentedly. He had a belly full of food, he was warm, his wounds were dressed, and for the time being he was safe. It was good. "Fool Deer will straighten arrows. But he will not loose them at me," he muttered. White Buffalo closed his eyes.

Moon Shadow, sewing a moccasin for Lost Eyes, paused in her labor. She had the feeling that even with his eyes closed, the shaman warrior watched their every move.

"Crow Striker is first in battle," the wounded man continued, "but around the council fire he must follow another's lead. Kills The Bear fears my power. It is the only thing he fears, but it is enough. It is the same way with the others. Go to the council. Tell them I have sent you. Tell them I have spoken and it is this—I will leave before the moon grows full. By then my wounds will have healed."

"I have no place at council," Lost Eyes protested.

"You do now. Go and bring my words to them."

Lost Eyes rose and started for the door flap. He couldn't

be in any worse trouble, so why not appear at council? Still he paused, wanting to understand one thing. "White Buffalo, you did not call to me."

"I am here, aren't I?" said the shaman.

Lost Eyes had only gone a few yards from his lodge when a pair of foot-long arrows thwacked into the dirt at his feet. He skipped back a pace and glanced around as two boys no taller than his waist trotted forward out of the gathering dusk. The boys wore breechclouts and doeskin vests and carried buffalo horn bows. Dabs of black war paint were a poor disguise, for Lost Eyes recognized the little ones as they hurried forward to gather their arrows. The two would-be warriors were the grandchildren of Crow Striker. The smaller of the two was called Turtle. He was a squat, thickset prankster of eight winters whose shaggy hair hung to his shoulders. His brother, Raven Takes Him, was a year older and an inch taller. He wore his hair in a topknot and braids like his Dog Soldier father.

"I told you it wasn't him," Turtle complained, angry that he had wasted his only arrow.

Raven Takes Him, who never liked to admit he was wrong, especially to a younger brother, merely shrugged. "I knew it to be so," he said, nodding wisely. "My arrow slipped loose."

"Your words fly as crooked as your arrows," Turtle chided.

Both boys stopped short as Lost Eyes snatched up the arrows at his feet and raised his hand aloft as if to hurl them at the brothers.

"Well, I will send them straight," he snapped. "Do you ride against me?"

"No *tsehe*," Raven Takes Him blurted out, momentarily cowed. Turtle shrank back behind his older brother, who struggled to regain his poise. As Raven Takes Him was the elder, more was expected of him. He timidly approached Lost Eyes. "We did not see in the shadows that it was you," the boy explained.

"No. You are much too small," Turtle added, peering past his older brother. "You could not possibly be him."

"Who is it you wait for?" Lost Eyes asked, suspecting the answer. He tossed the arrows at the brothers' feet.

"White Buffalo," they said in unison.

"We will fight him." Raven Takes Him threw back his shoulders and tried to make himself appear taller while Turtle dutifully gathered the arrows and returned them to his otter skin quiver. Bravado was one thing and losing two good arrows quite another. Let Raven strut, now Turtle had *two* arrows. "Our grandfather is Crow Striker. Our father is High Eagle. We too will be great warriors," Raven Takes Him bragged. Indeed, he came of good lineage and was quick to say as much.

"We shall kill White Buffalo and hang his scalp from our father's lodge pole," Turtle added matter-of-factly. He scratched his head. His round face wore a puzzled frown. "But how shall we know him?"

"Yes. Tell us, Lost Eyes. He is in your lodge. Tell us how we will know the man," Raven Takes Him insisted. He noticed Turtle had kept his arrow and promptly retrieved it from his younger sibling's quiver.

Lost Eyes folded his arms across his chest and his expression grew serious. "Ah, you will know him, if you are lucky." He tapped his lips and pretended to be uncertain whether or not he should confide in the brothers. He squatted down and continued his tale. The two boys gave him their undivided attention. They hunched forward as if to receive a secret for their ears only.

"He is a shape changer," Lost Eyes said in a dread-filled voice. "Before my eyes I saw him become a hawk flying circles around my travois and when his enemies tried to snare him, the hawk became a mountain panther with claws like knives and teeth sharper than any arrow. He was great and powerful, and when he roared the earth shook, and his eyes were like coals plucked from the fire."

Lost Eyes reached out and plucked imaginary coals from the thin air, and the boys jumped back. "And then White Buffalo changed yet again and became a wolf stand-

ing over the bodies of the dead. He howled the names of
those he had killed and my horse ran from him, for the
wolf bared his fangs and there was blood on his lips; the
blood of the four Crow braves he had killed dripped from
his fur and his breath blew hot and withered the grass
while he roared for someone to fight him, another enemy
for White Buffalo to kill and devour. And, in truth, I think
I heard him call two names." Lost Eyes pondered his
words, pausing to allow the scenario to sink into the minds
of the suddenly wide-eyed, pale youths. "Yes. I heard him
call the name Turtle. And another—yes, Raven!"

The brothers, speechless, hung on every syllable. Bow
and arrow slipped from Turtle's grasp, his fingers grown
limp at the prospect of confronting such a demon. Raven
Takes Him gulped and his Adam's apple bobbed like a
berry on a branch. He listened, mouth agape, while
visions of blood-eyed monsters danced across his imagination.

"Tuurrrrtle!" Lost Eyes' voice rose in pitch and volume.
"He howled for *you!*" Lost Eyes concluded his tale of
terror with a wolflike growl and half lunged for the boys.

Turtle jumped and managed to turn himself around in
midair and land at a dead run. Raven Takes Him uttered a
strangled cry and stumbled backward, tripped over his
bow, scrambled to his feet, and bolted away. He passed his
brother on the fly. Lost Eyes laughed and watched the
boys until they were nothing but blurs in the deepening
night, beating a hasty retreat for the safety of their mother's arms. Another voice joined in the laughter and Wolf
Lance stepped out from behind a tanning rack. Wolf
Lance was the larger, though he had none of Lost Eyes'
natural quickness. He was a quiet man, not given to
boasting. Of late, he had taken to wearing a wolf pelt cowl
that covered his shoulders and when pulled forward
concealed the upper part of his face.

"Well done, my friend," Wolf Lance said. "But from the
stories I have heard this shaman is truly a bloodthirsty
man."

Lost Eyes grunted and shook his head. He was grateful
for the company of a friend. "White Buffalo is a Blackfoot."

"You should not have brought him here. No good can come of this, for the village, for you . . ."

"I could not leave him for a Crow war party to kill," Lost Eyes protested. Wolf Lance was like a brother to him. But he refused to accept the bigger man's arguments. "I would have done the same for any of our people. I would have done the same for you. Is it not our way?"

"I have not killed a white buffalo and stolen its spirit," Wolf Lance argued.

Wolf Lance had received his visions almost a year earlier, which had not yet strained their friendship. Lost Eyes respected his friend's opinion, but he believed him wrong. Well, not entirely. It had been both right and foolish. But Lost Eyes was driven to see it through, and to defend himself before the council.

The drums had ceased. Lost Eyes listened to the quiet. The council had begun. "Let it be so, that I spoke for White Buffalo. And let it be so, that I spoke for myself," said Lost Eyes, his deep-brown eyes hard as the chiseled planes of his face.

"Wait here. I will bring you word," Wolf Lance pleaded. "I will speak for you."

"No." His firm resolve left little room for argument.

Wolf Lance stared at him as if he had taken leave of his senses. He fell into step with Lost Eyes. "That is not permitted. The chiefs will not hear you," Wolf Lance protested.

Lost Eyes answered with a mixture of wisdom and sadness in his voice, "Have they ever?"

The council of elders dominated the center of the village. The tribal chiefs had arranged themselves in a circle around a blazing fire. In a greater circle behind the chiefs a gathering of warriors watched and waited, taking keen interest in the proceedings. The drums had been still for the better part of an hour as each of the elders spoke what was in his heart. Many of the women of the village kept a silent vigil outside the perimeter of firelight. Although they had no formal voice in the decisions, their men knew how they felt. The children, of course, were tucked away in their beds away from the important event.

Crow Striker, in his buffalo horn headdress and beaded buckskins, strode to the center of the circle. He lifted a ceremonial pipe, tilting the stem skyward, and faced the four directions in turn, offering the pipe to the elements and the spirits of each direction. The bowl of the pipe had been carved of pink pipestone from the Black Hills in the Dakotas. The stem was two feet of carved ash. Symbols of thunder and rain and the morning star decorated its length.

Crow Striker inhaled the aromatic mixture of cherry bark and wild herbs and exhaled a billowing blue cloud of smoke. He studied the faces of the chiefs and the fifty or so braves behind them. Then he began.

"Kills The Bear has spoken of banishment. I agree; White Buffalo can only bring misfortune to our village. We must be rid of him. But we dare not take arms against him unless all else fails." Crow Striker wiped a hand across his mouth. His throat felt dry. He didn't have enough moisture to even spit. His gravelly voice grated on the ear. Many had to strain to understand him. But they made the effort, for there was none braver than Crow Striker and his opinions were respected.

Crow Striker glanced around. He caught the eye of Tall Bull and Black Fox, who were only waiting for one of the chiefs to call for White Buffalo's death. Black Fox and Tall Bull were young and hotheaded. They had never faced a man like the shaman. To battle with White Buffalo was to wage war with dark and evil spirits. If any of the other chiefs had spoken for death, Crow Striker would have joined them. But no one wished to take the lead. The village had driven White Buffalo out before, they would do so again, peaceably if possible. It was the easiest and best path to follow.

"I stand with Kills The Bear and Fool Deer," Crow Striker pronounced. He crossed the circle and took his place with the chiefs he had just called by name. Black Fox scowled at the news. Dog Chases The Hawk, a snowy-haired old sage, clambered to his feet. The old man's countenance was a war map of wrinkles, each line etched by sun and wind, by bitter cold and brutal heat, by joy and pain. He held forth an eagle feather and in a surprisingly clear and forceful voice spoke to the council.

"Who else will speak?"

Lost Eyes made his move from the rear of the crowd. Broken Hand recognized him and might have tried to block him, but Lost Eyes was too quick, and before any of the Blackfeet knew what was happening, the man without a vision had entered the council circle and stood before the chiefs and the warriors of the village.

Black Fox and Tall Bull and a handful of other braves advanced into the circle. An air of menace radiated from them as they drew war clubs and knives or picked up rocks from the ground, hefted their weight, and readied themselves to stone Lost Eyes if necessary. They would have if Dog Chases The Hawk had not placed himself in harm's way. He had known Eagle Runs Him, Lost Eyes' father; the two had ridden forth on many a raid and had stood together, back to back, and fought off a Shoshoni pursuit, allowing the rest of their companions to escape. Dog Chases The Hawk had been too close a friend to see that same friend's son clubbed from the council.

"Lost Eyes, why have you broken the circle? You have had no vision. Your words must be those of a boy in this matter and not for the ears of men." Dog Chases The Hawk faced down the would-be assailants. He pointed the eagle feather toward them; his hands trembled from age, but his gaze was iron. Black Fox and his companions lowered their eyes and retreated to the perimeter of the clear ground.

Lost Eyes breathed a sigh of relief and, realizing his fists were clenched, willed himself to relax his stance. "Honored One, I do not carry my own words but those of White Buffalo."

A ripple of excitement swept among the braves. Even the tribal chiefs seemed affected by the news. Their expressions changed. They had been prepared to have the

young intruder escorted from the council. But this news
bore listening to.

Kills The Bear, a broad-beamed, lumbering man with
thick black eyebrows and a bull neck, stood in his place. "I
will hear these words," he stated. His eyes ranged across
the assembly and he saw that others shared his opinion.
Kills The Bear looked around him and then sat and folded
his arms across his chest.

"Let him speak," Wolf Lance called out from behind the
chiefs.

"Let it be so," Broken Hand added. Despite his natural
animosity toward the one he still blamed for the death of
his friend, now two months past, Broken Hand was curious enough to break with tradition. Not so Fool Deer. As
far as Fool Deer was concerned, the youth standing before
them could only bring misfortune to the Scalpdancers.
Fool Deer found great evil in the fact that one whom the
All-Father had forgotten should have brought White Buffalo back to the village. And now this same brave defended
the shaman. Fool Deer rose from his blanket and entered
the circle and waited until he had the attention of the
elders.

"I am Fool Deer," he said. "Let my words fly as straight
and true as the arrows I make. Let my words strike your
hearts. I say I will not listen to Lost Eyes. I will not listen
to the trickster White Buffalo. They must be driven from
our village. Have you forgotten when the buffalo came no
more and our children cried from hunger and the Above
Ones turned from us? It will happen again if we allow
White Buffalo to remain."

"He does not intend to stay. He will leave before the
moon is full, when his wounds are healed," Lost Eyes
said. "These are his words." He spoke slowly and loudly so
that all would hear. "It is not our way to leave one of our
own for the Crow to torture and kill. That is why I brought
him here."

His words rang through the air and for a moment no one
seemed to have a reply until canny old Fool Deer spoke
again.

"And it is not our way to have a pup speak among men," the chief of the Bowstring Clan retorted. Now his expression turned shrewd. "But you have spoken and I have heard you." Fool Deer paused to allow the council to hang upon his words. If indeed White Buffalo could be trusted to leave without a fight, so much the better. Fool Deer had realized how he might have his revenge on Lost Eyes in the process. He opened his arms as if to embrace some invisible presence. A gust of wind tugged at his unbraided gray hair.

"Your words are those of the one you serve. Let him speak then for you both. Let his words be your words. And his fate, your fate." Fool Deer slowly advanced on Lost Eyes.

The father of Waiting Horse raised the eagle feather aloft and when he had closed the gap between them, he lowered the feather and brushed it across the younger brave's shoulders, first the left and then the right. Then Fool Deer touched the tip of the feather to Lost Eyes' chest, over the heart. The arrow maker returned to the fire in the center of the council circle. The flames fed greedily on the deadwood, and smoke rose as a sooty banner to blacken the stars. A crescent moon floated between clouds like faerie islands, ghostly and mist-swept.

Fool Deer held the feather above the dancing flames. "His fate be your fate," he repeated in a strong, clear voice that carried to one and all. And with that pronouncement he dropped the eagle feather, itself a source of magic and power, and sacrificed it to the flames. A rush of amazement swept through the Blackfeet. Fool Deer picked up the ceremonial pipe and held it out to the council.

Dog Chases The Hawk stepped forward. "Who stands with Fool Deer?"

Lost Eyes watched, speechless. He had set the trap and walked into it. He had baited and caught himself and allowed Fool Deer to snare him. Nor was Lost Eyes surprised when Black Fox broke from the throng and joined Fool Deer by the fire.

Black Fox took the medicine pipe and returned to the

perimeter of the council gathering. He raised the pipe aloft and fixed his victorious gaze on Lost Eyes. "I stand with Fool Deer," he said. Banishment for Lost Eyes. And in time Sparrow would forget him and find a suitable young man whom the Great Spirit had not forgotten.

Tall Bull got to his feet and, standing alongside Black Fox, accepted the pipe from Sparrow's brother.

"I stand with Fool Deer," said Tall Bull.

That too was no surprise. But Lost Eyes watched with sinking spirits as one after another of the braves rose and repeated the litany that had begun with Black Fox. Only Wolf Lance passed the pipe by and remained squatting cross-legged on the hard-packed earth. Lost Eyes grew angry and strode from the council circle.

He shoved his way through the braves, who only grudgingly gave ground. They jostled and elbowed the departing young brave, but at last he broke out of the ring and sought escape into the village. But the words hounded him, banishing him forever. Sparrow was lost to him . . . his own people . . . everything. He stumbled and stopped. He clawed at his chest and stared in stunned silence at the stars and the sinister moon while his mind raged.

All-Father, why?

But for Lost Eyes the question—like the ache in his heart—went unanswered.

9

It was time for the gathering, and the unmarried women of the village rode out on their sturdy mounts under the amber gaze of the morning sun. More than a dozen pretty maids, ranging in age from twelve to an "old" nineteen years, frolicked like fawns—much of the show made for the unmarried braves sure to be watching—and raced one another for the lead. It was good to feel life on a day in spring, good to smell the clean, sweet aroma of the pines upon the rain-washed air.

They rode together—Sparrow among them even though she would have preferred to go alone—to the east end of the pass, where the hills opened onto the plains and a line of aspen invaded a landscape once given over to the juniper. They were riding to where the creek grew shallow and widened its banks and at last disappeared, leaving a swath of mud where the waters seeped into the soil and returned to the land. Here, in spring, wild potatoes grew in thick profusion, wantonly trailing vines sometimes twenty feet in length across the plain, their wide white blossoms opening pink centers to the sun—but only for the first few hours of morning, so the women would have to hurry. Sparrow did not join in the songs or the prattling gossip. She ignored a challenge by Blue Cap. Blue Cap, three years younger than Sparrow, was slim and pretty and much sought after, and she wanted to show off before an audience of young bucks who had come to watch the women ride out. The braves loosed their war whoops and strutted among themselves like wild colts, their black manes braided with raven and eagle feathers, their coppery torsos hardening with muscle, having lost much of their winter fat.

"Come, Sparrow," the thirteen-year-old shouted, leaning forward onto the neck of her dun. "I will race you to the end of the valley." Blue Cap turned her pretty features toward the sun. "Let the young men see us riding to the light."

"Why?" Sparrow replied. "You have already blinded them." She rode with the mare, allowing the animal's movements to flow into her. She had no wish to impress anyone. Five days had passed since the council, and Lost Eyes' banishment weighed heavy on her mind. She was both angry and saddened by the outcome, one moment furious that he should have placed himself in such a position and then despairing because he would be gone before the next full moon.

"Poor Sparrow. She has ears for only one flute outside her lodge," a sharp-featured young woman taunted. This was Blind Weed and she was older than any of the others in the root-gathering party. She had ridden up opposite Sparrow and overheard Blue Cap's challenge. Blind Weed was a large-boned woman, comely enough but with an acid tongue that discouraged suitors. It was also rumored she had been intimate on more than one occasion with a warrior in the village who had already taken a wife.

"And you have ears for one flute too many," Sparrow retorted. She was in no mood to allow herself to be the target of Blind Weed's barbs.

Sparrow drove her heels into her mare's flanks and the animal bolted forward. Every woman within earshot of the exchange laughed at Blind Weed's expense. Though she was to blame for her own bad reputation, Blind Weed hated anyone who questioned her behavior. She loosed a pouch from her shoulder and flailed away at Sparrow, hoping to knock the smaller woman from horseback. She missed and Sparrow rode clear. Blind Weed, on a surefooted but slower pinto gelding, could do nothing but fume helplessly as she fell behind.

The unmarried women rode with wild abandon past the wives of the village, who now had duties of their own this day—to plant corn in the south meadow, where the crops were assured plenty of sunlight.

The Scalpdancers had learned the art of cultivation from the prairie tribes, who had in turn obtained knowledge from a Cheyenne village along the banks of the Tongue River. Most of the planting had been accomplished a few weeks earlier, but a few dozen shoots remained to be planted and the weeds and wild flowers need to be discouraged from returning. One of the women turned the soil using the shoulder blade of a buffalo for a plow. She had attached the shoulder blade to a pair of fresh-cut saplings. A mountain-bred mare drew the makeshift implement across the rich earth.

The married women paused in their labors and playfully insulted those on horseback. It was all in good fun. Yellow Stalk maneuvered herself to the fore and hurled a dirt clod at the root gatherers. Owl Bead and Berry joined in the assault, and the other ten women followed suit. Then the riders swept past and peace returned to the valley of the Scalpdancers.

Moon Shadow moved as silently as her namesake in and out of the lodge. She appeared solemn, said little, although from time to time she would chant a keening prayer song. She packed parfleches of dried meat and put together pouches of herbs and roots. And there was a buckskin shirt she wanted to finish and there was—there was—she needed . . . The tears began to flow.

Lost Eyes had just swept the flap back and entered the tepee and found her with tear-streaked face and bowed shoulders. He noticed White Buffalo's pallet was empty. He squatted by her and wrapped his arms around Moon Shadow's rotund body.

"Little mother, what is it?"

"I cry for you," she said.

"Save your tears then. I am not dead."

"You will be as one who is." She sniffed and swallowed and tried to regain the composure she had lost.

"Wolf Lance will be your son now. He will care for you," Lost Eyes told her, fighting a lump in his throat. For five days he had continued his life as if nothing had happened; the reality of banishment had yet to sink in. Somehow he thought the elders would relent, see their mistake and permit him to remain among the People. Moon Shadow, in her grief, brought the enormity of the loss home. She had been his mother. He would miss her terribly. She had been a good friend.

"Maybe one day I will return."

"No," the woman said. "After the full moon you will be considered an enemy and every brave you meet will ride against you. Do not return. Ride beyond the Backbone of the World. I will never see you again. I will cut my hair and bury my heart. And you will be dead."

She wiped an arm across her face and cheeks, then she picked up the shirt she had sewn for him. The brushed design upon the soft buckskin was incomplete, but a delicate pattern of trade beads and shells adorned the chest and when finished would depict a flight of arrows rising to the sun. Moon Shadow set to work, sniffing back an occasional sob.

Lost Eyes glanced toward the empty pallet. "Where is White Buffalo?"

"Gone."

"Where?"

"He hobbled out and called to his blaze, and the animal

came to him from across the creek. He rode back into the hills, where the Cold Maker comes."

Lost Eyes' brow furrowed with curiosity and he ducked out of the lodge and studied the north ridge. But if White Buffalo had indeed ridden that way, he was already lost among the trees. Five days and the man had already recovered enough to ride. Surely the shaman possessed great magic, whatever its source. But why should he ride up the back slope? Lost Eyes decided there was only one way to find out. He brought two fingers to his mouth and loosed a sharp whistle, and across the creek, out in the meadow, a big gray mare raised her head and shook her mane and trotted down from the sweet grass. The mare rode through the village and arrived at the lodge. The animal reared and pawed the air.

The young brave spoke softly to the animal, gentling the beast with a soothing litany. "Be gentle. Be still, my proud beauty. Be gentle."

He draped a blanket across the mare's back and fit a bull hide hackamore into place. He slung a quiver of arrows over his shoulder and, taking up his elkhorn bow, he leapt astride his mare and rode north. He looked to neither right nor left. He had grown used to the stares of the village women and children who watched him pass. Once they had been his friends, his people. Now they would be glad when he and White Buffalo were gone. What had been mere misgivings over his lack of a vision had turned to outright fear. He had inherited White Buffalo's sins and there was no mercy for him, today or ever again.

Nothing much had changed in eleven years, White Buffalo thought as he walked his blaze stallion out of a thicket of aspen and into tall timber that covered the steep slopes of Crazy Wolf Ridge. He could no longer see the village through the trees, but sounds carried and the scent of cook fires taunted his senses. He paused, lost in a reverie of how things might have been. He saw himself with a woman lying beside him in his lodge and she was

soft and warm and good to cling to, especially when Cold
Maker covered the land in forgetful snow and the world
slept. Yes, a woman and children, yes, strong sons to ride
with into battle and teach the ways of the Great Circle. He
saw children in his mind's eye: They danced before him
and ran naked in the sun, and he taught the boys to ride
and hunt, and the girls were beautiful and learned the
mysteries of womanhood from their mother.

Then he saw the white buffalo and replayed again how
he had taken its power: The beast was huge and shaggy
and stood tall like some great mound of snow. *The man
loosed an arrow, then another, and another, and the
wondrous beast bellowed and tried to flee, but the brave
rode in close and thrust his lance deep into the animal's
lungs, and the sacred buffalo died, its blood spilling onto
the ground. The brave washed himself in the blood and
ate the animal's heart and stole its power. . . .*

With that memory, the other dream died. It always
died. But maybe this time he might make it live again. He
would have his revenge on those who had banished him.
The Scalpdancers would regret the day they had driven
White Buffalo from their midst, for he had returned with a
purpose.

Eleven years' wandering had returned him to the Backbone of the World, where he forged an alliance with a
tribe of Shoshoni, the natural enemies of the Blackfeet.
These were the Shining Bear Shoshoni and they had
heard of the legendary White Buffalo, and he worked his
magic among them and slayed two of their chiefs and
another had died in his sleep just as White Buffalo had
predicted.

Afterward White Buffalo had walked among them and
told the warriors of how he would bring them to the fertile
meadows of the Elkhorn and lead them to victory over the
Scalpdancers. The Shining Bear people listened to the
shaman whose eyes held thunder and whose temper flashed
fierce as forked lightning. And like lightning, he promised
to strike down his enemies and theirs. Game was scarce in
the high country that year and the hunting grounds of

the Scalpdancers held a promise of a richer and easier
life.

It was a promise the Shoshoni accepted and White
Buffalo became one with them . . . or perhaps they became
one with him. White Buffalo had ventured once more into
the hunting grounds of the Blackfeet for the purpose of
discovering whether a back trail into the valley still existed.
Eleven years was a long time and the deer trail that
zigzagged like a jagged scar up the steep north face of
Crazy Wolf Ridge could well have been obliterated by
rock slide or erosion. White Buffalo considered with pleasure how being wounded had worked right into his plans.
Lost Eyes had provided the perfect key to entering the
Elkhorn valley. Once again the shaman's spirit power had
aided him.

Now he quit thinking and concentrated on the climb
that took him out of the aspens and scattered junipers into
the lodgepole pines, those tall, majestic trees so vital to
the survival of the village. Here an emerald peace descended
on the ridge and would have filled his heart had he only
allowed it. But White Buffalo's mind was on the future he
intended to shape and the revenge he intended to have.
He had no time for tranquil groves lit by slatted sunlight
and carpeted with pine nettles.

White Buffalo quickened his pace. He tapped his crutch
against the stallion's flank and the horse responded. In a
few minutes it brought its rider out of the tall timber and
out onto a rocky escarpment where massive granite boulders split by rain and ice and the heat of the sun formed a
natural line of fortifications and a veritable maze of narrow
passages and corridors. Yet in the center of the battlement
was a table of rock approximately ten feet in diameter.

The shaman warrior dismounted and hobbled to the
table rock, whose rain-worn surface rose a good three feet
above where he stood. As White Buffalo stepped up onto
the outcrop, pain shot through his wounded leg as the
muscles protested such abuse. He willed it to pass and it
did. He limped to the edge of the table rock and looked
down to what at first glance appeared to be a sheer drop of

some three hundred feet. On closer inspection though, he managed to discern a switchback of narrow ledges scrawled across the cliff face, barely wide enough for a man to stand upon.

Wide enough, the shaman reckoned. A magnificent ponderosa pine rose out of the dry rocky landscape about ten feet from the face of the cliff. The pine's long branches shaded much of the narrow switchback. The top of the cone-laden tree came to within a hundred feet of the table rock. As White Buffalo peered over the edge of the cliff, he dislodged a fist-sized chunk of granite that glanced off the side of the cliff and plummeted below. The noise of its passing rang in the clear thin air. A gray owl exploded from concealment among the ponderosa's branches and traced erratic spirals in the air above as it glided off in search of quieter surroundings.

The owl was the harbinger of death. A premonition made White Buffalo turn and instinctively grab for the knife at his waist. To his surprise he saw Lost Eyes, watching him from a granite boulder bordering the table on which the shaman stood. White Buffalo did not appreciate being spied on, but he subdued his own temper.

Lost Eyes left the reins of his gray mare hanging loose and scrambled down to the table rock. White Buffalo towered over him. But the shaman limped when he walked, and that vulnerability at least made him human. Yet when White Buffalo fixed his dark eyes on the youthful intruder, an aura of incredible power seemed to flow out of the shaman with almost palpable force. Lost Eyes had to retreat a few paces until his backside brushed against the boulder he'd been standing on.

"Why did you follow me?" White Buffalo asked in a deep, resonant voice.

"I don't know," Lost Eyes said. It was the truth, he realized. What indeed had drawn him to the shaman?

White Buffalo searched the line of trees and the trail he'd followed up the steep slope. Satisfied that Lost Eyes had come alone, the older warrior visibly relaxed. He drew close to Lost Eyes and touched the younger man's forehead with the tips of his fingers.

"I too was 'Lost Eyes,'" White Buffalo said. "The Above Ones did not speak to me. I received no vision quest. In the sweat lodge I fell asleep. The All-Father was blind to me." The shaman turned and held his hand aloft, indicating a northerly direction.

"I found the White Buffalo there in the country of Cold Maker, where the snow never melts and the land lives in Ever Shadow." White Buffalo's gaze grew distant with the memory; he was seeing a far-off country where he'd found the rare white buffalo trapped by a landslide. He could have freed the animal.

"But I killed it," the shaman said. "I used every arrow and even then I had to finish *Iniskim* with my war lance. I ate its heart. I drank the beast's hot blood. I slept in its skin. And that night I found my vision. I claimed the animal's sacred power as my own."

White Buffalo's features grew taut and firelight born of the shaman's own inner source flashed in his brooding gaze. He tossed his head back as if laughing, but he made no sound, and Lost Eyes' blood ran cold to see it. Then White Buffalo touched him on the shoulder.

"You and I are shadows of the same spirit," he said. "Perhaps I will let you sleep in my skin and share the vision. And you will no longer be Lost Eyes."

White Buffalo motioned for him to follow and started toward his horse. Lost Eyes looked back just for a moment. He wondered what the shaman had been doing in this lonely place. The young warrior had also spied the owl as it circled skyward past the edge of the cliff. The sight had unnerved him.

White Buffalo, as if reading his companion's thoughts, said, "I heard the owl call your name."

But the two of them had been present as the harbinger of death swooped away, its cry shattering the pine-scented peace of Crazy Wolf Ridge.

"Or yours," Lost Eyes snapped.

White Buffalo swung up on the blaze he'd left near the

table rock. "Perhaps one day we will know the truth," the shaman said, his features stretched in that blood-chilling silent laugh.

The ice in Lost Eyes' veins lingered long after White Buffalo had ridden away.

Lost Eyes moved like a shadow along the ridge south of the pass. After leaving White Buffalo he had spent the remainder of the morning dismantling the game traps and snares he had placed among the game trails that crisscrossed the forest-blanketed slopes from the granite battlements to the thickets of aspen and willow that almost completely obscured Elkhorn Creek. Only now and then through breaks in the trees or when the wind sighed could he glimpse the reflection of sunlight through the intertwined branches.

He had kept to the hillside and stayed well back in the woods until at last the voices reverberating through the pass lured him from his snares. He found a suitable outcrop of granite bordered by ponderosas and he scaled the backside of stone and cautiously peered above the speckled-gray surface.

Sparrow and the other young women were scattered along the grassy floor amid the flowers and the sweet green grass. Clouds scudding overhead cast patches of darkness upon the land.

He saw her, held her in the quiet of his heart. She was as warm as lost love, as ephemeral as twilight, and like twilight he must lose her to the night country. At the end of day, as the sun is going, a man clings to sunlight, especially when an eternity of night is all that lies ahead. A man slakes his thirst on amber warmth, clutches the lost golden rays to his chest because ever after the memory will have to do. It will have to be enough.

"No," said Lost Eyes. "I cannot leave her." His hand knotted into a fist and burrowed into his chest, as if by such a gesture he could grasp the pain and tear it from him.

And yet what recourse was left to him? What kind of life

was this for a woman: to follow a man without a home, a man whom the *Maiyun* had forgotten. The wind did not speak to him. No spirit animal entered his sleep and called him by name. Sunset and morning were mute; they hid their secrets well.

All the arguments melted away when he heard her laugh, when he heard her sad song borne on the stillness. Again he whispered, pressing his forehead to the cold and impervious granite, "I cannot leave her."

At noon I sing of winter hawks and white-faced owls and the secrets I have heard upon the wind. I have heard such secrets. And I could sing the songs of the children. But who will listen? I will sing as the berries ripen. But who will listen?

Sparrow shielded her eyes and paused in her work to watch the sun scale the big sky. It hung directly overhead. The flowers, hours ago, had folded their fragile blossoms in upon themselves. Among this fragrant litter the young women filled their baskets and deerskin pouches and draped the heavy bags over the backs of the packhorses. Sparrow's mind was far from her labors. Her thoughts were of Lost Eyes. And she spoke to him in her heart.

She was halfway through her third pouch when she paused to wipe the sweat from her forehead and cheeks. She glanced toward the distant hills. The hair rose on the back of her neck and she scrutinized the tree line. She had the distinct impression they were all being watched. It was hardly a comforting sensation, for the Blackfeet had many enemies—their hunting grounds were coveted by many tribes. She saw nothing and returned her attention to the task at hand but not before Blind Weed had spotted her and misjudged her actions.

"Do not look for him. He is as blind to you as he is to the Above Ones," the woman chided. "He can only see the sacred killer he brought to his lodge."

"Do not try to foretell the actions of a good man," Sparrow retorted. "You have not had the practice."

"But she has had plenty of practice with the other kind," Blue Cap added, enjoying Blind Weed's discomfort.

The young women around her laughed. Not Blind Weed though, she only scowled.

"Good man, ha! 'No Man' is a truer name for Lost Eyes." Blind Weed hoisted a sack of tubers upon her shoulder and made her way to her horse, where she swung her load across the skittish animal's back. The gelding shied and fought its tether line and pulled free, but Blind Weed caught the animal's reins and struck the gelding across the muzzle. The animal shied.

"Poor Blind Weed. She cannot even keep a gelding close. No wonder she has such terrible fortune with stallions," chided a round-cheeked girl of sixteen.

Blind Weed whirled around to address her tormentor but came face to face with a half a dozen cheerful, teasing girls, none of whom would take credit for the remark. Her expression hardened and she turned her back on them, lifted her smock, and showed them her naked buttocks in a gesture of contempt.

A handful of girls, taking Blind Weed's side in the matter, showered Blue Cap and the others with a volley of roots. They returned the attack in kind, retaliating with roots and handfuls of mud. Blue Cap scooped up a handful of mud and splattered Blind Weed's derriere. The older girl straightened up, screeched, and tried to wipe away the mud, but she only managed to smear it down her thighs.

Sparrow, who had tried to remain apart from the melee, laughed at the sight, just as Blind Weed glanced in her direction. The larger woman charged her. Sparrow was caught off guard and tried to back out of harm's way. She had been working near the mud where the creek played out and seeped into the soil. Her foot slipped and she slid, flailed at the air, then toppled over on her backside into the muck. Blind Weed lunged at the smaller woman. She missed completely and sailed past Sparrow—and belly flopped into the mud.

Sparrow didn't escape the morass. She rose up on her

elbows and grimaced as her hands sank wrist-deep in the mud. Water soaked in through her buckskin smock and the leggings she wore beneath. The ends of her hair were matted with grime. She managed to stand. She held her arms out from her body and walked stiff legged toward her mare. The other root gatherers doubled over with laughter at the sight of Sparrow and Blind Weed, who rose out of the mud and loosed another round of abuse at the Above Ones and all those who had made fun of her.

Sparrow was just as disgusted, but there was no gain in blaming the *Maiyun*. At least the creek was close enough that she could wash herself off before returning to the village.

Blind Weed wiped the mud from her eyes and spat a glob of wet sand. She raised her fists above her head. Her whole body seemed to swell as if she were about to explode. But the other women ignored her. They had seen her tantrums before. She had provided enough amusement for the morning. Blue Cap and the rest bid the two muddy antagonists farewell and turned their pack-laden mounts back toward the village. The echo of their passing reverberated through the hills. Blind Weed was unable to think of a suitable invective. She focused her attention on Sparrow and advanced upon the smaller woman.

Sparrow defiantly stood her ground. No matter that Blind Weed was larger and heavier by several pounds. Sparrow steeled herself, refused to show any fear. She was determined to match Blind Weed blow for blow if necessary. It seemed it would come to that when the two women came face to face, poised like two mountain cats. Then quite suddenly, Blind Weed's shoulders sagged and she shrunk in on herself and began to sob. She sank to her knees and cupped her face in her hands as her whole body trembled.

Sparrow's anger melted away, and was immediately replaced by pity. Blind Weed had always been dominant to a fault. She had kept her vulnerability well hidden. Now, all at once, her true self came rushing forth in a torrent of tears.

Sparrow was at first unnerved. She had been prepared for anything but this. She glanced over her shoulder at the mare and considered making good her escape. In that moment Lost Eyes came to mind and she remembered how he had been unable to leave the wounded White Buffalo. She began to understand a little of what he had felt.

Blind Weed had grown hard being the subject of gossip and ridicule of the women of the village. Yet today, something had snapped within her and left her vulnerable. She couldn't control herself; the tears spilled down her cheeks. She couldn't be strong anymore. But why did Sparrow remain? To offer comfort? Her actions left Blind Weed completely dumbfounded . . . and grateful.

"Run while you can," Blind Weed warned, slowly regaining her composure. She stood, stripped of her hardness, and wiped the mud from her eyes using the back of her buckskin garment. She patted smooth the front of her smock and her hands paused at her belly and rested there.

"I am carrying a child."

Sparrow lowered her gaze to the woman's abdomen and her breath ran shallow. Such news was worth poor Blind Weed's tears. To be with child and without a husband meant a terrible loss of station. What man would have her now?

"Whose child?" Sparrow asked timidly.

"Tall Bull's." Blind Weed sighed. It was a relief not to feel so alone. "You have seen Owl Bead. Plump as a beaver in the Leaf Falling Moon. He is no longer pleased with her. Tall Bull would take me to wife, but his horses are few. He has no suitable gift to bring my father."

And he never will have, Sparrow started to say, but she wisely reined her tongue. She had no use for Tall Bull. He was her brother's shadow, nothing more. Black Fox led and Tall Bull followed. True, he had taken Crow scalps in battle, but no one had seen those two braves he had supposedly killed. His actions caused Sparrow to doubt the man's claims.

"Why did you stay with me?" Blind Weed said. She rubbed her eyes and studied Sparrow.

Sparrow said, "I know what such a sorrow is. I too have wept."

Blind Weed now regretted her part in causing those tears.

"Better to be with the one whose name is in your heart and weep for the village you leave behind than to remain among your people as one already dead, for your heart will cease to sing," said Blind Weed.

She drew close to Sparrow and opened her arms to embrace the smaller woman as she would a sister. They held each other and both experienced a kind of healing, for Blind Weed had found a kindred soul and Sparrow had heard from another's lips the truth of what must be done.

Blind Weed stepped back and for the first time in a long while she felt like smiling. It was good to find a friend where once she had seen an enemy, or at least an outlet for her own dark thoughts. She was sorry for that. Anger and fear had clouded her sight and like her namesake made her truly blind to the gentle soul who stood before her.

"I will ride ahead of you," Blind Weed said. "It will be well for you not to be seen by the others riding in my company."

"I will ride with my friend wherever I choose," Sparrow told her. She shifted uncomfortably in her muddy smock and leggings. "But I shall bathe in the creek before entering the village." Sparrow fell in alongside Blind Weed, who had already started toward the horses. The animals shied nervously at the two women whose hair and clothing were caked with mud. They mounted their horses.

Galloping from a field of morning glories and serpentine vines, the newfound friends followed different trails. Only time would tell whether or not they rode toward the same destination. . . .

Sparrow lay naked in the middle of the creek, the sun-dappled water flowing over her shoulders and down along her slender legs. Her breasts were islands surrounded by rippling gold; her long hair wafted gently in the current where water sprites might dwell in the solitude of days. She lowered her head and the water rushed over her face. Only minutes ago she had discarded her muddy garments and immersed herself. After the initial shock she found the icy waters cleansed her spirit as well as her body. She submerged completely into utter stillness and only the flare of the warm sun overhead told her she was still in the world.

Then the sun darkened—as if in eclipse. She raised her head, brought her face out of the water, and opened her eyes. There was a man on the riverbank. Lost Eyes was watching her. Sparrow watched him, her features betraying her surprise. But she made no move to hide her nakedness.

"Lost Eyes," she said and outstretched her arms.

He moved reluctantly and lifted his hand to hers. Her fingertips brushed his and he trembled.

"I am not a man," he said.

"Prove it," she replied. She lifted her hands toward the sun. Her palms felt warm. Water streamed from between her breasts and gathered glistening in the curls below her stomach. "The sky is clear. And yet, beyond the hills, there might be thunder." She looked at him. "Is it any less a sky?"

"I have no vision," Lost Eyes protested weakly. His own rising passion threatened his resolve.

Sparrow shook her head. It was always the same with him. "I will be your vision now. Come. Let me fill you." She left the creek and lay down upon a carpet of green grass. Her flesh was cold from the water, but the sunlight helped. He removed his buckskins and covered her body with his own, and she was warm aplenty.

They needed no ceremony. The tribal music of wind in the branches of the willow, the call of tanager and crossbill nesting among the limbs, the playful courtship of otters splashing further up the creek, all were the music of their union.

After their lovemaking, Lost Eyes and Sparrow stretched naked on the creek bank and let the sun dry them. They held hands and they knew in their hearts there was no turning back.

"I will go with you," Sparrow said.

"Could I leave my heart behind?" said Lost Eyes. "Or my hand? Or any part of my body?" He eased over and placed his head upon her breast and listened to the life force beating within. "You are a part of me. As I am a part of you. And it will be so until the All-Father calls us by name and we stand in the Great Circle with the Above Ones. And even then we will be as one."

10

Rains came and for a time Elkhorn Creek overflowed its banks and flooded the willows. Boys played their games of war and hunt, and girls carried doeskin dolls on miniature cradle boards and sang them lullabies and rocked them to sleep. In all things the children imitated their parents. Boys learned how to stalk, to ride, and to kill with a single well-placed arrow. They learned how to speak to horses, to settle them with a word and a soothing tone. Girls learned of foraging, of the mysteries of roots and flowers and all wild growing things, and followed their mothers to the creek to capture the living water and carry it to their tepees. They learned to build a lodge, to care for it, to craft clothes from pelts and softened hides; they learned the mysteries of womanhood.

As the men of the village prepared their weapons, their thoughts turned to hunts and raiding parties into the land of the Shoshoni to the west or the Crow to the south. Women replenished their stores of medicinal herbs, tended the corn, and assessed what damage the wintry elements had done to the hide walls of their tepees. Some, like Yellow Stalk, the wife of Black Fox, prepared themselves for the new life they carried and dreamed of whether their first child would be a boy or a girl.

It was a time of lovers, when the renewing force of the world burned with fresh fire in the veins of the young men and women and turned their thoughts to the two-called-together ceremony.

For the aged ones spring brought memories of other blossomings, other futures that had become the past. It was a time of stories and song singings, a time to see the Great Circle with a new perspective, a time to dance the circle and enter the All-Father's loving song. Death and birth were part of the spring. Both were part of the song that had no beginning or end. Leaf after leaf, flower after flower, star after star, the song was there. All were born to hear it. Few were born to sing it.

White Buffalo had said he would leave when the moon hung full and silver-bright in the night sky. Yet the nagging fear remained among the Scalpdancers. What if his words were lies? Wolves had begun to prowl the ridges and this was seen as a bad omen.

Lost Eyes had grown to accept the judgment of the elders. Now it seemed almost a blessing, for Sparrow would be with him. The two could not be seen together and communication might have proved impossible but for Blind Weed. Through her, Lost Eyes and Sparrow plotted their escape. Ten days was an eternity to be apart, but there was nothing to be done for it. Black Fox must be convinced he had succeeded in driving an insurmountable obstacle between them. Indeed, he seemed to be completely taken in by the ruse.

So the days passed and Lost Eyes and White Buffalo readied themselves in secret until a night when the moon was not quite round in the sky, a night when none would expect them to ride out. Clouds like spiderwebs were draped across the sky, dimming the moonlight and painting the winding paths with patches of stygian dark.

Now was the time, with the village quiet and everyone

asleep. These days of rest had brought White Buffalo nearly to full strength. Why the shaman preferred to leave secretly puzzled Lost Eyes, but he didn't argue. The fewer people who saw him and Sparrow the better. If Black Fox were alerted, there would be bloodshed.

An hour after midnight Lost Eyes walked through the village. No one stirred. A camp dog lifted its muzzle and tested the scent of the shadowy shape gliding past. But Lost Eyes had long since familiarized himself with the dogs, and they knew him.

Lost Eyes made his way unchallenged by man or dog to the lodge of Blind Weed. He hunched down alongside a tanning rack and flipped a couple of pebbles against the entrance flap of the tepee.

Nothing.

Immediately his pulse quickened as he began to speculate on all the things that could have gone wrong. Black Fox might have discovered their plan. But how? Blind Weed had carried his messages to Sparrow. Lost Eyes had never even so much as approached the enclave of the Kit Fox Society much less Black Fox's tepee. What had he missed? What had alerted Sparrow's brother and kept her from spending the night in the lodge of Blind Weed's family?

He tried another pebble and glanced it off the weather-roughened hide. As his mind raced to form a new plan, the flap opened and Sparrow came through the opening, followed by Blind Weed. Lost Eyes sighed in relief. The women scrambled to his side. Sparrow carried a pouch of her necessities, extra moccasins, assorted packets of herbs, and the like. She found Lost Eyes' hand in the night and squeezed it reassuringly. Blind Weed draped a small medicine pouch on a thong around Sparrow's neck.

"It will guard you," she whispered.

Sparrow hugged her. "You are my good friend, Blind Weed—no, my sister."

Blind Weed blushed. She was grateful for the concealing darkness. For days she had acted as go-between, bringing messages from man to woman. Without her help Lost

Eyes could never have arranged to escape with Sparrow. He did not understand the strange and rather sudden friendship that had blossomed between the two women, and when he had asked Sparrow, she would only say that she had walked in Blind Weed's moccasins. Gratitude had kept him from pressing the matter.

Sparrow could think of nothing else to say. What else was there? A warm embrace spoke for her. For a brief second Blind Weed wished it were she, stealing off into the night with the father of the unborn child riding in her womb. She scurried back to the tepee and darted inside, returning to her bulrush bedding before her father stirred and noticed Sparrow's absence.

Lost Eyes led the way back through the village. The night grew brighter as the moon slipped free from its diaphanous bonds. Lost Eyes groaned. The last thing he needed was a well-lit escape route. Slipping past the sentries who guarded the entrance to the pass offered more than enough challenge for one night's work.

Another surprise awaited him at his own lodge, where the horses were tethered. White Buffalo emerged from the tepee dressed in his buckskins and carrying his rifle. A war club and knife were sheathed at his waist. What set him apart and marked him was the buffalo horn headdress that he wore. It covered his head and brow, and a white elkskin mask concealed his features. A coat of the white buffalo hide hung from his broad shoulders, making him a figure terrible to behold.

"You cannot wear such a robe," Lost Eyes protested. "There are guards in the hills."

"Let them see me. Whoever bars my way will die. And I will curse their flesh." White Buffalo seemed to tremble a moment; then Lost Eyes realized it was the man's own peculiar silent laugh. He shivered despite himself. Sparrow's hand tightened on his arm. She wanted him to tell the shaman what they had decided. Now was as good a time as any.

"White Buffalo, your way is not my way," Lost Eyes

said. "When we have ridden clear, Sparrow and I will leave together."

White Buffalo silently took a step closer. "I was going to teach you the truth, share my magic with you. We are alike."

"No," Lost Eyes said. "I would rather live my life without vision than steal it." He began to gather his belongings, most of which he had already loaded onto the pack animal.

"You are a fool. Even worse . . . a powerless fool. But go where you will." White Buffalo swung a leg over his blaze. He moved with such ease it was impossible to tell he had ever been wounded.

Moon Shadow emerged from the tepee. She handed Lost Eyes the shirt she had made for him. "When you wear the shirt, I will be with you."

"I will wear it often, little mother," Lost Eyes said.

"*Saaa-vaa-hey*," Moon Sahdow muttered. "You will forget me."

"Not as long as Cold Maker comes or the blossoms return with the Muddy Face Moon." The young brave hugged her big round form for the last time. Something caught at his throat and made it difficult to swallow. It was "good-bye."

Lost Eyes turned away and mounted his gray. The mountain-bred animal obediently held its ground. That was Sparrow's signal to leap astride her own mare. The moon drifted back into concealment and hid their features.

"Quietly—we stop for no one," White Buffalo cautioned. He reached down and caught the reins of the packhorse and headed out of the village. Lost Eyes and Sparrow, despite their misgivings, followed his lead. At last they were together, riding east toward the dawn of a new day.

An eagle left the safety of its nest high atop a craggy summit and cast itself upon the wind. The high-country monarch spread its regal plumage and rode the currents sweeping up from a narrow gorge far below, where three riders threaded their way. Dawn had changed the brooding night clouds to airy lavender wisps and brightened the ragged peaks with bronze and radiant gold.

The eagle glided effortlessly down from the cliffs. It dipped and soared, circled and darted, and owned all it surveyed. But the eagle was a hunter and it flew not for the joy of the morning—but to stalk and kill.

Lost Eyes rubbed the small of his back and, looking upward, considered the eagle and the beauty of sunrise. The gorge was a chilled gloomy place hemmed in by towering walls of stone. It was a place carved of violence and gave mute testimony to the forces of nature, the stresses and strains at play deep within the earth.

The eagle seemed to be following them, and Lost Eyes was reminded of another hunter who must track them before this day was done. Lost Eyes had no desire to fight Black Fox. He wanted to put as much distance as possible between them and Sparrow's brother.

White Buffalo turned his stallion to the west as he emerged from the gorge, and the walls fell away to either side. Lost Eyes took comfort in the warmth of the sun. He glanced at Sparrow. She managed a tired smile and from a shoulder pouch brought out a portion of pemmican, a mixture of dried chokecherries, buffalo meat, and meal pounded into fist-sized cakes.

Lost Eyes readily accepted the food and wolfed it down. Sparrow ate and allowed herself to drift a few paces back. She didn't feel like talking, not with the shaman so close.

They had remained with White Buffalo because he knew of a circuitous way west unfamiliar to the Scalpdancers. At least that was his claim. So far Sparrow knew precisely where they were; the course the shaman followed would eventually bring them just north of Singing Woman Ridge on the other side of the falls and the pool of spirits. She thought back on the day the shaman had ridden into their lives and forever changed them. She frowned, unable and, indeed, unwilling to hide her emotions. She had no love for White Buffalo and the sooner rid of him the better.

As if reading her heart and the enmity she held, White Buffalo twisted around and looked at the couple riding in his wake. How fierce he looked in the sacred headdress. His buffalo robe was too heavy to be comfortable here in the sunlight and he had draped it across his horse. Sparrow shivered as his gaze bore into her. Lost Eyes, made uneasy by White Buffalo's strange behavior, angled his gray between the shaman and Sparrow.

"When shall we rest?" Lost Eyes asked, hoping to break the shaman's concentration. The ploy worked. The older warrior gave a start, checked his surroundings for a moment, then answered.

"When the sun sleeps," White Buffalo replied.

The rattler issued its distinctive warning as it coiled to face the approaching riders. The reptile had been sunning itself amid the rubble surrounding a fallen boulder. The blaze stallion shied at the sound and danced skittishly to one side while White Buffalo strove to bring the animal under control. Lost Eyes took satisfaction in seeing the shaman struggle with the stallion. Sparrow's mare reacted in much the same way, but Lost Eyes' gray held her ground.

Lost Eyes spoke in soothing undertones and nudged his heels against the mare's flanks. The gray moved out of the snake's striking distance. A rifle shot startled Lost Eyes. The rattler's head exploded, and the body twisted and curled in its death throes. The gunshot echoed down the hills—announcing their whereabouts to one and all, Lost Eyes realized.

The shaman made it obvious that he did not care if he were found. He had nothing but contempt for his enemies. White Buffalo immediately began to reload.

"You have done a foolish thing," Lost Eyes said angrily. Sweat rolled down his cheeks and he hastily searched the hills for signs of pursuit. The sun had passed its zenith, and the few high clouds that remained did nothing to prevent the heat from reaching the earth.

"You worry too much," White Buffalo chided. He rammed powder and shot down the long barrel of his rifle and primed the weapon with a trace of black powder in the pan. Then he pointed to a line of hills they needed to cross over. "We will find water and a place to rest on the other side."

Lost Eyes studied the hills and estimated the distance. He turned to Sparrow. "Can you make it?" She nodded but her shoulders sagged. The young woman tried to straighten up. She wasn't fooling anyone.

"I can make it," she replied.

"Soon we'll be safe," Lost Eyes told her.

"Do we kill them now?" the Shoshoni brave whispered as he drew a bead on Lost Eyes.

Another Shoshoni standing at his side answered, "No." His name was Drum. He clapped his companion on the shoulder and retreated deeper into the thicket. An army could hide in these thickly forested gullies and ravines. Drum knew from experience. He had done it.

Drum rode at the head of over eighty Shoshoni braves, all of them painted for war and waiting back in the shadows. Three days' ride from this valley the rest of the Shoshoni village waited, encamped in a box canyon up on the divide. It was hard country, thrust high against the sky, but there they would wait for word that the Blackfeet had been driven out of their valley. No one wanted to consider the possibility of defeat.

"Wait," Drum said, studying the silhouettes as they materialized out of the woods farther up the valley. It was late in the day and Drum was tired and irritable, but not irritable enough to step into a battle when he didn't fully understand the situation. He was a slim, quick-witted man, who sat loose legged astride his mountain-bred horse. He reached out and forcefully lowered the rifle barrel of the man at his side.

Storm Bear, a squat, well-muscled brave, glared quizzically at his companion. Storm Bear was aptly named. His volatile nature could generally be counted on to stir things up. Unfortunately, he tended to act first and consider the consequences later. Right now, his rifle was cocked and primed and ready to explode, just like its owner. He grudgingly dropped his gunsight from the Blackfoot a hundred yards away.

"He is not alone," Drum cautioned. A woman—Sparrow—appeared, letting the reins rest easy in her hand. Her horse never swerved from the trail the gray mare ahead blazed through the scrub and thorny thickets.

"She is worth stealing," Storm Bear exclaimed. "I am glad to have lowered my gun. Let it speak thunder to all but her."

"You are wise," Drum answered, appraising the girl and finding her to his liking. What were these two doing alone? Were they lovers, fleeing a combative and vengeful father? It was too bad for the young man. He had ridden a long way just to die.

Movement continued behind a thicket of juniper. Drum held his breath as he caught a flash of white. And as if by magic a blaze-faced stallion poked its head around the thicket and the brief glimpse of a third man became instead a man garbed in the sacred hide of a white buffalo.

"It *is* he," Drum gasped. When the shaman had failed to return, Drum took it upon himself to lead his people down from the high country with its bitter winds and scarce game. He led them to war. And yet, without White Buffalo's magic to ensure their success, Drum had been worried. The Scalpdancers would fight for their hunting grounds. Many lives would be lost on both sides.

So Drum watched with elation as White Buffalo rode across the narrow gap in the trees where a rock slide from the ridge above had cleared a path through the forest.

"White Buffalo," Storm Bear muttered aloud.

Word spread throughout the war party. Eighty braves moved as one and emerged from the brush-choked stand of aspen into the slotted sunlight despite Drum's warning.

When his words of caution proved useless, Drum joined the warriors because he, like them, had given himself over to the shaman's sinister power in defiance of all he had once held sacred. If White Buffalo's magic won for them the land of the Scalpdancers, so much the better.

* * *

Lost Eyes reined in his mount and motioned for Sparrow to do the same as she drew abreast of him. White Buffalo continued into the rubble-strewn clearing.

"Do not fear," White Buffalo told them as he pulled ahead. "Come." He held up his rifle in a gesture of greeting toward the Shoshoni. "We are among friends."

"What are you saying?" Lost Eyes pointed toward the Shoshoni. "They are not my friends." He could see their painted faces in the sunlight and didn't bother to count their number. He saw a menacing group, bristling with war lances and bull hide shields. Some brandished flintlocks like the one White Buffalo carried, others held powerful ash bows, and still others great war hammers capable of crushing a man's skull with a single swipe.

Lost Eyes was filled with misgivings as he watched the Shoshoni slowly work their way up the treacherous incline. At his side Sparrow shared his concern.

"Have they come raiding for horses?" she wondered aloud.

"They have come for war." Lost Eyes glanced at White Buffalo, who continued to calmly await his adopted people. With sickening realization Lost Eyes began to understand the shaman's duplicity.

White Buffalo had hoped to have time to win Lost Eyes over to his side or to at least be rid of this headstrong young man and his woman. After all, Lost Eyes had saved his life. He turned, sensing the younger man's scrutiny. He didn't like the way Lost Eyes had unslung the elkhorn bow or the way the young warrior walked his gray to within arm's reach of White Buffalo.

"Our enemies draw closer," Lost Eyes said.

"A man chooses his enemies," White Buffalo countered.

The hooves of the horses clattered on the loose stone and debris left by the slide. Broken timber and shattered trunks forced the Shoshoni to cut back and forth and follow an indirect route up the slope.

"And his friends," White Buffalo added.

Lost Eyes judged the distance back to the cover of the forest. He knew what he could expect of the gray, for he had held her back and kept her to an easy pace. Still, the animal's strength had been sapped by the long ride. The gray was nearly winded. But she might have enough to get him over the ridge and down into the hills on the other side.

"And I chose poorly indeed. You are going to attack the village," Lost Eyes said, his temper rising.

White Buffalo's expression beneath the buffalo head-dress betrayed his disdain. He had been wrong about this brave without a vision.

"I see your thoughts," the shaman said. "The Scalpdancers have denied you as they denied me. But we are not alike. You cannot even carry your own hate."

Weak...cannot carry your own hate... the words echoed in Lost Eyes' skull, a challenge he must answer. It was as if a veil had been pulled from his eyes, permitting him to see at last. Suddenly the power of the shaman to influence him was gone. Lost Eyes tightened his grip on the elkhorn bow in his right hand; his muscles tensed.

White Buffalo never took his eyes off the young brave at his side as he lifted the flintlock rifle and thumbed the hammer back.

Lost Eyes caught the shaman completely off guard. Lost Eyes never reached for an arrow. Instead he swung the bow in a vicious arc that caught the shaman across the bridge of his nose and sent him tumbling off his horse.

Blood spurting from his broken nose, White Buffalo landed on his backside. The jolt caused him to tighten his grip on the trigger and the rifle discharged harmlessly into the air.

Lost Eyes whirled his horse about and almost collided with Sparrow as she fought to bring her own mount under control. She had not heard any of the interchange between the two men—but she knew there was danger from the approaching Shoshoni war party.

Lost Eyes didn't have time to explain. He pointed to a trail that began near the trees and skirted the slide area. The ground looked more solid there for the horses.

"Come with me!" he shouted. Behind him White Buffalo roared in pain and rage.

Sparrow needed no urging. She tugged savagely on the reins and turned her mount completely about, then lunged toward the path Lost Eyes had indicated.

Downslope the war party didn't understand what was happening, but with White Buffalo on the ground and out of the way, Drum, the Shoshoni war chief, gave the order to open fire on the two fugitives. A half-dozen rifles sounded in a ragged volley that peppered the hillside about the fleeing couple.

Lost Eyes ducked low over the neck of his horse. The gray seemed to know just where to run. It leapt a patch of loose gravel and gained the trail just behind Sparrow's surefooted mount. Leaden death ricocheted inches from the Blackfoot brave. He kicked his heels against his horse's flanks and tried to keep his weight forward to help the animal climb.

Down below, White Buffalo struggled to his feet. He looked up the hillside and saw the couple making good their escape, and he snapped his rifle to his shoulder and squeezed the trigger. Nothing happened. "*Saaa-vaa*," he muttered, remembering he had fired the gun when he landed on his backside. He grunted in disgust and reached for his powder horn. He poured gunpowder down the barrel and tapped it firm with his ramrod. Lost Eyes and Sparrow were in the shadows now—but they'd have to cross sunlit ground near the summit. White Buffalo fit patch and ball to the mouth of the barrel and rammed the load home.

Lost Eyes urged the gray mare to greater effort; only a few yards to go now and they'd be out of range.

The shaman dusted the pan with a trace of black powder. Behind him the Shoshoni guns spoke again, but either the range was too great or their aim too poor. White Buffalo shouldered his rifle, exhaled to steady his aim—

Sparrow crisscrossed the remaining distance and disappeared over the rim. Lost Eyes felt his heart soar and followed a similar serpentine path to the crest. For one brief moment he was skylined against the cobalt-blue horizon.

The shaman fired—

Lost Eyes started over the top as Sparrow waited, allowing her horse a second's rest.

He called her name as something struck the side of his head and plowed a path along his skull. Blood spurted from the wound and drenched the side of his head. Somehow he managed to cling to his horse as Sparrow cried out in horror. The gray plunged past her, carrying its nearly unconscious burden beyond the reach of the guns below.

Lost Eyes knew he had been hit. He knew he couldn't stop to find out how badly. He might never start again. The world reeled. He managed to ignore the worst of it; the pain would come later. Right now his head felt numb, but his cheek and shoulder were sticky with blood.

"No!" Sparrow shouted. She pulled alongside him just as he started to topple. She managed to take his bow and then shove him upright on the gray. He fought back from unconsciousness.

"Follow the ridge," he groaned, hoping she understood. Sparrow studied the terrain. The valley below looked unfamiliar, as if she were seeing it from a different perspective. The ground was hard packed and checkered with granite where rain and wind had eroded the thin soil. Unshod horses would leave no tracks over the table rock.

Time lost its meaning. A few minutes seemed an eternity as they galloped along the ridge until a suitable thicket of ponderosas and Douglas firs presented adequate concealment for a descent to the valley below. Sparrow looked over her shoulder. White Buffalo and the war party had yet to reach the summit.

Lost Eyes no longer gave orders; he needed all his strength and concentration to cling to his mount. His features were twisted with pain now, and he wore a mask of crimson. How much longer until he was unable to go on?

The trees . . . run to the trees. And then what? She

didn't know. Sparrow caught the horsehair reins as they slipped from between Lost Eyes' fingers. He took hold of the gray's long dark mane. They started down through the pines.

The pain welled in him now, like a cascade that split the hills and plummeted, crashing, churning into a cold pool.

Lost Eyes listened and realized for the first time that what he took to be the rushing wind was indeed a cascade, the sound of a waterfall somewhere in the valley below. He lifted his battered head and willed his eyes to focus on the valley.

They were above Singing Woman Falls, directly opposite the ridge they had crossed a lifetime ago.

He tried to tell Sparrow, or warn her to change her course. But his speech was slurred. Sparrow heard his sounds but didn't understand. He quit trying. He clung to the gray and prayed for the All-Father to grant him strength.

The pines seemed to open to envelop the wounded man and Sparrow, who never once looked back. The forested slope offered concealment, but the war party must search it sooner or later. We need a place to rest, to heal—her thoughts raced as she tried to contain her panic.

"But where?" Sparrow said aloud.

"Here."

The answer froze the young woman in her tracks. It had not come from her own mind. It had been spoken! She turned and glimpsed movement out of the corner of her eye. She tensed and grabbed for her own knife as a leathery hand closed around her forearm.

Sparrow gasped and looked down into the age-seamed face of a woman, her white hair streaming, her dry lips cracked by a broad smile. Old and brittle, this one, but with eyes bright and burning.

"Come," the old woman said and walked straight toward a massive jumble of boulders in the center of a nearby juniper thicket. She moved quickly for one so advanced in years.

Sparrow had cause to doubt her own senses. Was she

dreaming? Or was the old one a spirit of the hill and not a person at all?

"Come," the old woman said. "I have been waiting for you. Hurry." She stood beneath a natural arch of stones precariously balanced above a cleft in the hillside.

Lost Eyes slumped forward, oblivious to this strange apparition. He groaned but somehow found the strength to remain on horseback. He no longer cared where they were heading. It didn't matter now. He tried to tell Sparrow to leave him, to save herself. All he could do was grit his teeth against the pain and try to keep the blackness from engulfing him.

Sparrow reached the cleft and found it to be a cave entrance just tall enough and wide enough to permit a horse to enter. She guided the nervous animal into the passageway, followed a dark corridor that widened into a torchlit chamber.

The old woman left her then and hurried back for Lost Eyes.

Sparrow dismounted and took in the cavern. It was a chamber roughly thirty feet in diameter. The clatter of hooves rang upon the stone and echoed off the water-sculpted walls as the old woman reappeared leading the gray.

Lost Eyes wavered, lifted his head. He looked directly at the woman and amazingly his eyes seemed to actually focus, despite the terrible appearance of his wound.

The old woman grinned, displaying a row of broken crooked teeth.

"They will find the entrance too," Sparrow said.

"She can stop them," Lost Eyes said in a voice that was little more than a croak. He knew he spoke the truth. He had never seen this woman in his life, yet he sensed a kinship with her. Then he slipped from horseback and crumpled at her feet.

The old woman said, "Yes," in a voice dry as crackling flames. With hurried steps she returned to the entrance as Sparrow rushed to the fallen man.

The old woman began to sing and the song transformed

her rasping voice. It became winsome, unreal, lilting, and then strikingly familiar. Sparrow cradled Lost Eyes, taking him in her arms, and listened to the song in a language as old as dreams.

Nothing happened—at first—and then with a rumble the entrance collapsed in on itself. The boulders shifted and crashed against one another. The song trailed off, lingering in the faintest of reverberations, which in their dying gave birth to recognition.

"You are the one," Sparrow said, her heart pounding, her flesh cold. By all the spirits it was true! She was trapped beneath the earth with the ghost of Singing Woman Ridge!

11

Lost Eyes saw himself motionless, surrounded by a fog that swirled and writhed above the pool of water where the cascade plunged and spray billowed up from the surface of the water. The water was clear and the rocks upon the sandy bottom seemed inches from the surface when the depth was actually three feet. He heard an old woman singing and when he turned toward her, she acknowledged him with a wave and beckoned him through the rapidly thickening mist—but when he started to join her, the fog closed round, obscuring everything. It was then he began to sing and the spirit song filled him.

> "All-Father, as
> My voice is your voice,
> My desire your desire,
> Help me to find the way,
> That I may follow the
> Great Circle.
> By your secret name I

Call You.
Lead me.
Help me to see beyond seeing."

The mist dissolved, transformed in the turning of the hours and minutes, in the heartbeat of time. It became light and there were people around him, faces he did not recognize. He knew the old woman was there, standing beside him. She was called Singing Woman. Once she had had another name, long ago, before she walked in a dream. The light became brighter, white hot, and yet everyone continued to stare without going blind. At first Lost Eyes thought it was the sun, but the light increased and the words came to mind. Those surrounding him spoke in whispers and said the same thing: All-Father . . .

Lost Eyes opened his arms to the light, and the brilliance poured into him, transfixed him, and he cried out and went spinning up, up, up, into the light. The men and women lifted their voices until their songs filled the brightness and added to it.

He heard songs for the stillness, for grief, for joy, songs for the growing and the harvest, songs for the pleasure and goodness of life, songs that the world might not die.

Lost Eyes awoke and waited for his vision to clear before trying to sit upright. He touched his scalp, wincing as his fingers probed a tender spot near the bandaged wound. A concoction of roots and stems beneath the buckskin wrapping had already begun the healing process. His head throbbed a little, but mainly the wound felt warm.

He noticed Sparrow sitting near the entrance to the chamber. They were in another part of the cavern. Water flowed across the entrance and crashed into the pool, generating a permanent mist that with the cascade concealed the mouth of the cave. Lost Eyes had no doubt but the pool he gleaned through the rushing cataract was none other than the one below Singing Woman Ridge, only the voice of the mountain had come from an aged woman and not some spirit.

Sparrow had fixed her attention on the entrance. She rested in a patch of sunlight, her back to the stone. She turned, spied him sitting upright, and hurried to his side.

"You *are* alive," she exclaimed, as if for a long night and part of the morning she had expected otherwise. Sparrow began to explain to him just what had happened, where they were and who the old woman was.

Lost Eyes waved her to silence and patted her arm. "I know, I know," he said. Sparrow gave him a puzzled frown. "I walked in a dream."

Singing Woman edged around the falls and entered the cave and waited in the sunlit part of the chamber as her eyesight adjusted to the cavern's interior.

"Her dream," continued Lost Eyes, indicating the old woman.

The lead slug from White Buffalo's rifle had clipped Lost Eyes in the back of the skull and traveled around the side beneath the skin before exiting the scalp just above the ear. It was fortunate that the slug's velocity had been spent covering the distance. The wound itself was painful and had bled profusely, but it was not life threatening. Singing Woman's poultice had stanched the flow of blood.

Singing Woman chuckled to herself and, kneeling by the glowing coals of her camp fire, she filled a stone cup with a drink steeped from a combination of roots and herbs whose nature the old woman refused to divulge. There would be time enough to teach Sparrow the healing ways. She carried the cup to Lost Eyes. Sparrow intercepted their benefactor. She and none other would tend to the wounded brave. Singing Woman laughed softly in understanding. She too had loved and been loved. For her, though, the memories were like gray coals, dormant, waiting to blaze again in a night of dreams.

Sparrow tilted the cup to the wounded man's lips. Lost Eyes drank deeply of the bitter brew as he stared at Singing Woman, their eyes locked. He did not waver, nor did she.

"What is your name?" the old one asked.

"Lost Eyes."

"No," she said. "What is your name?"

The brave sagged against Sparrow's breast. With his cheek pressed close he could hear her quick heartbeat.

"What is your name?"

"Lost—" He shook his head, then gasped as the interior of the cave momentarily careened out of focus. He finished the contents of the cup and lay back upon a pelt-covered bulrush pallet.

"What is your name?" Singing Woman repeated.

"I—don't—know," the wounded man replied wearily.

"Then you must find your name."

"Where—do—I—look?"

Singing Woman placed her leathery palm upon his forehead. "In your visions."

He began to breathe more easily, regularly, and soon he was asleep. Sparrow watched the old woman with renewed respect. Indeed, Lost Eyes seemed in capable hands.

"I must go," she said. Singing Woman glanced up in surprise. "I must warn the people of my village."

"There is nothing you can do. The worst has already happened."

"No!" Sparrow exclaimed. "I can reach Elkhorn Creek in time. I know it."

"You can die," Singing Woman said. "Or stay here and live. Your people are no more. They are scattered. But one day they will gather again. Believe me. I have seen it in the flames."

Black Fox and Yellow Stalk, dear loyal Blind Weed and Moon Shadow, Wolf Lance . . . what had befallen them? She longed to know. But the time was wrong and she would be powerless to alter the circumstances.

"What can we do?" Sparrow said, desperation in her voice.

"Watch and wait," the old one sighed. "There is much for a Sparrow to learn."

He walked alone in a dream. He passed from the country he knew and climbed higher, crossed the Backbone of the World. He saw ridges and mountains in the mist, he saw winding valleys and thousand-foot gorges and heard the wind sough in a thousand trees, and he drank from streams icy enough to freeze his gullet. He followed the sun, each day alone, and by night he slept in peace and let the moon fill his heart. He listened to the earth and heard at last the meaning of the songs, and he glimpsed the great truth that no mouth can speak nor any tongue tell except in song.

And these things too he beheld: mighty waters that crashed upon the land and stretched out to the horizon where the sun dipped below the edge of the world; then he stood upon a hillside overlooking a mighty river, and before him rose a timber cross like the ones the Blackrobes brought with them years ago, and upon the cross hung a white man. Wind howling, lightning crashing, amid storm clouds, the cross rose against the sky. And the man on the cross looked into the eyes of the dreamer. Then the dreamer saw a long knife jutting from the grass where it had been thrust at the foot of the outstretched man. And there were long knives and guns, and suddenly blood began to flow, to mingle with the rain and the long grass.

The vision faded and dissolved into a fierce, bright illumination that drew him into itself. He heard laughter and saw children at play along a creek bank. Five naked little boys dived and splashed and emerged from the creek only to leap once more into the silt-churned water. As the children dared one another to greater deeds of bravery, one of the boys paused and looked up and met the dreamer's stare with eyes that never wavered, and the dreamer realized he was gazing upon himself. The boy started toward him, leaving his friends behind. He bravely approached until he stood before the man. The dreamer reached out, and as their hands touched, the boy vanished, leaving the dreamer alone upon a dusty plain.

He watched darkness and dawn; he listened and the storms shared their truth. He saw Cold Maker come all wrapped in deep-blue sky and gunmetal clouds. He saw snowflakes upon the land while the grass turned yellow, then brown, and died, and wildflowers curled into the soil.

Soon all the world was white. It was then he saw the great beast *Iniskim*, the white buffalo. The animal lay upon its side in the snow drenched with blood.

The dreamer cautiously drew near, for the sacred animal was not yet dead. Steam rushed from its flared nostrils and there was the power of death in its hooves and curved horns. The dying animal lay still and allowed the dreamer to come forward. Just as the child had stood before the man, now the dreamer stood before the dying buffalo, and the animal's large sad eyes beheld him and the dreamer began to understand something of change, of the sorrow of life and the joy of death.

The animal changed before his eyes into a pelt that covered a man. The man slowly stood and hid his nakedness in the skin of the beast. . . .

"White Buffalo," the dreamer said.

The shaman extended his hands and arched his back. A cry rose from his throat and echoed over the lonely snow. As the dreamer watched, the snow turned red and the cry of the shaman rose in pitch and volume until it became unbearable. And the dreamer covered his ears, but the cry burrowed deep into his mind and would not release him, but rather it held him prisoner. Panic filled him. He had to escape. How? The voice of the shaman held him prisoner.

The cry reverberated in his skull. He felt himself slipping away—then he heard the song. It came from within. Perhaps it was his soul that sang. The dreamer had no knowledge of the source, he only knew that the song was within him, and his spirit song, though tremulous at first, gave him courage. He sang for the dying earth and for the earth reborn. Power filled him and he sang. Peace filled him and he sang. Strength was his, and wisdom.

Red snow melted into rivers of blood. But the rivers seeped into the land and the grasses sprang forth and the world blossomed and was healed. Bitterroots bloomed among the sun-bleached bones of the buffalo. Nature had reclaimed its own. The dreamer knew that as long as he sang, as long as someone knew the songs and sang them, the world would not die.

The dreamer awoke. He did not know how long he had slept. From his pallet he saw Sparrow seated near the mouth of the cave, watching moonbeams glitter on the falls. The dreamer rose from his blanket and padded soundlessly across the cave. He wore only a loincloth in the cool night air. He ignored discomfort and continued to the entrance. His touch startled Sparrow from her reverie.

Her eyes widened as if she were seeing a ghost. His hand upon her shoulder held her in place; otherwise she might have fled through the curtain of water. Then he knelt by her in the moonlight.

"Open your blanket," he said. She complied and he sat beside her and shared her warmth.

"Your wound—" she began, touching his forehead.

"It will heal."

She sensed something different about the man from the moment he sat within her blanket: the way he looked, his expression of awe, of childlike wonder. Suddenly he crawled from her blanket and gingerly made his way to the edge of the pool and stretched his hand out into Singing Woman Falls. The force of the stream pushed his hand down. Ignoring his bandaged head, he entered the falls.

"Living water," he cried out as the stream pummeled him, bathing him in liquid moonlight. The bitter-cold shower took his breath away and left him gasping for air. He held himself in the falls, and beneath the noise of the plunging waters Sparrow heard a song.

When he emerged, he stumbled toward her and sank to the ground at her feet. She wrapped her blanket around him yet again.

"I have had my vision," he said through chattering teeth. He looked into her almond eyes and told her the truth of what had been revealed to him. "I must be gone for a time to find the Great Water that has no end, where the sun sleeps. I must make this journey. Alone. It is my vision quest."

"And I will wait here. You are not the only one who may be touched by magic," Sparrow said, trying to hide her grief. "Tell me you will return," she whispered, lying back and pulling him atop her.

"I will always return," he said.

Three days passed. Singing Woman left the couple by themselves as much as possible. Indeed, she was busy with her own tasks. She had found a grove of box elder trees surging with sap, and spent these days tapping the trees. The sap became quite sweet when boiled and the shavings from the inner side of an elk hide solidified when added to the boiling sap, producing a plentiful supply of candy, enough to satisfy her sweet tooth.

The old woman knew there was magic afoot and that the wounded young man had been touched by the All-Father and given sight beyond sight.

So it was no surprise when the young man of dreams announced he must follow his vision to where the sun sleeps. He readied his weapons and packed a little food, though in the end the land itself must nourish him if he were to survive. Sparrow remained quiet, withdrawn into herself and her own worries and speculations. There simply wasn't any more to be said.

And on the fourth morning the young man draped a blanket across the gray and slipped the hackamore over the animal's head. He allowed the mare a final drink from the pool at the foot of Singing Woman Falls. While the animal slaked its thirst, he nourished his own aching heart in Sparrow's embrace. His black hair hung long and unbound and blew across his face.

"Your dreams have taken you away from me," Sparrow whispered. "My love will bring you back." She opened her arms and retreated a step. How grand he looked in his buckskin shirt and leggings, his eyes aglow with life and vision in a bluntly handsome, scarred face.

He called out and the gray obediently abandoned the pool and trotted over to the young man. He leapt astride the mare. He heard a ghostly singing; an old woman's voice filtered through the falls, emanating from the earth and the forested ridge.

> "Peace before him.
> Peace behind him.
> Let peace be under his feet.
> May he follow a true path.
> May this lone walker listen
> With open heart.
> May this lone walker see with new eyes
> The spirit in all things.
> Peace before him.
> Peace behind him.
> Let peace be under his feet."

"Who are you?" Sparrow asked, voicing the medicine woman's question of a few days past.

The young man was caught off guard. He glanced quizzically at the young woman and started to answer "Lost Eyes," but the name died on his lips.

He lifted his eyes to the west and in his mind pictured the solitary journey that lay ahead, the journey he had already begun in his dreams. A name sounded in his heart, put there by a sacred song.

"I am Lone Walker."

PART III

Journeys

12

June 1814

Thunder rolled and shook the rafters of the Sea Spray Inn, but the storm Reap McCorkle feared most was the tempest brewing within his own walls. Thirty feet from front door to bar and seventy feet from west wall to east the Sea Spray Inn boasted the best rooms and the finest tavern in all of Astoria—indeed the *only* rooms and tavern in Astoria and for that matter in all of the Pacific Northwest. Reap McCorkle had gone to a lot of trouble; he'd cut the wood for every hand-hewn chair and table, he'd trimmed every white pine log and nailed every red cedar shingle into place. He'd personally hung the walls with ceremonial masks and fitted every lantern. The Sea Spray Inn had been a dream brought to fruition by the sweat of his brow and the money of John Jacob Astor himself. Reap didn't want his dream damaged, not one splinter of it. So he sat enthroned behind the spruce wood bar and rested his grizzled chin upon his entwined fingers and kept vigil, a wooden bung starter close at hand. If Captain Penmerry

had trouble in mind, friend or no, Reap McCorkle intended to end it.

Morgan Penmerry stared into the pewter mug at his
own image reflected on the last few swallows of rum. He
looked much the same as when he had fled Macao eight
weeks past. His chestnut hair was just as unruly, his nose
as askew and chin as squared; a close-trimmed black beard
covered the lower half of his face now and added a touch of
maturity to his features.

But Temp Rawlings, who knew Morgan better than any
man alive, had only to look into his young friend's eyes to
see the changes eight weeks had wrought. Temp was no
fool and kept his observations to himself. He knew trouble
when he saw it and he could read storm warnings better
than most. So he sat quietly and nursed his mug of rum
and savored the fire at his backside. Here along the south
bank of the Columbia, only twelve miles in from the
mighty Pacific's rocky coast, a blazing hearth felt good and
lightened a man's spirits.

Morgan ignored him. His rum-soaked thoughts were of
the high seas and the eight weeks in which he'd been a
"perfect gentleman" while bright-eyed Julia Emerson stood
on the deck of the *Magdalene* with her auburn hair
streaming in the wind and her cream-colored skin darkening
in the sun. Her emerald eyes mocked his discomfort,
playfully so, especially every time she'd bested him at
chess, a game for which she had a great knack. He
complained that a missionary's daughter had no business
being a master strategist. She countered, citing the war for
a man's soul was fought on the most treacherous battlefield
of all. She laughed and he would have to share her good
humor.

Much to his amazement they had become friends, a title
he had never given to a woman before.

Not that he was getting religion. Morgan Penmerry
considered the angels a dull lot, good for nothing but
hosannas and platitudes. The devil set a better table with
tankards of his brimstone brew and women whose lips
were hot enough to melt lead, whose kisses sucked a

man's breath away. A man could dance with the devil and forget about tomorrow because today had no end.

No end . . . and yet they'd sailed past Cape Disappointment and right up the mighty Columbia and brought the journey to an end. As the inlet opened itself to the *Magdalene* cutting effortlessly through the water, Morgan had experienced such a sinking of spirit. He would miss young Julia in a way he had never missed a woman before.

Morgan raised the tankard to his lips and drank deeply, not for the taste but for the effect. He wanted to get "blind-stinking-fall-down-and-forget-it-ever-happened" drunk. He wanted to forget the wreckage he had left behind in Macao: Chiang Lu and the Portuguese officer and Demetrius Vlad and the smoldering hull of the *Hotspur*. Oh yes, forget Macao, after all, he could never return. He wanted to forget the crossing and the sound of a young woman's laughter and the gentle way she had of leading him to question his life.

There was one thing more—he wanted to forget he was a captain without a ship. Morgan lifted his gaze to the window behind him. He stood and walked unsteadily to the shutters. He peered out at the night through a firing port, a slit large enough to admit a rifle barrel.

Lightning flashed and in the lurid glare of ionized air he glimpsed the *Magdalene* anchored fifty feet offshore, lifeless and dark, its sail furled.

A second ship rode the troubled waters alongside the *Magdalene*. This was the H.M.S. *Raccoon,* under the command of Captain William Black. The British warship had docked at the settlement on the thirteenth of December. British troops had disembarked and taken Fort Astoria without firing a shot.

Morgan shifted his stance as another flash of lightning illuminated the stockade itself, Fort Astoria now called Fort George. The Union Jack fluttered in the wind gusting over the walls. Morgan Penmerry closed his eyes and tried to blot out the memory of this day's landing, how a contingent of British soldiers had met the johnboat as it came ashore. The scene played over and over in his head and try as he might he could not alter the outcome.

"The *Magdalene* is my ship. You can't just take it!" Morgan protested.

Captain William Black was an astute and utterly polite gentleman in his early thirties. Splendidly attired in scarlet coat and white breeches, he doffed his black leather hat and bowed to the Emersons. The officer positively beamed at the sight of a woman so fair.

"I have already done it," he said, answering Morgan at last. He indicated his soldiers with a wave of his hand. A half-dozen marines were already boarding the *Magdalene* out in the river. "We are at war. I don't like it but—"

"I'm not," Morgan retorted. "I haven't an enemy in the world."

Julia had to turn away before the captain saw her choke.

Black turned and looked toward the ship. The English marines were already lowering the American flag. "I don't like it, either, but there you are."

Morgan fumed. War was for generals and admirals. His sole interest was in turning the debacle in Macao into a profit and he couldn't do that without a ship.

"I am not without compassion," Black continued. "Your men are free to come and go in the settlement. But that ship will fly the Union Jack and carry an English crew." He smiled toward Julia. He did not know how long he would be stationed in this godforsaken land far from home and the bosom of his loving wife and family. "My dear Miss Emerson, is it? You are a fair flower to this shore. I am totally at your service."

"We intend to bring the word of God and the peace of Christ to the savage tribes," Emile Emerson managed to interject. The soldiers made him a trifle nervous and the more rattled his nerves, the more pompous he tended to become. It was a fault he often regretted.

"Allow me to offer escort to you both," the captain said.

"About the *Magdalene*," Morgan interrupted. "Maybe

we could work out some kind of arrangement." He was desperate now. He needed that damn ship.

Captain William Black drew himself up and his gaze hardened. "The matter is closed!"

A broadside of thunder that shook the shutters and made the stout walls tremble shattered Morgan's reverie. Black's final words lingered in his mind. "Closed. The matter is closed," Morgan repeated under his breath.

He glanced around the tavern. Several trappers bellied up to their pitchers of ale and rum. Many of the *Magdalene*'s crew were scattered around the room, celebrating the voyage's end. And why not celebrate? The missionary had paid them off. Each man had just enough to outfit himself for the fur trade (under the auspices of the Hudson Bay Company) with a coin or two left over for a woman and a jug. Eight weeks of celibacy made a Chinook squaw appear mighty appetizing. There were several tepees in the vicinity and as soon as the infernal rain let up, talk was that the men intended to visit the encampment.

Along one wall three English seamen and a couple of marines noisily exchanged lies as they drained the contents of a keg and clamored for more.

"Show me the color of your coin," Reap McCorkle told them.

A gruff-looking marine sergeant shoved away from the table and lurched forward. He jostled a trapper, causing the man to spill his drink, but the trapper made no complaint. He hadn't drunk near enough to look for trouble with the King's own. The sergeant continued on to the bar. He fumbled at his belt and produced a money pouch that he blearily unlatched and held to the tavern keeper's nose. The pouch was empty.

"You've taken all my money but the scent; now give me a drink, there's a good lad," the sergeant muttered.

Reap McCorkle uncorked a jug of his own home brew, a fiery concoction brewed from wild berries and doctored with peppers and a sprinkle of spices. He passed the keg beneath the sergeant's nose.

"There you be, Sergeant." Reap corked the jug and set it back among his dwindling supplies.

"You mean the King's credit is no good?" the marine bellowed.

"I'll pour King George a drink anytime and he can have his fill and welcome to it. But you, sir, shall pay for yours."

The sergeant scowled and turned his back to the bar. Reap was tempted to bludgeon the man but resisted the impulse. He wanted no trouble and could care less which flag flew above the palisades. But by heaven the sergeant must pay for his drinks.

The marine fixed his gaze on Morgan, who had lost interest in the drunk and returned to his place by the hearth. Morgan refilled his tankard, ignoring the protestations of Temp Rawlins.

"I see," the marine said angrily. "Those two lads never showed you the color of their gold. Not once. Yet they guzzle their fill."

"They are my friends and I haven't seen them for better'n half a year." The owner of the Sea Spray Inn folded his well-muscled arms across his chest and ceased his explanation. He owed none to no man. The inn and the tavern were his, and he made the laws within these walls. "I come to these shores on the *Tonquin* back in the spring of 1811. My missus was the only white woman in the whole Northwest, I warrant you, least ways until the *Magdalene* anchored offshore this noon. I have paid to be here with my sweat and blood, and you, sir, will pay with a proper coin."

The English sergeant stepped back and wiped a forearm across his mouth, and then began slowly to applaud. He glanced at the men in the room, most of whom looked away. "Aye, you're a cheeky bunch," the sergeant shouted. "But look above the walls of the fort. It's the King and colors that protects ye now!" He turned and winked at his companions seated at the table, who cheered him on.

"That's telling 'em!"

"You put them in their proper places, Sergeant Chadwell!"

The sergeant waved and altered his course yet again and headed straight for Morgan's table. Chadwell stood approximately the same height as Morgan but was older by twenty years. His features were pockmarked and powder burned and creased from a lifetime of war and dissolute behavior. He hooked his thumbs in the pockets of his scarlet waistcoat. The brass buttons on his coat facings lacked luster as did his red-rimmed eyes.

"I know you." Chadwell's breath stunk of liquor. His shadow darkened the tankard in Morgan's hand. Morgan glanced at Temp, whose expression pleaded for patience. The British marine slowly circled the table.

"I said . . ." the sergeant repeated, then paused, uncertain of himself, his train of thought momentarily derailed. "I know you . . . the captain of the *Magdalene*. Lost one ship in Macao so's I heard tell and signed on board another and lost her too." Chadwell leaned forward, his fists on the table top, his backside to the hearth, his ugly face inches from Morgan's. "A captain without a ship—land-locked you are. And that makes you nothin' at all, by my seein'. I never lost a ship or a fight, but I pays for my drink while you take yours free. I can't abide such a lack of justice."

Morgan eased back in his chair. All eyes were upon him.

The British marine snatched the tankard from Morgan's grasp and examined its contents; not more than a mouthful sloshed in the bottom of the tankard, hardly enough to satisfy a thirsty man.

"You'll be pourin' me some run," Chadwell growled, mistaking the younger man's silence for fear.

Morgan smiled. His cold, unblinking gaze never left the marine. Temp Rawlins had seen that look before and he groaned inwardly and tried to reach the brown bottle, but Morgan beat him by half a second. He hefted the rum in his right hand, uncorked it with his teeth, and spat the cork into the fireplace.

"There's a lad, I'll have that rum and you can tell me

how it is to be a captain of a johnny boat with naught but a pulpit pounder, a bit o' skirt, and the graybeard here for a crew!"

Chadwell tossed his head back and roared with laughter. He was a man who enjoyed his own wit, what little he possessed. His compatriots joined in the merriment. Outnumbered within the confines of the Sea Spray Inn, the English were secure in the knowledge that the entire occupying force under Captain Black was quartered within the stockade barely seventy yards from the inn's front door.

Judging Morgan Penmerry to be suitably cowed, the sergeant leaned forward and bellowed in his face.

"Serve me the rum!"

Morgan served him. Temp, to his horror, saw it coming.

Suddenly there was an explosion of glass and rum as Morgan broke the bottle across the sergeant's skull.

The marine straightened and staggered backward, tripped, and sat down smack-dab in the middle of the open hearth. His rump landed on a blazing log. The sergeant erupted from the fireplace, eyes wide and sober, a howl on his lips.

He dove for Morgan, who darted aside, and Chadwell flew across the table, smashed face first into a ladder-backed chair, and landed on the cold stone floor. Smoke curled from the singed seat of his pants; blood streamed from a cut on his forehead as Chadwell rose yet again. The indomitable sergeant called for his companions, who shoved clear of the table and rushed to his aid.

Morgan braced himself. Well now, he'd found trouble after all. The rush of adrenaline left him jubilant, anger turned to strength. Nothing and no one could stand before him. Let Chadwell and his men try. They were sheaves of wheat and Morgan was the scythe. They were the sea and Morgan was a fast ship with the wind at his back cutting through their midst. Morgan the mighty, Penmerry the invincible, the scourge of Macao, charged his attackers.

That was the last thing he remembered.

* * *

The past three years had been hard for Faith Restored McCorkle. She had followed her husband to the north Pacific coast and labored beside him to build the Sea Spray Inn in the shadow of the stockade walls. Amid Chopunnish and Clayoquat, Klamath and Chinook, and a dozen other tribes Reap and Faith McCorkle had planted their roots. They intended to stay as long as the mighty Pacific pounded the shore and the great clouds washed in from the sea over the cliffs.

Faith McCorkle was a broad-shouldered, plain-spoken woman of forty, whose plain features beamed with pleasure at the thought of a houseguest. She would not hear of Julia Ruth Emerson staying in her husband's noisy inn with its hardcase trappers, lonely seamen, and boisterous British soldiers. No, these days the Sea Spray was no proper place for a young woman. So Faith added an extra blanket to the big feather bed she intended to share with the young woman. Poor Reap would have to sleep in the front room by the fire with Julia's father.

Faith tucked a few silver-brown strands of hair back in her bonnet and paused as Julia finished tucking in a sheet. Julia sensed the woman's scrutiny and glanced up, her eyes questioning whether or not she had done something wrong. Faith dabbed her apron to her cheek and wiped a tear away and smiled.

"It's nothing," she said in a husky voice. She was coming off an attack of the grippe, and her chest was still sore from coughing. Ailments were the least of her worries. Loneliness had taken its toll. The tears were from gratitude.

"I've been the only white woman along the whole north Pacific coast," she explained. "To have someone—another woman to talk to, to share with . . ." Faith turned and sat on the edge of the bed and began to cry softly.

Julia had taken an instant liking to the woman and came around to sit beside her.

"I too am happy. It makes everything—all the changes— less frightening."

Julia said nothing of her own pain though, the loss she felt now that an ocean had been covered and Morgan

Penmerry was out of her life. "Good riddance," her father had muttered. But his ill temper was transparent and did not hide the grudging respect he harbored for Morgan Penmerry. He was jealous and overly protective of her. This was a side of her father she understood and had come to respect. A motherly woman like Faith Restored McCorkle was just what a confused, frightened missionary's daughter needed. Julia found hope in the work-roughened hand she held.

Faith sighed and rose from the bed. "Come with me, dear. I'll show you something."

She led Julia into the front room. Reap McCorkle had patterned his house after the sloped-roof lodges of the Salish Indians. It was rectangular in shape, sporting three oversized rooms big enough for a man "to stretch his legs in": a bedroom, a front room for visitors, and a large kitchen, where they also took their meals. A quilting frame was suspended from the ceiling in the front room, but scraps of suitable cloth had been scarce of late.

Faith McCorkle walked across "her sitting parlor," as she called it, and approached the mantel Reap had constructed of gray-black stones smoothed and polished by the sea. A rack of carved driftwood rested upon the mantel, and on it was arranged an orderly row of twelve ornately molded silver spoons. Each spoon was approximately six inches in length and polished to a fare-thee-well. The stems had been molded into twin vines intertwined and tipped with either an intricately detailed rose or tulip. There were six rose spoons and six tulip spoons in the set. The bowl of each spoon bore the name of one of the twelve Apostles of Christ.

Julia had noticed the spoons on entering the McCorkles' house but was pleased to examine them more closely. They were the product of a master craftsman and the young woman said as much.

"Reap melted our silver teapot into coins to pay for the first winter's supplies. Neither of us wish to be beholding to Mr. Astor any longer than is necessary," Faith explained. "But I begged him to spare the spoons and he did." She slowly exhaled, shook her head, and touched the last spoon on the rack. It was the only one to bear an imperfection. "There's even a Judas spoon," she added, indicating the "blemished" rose.

"They are lovely," Julia complimented her.

"Mind you, I have not regretted our decision to come here. Only it has been lonely." Faith replaced the spoon. "You won't be lonely. The men will make a fuss over you, mark my words. Captain Black has already taken an interest. I saw the way he looked at you when he brought you here."

Faith laughed as Julia turned away, blushing from embarrassment. Indeed the English officer has been most cordial, but then weren't all English gentlemen? Still, any man so far from home would yearn for a woman's softness and a woman's touch. There was no denying she had immediately awakened his interest.

Thunder rumbled and roused Julia from her thoughts. She wrapped a shawl about her shoulders, walked to the door, opened it, and stepped into the porch that ran the entire length of the house. Rain dripped from the eaves of the flat roof overhead and trickled down the sturdy columns of Douglas fir, two feet in diameter and with the bark still on, much like the man who'd felled them. The column supported the porch roof and provided Reap McCorkle with a place to hang his traps and dip nets. In the past the porch had served as an informal courtroom, for Reap, as a representative of the American Fur Company, was often called on to resolve disputes between trappers.

Tonight the porch served for a young woman to keep her silent vigil. She studied the tavern about fifty yards down the hillside. Lantern light filtered through the rain.

Julia adjusted the shawl and pulled it close around her shoulders. Even in early June the wind blew cool. Rain continued to splash the front edge of the yellow cedar decking. The porch at eight feet wide permitted Julia to keep a safe distance away from the downpour. A figure loomed in the storm's garish glare and for one brief moment her heart took flight and soared with the possibility that Morgan Penmerry had come to find her.

She started to call his name and caught herself in time. Jagged bolts of electricity severed the black sky and lit the path leading uphill and the hunched, sodden shoulders of Emile Emerson.

The reverend trotted the remaining distance to the porch. He slipped once and lost his shoe in the mud. He managed to retrieve it, stepped his stockinged foot in a mud puddle, and then hopped the last few feet to the safety of the porch.

"Dammit to hell," he cursed as he darted beneath the roof and plopped down on a half-log bench resting against the log wall. He sheepishly avoided his daughter until he brought himself under control. "Uh . . . what I meant—"

"Just what you said," Julia flatly stated, moving toward him. She removed her apron and passed it to him to use on his muddy foot.

"I suppose," he conceded. Emerson dried his foot, grateful for the apron. His greatcoat dripped water on the wooden deck at his feet. A puddle quickly formed beneath the bench, but Emerson had his shoes on again and did not care. He brightened, remembering the good news he brought as a result of a visit to Fort George.

"Oh Lord," the missionary exclaimed, discerning his daughter's thoughts as she returned her gaze to the settlement below. "You're looking for him, aren't you?"

"Yes, I admit it. And no doubt in vain if that makes you happy." Julia saw no reason to hide anything from him. They had been together too long for that.

"I don't want to see you hurt, daughter." Emerson leaned back and closed his eyes. He enjoyed the aroma of freshly baked bread that wafted through the shuttered windows to mingle with the scent of rain-washed pines and the ocean. "I have known such men before. Irresponsible men. Oh, they do not act out of meanness. But they are wanderers whose truth today is a lie tomorrow."

"Morgan Penmerry is different," the young woman

protested. "Granted, he is no gentleman like Captain Black," she added facetiously.

"Mockery is poor reward for the Englishman's generosity," Emerson countered.

"He took the *Magdalene!*"

"But not the stores. I've just come from him and he will permit us to unload everything, all the goods. Everything we need to bring the word of God to the poor red children. The captain is a Christian and will not interfere. We can have our school; we can have the mission again." Emerson approached his daughter and touched her arm. "It can be as it was."

Julia closed her eyes and listened to the rain. It sounded like the voice of creation singing to the fertile earth. Why couldn't her father see the change and accept it, as she was learning to do?

"It can never be as it was," she said without rancor.

Nothing can ever be as it was, but it can be better. In a way, Morgan had taught her such a lesson by his own example. He had endured his misfortune in Macao and come away with his eye upon tomorrow. Whatever despair he must be feeling would not last. She was certain he'd view his loss of the *Magdalene* as just another opportunity for his irrepressible spirit to rise to the occasion. Morgan Penmerry would make the best of the situation, of that she was certain. She was sure that things couldn't get any worse.

But at that precise moment they did.

13

He dodged a thrown stool, shot up, and head-butted his assailant. Another face appeared to his left. He swung out, then dodged, blocked a vicious inside jab, danced back. Someone pinned his legs; he lost his balance and crashed to the floor. Bodies piled on him. A fist caught him on the side of the head; a hand reached out to choke him. Morgan bit the outstretched fingers. Someone kicked him in the side and pain flashed the length of his body and lit up the inside of his skull.

Morgan saw a nose and broke it. He struck out and buried his fist in someone's groin. He almost fought his way to freedom, and, laughing through his bloodied lips, he hurled insults at the English seamen and dared them to fight on.

Blood and bone and battered breath . . . he saw the foot coming; like a lead ball shot out of a cannon, it filled his sight and there was no escaping. He squirmed and struggled right up until the foot cracked against his skull and an avalanche of bright blue rocks came tumbling down in *his mind and buried him alive. Faces, out of focus now, leered at him. With the last of his fading strength he swung his hard fist.*

It cracked against the log wall and woke him up.

"Yeeow!" Morgan groaned and rolled over on his side, curled up, and cradled his bruised fist. He'd skinned the hide off his knuckles. "Good Christ," he muttered and opened his eyes and saw Temp Rawlins squatting on the floor across from him. Temp had two black eyes and dried blood beneath his nose.

"You look like shit at low tide." Morgan grimaced.

"You should see you," Temp countered.

Morgan wondered if he looked as bad as he felt. Probably worse, he decided, gingerly probing the swollen lump on his scalp and his split lips. He glanced around at their confines, a tack room—he inhaled—off of a stable no doubt. The air was thick with the scent of hay and manure, horseflesh and leather.

"Where are we?" He sat upright, using the wall for a backrest, his legs outstretched. Rolling up his pant leg, he spied a row of teeth marks about four inches below his knee.

"One of those damn sailors bit me," he muttered.

"That or one of the marines. Seems I saw one of them latched onto your ankle before you went down." Temp shook his head in disgust. "I knew trouble was brewing. You were primed and waiting for someone to pull the trigger. If it hadn't been Chadwell, it would have been someone else." Temp ran a hand through the silvery remains of his hair. Big bushy eyebrows arched as he gingerly touched his left eye.

"Those are beauties," Morgan observed.

"And you can take credit for this one," Temp grumbled as he ran his fingers over his discolored cheek just beneath his lower eyelid. "It's your handiwork."

"Me?"

"I pulled a roisterer off your back and this was my thanks." Indignation transformed Temp's burned features into a mask of wrinkles that made him seem suddenly old and weary.

Morgan crawled to his feet. His knuckles were raw, his neck hurt, and it felt as if someone had put a live coal inside his rib cage. Dried blood matted his right sleeve; a similar stain darkened his trouser leg where a six-inch tear and a nasty wound showed someone had gotten careless with a carving knife during the tavern brawl. Morgan inspected the cut by the light of the single candle burning on an overturned nail barrel, the room's only furniture.

Morgan decided his leg would heal, but he'd walk stiffly for a while. He studied their humble surroundings. The space was barely large enough for the two of them. It had no windows and the only way out was through a solid-looking door bolted from the outside.

"Suppose they'll shoot us?" Temp wondered. "Striking an English soldier and all?"

"They only kill you for striking a gentleman," Morgan said. He peered through a knothole in the tack room wall and glimpsed sunlight and the dappled rump of a brown mare and dancing dust motes swirling in the fragile light. While ruminating on his chances of kicking a hole in the wall without alerting any British sentries, Morgan heard the bolt slide back and the door scrape the earthen floor as it swung ajar.

A British corporal stood in the doorway. He was short and stocky with an air of complete distaste for the prisoners. Four marines waited behind him, their rifles cocked and primed. Unlike Sergeant Chadwell at his drunken worst, these men looked more than capable.

"Please come with me." The corporal turned on his heels. "Try to escape and it will be my pleasant duty to shoot you outright."

"Polite," Temp muttered. "And with a sense of purpose."

"Just as well. I'd hate to meet my maker at the hands of a rude man," Morgan replied and limped through the doorway and out into the stable. Slanted beams of sunlight flooded through the gaps in the mud-chinked walls.

Dry yellow straw crackled underfoot. Flies swarmed the droppings, buzzing in ever-tightening circles. The barn sheltered a dozen horses and the animals whinnied and pawed the hard earth. Near the front of the stable stood the blacksmith's forge, its rock chimney rising through the roof. A couple of iron wheel-rims rested against an anvil. The forge itself was cold and from the look of things hadn't been worked for quite a spell.

"Where's Robinson?" Morgan asked.

The corporal glanced back at his prisoners, his round face registering surprise. "The smithy? Poor bloke crossed himself with one of Chief Comcomly's daughters. 'Twas me and some of me mates as found his body back in the hills. His head crushed in like an egg, it was." The corporal hooked his thumbs in the cartridge belt around his waist and sighed forlornly. "Been a long time since I had an egg. Fancy them, I do. Used to snitch 'em as a lad, a regular fox I was."

The stockade walls of Fort Astoria, now Fort George, were built of Douglas fir. Each side ran approximately two hundred feet in length. The walls stood ten feet tall, a little more in some places, less in others, depending on the cut of the timber. Barracks for the sixty British marines and thirty seamen ran the length of one wall. Another backed a long row of buildings that housed a hospital, a supply house, and quarters for the officers. The stable dominated the third wall, while the powder magazine had been dug underground in the center of the courtyard to avoid any nasty accidents and damage to the stockade proper.

To Captain William Black's credit Fort Astoria had been taken without firing a shot. The American Fur Company had allowed the post to become severely undermanned in recent years. Most of the garrison had abandoned their duties in favor of the lucrative trade in pelts. The woods were teeming with otter and beaver and prime fox. A fortune could be made. The Indians were for the most part friendly unless provoked. They seemed perfectly willing to trade with Reap McCorkle, the fur company's representative. What need had there been of heavily armed troops?

Morgan had learned that Black's contingent of marines had quickly rounded up the fort's command, thirteen men in all, and paroled them into the settlement after confiscating their weapons and ammunition. But all that was history—and Morgan's chief concern was the present.

Out in the open now Morgan slowed to breathe in the rain-washed air and to gaze northward in awe at the majestic ridges beyond the stockade walls. For a moment he paused, spellbound by a calling he'd only sensed upon the sea.

A marine behind him jabbed the butt of his rifle in the small of Morgan's back. Morgan spun about, his fists clenched. The marine, a fair-haired young man no older than Morgan, jumped back in alarm and raised his rifle as if to ward off an attack. Morgan laughed in the frightened man's face, winked at Temp, and rejoined the procession across the stockade grounds. The corporal shook his head in exasperation, his hand upon the pistol thrust in his belt.

"Do me a favor?" Temp moaned. "Don't go and get us shot before our time." Lack of sleep and cramped quarters may have taken their toll on Temp's weathered limbs, but he still preferred discomfort over death.

Captain William Black sat stiffly in the chair behind the log table that served for a desk. He had not slept well. In fact, his nights had been filled with restlessness since coming to the Pacific coast. It didn't matter to him whether the Hudson Bay Company or the American Fur Company ran Astoria. England would survive the loss of a few shiploads of fur. It was the war he longed to be a part of. In war a man could win glory, a man could advance his station.

Black was a long-featured, clean-shaven, fair-skinned man painfully thin from a current bout of stomach troubles. Generations of his family had proved their mettle on the battlefield or the high seas. Now it was his turn, and all he could manage was loose bowels and the occupation of Astoria. The locals hadn't even put up a fight. Free trappers didn't care who bought their furs. Hudson Bay silver spent as good as American Eagles.

Black shifted uncomfortably behind the table. Across the confines of his office Emerson pretended not to notice the captain's discomfort and fixed his gaze on the floor before him. Emerson still could not believe the reason he had come to see the English captain. He ought to request that Black forget the whole arrangement. It had been a mad suggestion anyway. Then suddenly it was too late. An orderly appeared in the doorway and announced the arrival of the prisoners. A moment later Morgan Penmerry and Temp Rawlins were led into the room. Black dismissed the corporal. Morgan and Temp greeted Emerson, surprised by his presence.

"Come to read words over us?" Morgan growled. "Here I am, a Cornishman, fixing to be executed by my own kinsman. Now that's the luck for you. And what words have the angels for me?" He was in no mood to be cordial. The friction between the two men had only increased the closer Morgan and Julia became.

"Never underestimate the power of prayer," Emerson replied, and he produced a timeworn Bible passed from father to son, generations of Emersons inscribed inside the cover. He patted the leather spine and eased back on the bench seat, a half log split flat-side-up and supported by four thick limbs stripped smooth of bark.

"Ahem!" The man behind the table cleared his throat.

Morgan and Temp turned toward the captain. Morgan calculated his chances and decided if worse came to worse, he'd make a try for the flintlock pistol Black had placed within his own easy reach.

"Gentlemen," Black said. "You have placed me in an awkward position."

"Awkward? You ought to try sleeping in that tack room, beggin' your pardon, sir," Temp said.

"What Mr. Rawlins means is that we were forced to

defend ourselves," Morgan explained. He paused, unable to figure the captain.

Black chuckled softly, accurately reading Morgan's confusion.

"No, I am not the villain you take me to be," Black replied. He eased back and folded his hands across his flattened stomach; his fingers toyed with the shiny brass buttons down the front of his waistcoat. "Or wish me to be," he added. His eyes followed the flight of a bee that had intruded through an unshuttered window. The insect skimmed past the rafters and finally followed the sunlight to freedom.

"I could have you hanged for striking a British soldier," Black finally said. "However, Sergeant Chadwell is one man who needs striking from time to time. He is a bully and a drunkard. Still, it would be terrible for the morale of my command if this incident went unanswered."

Black studied the two men a moment and then glanced at Emerson. He nodded at the reverend, who at that signal rose and stood alongside the prisoners. He tucked his Bible beneath his arm.

"Dr. Emerson intends to build a mission upstream on the south bank of the Columbia. To that end you shall be paroled into his custody. And you will remain in his service until his mission is built."

Morgan's eyes widened in amazement; he looked at Emerson, then at the captain, as if expecting them both to break out laughing. Neither of them did.

"Or I could just have you hanged," Black said. "Either way, old boy, we simply must have the use of the tack room."

"It will be a cold day in perdition—" Morgan snarled. Temp cut him off and stepped forward.

"Before we break parole, Captain. You can count on us," Temp exclaimed. "Me and the younker here will see to rounding up a wagon from McCorkle and loading the reverend's things aboard." Temp knuckled his forehead in a hasty salute and, taking Morgan by the arm, all but dragged the younger man from Black's office. Emerson started to follow them, when the captain called him back.

"The second favor I've granted you," Black said.

"God will reward you. 'Whatsoever you do to the least of my brothers that you do unto me,'" Emerson replied, nervous despite himself. Something about the Englishman disturbed him. Perhaps it was just the way Black kept turning the conversation around to Julia.

"I am an impatient man, Dr. Emerson. God often takes too long. Perhaps I shall come calling when the church is completed—and Julia will receive me, eh?"

"We will always be glad to see you, both of us." Emerson started toward the door.

The corporal and the captain's aide were warily keeping tabs on Morgan and Temp. Emerson hastened to join them on the porch and together the threesome hurried across the stockade.

"Dr. Emerson, that was a smooth trick," Temp said once they were through the gate. Fifty yards away the mighty Columbia rushed to the sea, completing a journey that had covered hundreds of miles and dropped thousands of feet in a chain of pristine waterfalls and plunging cataracts.

"It helped that we are both admirers of John Wesley," Emerson added. "And I like to think the Holy Spirit had something to do with it." They climbed the hill toward the Sea Spray.

"Tell me, Dr. Emerson." Morgan drew up. Anger in his voice, he caught the missionary's arm and spun him around. "Was it the Holy Spirit or maybe just the notion of free labor that brought you to Captain Black?"

Emerson met Morgan's angry gaze. "It was my daughter who forced my hand, sir." Emerson fished a clay pipe from his pocket and clamped it between his teeth. "I've a wagon to load. I expect you'll be helping me, gentlemen."

"Now that's how it should be," Temp Rawlins said, glancing over his shoulder at Julia and Morgan walking together well back of the dust kicked up by the wagon. "The young'uns walk while the elders ride."

"There's times I'd sooner it be the other way. Or in the least, have my daughter at my side," the reverend said. He kept his eyes on the twisting set of wheel ruts Reap McCorkle had shamelessly referred to as the West Road. Road indeed! The wagon lurched to the right, then leveled sharply with a thump that popped their spines.

"Careful of that boulder," Temp muttered through clenched teeth. Though a bit tardy in his warning, he felt compelled to make a point. He glanced at the tempestuous surface of the Columbia River as it spilled over massive chunks of basalt and broken tree trunks near the banks. A half-dozen nearly naked Indians maneuvered with catlike grace, dip nets in hand, across slippery boulders at river's edge and paid no mind to the wagon inching its way up the shore trail.

"Clayoquat," Emerson guessed. He had chosen a mostly cleared knoll about a quarter of a mile from the settlement and halfway between Astoria and the Clayoquat village. "I hope to bring them the Word of God." He looked around to check on his daughter.

"Whether they want it or not," Temp observed. He pointed toward a rain-eroded gap in the trail. "Mind the path here."

"I see it," Emerson curtly replied.

"I wasn't sure, the way you keep checking where we've been." Temp clapped Emerson on the shoulder. "Relax, Dr. Emerson. After all, Morgan behaved right proper aboard the *Magdalene*, now didn't he?"

"Yes," the reverend grudgingly admitted. "But things are different now."

"They sure are. And nothing you can do to change things back to like they used to be."

"I do not know what she sees in that man," Emerson sighed.

"Maybe the same things you oughta be looking for," Temp said. "Or have you been reading Scriptures for so long you've forgotten how to read people?"

Emerson touched his whip to the rumps of the mules as they hesitated at the last moment. The animals balked;

Emerson cracked the whip and popped the stinger inches above their heads, displaying a skill usually attributed to freight men. Temp appraised the missionary with renewed interest and respect.

The wagon rolled across a nasty gully, almost dislodging Temp and the reverend, then righted itself as the mules hauled their burden on to firm and level ground. Once safe, Emerson checked on his daughter again. She and Morgan were about a hundred feet downriver, voices drowned out by the noisy rush of the rapids.

Julia matched her stride to Morgan's slower pace. "Papa's story is kind of like Paul's on the road to Damascus. The Emersons owned a good deal of property around Boston and a coal mine somewhere in Pennsylvania. He was an only child and the sole heir to his family's estate.

"But like Paul, one day Papa experienced a revelation. He heard God's call. He studied in the Methodist tradition and became a minister. About the same time he met and married my mother. When his studies were complete, he sold everything and he and mother left together, to bring the light of Christ to the dark corners of the world." She watched the shadows melt and re-form with the passing sun. "China was the first dark corner. It cost us mother and most of his fortune. This is the second, and the last, I suppose, and no telling what it will cost. But I am willing to pay it."

Indeed, this was beautiful country; it inspired her. Julia looked forward to the challenge, even more so because Morgan would be close at hand. She sensed him studying her. "My, but it is warmer here than I would have imagined," she softly exclaimed as if to herself. She untied her bonnet and let her auburn hair spill across her shoulders.

She turned and met his gaze. "I do hope you prefer a few weeks of indentured servitude to hanging, Captain Penmerry."

"Maybe it will be an education for us both," Morgan said.

"Remember, you promised my father you'd be the perfect gentleman."

Morgan glanced toward the wagon, saw that Temp and her father were preoccupied, and then in a single fluid motion pulled Julia to him and planted a kiss on her sensuous mouth. He released her. Julia gasped, completely at a loss for words.

"We aren't aboard the *Magdalene* now," Morgan said.

He resumed walking. Julia hesitated, then joined him. They continued in silence. But Morgan noted the absence of a protest or any display of disapproval. He had a feeling he was going to like indentured servitude.

Reap McCorkle was waiting on the hill as Emerson's mule wagon climbed the last fifty feet of the shore trail and rolled out onto the shaded summit through the lush grass and past a cedar grove. The clearing was ringed on three sides by towering firs. There would be plenty of timber close at hand for the mission.

Reap McCorkle had tethered his mount to the branches of a fallen log. He had already started a camp fire and smoke coruscated upward into the pristine sky. The trader was not alone. He had been joined by several Clayoquat braves and their chief, a barrel-chested, white-haired man wearing a woven-grass shirt, a loincloth, and hide leggings. A string of brightly colored shells encircled his neck. He wore a headdress of feathers and wood inlaid with shells that gave him him the appearance of a barbaric monarch. The other braves were more simply attired, and though all were armed with spear or club, their casual attitudes were reassuring to the newcomers.

Reap gestured to the fire and the black enameled teapot on the edge of the coals. "Your first cup of tea at the mission, Dr. Emerson. With some members of your new congregation," he said.

Emerson climbed down from the freight wagon. Temp had no use for "savages," even supposedly friendly ones, and kept his hand close to the pistol jutting from his belt as he alighted. He kept the wagon between himself and the closest man with a spear. Behind him Morgan and Julia reached the clearing. The missionary's daughter hastened to stand at her father's side as Reap handed the man a cup of strong tea. Morgan went to the camp fire. He stood alongside Julia.

The Clayoquat natives seemed to take a special interest in Julia's auburn hair. The braves drew closer; their chief came within arm's reach. He reached out and touched the girl's hair, nodded appreciatively, then turned to Emerson.

"I am Comcomly," he announced. "These are my people."

Emerson, surprised at the chief's mastery of English, glanced quizzically in Reap's direction.

"You'll find most Indians speak a smattering of English or French. The Jesuits have been all through the north country. Also, Canadian voyagers have traded with many of the tribes," Reap said.

"And you are a medicine man," the chief said. "The trader has told me. You speak of the Above Ones?"

Emerson appeared momentarily caught off guard. No telling what McCorkle had told the chief of the Clayoquats. "I pray to the Lord. I suppose that is speaking in a way. So yes, I do talk to God the Father and the Father speaks to me."

"The All-Father? It is good. You may tell us what the All-Father tells you." He motioned toward one of his braves, a young man who immediately trotted forward carrying a rack of smoked salmon. The orange-pink flesh glistened in the sun. He set the rack by the fire.

"My people will teach you the ways of the Great Water, our mother. We will learn from each other." Comcomly handed Emerson a wooden pipe that had the carved head of a seabird for the bowl. "Keep this with you and all will know you come in peace."

"Thank you, Comcomly," Emerson said. He turned and signaled to Temp. "Mr. Rawlins, please bring the blankets, now there's a good man."

Temp dug a half-dozen coarsely woven blankets out from under one of the reverend's trunks. They were rough blankets, heavy and warm. Temp grudgingly came forward and passed them over to one of the Clayoquat men. He

immediately retreated to the corner of the wagon and
once more took up a defensive position.

Comcomly seemed pleased with the exchange of gifts
and held out his hand, as Reap had once shown him. With
a dramatic flair he shook Emerson's hand. Up and down,
up and down, he almost dislocated the missionary's right
arm. The other braves continued to eye Julia. And when
Morgan took up a position close by the girl, the braves
frowned angrily at the bearded white man. When their
chief turned to leave, the braves fell in line behind him.

"You did well, Dr. Emerson," Reap said, watching the
Indians depart. "I think Comcomly likes you. At least he'll
let you stay. Just see you keep clear of his daughters,"
Reap added with a wink.

Emerson blushed, taken aback by the trader's suggestion.

"It appears I'll not have to warn your young friend,
however," Reap said, taking quick note of the way Julia
and Morgan looked at each other.

Emerson glowered at Morgan. "Unload the wagon.
There's enough of the day left to lay out the groundwork."

Morgan for a moment was locked in a contest of wills
with Emerson, a contest that Julia put an end to by
stepping between him and her father. She took the cup of
black tea from her father's grasp, took a swallow, and
passed it to Morgan.

"Drink," she said. Her expression added "please" and
the man could not refuse her. He tilted the cup to his lips
and drained the last of the contents. The liquid warmed
his gullet.

"Now we have drunk from the same cup. We are in this
together," Julia said. "All of us." She looked from Morgan
to her father while, above, the lonely lemon sun drifted
westward. "'Blessed are the peacemakers,'" she said.

"'For they shall see God,'" Emerson finished, surrendering
to his daughter's appeal and unable to escape the wisdom
of the Scripture.

"Will you help us please, Master Penmerry?" It wasn't
an order this time, though Emerson nearly choked on his
own pride to address this rogue in such a fashion.

Morgan let his actions speak for him. He walked around to the rear of the wagon and hefted a heavy roll of canvas onto his shoulders.

"Where do we pitch the tents?" he called out.

Emile Emerson hesitated. Could he really trust this man enough to lower his own defenses? It seemed a leap of faith was required.

"I believe my daughter can show you the way," said Emerson.

14

In the waning days of June, in the time of the Faltering
Moon, Singing Woman rested her tired limbs and sat back
upon her heels as she squatted in a patch of sunlight
filtering in through the waterfall, lulled into a trance by
the rippling patterns upon the cave's stone floor. Like
shadow snakes they writhed and coiled, and though her
eyes remained open, she entered the dream.

She saw mountains with craggy summits tipped with ragged wisps of clouds. She saw darkness and a full moon and
silver light. She saw red glaring wolves and blood on a patch
of pine nettles—and even in her sleep, if sleep it was, she
began to chant, for she knew at that instant all that
was revealed to her came from beyond the Backbone of
the World.

She saw all these things, this far country, through the
"lost eyes" of a man.

"All-Father,
I sing for warmth against

The cold.
I sing for the lost ways that
They may be known.
I sing for the vision at the
End of a long journey.
I sing for peace in the far
Land where the sun sleeps."

Suddenly the vision faded and in its place emerged a single terrible figure wrapped in a white buffalo robe, his eyes ablaze beneath the horned headdress. And the figure pointed his rifle directly at her and flame spat from the barrel. Thunder cracked the silence. Singing Woman gasped and cried out a secret name, his name.

A half mile from the hidden cave, in the heart of the pine forest, Sparrow heard the crack of a rifle shot and dropped to the ground. She burrowed beneath the nearest shrubbery, where a cluster of leafy green fronds flourished in a patch of olive-amber sunlight. The rifle shot had sounded frighteningly close. The ponderosa pines successfully distorted the sound. She pressed her ear close to the pine-fragrant earth where tiny blue flowers flourished in the thin soil. She waited patiently, knowing a hunter must bide her time and listen to the cool ground. The forest would tell her when it was safe to move. Singing Woman had taught her well to hear what others would not.

So Sparrow waited, and soon she heard the drum of hooves, the frantic tread of an approaching animal. A white-tailed doe crashed through the underbrush a dozen yards away. Its once graceful leaps became ungainly as it fled humankind. The doe, once nimble and fleet of foot, could not escape its fate. Even as the doe sought the safety of the forest, the animal's lifeblood matted its reddish coat and frothed at the puckered wound where a rifle ball had punctured the lung.

The whitetail staggered in its course, then ran a few frantic yards, leapt, and crashed against a tree trunk. The animal paused on trembling legs and took its bearing; the doe's large brown eyes ranged the woods. It found no release from the fear and the pain and the terrible weakness it felt struggling for breath. The doe spied the cluster of underbrush and took a hesitant step toward Sparrow's place of concealment.

"*Ahwahkis*," Sparrow whispered, calling the dying animal by name. "If you approach me, it will mean my death." The doe's gaze fixed on the patch of shadow that was the young woman—only a stone's toss from the trail. The doe shuddered but came no closer, its eyes fixed on Sparrow's. The doe pawed at the pine needles, then collapsed.

A momentary quiet settled over the forest where gray squirrels had chattered and kinglets had dashed among the branches of the conifers. A gust of wind stirred the brush and a warm breath of air fanned Sparrow's cheek as if she had been brushed by some invisible creature bounding past.

She waited, remained vigilant, one minute, then a dozen, and was rewarded by the tread of an approaching horse. Sparrow dug deeper into the vines and soil when she caught a glimpse of a white robe further up the slope. It was all she could do to keep from fleeing for her life when White Buffalo walked a big brown gelding through the ponderosas and dismounted alongside the doe. He landed soundlessly despite his bulk and knelt to inspect his kill. He went to work with his knife.

Sparrow stifled a gasp. She recognized the gelding; it had belonged to Broken Hand. The young brave would never have surrendered his mount while alive. The woman's heart sank as she wondered how many of her people had died. White Buffalo tore a morsel of liver from the tip of his knife and chewed contentedly, one elbow resting on the carcass. Then he tossed the liver aside and wiped his red lips on the sleeve of his buckskin shirt. He grabbed his rifle, cocked the weapon, and turned in Sparrow's direction.

The woman stiffened and closed her eyes, knowing that

to make eye contact with the shaman was as good as standing and announcing herself. She cleared her mind too and imagined herself safe once more in Singing Woman's company. She pictured the medicine woman's kindly wrinkled visage, and her heart ceased to pound so wildly in her breast. She clung to the mental image of the aged one, sensing safety in that presence.

How long she remained staring into the blackness of her own shuttered eyes, Sparrow did not know. But when she at last chanced a look, White Buffalo and his kill were nowhere to be seen.

Sparrow cautiously got to her feet and started downslope at a brisk trot, anxious to distance herself from the evil shaman. She ran easily, her body a fluid shadow, quick as her namesake flitting overhead in the branches of the aspens and ponderosas. She reached a gully at the bottom of the slope and changed direction, keeping to the gully and working her way toward Singing Woman Ridge, rising to the north.

She leapt brambles and ignored game trails. She had no desire to rig her snares where White Buffalo was likely to hunt. She had to pause twice, for the gully did not look familiar. She had taken a different route home, one that almost caused her to backtrack rather than to press on, for the dry watercourse was littered with sharp stones that punished her moccasined feet. She considered climbing out, but cover was scarce here along the valley floor. It offered little but an occasional clump of aspens and plenty of buffalo grass drying in the sun. An occasional prickly pear cactus reared its spike paddles to wound the unwary. Sparrow was so concerned with the trail, her eyes fixed on the ground, that she failed to use her other senses until too late.

She blundered into a cold camp.

Squat, crudely constructed shelters clung to a barren hillside. Children waited in the shadows of the shelters, their poor thin bodies showing the effects of hunger.

One of the few braves visible took up bow and arrow and placed himself between Sparrow and the women gathered about the lifeless ashes of a camp fire. There could not have been more than twenty people, counting men, women, and children, in this narrow canyon. And Sparrow, to her horror, knew them all.

The brave facing her was Wolf Lance. He notched an arrow and waited for her to come closer.

"Where is Lost Eyes?" a voice behind her said. Sparrow turned and faced her brother, Black Fox. "Where is he who betrayed us? I will kill him." From the hillside Black Fox had spied her approaching along the gully and hurried to intercept her.

"Lost Eyes is no more. He has received his vision. He is Lone Walker, now," Sparrow said.

"Then I will kill Lone Walker," Black Fox said. His hand shot out and slapped her full in the face and knocked her down. The gravel and loose shale gouged her back and shoulders, the blood flowed where she bit the inside of her mouth.

"Black Fox, no!" Wolf Lance called out and ran toward them.

Sparrow sprang to her feet, pulled a knife, and crouched menacingly, her eyes ablaze.

"White Buffalo is near. He hunts the ridge. I would be careful. He might come and kill you. But if you raise a hand to me again, I will cut it off."

Black Fox retreated a step, taken aback by his sister's ferocity. The delay gave Wolf Lance time to approach. He immediately inquired and she told of Lost Eyes' vision quest and his new name.

Sparrow looked around at the people in the encampment. How listlessly they moved, coming forward to see for themselves this new arrival. Fear showed in their dusty expressions.

"White Buffalo and the Shoshoni were upon us before we knew it," Wolf Lance recounted, bitterness in his voice. "Before us and behind us, everywhere. The power of White Buffalo was with them. They slaughtered our elders and our braves, captured many of our children and women. We are all that remain."

Sparrow walked toward the crude shelters, paused. The faces of the survivors were familiar to her. But too many were missing.

"Yellow Stalk is near birthing time," Black Fox said, stumbling forward, his anger gone now. It had been a momentary flash, like lit gunpowder, a burst of flame, then nothing. He shaded his eyes and studied the ridge behind them; imagining White Buffalo so close filled him with dread. "I should have died with the others," he said. "But instead I fled. I took Yellow Stalk and I ran from battle. Now we are here in this dead place. And I do not know where to go."

Sparrow's cheek still burned from his slap, but she sheathed her knife and faced him. His head hung low, defeat evident in every muscle and in his bleak expression.

Sparrow had no choice. She lifted her gaze to Singing Woman Ridge and said, "I know a place."

It was a time of labor, a time of building dreams. The west wind sang in the hills; rain showers washed the verdant land. There were nights the thunder bellowed and lightning flashed. Undaunted, Emile Emerson remained. He had come to bring the Word of God to the north country and, by heaven, he intended to stay. No task was too great, no travail impossible to endure, said Emile Emerson. The failure of his mission in Macao seemed to have been eliminated from his memory.

"Here we remain."

He spoke these words in early August, standing on the steps of his empty church. It was a long, low-beamed house made of logs and mud chinking with a red cedar-shingle roof. A rock chimney rose atop one end of the structure four feet above the roofline. To his left the sound of women singing emanated from his cabin, a three-room structure built much on the order of Reap McCorkle's house though smaller. If its exterior might seem rough-hewn by civilized standards, to Emerson's beaming eyes this was home. Sweat and untiring effort had made it possible. The dream had been wrought by more than his hand alone: Morgan Penmerry and Temp Rawlins had labored alongside him, had been burned brown by the sun and hardened by long hours of felling trees and trimming logs and setting timber into place. The shipmates were a pair of irascible rogues, but, by God, they had worked. Emerson couldn't help but feel grateful. He'd begun to see Morgan Penmerry in a new light, as much as he hated to admit it.

Think of the devil and here he came, Emerson reflected, hearing the crunch of boots. He peered past the edge of the porch and spied Morgan on the trail.

Morgan was dressed in a coarse linsey-woolsey shirt, black pants, and deerskin boots he'd won off a trapper during a game of "three thimbles." He appeared much the woodsman save for the cutlass sheathed at his waist. He wore a brace of pistols and carried a double-bladed ax upon his shoulder. Black allowed the trappers their weapons as long as there was no trouble. The country was too dangerous to travel unarmed.

"A fine morning, Dr. Emerson," Morgan called out. He wiped a forearm across his brow, taking a furtive glance toward the cabin in hopes of catching a glimpse of Julia. "Thought I'd cut some wood for the smokehouse today. Spied some suitable timber back in the hills by the spring." He relayed his intentions at a distance, hoping the woman in the cabin might overhear.

"It's the Sabbath." Emerson hefted an enameled cup of tea. "A day of rest."

"I'll do my resting when it rains," Morgan said, drawing close to the porch. The steps rose three feet to the crudely planed decking. With rain in such abundance, they'd built the church with a decent crawl space beneath the floor. Solid timbers of Douglas fir anchored the cabin. The Pacific coast was no place for a dirt floor. Even the cabin sat a foot above ground. "Seems mighty quiet for a Sunday. You fixing to preach to an empty church?"

Emerson glanced wistfully at the church's interior, which housed ten long benches and a pulpit fashioned of driftwood and barrel staves. He chuckled softly and climbed down to sit on the steps.

"You must think me mad, eh, young man?"

Morgan shrugged. "No. Every man ought to do what he believes in. I've found it the only way to live. I meant—you must be disappointed."

Emerson shook his head. "Hardly. The church is built. The cabin too. The rest will happen in its own good time. The people here must get to know me, to trust me. White man and red. When that occurs, great things happen. But before I can expect the Clayoquat to come to me, I must go to them. Before I can teach, I must be taught. Before I can speak, I must listen." The reverend's features all but glowed as he spoke. For a moment it was as if he could see beyond the present to the future, to the possibilities waiting to be experienced. His heart felt buoyed by a sense of joy. He was a man with a purpose again. Emerson suddenly grew self-conscious. "Well, you see, I preached a sermon after all," he admitted sheepishly.

"You alone?" he asked, glancing back at the river trail for the sight of Temp Rawlins struggling up the path. The two men had taken to sharing black tea and biscuits of a morning.

"He stayed at the Sea Spray," Morgan said. "Captain Black took a ship and half his men downriver. Another schooner's been spotted prowling the coast. No doubt Black figures to increase the size of his fleet yet again. Reap's tapped a keg to celebrate the captain's departure." Morgan hooked a thumb in his belt and stepped back. "I don't see a need to celebrate, 'cause Sergeant Chadwell's in charge of the garrison. There's even talk of storming the fort. Trouble is, no one wants to get himself shot. Temp has never been one to pass up a good time. I'm sure they'd be plumb happy for you to join them; you might even say a few words as a sort of blessing for all the pelts stacked up at McCorkle's. Maybe a few holy words would help them bring a better price from the British."

"Perhaps later," Emerson said, finding some merit in the idea. "I have other duties this day. And here they are."

The reverend stood and set aside his cup. Morgan looked around and saw Chief Comcomly standing at the edge of the clearing. He was dressed in a coat of woven grasses and wore an otter pelt cap upon his head. Again he came with a retinue of a half-dozen braves, who, Morgan had learned, were the old chief's sons.

"I've been invited to witness their fertility ritual, as several young girls have passed into womanhood. It is the day of the ceremony." Emerson gulped and straightened his shoulders and descended the steps. He raised his open palm in salute to the chief of the Clayoquat. "Reap tells me it is quite an honor," the reverend added under his breath, keeping a smile upon his face.

"Never can tell what you might learn," Morgan said with a grin.

"Oh, God," Emerson muttered, thinking of the possibilities.

"I've been to islands where the holy man is expected to bed every lass who comes of age. It's quite an initiation."

Emerson bravely kept his smile plastered on his face. His expression briefly wavered when he heard the tribal drums begin their cadence in the village upriver. He clutched his dog-eared Bible and took courage. He hurried across the clearing.

"Be fruitful and multiply!" Morgan called after him. Emerson winced as if struck between the shoulders, but he made no reply.

Faith McCorkle put her curtains aside, and needle and thread quickly followed. She took up the curtain Julia had been working on—and hadn't touched a stitch to since Morgan entered the clearing. Julia, in a simple deerskin dress, a gift from one of Chief Comcomly's wives in return for a small hand mirror, stood by the cabin door, just enough in the shadows of the front room to remain out of sight.

"Daughter, this isn't Philadelphia," Faith chided gently. "Proper rules of courtship have no place here. Listen to the drums. They'll tell you what to do."

"Courtship?" Julia feigned surprise, watching her father depart in the company of the Clayoquat chief. She heard the distant drums but did not understand their meaning. Not yet. She peeked sideways at Faith, who maintained such an incredulous expression that Julia had to laugh. "Am I so obvious?"

"Only to a person with eyes," Faith declared merrily. Julia's cheeks reddened with embarrassment. "You've much to learn of needle and thread. Speed for one thing. I'll have all the curtains sewn in the time it takes you to gather a basket of wildflowers for the table."

"I hate to leave you alone," Julia said.

Faith had presented an opportunity the missionary's daughter couldn't refuse. She could not express her gratitude. Morgan had already disappeared behind the church. But Julia had heard him mention a spring and knew precisely where he'd be. Then forlornly Julia thought of how poorly she must look, dressed like a red Indian, and she considered a more appropriate dress. But her trunk held a few dresses and skirts in grays and blacks and some rough-woven blouses. These past months she had worn her buckskin dress and ankle-high moccasins, finding such attire more appropriate for work. She stood in the doorway of her room and stared at the unopened trunk at the foot of her hand-hewn bed. Perhaps a ribbon to tie back her hair?

"It's a man you'll be seeing. Not some cavalier," Faith said. "I've seen you both working together; I've seen the way Mister Morgan watches you. I'm wishing my own sweet husband would look at me like that. Just once like he used to." Faith made a kind of clucking sound as her mind became filled with youthful fantasies. She crossed the room and touched Julia's shoulders and turned her around.

"You'll find nothing in that trunk that will do for the likes of Penmerry more than the natural gifts God gave you," Faith McCorkle said, her hands on her solid hips. She wore a work shirt and breeches, both of which belonged to her husband. An elaborate necklace of shells

and brightly colored glass beads and a tuft or two of
seabird plumage was her only claim to vanity this day.
Faith stepped back and gave the younger woman an
honest appraisal.

The buckskin dress did little to hide her figure and
Julia's trim well-shaped calves were certainly pleasing to
the eye. No doubt Morgan had already noticed, having
worked alongside Emerson's daughter lo these many weeks.
He must have watched and wanted to run his hands
through her thick auburn hair or kiss her wine-red lips.
It was a hard world with precious few moments for a man
and a woman to find love. Faith McCorkle wasn't about to
stand in the way of Julia and Morgan. Let them find each
other and let tomorrow bring what it may.

"Go, child—and if your father should ask..." She walked
to a window and fumbled with the curtains. "I'll just say I
was tending to the curtains and when I turned around..."
Faith peered over her shoulder. She was alone. She heard
footsteps outside the cabin.

When Sergeant William Chadwell came to the Sea
Spray Inn, he came alone to prove he feared not one man
among the trappers who worked the coast. He arrived just
as Trey Frugé, a French Canadian, was displaying his skill
with a tomahawk, much to Reap McCorkle's displeasure.
Frugé and Temp Rawlins were arguing the merits of a
hand ax versus a stout cutlass.

Frugé hurled his tomahawk across the room and buried
the blade in one of the wooden ceremonial masks hung
near the door just as Chadwell made his entrance. The
British marine leaped aside as splinters showered his red
tunic. He grabbed for his pistol, tripped over a stool, and
landed on his ample rump, much to the amusement of the
half-dozen men gathered at the bar. Reap McCorkle had
hoped if he could get enough men filled with whiskey
courage, he might be able to lead them in storming the
stockade and recapturing the fort.

To his dismay most of the trappers had left for the high
country and those who remained were far more interested

in draining the last of his whiskey. Frugé and another
trapper, a hard-bitten trader named Nick Roemer, had just
brought in a load of prime pelts for Reap to store until the
Hudson Bay Company representative arrived from the
Vancouver settlement to the north. Neither of these new
arrivals were interested in the fight to preserve Astoria. As
for the others, men who Reap considered friends, only
Temp Rawlins was game. The seaman would have been
willing to storm perdition itself, anything to escape building churches. So Chadwell's mishap lightened an otherwise dour mood. It wasn't until they recognized Chadwell's
pockmarked features rising past the edge of the table that
the laughter died. Temp and the others had glimpsed the
uniform, not the man. Only a fool would knowingly mock
the mean-tempered sergeant now that he was in command
of the fort.

Chadwell looked around, spied the tomahawk, and
wrenched it from the remains of the mask. Frugé gulped.
He turned toward the bar and reached for the whiskey.
Reap slid the bottle out of the man's reach and placed a
jug of his home brew in Frugé's grasp. As the French
Canadian wasn't about to take part in a rebellion, Reap
saw no point in plying the man with the last of his whiskey
stock.

Frugé loosed an audible sigh. "*Sacre bleu*, but you are a
cruel man, monsieur innkeeper," he said in a wounded
tone. He motioned for his partner to join him at a nearby
table. Reap shrugged and started to remove the home
brew. Frugé caught his arm and confiscated the clay jug.

"It will do, *mon ami*, though you've spoiled my taste for
it," Frugé remarked. But the French Canadian could be
philosophical. The American Fur Company always sent a
supply ship in August. He'd bide his time and steal a
barrel of spirits for himself right off the boat if need be.

Chadwell sauntered the length of the tavern, enjoying
the attention he received as the several men who had
gathered for a morning of strong drink and tall tales turned
guardedly silent. The men warily waited for the sergeant
to announce his intentions.

Chadwell paused at Frugé's table and placed the tomahawk in front of him.

"You lost this, mate."

Frugé steeled himself, waiting for the explosion. Chadwell's
temper was widely known. To his surprise the British
marine let the matter drop. Beneath the table Frugé's
thumb gently lowered the hammer of the pistol he had
kept aimed at Chadwell's groin.

The marine crossed to the bar and stood face to face
with Reap McCorkle.

"Twas a sad day when we buried poor leftenant Briarwood
who died of the fever. A sad day for you, McCorkle.
'Cause that meant Captain Black would have to leave me
in charge." The sergeant grinned like a big ugly alley cat
standing over a broken-winged robin. His eyes narrowed
into tiny black beads; a grin split his features, crinkling his
already scarred flesh. He slowly reached out and hefted
the whiskey bottle on the countertop and tilted it to his
lips.

Reap held himself in check. The innkeeper's celebration
had been premature. With Chadwell in charge things had
gone from bad to worse. The sergeant placed the bottle on
the counter and slapped the bar top.

"Bless my soul, now there's a drink fit for lords and
admirals," Chadwell remarked, smacking his lips as the
whiskey coursed down his gullet. He cocked his head and
scrutinized Temp standing a few feet away. "The sea
hound is here. But where's the pup?" Chadwell glanced
around the tavern and shoved his black cap back off his
forehead. "Well, no matter. Our paths are bound to cross
before Captain Black returns." He looked back at Reap
McCorkle. "I'll see the hides you've stored, innkeeper."

Reap's eyes widened. Black had promised to allow Reap
a profit on the sale of the furs. It wouldn't be his usual
commission, still, better than nothing. Reap kept them
stored in a cellar below the tavern. Chadwell went behind
the bar, knelt, and curled his fingers through an iron ring
on the floor. He straightened and the trapdoor groaned
open. Chadwell lit a lantern and held it before him and

ducked partway through the portal. The light of the lantern played on the sleek pelts—otter, fox, beaver, and wolf—silky, soft, shining in the amber glow while shadows danced upon the wall like animal spirits of the dead.

The sergeant whistled through his teeth. "I heard you stored 'em below. Someone could wind up a wealthy man with all them pelts." His close-set eyes peered above the lip of the trapdoor. "I wonder who."

The conifer forest muffled the sound of the Clayoquat drums. Where the icy spring bubbled out of the ground to form a shallow pool, the distant drums could be felt more than heard, and became the very pulse of this evergreen world waiting in the August warmth.

Slanted sunlight bleeding through the vaulted ceiling of the firs only added to the magic, linked heaven and earth.

Through this cathedral of silence and magic a shadow man moved with all the stealth of a hunter. Thirst had overruled his own common sense. It was too dangerous. But the shadow man had to trust his senses. Were not his eyes sharp as a hawk's? He could see no one was about. He had ears, did he not, that could alert him to the approach of a stranger?

The shadow man detached himself from the safety of the emerald gloom and entered the light. He hurried to the pool's edge and knelt on the moist soft earth amid the tracks of elk and white-tailed deer, otter, squirrel, red fox, and badger. Water was the source of life for them all.

He saw himself reflected upon the water and he hesitated, staring into the face on the pool's rippling surface, and words formed in his mind. He spoke them, softly:

> "I am the watcher in the woods.
> I am the hunter in the dark.
> I am Lone Walker."

15

Morgan Penmerry didn't notice the moccasin prints near the spring. His mind and heart, and so his eyes, were elsewhere, ranging the trail that wound off past clusters of calico flowers thriving on the transitory light of midday. His ax, sheathed cutlass, and brace of pistols lay a few feet away, where he had dropped them, unbuckling his belt and spreading a blanket wide enough for two.

It was no accident that brought Morgan to the mission just as Emerson was preparing to depart. Julia had told him the day before of Chief Comcomly's invitation.

Morgan knelt by the spring and cupped the chilled water to his face and doused his head. He emerged with his hair streaming water. He circled the spring to burn off his nervous energy and was amused at his own antics. Merciful heaven, was this Morgan Penmerry, the dashing China trader, a man who'd sailed around the Horn, brought to such a terrible state, to prowl and pace like a milk-faced lad at the notion of a young woman's arrival?

He looked up and saw her standing near the blanket.

Sunlight played upon her unbound auburn hair. He skirted the shallow spring, disturbing a swarm of hovering bees near the water's edge, and stood before the missionary's daughter. She reached up to touch his clean-shaven face.

"I like that," she said, looking up with liquid green eyes. She brought a hand to her mouth, a demure gesture to cover a teasing smile. "You looked almost frightened to see me, Master Penmerry."

"Maybe I thought you were a bear," Morgan said. "Anyway, it's you who ought to be frightened, lass. There you be, comely as a siren and alone in the forest with the likes of myself."

Julia turned with a flip of her auburn locks. "I'm not worried. After all, I have accorded you the trust that comes with friendship. And I can trust you, Morgan. You proved that in Macao!" She sat on the blanket and tucked her legs beneath her. Julia smiled remembering the tryst that never quite happened and how she had passed the night in a drunken and very innocent stupor.

"Oh," he said, somewhat dismayed by her reply. She would have to bring up "friendship" and "trust."

He knelt beside her and lost himself in those green eyes. For one brief moment he experienced a peculiar sensation, an almost unbearable sadness, and the sadness filled him and brought him almost to the brink of tears before it changed to a fire that consumed him, burning away the pain and the strange sadness. Obeying the flames, he pulled her to him. He would not burn alone but must let the fires engulf them both. The sadness turned to urgency, and wordlessly Julia clung to him, sharing his need. The beat of their hearts became one.

Clothes were swept aside as flesh yearned to explore and touch and taste. Their passion was playful, wanton, freely given, freely shared.

They kissed—mouths hungry for each other—and kissed again. With the beat of passion and the trust of reborn innocence they nurtured each other, brought each other to almost painful yet sweet fulfillment. Love was the journey and they were willing wayfarers down a road neither had ever traveled before.

Passion was a song of light and life to rage in the face of night. Ecstasy was a tide that bore them away. Julia's hands clawed at Morgan's back as his warmth filled her. He groaned and repeated her name like a litany as their bodies were joined like hands in prayer.

In the shadows of the forest Lone Walker watched, not as a voyeur but as a man whose own love lay beyond the mountains, across hundreds of miles of hard country. He saw himself and Sparrow in the place of the lovers by the spring. He closed his eyes and his right hand burrowed against his chest in an effort to ease the pain.

His eyes were deep set now from his being ever vigilant and never relaxing his guard. He was leaner, his belly flat and hard. But his soul was the same and his heart was the same, and he longed for Sparrow. He had crossed the Backbone of the World and followed the sun, and still he had not reached the end of his quest. Lone Walker wondered if he ever would. His legs buckled as he propped himself upon the thickest branch of a storm-shattered tree lying on its side and overgrown with purple flowers and camouflaged with moss. The branch cracked beneath his weight and deposited the young Blackfoot on the ground. The noise disturbed his gray mare, who was grazing quietly several yards from the spring. The animal lifted its head and neighed in protest.

The crack of timber and the sound of a horse hidden in the trees brought Morgan scrambling into his breeches. Julia blinked awake and rubbed at her eyes.

"Morgan . . . what—"

He tossed his belt and brace of flintlocks onto the blanket beside her and brought his finger to his lips, signaling her to silence. Then he drew his cutlass and tossed the scabbard aside and began walking barefoot in the direction of the sound.

Lone Walker slowly brought his legs beneath him and stood. The movement alerted Morgan and he altered his course and headed toward the patch of shadow that concealed the Blackfoot in its depths.

Lone Walker readied his elkhorn bow and notched a black-feathered arrow to the sinew string. He could draw the bowstring and loose an arrow in an instant if need be. But though he held his arrow at the ready and could kill the white man at a distance, he did not take his shot. He was poised yet could not act, rooted in place by the white man's familiarity. Lone Walker studied the man's face, then looked at the long knife Morgan held.

Morgan entered the shadows. For a moment the patterns of fragmented sunlight and the colors of the foliage conspired against him. But at last, even to his unaccustomed eye, the shapes and silhouettes sorted themselves and he was brought up sharply in his tracks at the sight of the Blackfoot warrior standing a stone's throw away.

The warrior could have killed Morgan at any moment as he blundered forward, and Morgan realized this. It puzzled him.

Morgan sensed that this brave was different from the coastal Indians he'd encountered. The man seemed to have done some hard traveling, judging by the trail-worn condition of his buckskin shirt and leggings. His hair hung long and straight and black as night. His features were burned dark by the sun, and he had a lean and hungry look.

"Well, boy-o, you certainly got an eyeful," Morgan muttered. He glanced at the bow and arrow and wondered if the warrior meant to use it. Why was the brave staring at him like that? Morgan took a chance and thrust the steel-tipped blade into the ground. "I'd have probably stayed for a look-see myself," Morgan added with a grin.

Lone Walker tried to follow the man's speech. He understood a smattering of English from the rendezvous he'd attended with trappers down on the Wind River. And the black-robed Jesuits who had ventured into the north country had left in their wake a rudimentary grasp of French and the words of the white man's God who had lived long ago.

Am I dream-walking? Lone Walker pondered. He had to know whether this was a vision or a flesh-and-blood man. Either way, Lone Walker had seen him before. As Morgan discarded his cutlass, Lost Eyes dropped his elkhorn bow and gingerly approached him. He outstretched his hand and, hesitant at first, probed the white man's muscled shoulders.

"I must look worse than I think," Morgan observed dryly.

"I know you," Lone Walker said, struggling with the English words. He placed a hand on his chest. "I am Lone Walker."

"I'm Morgan Penmerry and you chose a rotten time to make my acquaintance." Morgan glanced over his shoulder and saw Julia had already dressed.

"I know you," Lone Walker said. He repeated the statement in French. Morgan understood him both times. How could it be? Their paths had never crossed. Morgan didn't know him from Adam.

"You know me? How?" The hairs rose on the back of Morgan's neck; the brave seemed so earnest.

"Our spirits walked in a dream." Lone Walker turned his attention toward the girl. His expression changed, became curious at first and then, suddenly, disturbed. He felt cold standing there in sunlight and shadow, cold in midsummer with a warm breeze at play in the treetops. The Blackfoot quickly looked away and retreated a pace. "You must show me where the sun sleeps," he said to Morgan.

Lone Walker had been following the Columbia for days now, skirting villages, passing as a shadow through the forests. Today, in the presence of the white man, Lone Walker sensed the end of his journey was near. He used a mixture of English and French that Morgan had to struggle to comprehend. The young brave's intensity was all but overwhelming.

"Who is he? What does he want?" Julia came up beside Morgan. She carried his pistol belt draped over her shoulder. She handed him his shirt and black boots.

"As best I can figure, he claims to know me," Morgan said, scratching his head. "He wants me to show him the sleeping sun or where the sun sleeps or something. He's been watching us for some time."

"No!" Julia choked on the word. "Oh, my God in heaven." Her hand fluttered to her mouth. Blood rushed to her cheeks and forehead. She bolted toward the spring. She splashed across the pond, her skirt held high. She emerged from the pond and continued down the path toward the river, unable to face either of the men.

"Shit," Morgan growled, watching her flee the clearing. Julia would never be able to outrun what had happened between them. Maybe it was for the best that she left, before he made a fool of himself by declaring his undying love. What would have been her reply?

"Where does the sun sleep?" Lone Walker said, trying to make the white man understand.

Morgan had other things on his mind right now, words he'd wanted to say—but now the moment was lost. He considered leaving the Indian to his own devices, yet the urgency in the warrior's voice demanded Morgan try to help, though he wasn't sure just why. Where did the sun sleep? Perhaps beyond the ocean. It was worth a try. Morgan figured he'd have to borrow a horse on the way to the shore, but he knew just the camp. Old Boudins Reasoner would be right on the way.

"Come with me," Morgan said to the Blackfoot warrior. "Follow." He motioned for Lone Walker to fall into step and started off through the woods. His eyes darted only once to the empty blanket by the spring. It was enough to fill him with warmth all over again. I'm in love with a missionary's daughter? He tried to sort through his feelings as he watched the brave lead the gray mare toward him.

So it came to pass in the time of the Breeding Moon, Lone Walker left his horse where the forest thinned, and pressed on the last few yards alone. His weary body trembling, he followed the sound of the crashing waves until he stood upon the edge of the world. The tremendous expanse of the Pacific stretched on forever to meet the dancing clouds that rode the wind out of the cerulean horizon and swept across the cliff to engulf the man on the heights. Lone Walker opened his arms and breathed deeply. The moist whiteness enveloped the broken cliff face overlooking the ocean. Waves dashed upon the rocks below.

Lone Walker stood transfixed, arms open, his entire body absorbing the vista. Morgan waited a few yards behind. His borrowed animal grazed contentedly alongside the gray mare.

The sun continued its descent. The sky changed from pink vermilion to crimson and azure and became streaked with royal purple. Minutes passed; the colors melded into a golden light that bathed the world in its purity.

Lone Walker could not tear his eyes away. The sun danced and shimmered before him. It swelled in size, shrank, and swelled again. He raised his arms, hands palms outward, and breathed the golden air while he praised the dying light. He stood with muscles taut. He felt as if he were floating into the heart of the radiance. Flesh and bone seared away and he became a soul of light, drifting on the sea breeze.

Joy filled him. Wonder held him fast. Magic transformed him, sealing his name—and his fate.

As for Morgan Penmerry, he had seen sunsets before. He knew a man could sail the sea and find the sun again. He had tempted the cruel mistress of the sea and come away scarred perhaps but alive and ready for another challenge. Yet in Lone Walker's company Morgan saw the sunset with new eyes.

He heard the warrior's gentle sibilant song and though he knew none of the words, it was as if their meaning were etched in his soul, demanding he remain.

Lone Walker sensed his nearness and turned for a moment. Morgan trembled despite himself, for in that briefest of moments he could have sworn the Blackfoot's eyes became imbued with a dazzling and unearthly light, pulsing like miniature suns.

Lone Walker faced the sunset as the molten orb poised upon the surface of the waves, casting a path of liquid amber across the living water. Ephemeral figures moved along the path; some beckoned to him, others sang, still others could do naught but embrace the dying light. He heard his name spoken on the wind; he saw the faces now, the living and the dead, the spirits of the shamans and the spirit singers who must add their voices to the song of the Great Circle, for in their chanted prayers were the secrets of morning and night, life and death, chaos and peace.

The sun dipped below the horizon. Lone Walker watched as the spirits shook free and escaped the golden shackles of the sun and sped toward the cliff in an onrush of abandoned souls.

"Aaaahhhh!" Lone Walker cried out. He tried to withstand them but reeled before the Above Ones and collapsed, unconscious.

Nearly a thousand miles away White Buffalo bolted upright, and in the night-darkened lodge stared into the heart of a sphere of fire, painful to look at, blinding in intensity, yet he could not tear his eyes away. He struggled to breathe. He struggled to ward off the molten light and caught up his war hammer.

"No!"

The light vanished, leaving him to the darkness that mirrored his own bleak heart. Perspiration streaked his cheek and dripped from his jawline. He sucked in a lungful of air, grateful that he was still able to. His magic, the power of *Iniskim*, had saved him. Still, the vision had left him shaken.

"He's alive," White Buffalo said aloud.

The form beside him stirred. Blue Cap rose up on her elbows. The blanket slipped from her small, pointed breasts. Taken captive, she had immediately ascertained where the power lay. Unable to resist the shaman's personal magnetism, she had come to him willingly.

Blue Cap caught his arm. She hoped to remind White Buffalo of what they had been doing before the strange mood came over him. She took his hand and placed it between her legs.

The shaman shoved her aside. "He's alive!" he repeated. The vision had been a warning. And now that he knew, he would be ready.

Singing Woman bent to fill her water bag alone in the comforting quiet of the summer's night, beyond the reach of her noisy cave-home with mewling infants and fretful children and long-suffering adults, all of whom she considered tedious intruders. It was too late to do anything but endure now and have faith that the intrusion of her kinsmen would not last forever. Her fear was that White Buffalo might locate the natural caverns what with all the activity around the spring.

She sighed, content in the silence, as air bubbles rippled the surface of the pool and the spray from the waterfall cooled her flesh. Her silhouette upon the dark surface of the pond faded and in its place the fire glow of a miniature sun seemed to dance before her eyes. She experienced such elation, it made her heart young again.

She hobbled as fast as she could back to the cave, her silver hair streaming behind her like a cape.

She picked her way through the huddled sleeping forms curled in their blankets upon the grass-littered floor, and found Sparrow and hurried to her side and shook her awake.

"Lost Eyes is dead," Singing Woman said.

Sparrow covered her mouth to stifle her outcry as Singing Woman continued.

"He is truly dead. Now there is only Lone Walker." Singing Woman patted the girl's arm.

Sparrow embraced the old woman. They clung to each other, and Sparrow wept. "Are you sure? How do you know?"

"I have seen with his eyes," Singing Woman replied.

Boudins Reasoner had stopped by Emile Emerson's mission to reclaim the horse he had loaned Morgan. He stayed to identify the semiconscious Indian Morgan had delivered to the church. Morgan had no intention of trying to convert the intense young man. The mission church simply offered shelter and relief from the rain that had begun to fall during the ride back from the coastline.

"I don't know what I'm doing with him," Morgan snapped in exasperation. "He showed up at the spring, said he knew me. I haven't been able to cut free of him. I took him to the coast—and now here. . . ." Morgan threw up his hands and began to pace.

"He's a Blackfoot," Boudins Reasoner said. He sneezed and wiped his mouth on the sleeve of his greasy capote. He was a rail-thin, gamy old soul who had tempted fate more than once, having headed into the mountains purely out of curiosity about what lay on the other side. "To have come this far he's probably on a vision quest. I've seen his kind before, other warriors who have heard the gods tell them to go off alone and do something special."

Reasoner scratched at his hooked nose. He had a hankering for a smoke, and pulled a clay pipe from a raccoon-head pouch dangling from his belt. He filled the bowl of the pipe with a mixture of tobacco and local roots the Clayoquat used in their ceremonial smokes. He speared a glowing ember from the fireplace with the tip of his dagger. He puffed clouds of blue-white smoke, sucking furiously to keep the pipe lit.

The action brought Lone Walker out of his trance. His eyes focused. Like a man emerging from a dream, he could remember none of what he'd seen in his mind's eye or where in his soul he had journeyed. Images would return to him throughout his life, allowing him to grasp more, just a little more, of all he had witnessed. Suddenly he bolted upright, seeing the white faces surrounding him. His hand closed around the hilt of his knife and he looked wildly about, trying to make some sense of his surroundings.

Reasoner moved closer. He limped when he walked, the legacy of a hostile Blackfoot encounter up in the high country. But Reasoner held no grudge. It was the way of the wilderness, one of the harsh lessons of survival a man must learn. And if all a man suffered was a clipped wing in the process, that man could count himself lucky. There were far worse fates. Reasoner had lived. He had faced down death, looked it square in the eye and grinned his broken-toothed grin.

"You are in the lodge of friends," Reasoner said in Lone Walker's own tongue.

"A Scalpdancer has no friends among the white men," the Indian replied. He had never been in a lodge so large as the church.

"You have come to a far place," Reasoner replied. "It is not the same here." He indicated the reverend, who had emerged unscathed from his initiation into the Clayoquot rites of passage. Julia too was present, but she blushed every time the Indian looked in her direction. "They wish you to be their guest. You can rest here. Find food and living water here," Reasoner said.

Lone Walker did not reply, but his gaze centered on Morgan Penmerry.

"Mor-gan," the Blackfoot said.

"There he goes again. What have I to do with anything?" Morgan blurted. The whole thing was eerie. First the brave appears out of thin air and says he knows him, then the strange behavior on the cliffs—and now this. "What does he want from me?"

Boudins Reasoner relayed the question and translated Lone Walker's response.

"He doesn't know, younker." Reasoner sucked on his pipe, but the tobacco had already burned itself out. The trapper helped himself to another ember and blew another cloud. He offered the pipe to the Blackfoot.

"It may not mean much; then again it might keep him from slitting your throats while you sleep." Reasoner held the pipe steady, insistent, refusing to be tricked by the Blackfoot's seeming indifference. At last Lone Walker accepted the pipe. "Good," Reasoner said. "Smoke with him. It will seal the peace between you." The trapper cocked an eye toward Julia. "You won't need to, Missy. His kind don't make war on women."

"I am glad to hear it." Julia glanced over at Lone Walker. A smile touched the corners of his mouth. Julia instantly reddened and averted her eyes.

Lone Walker turned his attention toward Emile Emerson, focusing on the small wooden cross the reverend had taken to wearing about his neck. He immediately recognized the symbol.

"Where is your black robe?" Lone Walker asked in English, pointing at Emerson, who appeared at a loss for words.

"He thinks you're a Jesuit," Boudins Reasoner explained with a wink.

"Oh, heaven forbid." Emerson glowered, thoroughly insulted. "I am a Methodist. A *Methodist!*" He could tell the Indian did not appreciate the difference, the term unfamiliar to him. "Tell him for me, Mr. Reasoner."

Reasoner shrugged and turned to the brave, wondering how best to convey Emerson's remarks. Finally, he just shrugged and told the warrior that Emerson once had a black robe, but he had lost it, and that he was still a medicine man and could call the white man's God by name. Lone Walker relaxed his guard. He pulled himself upright and made an attempt to stand. The room swayed for a moment, then steadied. The brave glanced toward the blazing fire close at hand. His belly growled, but he was too proud to ask for food. He made his way unsteadily past the benches and down the aisle, his steps slow and measured. When he reached the door, he unslid the bolt and opened it and walked out onto the porch. A curtain of rain spilled from the roof and black clouds obscured the stars. No one followed him. The noise of the cloudburst flooded the room. Thunder reverberated within the walls of the church.

"Reckon, if you don't mind, I'll sleep out the storm as well," Reasoner said, dismissing the notion of trying to return to camp. Something cooking smelled mighty good.

"You are more than welcome." Emerson gave the trapper a stern look. "Just see you uncork whatever jug you've hidden in your possibles, outside on the porch. There will be no consumption of liquor in the house of God."

Reasoner's weathered features assumed an air of innocence as if he'd never consider such a thing, but Emerson wasn't buying his act.

Julia crossed to the fire and with a long enameled spoon lifted the lid on a black kettle she had hung above the flames. The delicious aroma of venison stew wafted through the church. She filled several wooden bowls with meat and gravy and set them on a small rectangular table where she had also placed a round loaf of crusty bread and a heavy knife.

Morgan was the first at the table; he helped himself to a bowl and whispered, "We must talk."

The other two men, Boudins Reasoner and Julia's father, gathered round before she could reply. Summoning her courage and what was left of her pride, Julia took one of the bowls in hand, added a chunk of bread, and walked down the aisle of the humble church to the porch, where Lone Walker watched the rain, his thoughts turned to the miles behind him and the miles that lay ahead.

He failed to notice the woman at first, for his attention was on the storm and his own disturbed heart.

Julia touched his elbow and Lone Walker reacted as if he had been burned; his arm jerked on reflex and he leapt back from her. Then he realized who she was. She offered him the wooden bowl of food. His stomach continued to growl and betrayed his hunger. Still he resisted, cautious to a fault. Several seconds passed; they were hours to Julia Emerson.

"Well, I don't intend to stand here all night," she snapped and set the bowl in the palm of his sun-brown hand. "Eat or throw it out for the owls, Mister Lone Walker."

She turned to leave. Lone Walker caught her and spun her around to face him. Her auburn hair spilled down over her shoulders as a gust of wind whipped the porch and momentarily sprayed them with a fine sheen of droplets.

Julia gasped, half expecting the Indian to plunge a dagger into her breast. Instead, this strange newcomer smiled. Her spirit reminded him of Sparrow.

"It is good," he said in labored English. He thought a moment, then continued. "My woman—is—many walks from here." He wanted to tell her of the distance and the longing, of Sparrow's own fiery spirit and her gentle ways. He had no words to hold his meaning, to express his loneliness and his longing. He released her and turned to face the rain-driven night.

Julia left him in the privacy of his pain. She thought Lone Walker yearned for what he could not have and grieved for himself.

She was wrong.

16

With the first light of morning the song began. Julia heard it and, rising from beneath her down comforter, she unlatched the window and opened the shutter. She saw the Blackfoot was standing in the middle of the yard. Moisture sparkled on the trampled grass; puddles of rainwater glistened in the wagon-wheel ruts that crisscrossed the cleared ground. Lone Walker had taken a position near the river trail, where he could look across the Columbia to the forested hills lining the northern shore. Sunlight gleamed like the first morning in Eden, and Julia, after a troubled night's sleep, was grateful for dawn. On the previous night she had been unable to slip away with Morgan, and so whatever he needed to say had gone unsaid.

She knew she was supposed to feel immeasurable guilt for what had happened in the woods. Yet Julia knew only completeness and love. Yes, she loved Morgan Penmerry and refused to harbor regrets. She had given herself to him and he had reciprocated. How could it be a sin to celebrate the love God had placed in their hearts? Last night she had yearned to be with him, and this morning she wished he were at her side.

Julia was surprised to see her father appear on the front porch of the church and wondered why he had left the cabin without waking her. Did he suspect something? She prayed not. Then the source of her unrest emerged alongside her father. Morgan's labors here were finished. The church was built and that was all he had committed himself to. She had never asked him to change his life. She knew all too well that the sea was a jealous mistress and would vie for his affection and indeed his very life. Julia closed her eyes and listened to the warrior's song, whose words were a mystery to her ears.

"Appears you ain't the only holy man in these parts," Boudins Reasoner said as he walked out from the shadowy interior of the church. He rubbed the sleep from his eyes and scratched at his buckskin shirt. "Reckon I ain't the onliest one in this shirt." He winced as if bit, and scratched energetically at his armpit.

"What do you mean?" Emerson asked, his eyes on the Blackfoot.

"The Injun's making some kind of prayer." The trapper sniffed the air and noted with regret no one had started breakfast. Maybe there was some cold venison left in the pot. He decided to take a look-see before either of the others thought of it. He ambled back inside.

Emerson climbed down from the porch and sat on the steps. Morgan lingered behind him. They listened to Lone Walker as he lifted his voice in thanksgiving and praise.

"I've something to tell you," Emerson announced. He searched his waistcoat pocket for his cross and brought it out and gripped it in his fist. The Clayoquat ceremony flitted through his mind: vivid images of red-skinned young girls in woven grass or deerskin dresses, their virginal flesh dabbed with paint, necklaces of shells draped about their slender throats. There was singing and feasting

and ceremonial dances that mimicked the mating rituals of
forest animals. The girls were becoming women, passing
into adulthood and leaving their parents' lodges. He could
not help but reflect on his own dutiful daughter, who had
passed from girlhood to womanhood—so soon.

Emerson wanted to tell Morgan Penmerry that he was
free to call on his daughter. But the words died aborning,
the ties too close to be severed in a single blow. They'd
have to be undone thread by thread. It was the best he
could do.

Morgan stepped off the porch and came around in front
of the reverend. He hooked his thumbs in the broad
leather belt circling his waist. "I'm listening, Dr. Emerson."

"Yes... well... I just wanted..." Emerson cursed his
own failing courage. He was handling it poorly indeed. "I
wanted to thank you for your splendid effort. For all your
help."

"I was paroled to you." Morgan shrugged.

"No more than you agreed to be," Emerson reminded
him. "I am indebted." He held out his hand. Morgan
enclosed the reverend's stubby calloused fingers in his
own hard grip.

"My daughter might need help, wood for a breakfast
fire and all. I think I'll ride on down to McCorkle's. Maybe
I can drum up a little business for the Lord." He started
toward the river trail, keeping a distance between himself
and the Blackfoot.

Morgan, scarcely able to believe his good fortune, hurried off toward the cabin. Emerson spied Julia in the
doorway, a robe pulled tight around her buxom figure.

"Wonder what I can trade for a Clayoquat ceremonial
drum," Emerson dolefully said under his breath. "I have a
feeling I'm going to need it."

The summer kitchen was a newly completed shelter, a
pole construction whose cedar roof was supported by four
stout columns of white pine. A stone fireplace was built at
one end of the shelter. An eight-foot-long table with
split-log benches to either side doubled as a dining room
setting and a workbench.

Morgan carried an armload of kindling and deadwood branches to the fireplace just as Julia arrived from the cabin in her buckskin attire, her auburn hair gathered in a bun at the back of her neck. She balanced a tin of tea, a clay jar full of freshly gathered wild honey, and a large round loaf of crusty bread. There wasn't a place for her to set anything down, as the table itself was inch deep in shavings and littered with hammer and adz, wooden pegs, and other tools of Emerson's carpentry. A seven-foot wooden cross rested on its side, propped against one of the poles.

Morgan dropped the branches and kindling and hurried to clear the table. He shoved Emerson's tools aside and swept the shavings onto the dirt floor.

Julia dropped the tin tea box. It was painted black with gold snails crawling amid delicately etched flowers on the lid and sides. Tea leaves spilled onto the table. She managed the jar and the loaf of bread without mishap, but when she tried to brush the loose tea back in the tin, she accidentally nudged the jar of honey and tipped it over.

Morgan and Julia reached out at the same time. Their hands met and they righted the jar together. Honey glistened on her knuckles.

"I've always been clumsy," she admitted.

Morgan lifted her hand to his lips and licked the honey from her hand.

"I wish you wouldn't do that," she said.

"Why?"

"Because it makes me want to . . . do this," Julia stammered. Her mouth covered his; her arms encircled his neck.

When the kiss ended, Morgan retreated a step to catch his breath. "I came to talk to you."

"What is there to say?"

"I thought I knew," Morgan said. "But now I'm not sure. By heaven, girl, you've gone and driven it out of my head."

"Then perhaps it wasn't important," she replied.

"I wanted to explain about—" Her fingertips traced the

line of his jaw. He had to reach up and catch her wrist. Julia frowned and advanced on him, forcing him back.

"Explain about what happened between us. About yesterday, about—how everything was your fault. Well, Mr. Morgan Penmerry, it wasn't. And don't you dare try to explain about anything!"

He tripped over the kindling and landed on his rump in the dirt.

"By heaven, you are quick-tempered. You show more sparks than a mountain of flint." She didn't respond but looked past him as a shadow fell across the man sprawled upon the ground. Morgan scrambled to his feet, dusted himself off, and faced the Indian on horseback who had ridden up to the summer kitchen.

"This is becoming a habit with you," Morgan said. The Blackfoot might not fully understand the words, but the white man's expression and tone of voice carried enough meaning.

"Go from this place." Lone Walker walked the gray mare almost under the cedar roof. He slashed the air with his elkhorn bow. "No good here. Leave!"

Julia gasped. She took the man's gestures as a threat. Morgan caught the horsehair reins and forced the mare back onto the grass out from the shaded ground.

"Leave! I have spoken!" Lone Walker repeated. He tugged free of Morgan's grasp.

"No," Julia said, shaken.

"This is her home, you crazy red stick! Mine too!" Lone Walker tried to ride around him. Morgan blocked his path.

The brave raised his bow as if to strike him. Morgan tugged a knife from his boot top.

"Just you try it, laddie buck, and I'll carve you from nose to toe," Morgan threatened.

The two men confronted each other across a gulf of silence and sudden suspicion, the pragmatic sea captain and the Blackfoot warrior and spirit singer.

Lone Walker whirled his mount and showered Morgan with a spray of dirt and grass kicked up by the hooves of the mare. Morgan dusted the debris from his clothes as the Indian galloped off toward the river trail. Was he riding to the sun once again? Morgan felt a chill creep along his spine. Julia quickly warmed him, standing near enough so her breath tickled the back of his neck.

"By my eyes that's one heathen who's been to the sun once too often," Morgan said, returning the knife to his boot top.

"My gosh, I thought he might attack you. Why did he want us to leave?"

"Maybe he wanted to convert you to his 'heathen' ways," Morgan said. "Maybe he just saw something yesterday in the woods, something he liked, and wanted to take you back to his village as his squaw."

"Don't make fun," she chided.

Morgan lifted her into his arms and carried her toward the cabin. "Come to think of it, I saw something in the woods I liked," he said.

"Morgan—no," she protested, but her heart wasn't in it.

"The good reverend is gone to read from the Good Book at the Sea Spray Inn. If those godless trappers won't come to church, he'll go to them." Morgan carried Julia out from the shadows of the summer kitchen and never broke stride as he made his way up to the cabin door.

"What of Mr. Reasoner?" Julia blurted out the name in a last-ditch effort to dissuade. Quite by chance and completely on cue Boudins Reasoner's voice reverberated within the confines of the church as he mutilated one liturgical hymn after another.

"I left a bottle of McCorkle's brew near the stew pot," Morgan admitted. "And Boudins is a man with a thirst." He glowered menacingly at the girl in his arms. "Now before I step one foot across the threshold of this cabin door, you name your objections, Julia Ruth Emerson." He held her in his arms and waited in silence, unwilling to proceed unless she wished it so.

"You're a rake and a rambler, I fear, Morgan Penmerry, and like as not you'll be breaking my heart, but I love you." Julia's eyes no longer teased, they sparkled. "Objections? None, my love, my own dear—none."

By midafternoon Lone Walker had developed quite a thirst. Where he sat atop Cape Disappointment, a strip of land jutting out into the mouth of the Columbia River, he had the roiling wind-whipped swells of the Pacific on his left and the churning current of the Columbia on his right, where freshwater battered the incoming tides.

From his vantage point he watched seabirds dive and swoop down the face of the cliffs to become glimmering blurs of snowy plumage before rising on the wings of the wind like prayers to the All-Father.

Lone Walker listened with his ears and with his heart and heard the wind and the ocean speak. Even the willful sun revealed its secrets to this young spirit singer. He laughed at the antics of three young otters frolicking along the banks of the river.

He thought of the young white man, "Mor-gan," and his woman. What did he know of them? Nothing. Yet they had come to represent himself and Sparrow. Lone Walker needed no translation. But they could not see beyond seeing. They were white-faced ones whose god had died long ago and no longer spoke to them in the wind and the rain and in the silence atop the Backbone of the World.

He lifted his gaze to the horizon, where gray clouds billowed, formed and re-formed against the cobalt sky. Lone Walker watched the turbulent forces of nature at work against a seemingly limitless expanse until sea and sky and earth became one unbroken pattern of energy flowing into and through every living thing.

"All-Father,
I am here among the white faces.
Their ways are strange to me.
Yet I am drawn to them and do not know why.
What must I do among them?
Show me the path I must walk.

Do not keep me here. My heart
Longs for Sparrow.
The way behind me is long;
The way before me is long.
That is the way of the Great Circle.
It is the way of living.
I sing for the journey."

His voice carried to the whirling gulls and echoed down the broken hills. The crashing waves added their chorus, and the wind swept it all away.

His vision cleared, the world slipped into definition, became an increasingly storm-laden sky. A shadow-patched sea dashed itself against lichen-spattered boulders with increasing intensity. Seaweed, sodden leavings abandoned by the foam-flecked waves, was strewn along every clear interval of moist dark sand.

A three-masted bark rounded Cape Disappointment and entered the mouth of the Columbia. It was a sleek, deep-drafted vessel, its mainsail unfurled to take advantage of the oncoming storm. Lone Walker had seen the *Magdalene*—now called the H.M.S. *Cornwall*—anchored offshore. To watch one of the vessels glide silently across the water filled the young shaman with awe. Its sails were like the wings of a soaring eagle. The ship cut through the current as if it were alive. Its bow rose and fell as it rode the turbulent waters toward Astoria harbor.

As Lone Walker sat in solitude, the river itself darkened. A dense cloud-bank overtook the sun and obscured its solar energy. The darkness seemed to spread out from the boat in the river and took in the riverbank and the steep promontory where the Indian kept his vigil.

A "civilized" man might have declared the approaching storm a natural phenomenon, especially here along the Pacific coast. But Lone Walker read a warning in the night-shrouded air and the suddenly ominous presence of the craft.

It was none of his concern. Let the white-faced man and woman take care of themselves without his help. And what of the vision he had received? The All-Father would not let him turn away. Mor-gan was a big, strong man, larger and more powerfully built than Lone Walker. He certainly appeared capable of handling himself no matter what.

The Blackfoot might have dismissed his worries had he not turned and in that moment found a dead gull near a basalt outcrop in the tall grass at the edge of the cliff where a portion of the hillside had slid into the sea. The bird had been dead for hours, its mottled wings outstretched. The gull's beak lay open as if to add its own raucous melody to the smiling, soaring symphony of the birds. But this gull was dead. Ants had eaten the eyes and tongue from the carcass. The meat had begun to rot.

Lone Walker knelt by the gull; his fingers probed the bird's lifeless form. Suddenly he straightened, recognition in his eyes. The warrior called softly and the gray mare abandoned its grazing. Lone Walker grabbed the animal's mane as the mare broke into a run. The animal's momentum swung the Indian up onto its back. Lone Walker clung to the animal's back and urged the horse on to even greater effort. He was racing the storm now and couldn't afford to lose. It was a matter of life and death.

"Do you know the legend of St. George and the dragon?" Emile Emerson asked Temp Rawlins and his mates over a pewter cup of rice wine. He refilled his cup, emptying the contents from a clay bottle—one of the bottles he had loaded in Macao and traded to McCorkle for lodging and the amenities to make an adequate household for himself and his daughter. Emerson had built up considerable credit waiting for the supply ship from New York, which was long overdue. Then again, the British might well confiscate everything aboard. A Hudson Bay Company supply boat was also scheduled to arrive. And though Reap McCorkle desperately needed to replenish his stores, the trader would have to resign himself to bartering at a disadvantage. The Hudson Bay Company, under the protection of the English occupation, paid a third of what the furs were valued. Reap was given a commission for storing and baling the pelts and preparing them for shipment.

Tim Britchetto and his two partners, all of them former members of Morgan's crew, sat in sullen silence as Reap tabulated their furs and prepared to quote them the Hudson Bay price.

"I never heard of either of 'em," Tim replied glumly and slid his chair back from the table. His two companions— men in their mid-twenties, quiet, earnest, plain-spoken souls who like Britchetto were attempting to learn the trapper's trade—followed Tim over to the bar, where Reap was judging the quality of the otter pelts the lads had brought him.

Emerson turned his attention toward Temp Rawlins, the last man at the table. Temp shook his head no and gnawed an antelope rib he'd snatched from a platter of ribs Reap's wife had intended for the newly arrived trappers. Faith had left them at the bar with a stern warning to her husband that Temp Rawlins needed to either work for his keep or eat and sleep elsewhere. She wasn't being unkind, only practical. With the current state of hostilities between England and America a wise person made a profit whenever possible. Faith McCorkle clung to a fragile optimism and prayed for better days.

Temp Rawlins munched contentedly and waited for Emerson's story; he knew one was sure to follow. He did glance up toward the stairs just once and spied Faith glaring at him from about midway up. She spun around and in a huff continued upstairs, her hands thrust into the pockets of her voluminous apron. Temp sighed. What did she want him to do, starve?

"I used to fancy myself a kind of St. George come to slay the dragon of faithlessness and paganism."

Emerson rested his hand on the Bible he had not opened since morning on his way to the McCorkles' inn. He had lied about coming to win souls. It had been an excuse to leave his daughter and Morgan alone. All the previous night the two had not even so much as exchanged pleasantries but averted their eyes and avoided contact. Had they quarreled? No, this wasn't a hostile silence. It was more like two people with so much to share, they feared even the simplest exchange might unleash a flash flood of emotion. They both were striving to hold back and that made the reverend extremely suspicious. Better to let them work their problems out, Emerson had decided. His daughter, after all, was no longer a child. But leaving the mission site had been one of the hardest things he had ever done.

"Maybe life is meant to be a battle," Emerson continued. "Sometimes we are St. George and at other times the dragon. The trick is knowing who we are and accepting it." He added, contemplatively, "And who our children are and accepting them." He tilted the cup to his lips and took a swallow of its bitter contents. "Do you, my good man, in some small measure, understand what I am saying?"

Temp nodded. "Sure, Dr. Emerson, you're telling me I've lost my boy. He's trimmed his sails and he'll not be slippin' out again." Temp snorted in disgust. "Women. They'll do it every time."

Aye, females had sunk more sailors than any squall that had ever blown. Women with their tricks and their wiles kept men land bound. He'd recognized the inevitability of such an outcome right from the start, from the way Morgan's eyes had danced with light when describing Julia a lifetime ago in Macao.

"I fear I've lost my shipmate," Temp said.

"And I my daughter," Emerson added, staring at his folded hands upon the tabletop. He started to laugh; it began deep in his chest and burst through his gloom. "Look at us, Mr. Rawlins, like two old mother hens fussing over our chicks." Tears sprang to his eyes; his cheeks grew red. He struggled to breathe. His belly shook from the spasm as he tilted back in his chair. His humor was infectious, and soon he had Temp Rawlins in the same good humor.

"By heaven, Dr. Emerson. You're right," Temp said. "Couple of maiden aunts, that's us."

Reap McCorkle paused in his assessment of the pelts covering the bar top and studied Emerson and Temp.

"Maybe I underestimated that rice wine," Reap said.

"You underestimate me if you think I'll give my pelts away," Tim Britchetto grumbled. He'd quickly learned to set traps and where to look for fox and beaver. The past two months had proved fruitful and he wasn't about to be robbed. "I'd sooner burn them than have 'em stolen by such as you."

Reap McCorkle's work-worn features darkened and his forehead became as furled as a new-plowed field. His frown silenced Tim's companions before they could add a similar sentiment.

"Burn them and be damned. Hudson Bay holds the purse strings, not I." Reap shoved a mound of pelts onto the floor. Tim tried to stare the agent down, but it was he who backed off, his bluff called. Meekly now, he knelt and gathered the pelts and placed them back on the counter. "Stout, Bedlow, help Mr. McCorkle here carry the pelts below." The men at the counter nodded glumly. "We'd be fools not to have something to show for our troubles."

"It don't seem right," said Zekial Bedlow, the taller of Tim's companions. He wore his dissatisfaction like a badge. But he was not a leader, and when Tim acquiesced, the narrow-faced man in the short-brimmed cap gathered a mound of beaver pelts in his long-armed embrace and started for the stairs.

Meanwhile, young Tim sauntered across the empty tavern. His worn-at-heel seaboots beat a lazy cadence as they tapped the wooden floor. He stood in front of Emerson's table, where the reverend and Temp were only just subsiding in their humor.

"I don't see what the devil is so funny," he snapped.

"Give yourself time, lad," Emerson replied, drying his eyes. God, he felt better. "You will."

It was about then that they heard the gunshots. For a moment no one paid them any mind. Then Faith McCorkle appeared at the top of the stairs. "They're killing them. They're killing the British!" she gasped.

The men below shoved away from the tables and headed for the front of the inn. Emile Emerson and Temp Rawlins were the first to reach the door, throwing it open and stumbling out onto the porch. Out in the river a sleek, three-masted bark had anchored alongside what had once been Emerson's ship. Several johnboats were pulled up on the shore and roughly two dozen men, brandishing an assortment of rifles and pistols and cutlasses—the steel blades flashing in the sunlight—had disembarked and arranged themselves within range of the English marines manning the stockade walls.

Two red-coated soldiers were sprawled on the sand and another three, including Chadwell, who no doubt had come to meet the longboats, stood with their hands in the air. A fourth man, a bound British officer, was kept in full view of those manning the walls of Fort George. The officer was Captain William Black. It was obvious that any attack mounted from the fort would result in the death of Black and the others.

"By God, it's the Americans come to claim Astoria!" Tim Britchetto cheered from the window and slapped the sill with the flat of his hand.

"I don't think so," Emerson replied as a detachment of the men on shore started up the hill toward the Sea Spray Inn. The man leading them looked strikingly familiar to both the missionary and Temp Rawlins standing at his side.

It was Temp who burst into action. He ran back inside the tavern, brushing past Reap McCorkle in the process. "Americans nothing. Them's raiders. And they ain't come for the redcoats; they come for the pelts."

Tim Britchetto glanced at Bedlow and Stout, then turned back to Temp. "Are you certain?"

Emerson darted through the doorway and slammed the door and slid the bolt home. "As certain as that's Demetrius Vlad!"

Gunfire punctuated his statement. Rifle balls thudded into the door, buzzed through the unshuttered windows, and ricocheted off wooden beams. A lantern dropped to the floor and shattered. Zekial Bedlow groaned and clutched his throat. He toppled backward onto a table, blood spurting through his fingers.

Faith rushed forward to close and bar the shutters. Reap McCorkle headed for his rifle rack. Faith returned to the dying man's side. There was nothing she could do. Emerson sagged against the door, his features drawn and bloodless in the wake of what he had seen.

"We'll need help," he said in a weak voice. Sometimes courage needs a second wind to get started. It was that way with Emile Emerson. He had to dig deep in himself. He muttered the Lord's Prayer beneath his breath, took hold, and hurried across the room to Tim Britchetto.

"Are there any camps close enough for you to reach?"

"Frugé, you know, the French Canadian, he and about a half-dozen men set out for Miles Point this morning."

"Bring them back," Emerson said. "Use the side window. Hurry before they surround the tavern."

Three rifles roared in unison as Temp Rawlins, Reap McCorkle, and the trapper known as Stout opened up on the approaching raiders. The triple blast deafened everyone in the tavern but served to scatter the men coming up the trail from the fort.

"Hurry!" Emerson told the younger man. Tim ran to the rear of the tavern, then paused to look back. The cellar below was stacked high with prime pelts awaiting shipment and the Hudson Bay representative with his bag of silver. Losing the pelts to raiders would be a disaster all the way around.

"I'll bring 'em on the run," Tim said and climbed through the window. Faith set down an armload of pistols and closed and barred the portal behind the young trapper. She remained at the gun port until Tim made good his escape and disappeared into the heart of the forest. She gathered the pistols and powder flasks and hurried to the front of the tavern. Emile Emerson took his place alongside Temp Rawlins. The old sea dog handed the missionary a pistol, smoke curling from its barrel.

"Load and prime, Dr. Emerson. Load and prime,"
Temp said.

For the first time in his life Emile Emerson was grateful
his daughter wasn't with him. Demetrius Vlad had probably recognized him. Emerson had to hope and pray Vlad
didn't learn of the mission site and the man and woman
who were there. Morgan and Julia wouldn't stand a chance
against Vlad's men.

He swabbed the gun barrel, tamped in powder, patch,
and shot, and dusted the pan with gunpowder, then
exchanged the gun for the one Temp had just emptied.
Ears numb, the stench of powder smoke burning his
nostrils and lungs, the reverend loaded and primed, loaded and primed—and prayed for help.

17

Morgan rolled out of bed and tugged his trousers and boots on. He'd heard the distant sound of scattered gunfire. For a few minutes after it had stopped he waited, silent and listening, expecting the gunshots to resume. Either some of the fur trappers were having a real celebration or Reap McCorkle had finally talked some ignorant yahoos into storming the fort. He hoped Temp Rawlins wasn't among their number. The more Morgan thought on it, the more worried he became. Temp could act mighty foolish at times and had been known to tempt the Fates on more than one occasion.

He ran a hand through his chestnut-colored hair and scratched at his craggy jaw and rubbed the back of his neck. Maybe he had better go check.

Julia rose and quickly dressed, blushing beneath his appreciative stare. She pulled the buckskin dress over her head, slipped into her moccasins, and crossed around to stand at the foot of the bed.

"I love you, Morgan Penmerry. Now what do you think of that?"

"I think I'd better talk to your father," he replied. "A marrying ought to break in his church just fine." His thoughts were still on the gunfire.

Morgan Penmerry left the bedroom, stepped out through the front door and into the amber glow of late afternoon. He thought to himself how good it was to be alive and to be loved, to feel so full that another minute of such contentment must burst his heart for sure. He looked toward the church and imagined Boudins Reasoner blissfully asleep beneath a bench, a bottle cradled (with all the care of a newborn infant) in his grasp. Morgan congratulated himself on his own cleverness. Julia emerged from the cabin and joined him, working her arms around his middle. Her auburn hair was tousled from sleep and in Morgan's eyes made her look all the more fetching.

"My father—" she began.

"Will give us his blessing," Morgan finished. He turned to face her. "And if he won't, then, by heaven, I'll take it. Either way, I'll have you for my wife." He ran a finger down the side of her neck, then beneath her chin, tilting it and kissing her.

"How very touching," a silken-tongued voice purred. A familiar figure rounded the corner of the cabin.

Morgan recognized the voice before he turned and looked into the scarred visage of Demetrius Vlad.

The Russian exile doffed an imaginary hat and, mocking the couple, bowed in a grand gesture of courtesy. The mark Morgan had left on him was a boldly livid slash that ran from Vlad's forehead to his left cheekbone. It was an angry inflamed reminder of the only time Vlad had ever been bested with a sword.

Morgan froze, astonished at the sight of the man who so casually stood there, hands thrust in the pockets of an acorn-colored waistcoat. Unlike Morgan's rough-spun garments, the Russian wore a ruffled white shirt and green silk pants molded to his lower torso and thrust into high-topped boots.

"Imagine my delight when we anchored alongside the *Magdalene*. I recognized the ship."

"What the hell do you want here?" Morgan tensed like an animal preparing to strike.

"I came for the furs, of course," Vlad said. "I'll take them too. Only there's a slight problem." He took a step forward and smiled at Julia. "A handful of stubborn fools led by her father have barricaded themselves in the tavern on the slope above the stockade. They will not surrender even if I threaten to execute a few English soldiers." Vlad paused just out of reach. "That's where you come in, my dear," he addressed Julia. The Russian extended his slender hand to her as if he were a gentleman come calling to escort her to a ball. "Sergeant Chadwell told me where I might find you. Just before I slit his throat." Vlad chuckled. He curled his fingers, motioning for her. "Hurry now, my pretty. I dare say, your father will throw wide the blockhouse doors to save your life. And we'll take Morgan with us; after all, he knows your worth better than any man, I imagine."

Vlad flashed a leering grin. Morgan's fist landed right in the middle of it.

Once again, Demetrius Vlad had underestimated the large man's quickness. He tried to duck and pull one of the small-bore flintlocks secreted in his waistcoat pocket, but the frizzen caught on a loose stitch in the lining as Morgan's big fist crashed into his mouth. Vlad landed flat on his back.

He spewed a mouthful of crimson. "Take him!"

"Morgan!" Julia screamed.

Morgan spun around as Abdul and Vlad's first mate charged from the opposite direction. Abdul held a musket as he darted inside a wild punch. The musket stock shot up and clipped Morgan just beneath his chin. Morgan's head snapped back. The blow brought him up on his heels, and the world fractured like a broken pane of glass. Abdul's black features became a pool of darkness spreading across the sky, blotting out the light. Now the world turned and tumbled. The darkness was below, a place of utter peace beckoning—Morgan dived into it. He heard someone laughing—Vlad, damn him! And he heard Julia calling him by name, throughout the long free-fall.

On the banks of the Columbia where the johnboats were drawn up on the shore, they crucified Morgan Penmerry by the light of the dying sun. Two of Vlad's crewmen lashed Morgan's arms to the cross beam, then Abdul and another man lifted the cross and secured it to the raised singletree on one of Reap McCorkle's wagons. A bucket of water dashed in the face of the unconscious man washed the blood from his bruised face and brought him around.

Morgan sputtered and gasped and struggled against the bonds, then sagged against the rough wood. The weight of his body wrenched at his arm sockets and a groan escaped his lips. But the pain cleared his head. He looked down at Vlad's smug expression and tried to kick it in. The Russian easily avoided Morgan's clumsy attack and he slapped the flat of his saber across the crucified man's belly in return. Morgan groaned and tried to work his wrists free but only succeeded in peeling a patch of skin off his arm.

"Well, my friend, we meet again. Emerson's destination was common knowledge in Macao. You did not think I would follow?"

"I knew you were a bastard, Demetrius," Morgan said, at last giving up the struggle. "But I didn't think you were a sacrilegious bastard."

"On the contrary, my friend, the cross suits you."

"You use that word 'friend' like a whore uses powder; it doesn't hide what you are."

Vlad's expression stiffened. He touched the scar on his face and then moved in close.

"Look up the hill, Morgan; see her, yes?"

The river behind him, the path to the inn before him, Morgan lifted his eyes. He saw a bound-and-gagged Captain William Black and three other British marines under guard a stone's throw away. More of Vlad's men busily lined the path with torches, anticipating they would soon be supplying their ship from the inn's storage and making off with a cargo of fine pelts McCorkle always had at this time of year.

"Ah, you notice—Captain Black." It gave Vlad pleasure to recount his successes. "I flew England's colors from the mainmast and when his ship closed with us, I sent word our own captain was grievously ill and could he help us. Black, being a gentleman, came across with his own ship's physician." Vlad winked at Abdul, who grinned, flashing a row of white teeth. The Moroccan's ebony features were beaded with sweat. He patted Morgan's own pistol belt draped over his shoulder; another pair of ornately carved weapons were thrust in the scarlet waist sash he wore. "Those in the fort will not lift a finger to help, being loath to risk the life of the good captain. As for those in the blockhouse, Black means nothing to them. But the girl does."

The Russian raised Morgan's head, placing the saber beneath his chin.

"Do you see her now?"

Morgan noticed a half-dozen brigands within hailing distance of the blockhouse. Julia Emerson stood among them, defiant yet completely at their mercy.

"She is the key that will open the blockhouse door. Wait and see, Morgan Penmerry, I'll have what I came for, wealth and vengeance. No, I won't kill you. But I'll mark you for the rest of your days, on my oath. Whenever you think of her, you'll remember me as well and think of this night. It will burn in you until love and hate become indistinguishable."

"Leave her alone," Morgan said, shaking with fury. "Demetrius, so help me, God! You harm her, I'll see you dead."

The Russian pirate motioned to the crewmen near the longboats to come forward. "Load our English guests into the wagon." As the raiders hurried to gather up the bound Englishmen, Vlad turned to the most loyal of his men. "Abdul?"

"Yes, my captain?"

"Remain here with our friend, Captain Penmerry," Vlad said. "Allow no one to approach him."

Abdul flexed his powerful physique. "It shall be as you command, my captain."

Demetrius Vlad looked up at Morgan, pausing as if there were more to say. But he could think of nothing else. He turned and studied the stockade walls yet again and the silhouettes of the marines arrayed along the walls.

As if daring them to open fire, Vlad sauntered along the slope until he stood within easy range of the muskets leveled at him. He did not even need to shout to be heard.

"I and my men will soon be gone. As long as you do not interfere, your captain will be as safe as if in the arms of his own mother. Remain within these walls. Venture forth and Captain Black and the others will have their throats slit from ear to ear. Is that understood?"

"We hear you, mate," a sullen voice drifted down to him.

"Good." Vlad turned his back on the marines, many of whom were sorely tempted to blast the man from the earth. But no one wanted to be responsible for the death of Captain William Black, who came from a family of wealth and influence.

Morgan watched helplessly as Vlad continued from the stockade up the path worn into the hillside that led to the front steps of the Sea Spray Inn. He sagged against the crossbeam and turned to watch as the marines were dumped like so many sacks of grain into the wagon. Black's eyes were ablaze with hatred.

Morgan noticed a familiar figure among the raiders who had come from the longboats. Jorge Rossi, the Portuguese commandant of Macao, lowered his head and tried to avert his face from Morgan.

"Capitano Rossi, you've come a long way from China just to turn pirate," Morgan said in a voice thick with pain.

Rossi held out his hands in a gesture of helplessness and drew close. He glanced nervously at the Moroccan, who took the opportunity to urinate in the shadows beyond the wagon. Rossi and another guard, a quarrelsome sea wolf named Oberon, had been left to guard the wagon with Abdul.

Rossi was thinner now and his flesh had a sickly pallor. His hands trembled, betraying his desperate need for a tankard of rum. His former aristrocratic bearing had crumbled beneath the weeks of abuse he'd endured as a common seaman.

"I have fallen among hard men and unpleasant circumstances," Rossi said.

Oberon, who had no use for aristocrats or Englishmen or anyone but himself, leaned on his musket and munched a hard biscuit, ignoring Rossi and the man on the cross.

"You don't have to stay among them." Morgan groaned. His arms felt as if they were on fire; his shoulder joints throbbed. His spine felt as if it were slowly being pulled apart. But none of it could match the horrible feeling of helplessness that was his as he watched Vlad take Julia's arm and lead her toward the darkened blockhouse.

"Demetrius murdered Chiang Lu," Rossi said. "It doesn't matter, my telling you. I think you are a dead man." Rossi shrugged. "I am a part of it all. There is no going back."

Rossi turned and ambled over toward the camp fire a few yards from the wagon. He was never warm enough these days and wished he were in warm country. Maybe with his share of Vlad's booty Jorge Rossi could find his place.

Boudins Reasoner held Rossi in his rifle sight. Reasoner stood in the shadows beneath the walls of the stockade and tried to steady the weapon in his hand. He'd chosen Rossi because, outlined by the camp fire, the Portuguese offered the best target. Reasoner had watched the capture of Morgan and Julia from the safety of the church. But he'd sated himself with too much drink to be able to offer assistance. A douse in the cold waters of the Columbia had cleared most of the cobwebs from his head and enabled him to follow the trail left by Vlad and his prisoners.

He had no plan. A simple man who rarely thought beyond the next sunrise, he thought it made perfect sense to pick off one of the thieves, run and hide, and return to kill another—and to keep doing that until the bastards weighed anchor and departed. They'd pay for his pelts in blood, by heaven. The gruff old trapper sucked in his breath and slowly exhaled. His finger tightened on the trigger. A hand shot out and closed over the flash pan and forced the barrel down.

Reasoner whirled, dropped his rifle, and reached for his knife. He was filled with dismay that any man could have sneaked up behind him, especially a damn pirate fit only for the rolling deck of a ship. Heart pounding, he struggled in his attacker's imprisoning grasp. He gasped as a demonic face peered into his own grizzled visage. He started to cry out, but a second hand cut him off, closing around his windpipe.

He waited for the killing blow, the whisper of a knife blade, the sudden fatal pain of cold steel in the pit of his stomach . . . maybe a crushing blow to the skull . . . a muffled gunshot and the numbing bite of a lead slug slamming into his heart. . . .

Nothing.

Then he caught the smell of buckskin and smoke, and the demon's face became a set of war-painted features. He recognized his attacker. Lone Walker had come to kill, but not Boudins Reasoner. He was painted for war: Half his face was black, the other half a sulfurous yellow. He caught up Reasoner's rifle and handed it back to the trapper.

"Not yet, old one," the Blackfoot signed.

The man on the cross would be helpless if a fight broke out now. Mor-gan must be freed and the white men in the wagon as well. But Lone Walker's eyes were fixed on the cross.

This had been part of the vision he had followed to the edge of the world. He had arrived atop the hills above Astoria as Vlad returned with his prisoners. Lone Walker waited and watched as darkness settled over the land. He had prayed and sung a song of war and preparation for battle and applied war paint to his features. He had placed a black hand and a yellow hand upon the rump of his gray to protect the animal in battle. And when all these things had been done, he had cleared his head of dreams and come down from the mountain.

Reasoner was no fool; he quickly grasped the brave's intentions. He pointed toward the British soldiers imprisoned in the wagon. "You free them there lads and I reckon the other'll feel free to come out and join the fight," he whispered. "You got your horse?"

Lone Walker led the trapper back along the stockade wall. They crept around a corner and a few seconds later arrived at the ground-hobbled mare.

The gray lifted its head and softly neighed at the scent of a stranger, then quieted under the Blackfoot's gentle hand. Reasoner climbed upon the animal's back while Lone Walker held the animal steady. He paused only once, curiosity getting the best of him.

"Tell me, bucko, I got to know. Why are you mixing in this?" He spoke in English and signed along with the words. "What is Morgan Penmerry to you?"

Lone Walker pondered a moment, wondering how best to describe in words what he knew or what he had seen of the long knife and the man outstretched upon the cross, *Mor-gan*.

"He is part of my song," the Indian said.

Reasoner scratched his nose, then patted his raccoon-head pouch for luck. He stood on the mare's back and stretched his thin body until his bony fingers found a handhold, and he hoisted himself up and over the wall.

Lone Walker quickly, quietly, stole away from the stockade, and ran like a panther straight for the river.

Julia Emerson was much too proud to show fear to the ruffians who surrounded her. Their watchful eyes appraised her like one of the pelts they hoped to steal. To such men as these the missionary's daughter was something to be sold or traded and in the process used. She had no illusions as to the treatment she would receive at their hands. Demetrius Vlad was the worst of the lot, of that she had no doubt.

The Russian came to her side and bowed courteously with a flourish of his dark-green cape. "How good of you to wait for me," he said, the soul of refinement.

"Sweet words from a foul heart." Julia stood proud and erect, her head held high. She refused him the satisfaction of even one single tear, though her own heart broke every time she looked to the river and Morgan hung upon the cross. "What blasphemous cruelty," she said, fixing Vlad in a venomous stare. "Your sins will find you out."

"And until then I shall enjoy them, as shall you."

At a gesture from Vlad, fifteen pirates arrayed along the hillside readied their weapons and took aim at the windows and door of the Sea Spray Inn. The Russian forced Julia into the glare of the sputtering torches. The wind had begun to gust now and the flames of the torches flickered like banners, fluttering in the night. A handful of stars glimmered through the cloud cover; then they too disappeared, winked out one by one.

"You see who I have, yes?" Vlad shouted. Julia struggled in his grasp, but her wrists were bound and there was little she could do. He reached out and caught her hair and with his right hand jabbed a gun in her side.

"I will count to five, my friends. If the door does not open, permitting us to enter, then I shall leave her here for you to bury." He leaned in toward the young woman. "Don't worry, I'll count slowly," he added, a smile scrawled across his ruined face. "One!"

The Russian's voice carried through the solid walls Reap McCorkle had built. Smoke from the black-powder rifles clung to the cross beams and rafters above the heads of the inn's defenders. Reap McCorkle, Faith McCorkle, Temp Rawlins, and the trapper Hector Stout sat by their firing ports and watched Emile Emerson, who slumped forward in defeat, his head in his soot-streaked hands. The missionary's resolve collapsed the moment he had recognized his daughter in the clutches of the renegades.

"Only one thing to do," Temp muttered. "But it's like salt in a wound."

"Two!"

Reap McCorkle slammed his fist against the wall alongside the shuttered window. Faith jumped at the sound. A Klatsop tribal mask clattered to the floor.

"I built this place to last. It's a fortress," Reap said. "I figured to be able to hold out against anybody." He set his rifle against the wall.

"Three!" the voice intoned, tolling ominously the last few seconds of a young girl's life.

Emile Emerson heard the rasp of wood on wood and glanced up as Reap unbolted the door, sliding a length of timber out of the door latch. He pulled on the latch and the door swung open. He retreated from the doorway and headed for Emerson's table.

The missionary looked up at them in gratitude, his eyes red rimmed.

"Well, hell," said the trapper by the window. Stout tossed his gun aside and headed for the jug of rum on the bar. He uncorked the jug and gave it a shake to reassure himself of its contents. He wiped his round cheeks and pale lips on his forearm and hefted the jug to his mouth and began to drink. After a couple of swallows he lowered the jug and belched. "Just 'cause they take my pelts don't mean I have to watch." He tilted the jug and began to drink himself into sweet oblivion.

"Four!" a voice cried out.

Boots clattered on the porch, commands were shouted, shutters were battered aside, and muskets jabbed through the open windows. Then a trio of hard-bitten rogues crowded the doorway and shoved their way into the room, eyes wary and pistols cocked. Lamplight flickered along the curved blades of their cutlasses.

And behind them, Demetrius Vlad strode into the tavern, brushed his own men aside, and dragged Julia forward and hurled her into her father's outstretched arms.

"Five!"

* * *

Morgan dreaming, reflecting images on the cold, clear surface of his mind. Pristine images shimmer, re-form, become the mother who had loved him, who had tried to care for him, and who died, in poverty, crushed beneath the wheels of a runaway carriage. He sees a boy alone. It is himself and watches the lad steal aboard an American merchant ship leaving England forever.

Morgan dreaming, sees a storm-tossed sea and the violent spin of the ship's wheel as the pilot is driven to his knees by a wall of water. Lightning in slow motion melts down the sky and covers the sea and the ship in its fiery sheen. Flesh becomes bronze in color and the air is thick to breathe as the ship fights for its life.

Morgan dreaming, watches the swollen sea solidify, transformed into forest-covered hills. The boy is gone and Morgan, the man, stands in his place. There is a wild rushing river. There are mountains beyond mountains. There is a woman made of sunlight and shadow hidden in ethereal mists. Her auburn hair billows out to frame her features in roan-red beauty. Morgan calls her by name, Julia. Julia.

Beyond her a speck of crimson expands, slowly, inevitably engulfing everything in its path. Julia is the last to go no matter how Morgan strives to spare her. And yet even this is not the end, for the void itself frays and tatters and parts like a threadbare blanket to reveal a hilltop and a solitary figure outlined against the purple hills. The warrior's song reaches out to Morgan, draws him closer, binds the visions to the man, and the man to the Great Circle.

"Lone Walker!" Morgan shouted.

His head snapped forward, popped his neck, and Morgan woke to the gentle caress of a pattering rain. He gasped and gathered his faculties and tried to make sense out of the world around him. The hemp rope binding him to the cross beam cut into his flesh. How long had he been unconscious? His shoulders and arms were numb. But the misting rain felt good on his face and with the gusting wind revived him. He could hear the distant thunder.

Morgan spied movement out of the corner of his eye and turned his head toward the dancing shadows on the edge of the firelight. Someone or something stirred on the edge of night; this lurker in the dark, unseen, waited, biding its time, no, *his* time. Suddenly Morgan knew. He didn't know how, but he knew just the same. A vision from his tortured mind had materialized and come to kill.

One of the johnboats was already on its way to Vlad's ship. The men who had loaded it started up the hill path, filing back to the inn for another load. McCorkle, Hector Stout, Rawlins, and Emerson had been impressed into service and had just deposited a load of pelts, two barrels of gunpowder, and a larger barrel of salted fish in another of the boats. They heard Morgan cry out. Emerson and Temp started over toward the man on the cross.

Abdul noticed them and ordered Rossi to intercept the missionary and his companion. "Return to your own work," Rossi snapped officiously. He had taken the English officer's red coat to wear and the change in attire had restored a bare semblance of his frayed dignity.

"For the love of God, cut him down," Emerson pleaded. He was horrified at the use Vlad had found for the mission cross.

Temp tried to step around Rossi, but the former *capitano* of Macao pulled a flintlock pistol from his belt. "I don't know what you are doing among such men as these, Capitano Rossi. But this is wrong. And you know it."

"I cannot believe you would approve such a thing," Emerson said.

"It makes no difference what I approve. I sail with Demetrius Vlad." Rossi scowled, brandishing the gun in his hand. The weapon looked abnormally large in Rossi's slender hand. "I bear you no malice. But do no try me. The man I was is gone forever."

"You were never a man." Temp lunged for Rossi's gun, catching the smaller man off guard. But Jorge Rossi proved tenacious, and held on to the pistol as Temp Rawlins dragged him to the ground.

Abdul stared at the two men in disbelief. Firelight

gleamed on his ebony scowl. "Fools," he muttered. "Kill the old one," the Moroccan ordered his companion, Oberon, a Spaniard whose skill with a rifle was legendary among Vlad's crew. Yet no gunshot followed Abdul's command even though the Spaniard had an easy target.

"Kill him or I'll lay open your back with the cat, by my oath," Abdul cursed.

Oberon made a choking sound for a reply. Abdul glanced up and found himself looking into the face of a dead man. He rolled over on his backside as the rifle slipped from Oberon's dusky fingers. He wore a look of utter surprise for the end of his life. Too late now. The Spaniard twisted and collapsed face forward into the fire, landing in a shower of sparks, an arrow buried between his shoulder blades.

The Moroccan scrambled to his feet and drew his pistols and turned to face his unseen attacker. Lone Walker charged out of the night, materializing in the pool of firelight surrounding the wagon and its prisoners. He rode low, leaning over his horse's neck, and he loosed a wild high-pitched cry that raised the black man's hackles.

Abdul heard the twang of the elkhorn bow and saw the arrow that corkscrewed in the air for a few seconds, no more. He tried to dodge the missile and almost succeeded, but the shaft ripped through his side and glanced off a rib. He yelped and staggered forward clutching his wound as the gray mare filled his vision. Abdul hesitated, uncertain which way to leap. A great gray mass of horseflesh smashed into him.

The Moroccan screamed and fell beneath the mare's flashing hooves and bared teeth.

A few yards away Rossi fought free of Temp Rawlins. He bit the older man's wrist and when Temp loosed his hold, Rossi retrieved his pistol. Behind him Emerson picked up a stone the size of a whiskey jug and, holding it high overhead, dropped it on Rossi's skull. Rossi collapsed on his side. Temp rolled out from under him.

"May God forgive me," Emerson said.

"Don't worry, he will." Temp stripped the former *capitano*

of his weapons. Lead shot began to fan the air around them, and the two men scampered toward the prison wagon.

Lone Walker whirled his horse about and rode straight for the man on the cross.

Morgan, for all his hallucinations, still couldn't believe his eyes.

The Blackfoot yanked an iron-bladed tomahawk from his belt and hacked at the ropes binding Morgan to the cross. In a matter of seconds Morgan dropped to the ground, his arms dangling limply at his side. Lone Walker leapt from his horse to the wagon and began to free the soldiers.

By the fire Abdul lifted his broken, battered body from the ground. His fingers closed around the razor-sharp scimitar sheathed at his side. He saw Morgan lying against the wagon, flopping like a wounded bird as he tried to work some feeling back into his arms.

The Blackfoot did not notice the black man, and the English soldiers quickly dived over the far side of the wagon as bullets began to concentrate on their position. Emerson and Temp ducked down behind the riverbank and worked their way over to where Captain William Black waited with his men. Black was shouting to the marines garrisoned in the stockade, letting them know he was momentarily safe. He was grateful to see that the reverend and Temp had brought along Rossi's brace of pistols and an ammunition pouch.

Morgan, still on the opposite side of the wagon, struggled to stand. His arms had begun to hurt as blood found its way to his fingertips. Concentrating on his limbs, Morgan failed to notice the hulking figure standing over him until it was too late.

The scimitar sliced through the air. Morgan ducked low and inside, and the razor-sharp curved blade clanged on the wheel rim behind Penmerry. Blood seeped from the Moroccan's chest and side, but he wasn't dead yet and he had his orders: Morgan must die. He drove in for a killing thrust, missed, and momentarily left himself open as his

scimitar caught in the wheel spokes, hung there, missing
Morgan's throat by inches.

Lone Walker rose up past the wagon siding and sank the
iron blade of his tomahawk deep into the base of Abdul's
neck. The black man loosed a startled scream, clawed at
the hand ax, and staggered backward into the fusillade
loosed by a dozen pirates who rushed to quell the prisoners' try for freedom.

Wood popped and splintered as lead rained into the
prison wagon and gouged pockets of earth at the feet of
the newly freed Englishmen.

Abdul shuddered as the slugs ripped into him and he
sank to his knees, cursing his own men, who in their panic
had finished him. He dropped forward, his cheek to the
ground. Pink froth formed on his lips as his eyes dulled
and his fighting heart beat its last.

Morgan dodged past the black man's corpse as the
oncoming raiders hurried to reload their muskets or brought
their pistols to bear on him. He reached the musket
Oberon had dropped. Willing his arms to work, he managed to gather up the musket and the Moroccan's pistols.
He tore loose a powder horn and shot pouch from Abdul's
corpse. He glanced up as a dozen men lowered their
muskets at him. Flame spat from the barrels as the pirates
fired in ragged succession.

Morgan propped Abdul's body upright and ducked behind the fallen man, allowing the man to take the brunt of
the assault. Musket balls thwacked into the dead man's
torso.

Morgan struggled to his feet and took off running. Lone
Walker stood on the wagon, methodically firing his arrows
at the raiders. Another twenty heavily armed men hurried
down the path from the inn to join the fray.

Demetrius Vlad stood on the porch and admonished his
raiders to recapture the Englishmen whatever the cost.
He worriedly checked the stockade walls, hoping the
leaderless marines might be reluctant to enter the fight.

Julia stood at his side. She had no choice. A twisted
length of rope encircled her wrists and prevented her

escape. The Russian exile kept the other end of the rope firmly in his grasp.

"You are finished," Julia told him. "All your plans crashing down like the walls of Jericho." Julia's heart raced as she saw the Blackfoot free Morgan. The gunfire erupting near the riverbank gave her hope that the prisoners were making good their escape.

Thunder reverberated along the valley, following the river; a jagged bolt of lightning livid as the scar on Vlad's face transfixed the clouds black as cauldrons. As if in answer to the oncoming storm, a burst of rifle fire lit the shadows beneath the walls of the stockade.

A double line of British marines advanced toward the pirates, firing a volley as Morgan dived beneath their guns for the safety of the wagon. Lone Walker, his quiver empty, fell down alongside Morgan.

"You pick the damnedest times to show up," Morgan said, working the stiffness from his shoulders and finger joints.

Temp Rawlins opened fire with his pistol. A man screamed and Temp grunted in satisfaction. Morgan continued to work the circulation into his arms. He had to be ready for Demetrius Vlad. Emile Emerson kept a worried watch on the hillside. He prayed silently for forgiveness and for his daughter's safety.

"That's got them on the run, lads," Black shouted. He dashed past the wagon and with his men hurried to join the marines as they lowered bayonets and charged.

Vlad's men turned and fled, unable to stand before a disciplined force. Brigands pitched forward clutching at their shattered limbs or crumpled to the ground mortally wounded. The raiders closest to the wagon broke ranks and ran up the hill path toward their companions.

High on the stockade walls old Boudins Reasoner had been waiting for just such a moment. The English corporal had left him in charge of the fort's only cannon, a nine-pounder the marines had rolled into a parapet and loaded with grapeshot to sweep the hill path.

Men died on that hillside in the settling dusk. Men cast

aside their cutlasses and pistols and raised their empty hands aloft. Men darted away toward the false safety of the forest, chancing a cruel wilderness that would swallow them up and seal their fates in mystery.

From his vantage point on the porch of the Sea Spray Inn Demetrius Vlad witnessed his best-laid plans unravel, and his thoughts were as turbulent as the oncoming storm. What went wrong and who was the Indian? He shook his head. No man could understand the cruel vagaries of fate. If he knew anything of life, he knew that. But the drama had yet to run its course. One act remained before the curtain lowered.

"Well," he said and, glancing over his shoulder, motioned for Faith McCorkle to come out from the tavern. "You go ahead, my dear, and tell Morgan Penmerry I'm waiting for him. Tell him he must come alone or I shall kill the girl."

Faith stifled a gasp. She lifted her woolen skirt to free her ankles as she hurried toward the river. Julia watched the woman go, her heart sinking. She felt very much alone.

18

It had ended as quickly as it had begun. The British marines were once again in control of Astoria, but Captain William Black knew only too well it had been a combined effort that won the day. His men stood in formation at the river's edge where the last of Vlad's crew had come ashore to surrender. Tim Britchetto had arrived with a half-dozen trappers who were put to work gathering the pelts and supplies littering the riverbank. The storm continued to threaten. Clouds crashed; lightning cracked and split the night sky. Wind gusts carried the scent of pines and the sea, yet even the mist had ceased to settle on the hungry earth.

Morgan loaded and primed a brace of pistols and tucked the weapons in his belt. Temp Rawlins waited off to one side.

"I don't see why you must do this." Temp grumbled, trying to think of a good argument.

"Ask him," Morgan said, indicating Lone Walker, who waited by the gray mare. "He knows."

"Damn fool business," Temp said. He held out a small bottle of sipping brandy he'd found in Rossi's coat.

The Portuguese man still lived, much to Emerson's relief, although the former *capitano* would have a terrible headache for a while. He'd been taken away in irons along with the other survivors of Vlad's command.

Morgan gratefully took the bottle and gulped its contents, allowing the warmth of the brandy to infuse his limbs with life. He handed the empty bottle back to Temp, who was less than pleased that Morgan had drunk it all.

Morgan clapped his friend on the shoulder. He noticed Emerson standing near the fallen cross by the wagon and considered offering the missionary some encouragement. But maybe those words had to come from a greater power than Morgan Penmerry. He walked away from the missionary and past the marines, who watched him with curiosity and admiration as he started up the path. He saw Reap and Faith McCorkle, their features etched with concern. Reap's arm was bandaged, but he would recover. He passed them without speaking. Black waved for him to hold a moment, and Morgan paused as the captain approached.

"What do you intend to do?" Black said.

"What I have to," Morgan replied.

"By heaven, this is a bloody awful impasse," the captain said. "I'd storm the place and hound this Demetrius Vlad all the way to the hangman's noose. But I dare not risk the girl. Not unless I have to."

The implication was clear. Black would indeed order his men to capture or kill the Russian if Morgan failed. "She's a lovely girl," the English officer observed dryly. "You fancy her quite a lot."

"Yes."

"And she fancies you?"

"Yes."

"I say, more is the pity for me." Black held out his hand. "Good luck then."

Morgan shook hands and continued on his way. But he'd

only taken a few steps when he heard the sound of an approaching horse and without turning knew it had to be Lone Walker.

"I go with you?" the warrior asked.

"Stay here. This is between Vlad and me." Morgan stopped and turned to look at the Blackfoot. "Somehow, you knew all of this would happen. That's why you tried to warn me."

"I do not know all," Lone Walker told him. He tried to find the right words, to make the white man understand.

Morgan thought of the cross and the images he had seen while bound to that cruel tree. "I too have walked in a dream."

Morgan resumed his climb, past wind-whipped torches and quaking trees, past barrels and pelts that had been cast aside. In the bone-white glare of a lightning flash he saw dead men lying on the earth, their sightless eyes open to the approaching storm. They had come for plunder but found another end.

Morgan drew the pistols from his belt as he approached the Sea Spray Inn. True to his word, Demetrius Vlad waited on the porch, a pistol in either hand, with Julia at his side. The couple were outlined by the leaping flames that had begun to lap at the outer walls of the tavern. Vlad had set the place afire in one final angry act of vengeance toward the settlement.

Vlad and the girl left the porch and moved away from the burning building as the heat intensified.

"Julia . . ." Morgan called out. He glared at Vlad. "I'm here, you bastard. Let her go."

"So be it," Vlad said and sidestepped a few paces, permitting the girl to stand alone. "You see, I'm hardly the villain you think I am. Go to him, girl. Go to your love."

Julia flashed a questioning look at her captor, then started toward Morgan. The roof beams groaned and crashed in on themselves. Demetrius Vlad watched the flames and thought them a fitting pyre. Julia was running now, her arms outstretched, her hair streaming.

"You'll remember this climb uphill; you'll remember this night all the rest of your life," Vlad said, striving to be heard above the thunder. "And you'll wonder what you should have done, and curse yourself."

Morgan never heard the gunshot for the storm. But he saw fire and powder smoke spew from one of Vlad's pistols. Morgan snapped up his own guns and fired both simultaneously. The big-caliber pistols bucked in his fists. Vlad twisted completely around, blood pumping from his chest. He fired his second shot into the air and staggered blindly, then toppled forward. For all a lifetime of scheming and deceit, he was dead in a matter of seconds.

"Morgan . . ." Julia called to him; she wasn't running now. She moved awkwardly. She reached out to him. A raindrop splattered in the palm of her hand. She beheld it as something miraculous. She caught another and lifted her hands to the sky.

Morgan ran to her and wrapped his arms around her. He felt a moist stain spread along her side. He pulled his hand away and found it covered with blood.

"Oh, God, no," he whispered.

"I love you, Morgan," Julia said, her voice weak.

"Oh, no, please, no!"

"I love—" She sagged against him as the rain fell from the angry sky.

Morgan looked down at the grave, at the name on the headstone. He said the name aloud: "Julia." He raised his eyes to the river and the hills beyond and thought to himself that there were worse places to spend eternity. He'd heard the words and endured the prayers that Emile Emerson had spoken in his trembling grief-laden voice. Morgan had played the role of grave digger. He'd done everything he was required to to. And it had not been enough.

"C'mon, lad," Temp Rawlins called to him, standing off to the side at a discreet distance. "There's nothing you can do for her now." The old sea dog sniffed, and wiped a forearm across his eyes.

"Nothing I could do for her when she was alive," Morgan said bitterly. He knelt, placed his hand on the freshly mounded earth, and closed his eyes. "I am so sorry." Then he straightened. He looked down the river trail to where Reap and Faith McCorkle waited in their wagon. Reap had already begun to rebuild his inn. Captain William Black was there and many of the trappers, who had come out of a gesture of sympathy. They all stood together. They all waited.

Morgan started toward the horse he had ridden up from the stockade.

"There you be. Some things is best left behind," Temp said, encouraged by the young man's actions. Morgan had not even spoken since the fight. He had not wept at the funeral.

"Good-bye, Temp," Morgan said.

"Now, lad. It's rough seas, I know, but you'll come through it."

"I mean really good-bye."

Temp stepped back and studied him. The look in Morgan's dark eyes told the seaman that nothing would ever be the same again, that the younger man was leaving. No. He had already left. "Good-bye," Temp managed.

Morgan mounted the sturdy brown gelding and rode away from the grassy hill overlooking the river. He guided the animal toward the mission church and Emile Emerson. The missionary was using the same shovel that had dug his daughter's grave. The large wooden cross lay on the ground close at hand. The reverend intended to raise it upright today. He had refused any help. He would do this alone. Morgan could understand his reasons. But planting a cross wouldn't heal the hurt Morgan felt deep in his heart.

Emerson worked the shovel like a man possessed, pausing briefly to wipe the sweat from his brow on the sleeve of his shirt. But he noticed Morgan approach and he stopped to face him. Emerson's eyes were red rimmed, and moisture streaked his dirt-smudged cheeks. The frock coat he had worn for the funeral service lay folded on the ground. His Bible was open face down on the coat. His sleeves were rolled up to his elbows; in truth, he looked more like a laborer than a minister. Emerson leaned on the shovel and looked up at the man on the horse.

"I'll have it in the ground by afternoon," Emerson said, with a quick look toward the cross. "Then the difficult work begins."

"What's that?"

"Living." Emerson closed his eyes for a brief moment and grew very attentive, as if listening to some private inner conversation. He then returned to work. Morgan left him with his cross and his graves and his dreams.

Lone Walker had come to bid farewell to the spirits of the Great Water. He had come to stand upon the edge of the world for the last time. He had come to sing the song of sorrow for a woman he had barely known. She had not been of his people, yet he felt her death. And he prayed she might find peace and be allowed to enter the Great Mystery singing.

It was late afternoon. Already the sun had begun its earthward slide to the rim of the world. Lone Walker made a sacred fire, gathering twigs and dry grass and setting them afire with sparks from a flint. Then he opened his medicine pouch and took a pinch of sacred soil and sprinkled the cheerful little blaze. And when the prayer smoke began to spiral skyward to be gathered by the drifting clouds, Lone Walker began his chant:

> "It is done, All-Father.
> I have fulfilled the vision.
> May I return to my people?
> My heart aches for the woman
> Who walks in my soul."

He reached into a shoulder pouch and brought forth his reed flute and began to play upon it a series of softly trilling notes. He played the flute, and the music was his song and his prayer. As he played, he saw Sparrow's face and he knew joy. But the joy was short-lived, for White Buffalo appeared in the shadows behind her and he was a fierce and terrible figure in his sacred robes, and Lone Walker seemed to hear the shaman speak. And he said, "My magic is strong, my power is strong, and none can stand against me."

The image faded and Lone Walker saw a high-country trail where the new-fallen snow lay thick upon the hard earth, covering the wind- and rain-eroded boulders with a sheet of ice as smooth as glass. Lone Walker knew then he was homeward bound. He could even see his shadow cast upon the pristine snow as he rode east across the Backbone of the World. No . . . two shadows shimmered silently across the drifts. This puzzled him, and he asked more of the vision.

"Lone Walker." Morgan's voice broke the spell. The images faded and the Indian opened his eyes. He took the flute from his lips. The horizon was tinged with scarlet and vermilion. The clouds themselves became vessels of burnished gold. Lone Walker beheld Morgan Penmerry through a haze of sacred smoke.

"I am going with you," Morgan said.

A journey ends, another begins, such is the way of the Great Circle, ending and beginning, ever changing, ever the same.

The second shadow was Mor-gan.

Lone Walker replied, "Let it be so."

PART IV

The Return

19

October 1814

The last thing Singing Woman wanted in her bed on a frosty night in autumn was an albino sage lizard with spiny claws and eyes like drops of blood. The startled reptile crawled under the blanket and ran up the old medicine woman's naked legs. The creature attempted to burrow beneath her smock. Singing Woman yelped and shot out of her blankets with the speed and agility of a person thirty years younger. She leapt to her feet and slapped at her buckskin smock. Seven inches of terrified lizard dropped to the cave floor and scampered toward the nearest patch of darkness. The old woman headed in the opposite direction and stumbled onto the two culprits responsible for the lizard's intrusion.

Raven Takes Him rebounded off his brother Turtle and the two youngsters leapt over each other in an attempt to escape the old one's clutches. They scrambled toward an inner chamber of the cave where the rest of the survivors of the Shoshoni raid lived by torchlight amid limestone columns and draperies of travertine.

"Run, jackrabbits, hide if you will, but you cannot escape my magic!" the irate woman shouted as she chased them into the chamber.

"We aren't afraid of you," Raven Takes Him called over his shoulder. It was easy for him to say, for his long-legged gait put him well ahead of Singing Woman. However, she caught Turtle by the ear and dragged him to a halt.

"By the light of my spirit fire I'll conjure the eaters of the dead to pluck this hide from your bones," she told him and pinched the fat on the underside of his arms. Turtle squealed for help and fought her efforts to drag him back into the outer reaches of the cave. Their commotion woke the other children, including the recently born son of Black Fox and Yellow Stalk, a baby they had taken to calling Little Elk. The smaller children, once awakened, began to clamor for their weary mothers, who themselves had just curled up on beds of evergreen needles beneath blankets of hide or fur pelt, bearskins, and buffalo robes.

Black Fox, who had been enjoying his wife under their blanket, sat upright and began to pelt the old woman with pebbles from the floor. A couple of other men joined in, anxious to drive the intruder from the room.

"Leave him alone, old mother," Black Fox said. One of his stones caught Singing Woman on the tip of the nose. She released Turtle and wagged an accusing finger at the lot of them.

"Be gone, ungrateful dogs!" Blood oozed from the tip of her nose along the jagged little cut. "Once I heard only the wind and the song of living water that hid me from you and all the others like you. I was happy and did not know it," Singing Woman said in disgust.

Wolf Lance entered from a side chamber where the horses were kept. He wore a coat of gray wolf pelts that added stature to his already bulky form. He hurried to the old woman's side.

"Enough," he roared. "Singing Woman risks her life for us. Is this how you repay her kindness?"

Yellow Stalk cradled her infant to her breast. Little Elk

found his mother's nipple and began greedily to suck it. Yellow Stalk tugged at Black Fox's arm, but he pulled away.

"The Above Ones have touched her," he said. "She is crazy." The baby, frightened at his father's ranting, began to howl.

"Touched me, yes, long ago," Singing Woman said. "I abandoned my people and came here to live." The old woman moved through the chamber, carefully skirting the huddled forms of the men and women who were trying to sleep.

When she came alongside Yellow Stalk's bed, Black Fox raised a hand to stop her. He was a proud man, but Singing Woman could see through him to the angry boy within. She wasn't cowed by him, and she understood his worries. He had a new child and yet must live in hiding. White Buffalo and the Shoshoni were searching for the remnants of the tribe they had nearly destroyed. How long could they elude capture? Where could they go? The Scalpdancers had become a people without vision, a defeated people whose days seemed numbered.

Singing Woman crossed in front of Black Fox and knelt by Yellow Stalk and her fussy infant. Singing Woman took a small medicine pouch from her neck; she sprinkled a pinch of dust and ash on the infant's belly and chest. "Now he will be able to ignore his father's bellowing as do I."

The sacred dust settled on the baby's plump flesh and the child quieted and began to coo and giggle as the old woman sang a soothing little chant. Black Fox scowled at her insult.

"I have had my fill of magic," the warrior grumbled. "And this cave."

"Then go," Singing Woman told him. They were watching her now, all of them. She unnerved them; she was too strange. "Go, I say. But leave my blanket here." Her hand shot out and grabbed a fistful of the blanket Black Fox had wrapped about himself. She spun around and pulled.

The Blackfoot brave was caught completely by surprise

and before he could tighten his hold, the blanket was yanked completely from his grasp, leaving him standing totally naked in front of everyone. He dived for the extra blanket he'd shared with Yellow Stalk much to the amusement of the entire chamber full of people.

Singing Woman left Black Fox to the good-natured derision of his clan and returned to her own quarters. Wolf Lance followed her, looking older than he had a right to. Singing Woman draped a worn and ratty trade blanket across her shoulders. The lizard that had instigated the uproar scurried along the wall opposite her bed. She grabbed a parfleche of dried hollyhock and fleabane and hurled it at the intruder. The lizard became a pale blur and escaped through a crevice in the limestone wall.

Lying still, one could hear the droning of the waterfall as it spilled into the pool at the base of the ridge. Come winter, the plunging cataract would be reduced to a trickle when temperatures dipped below freezing and remained there. It too would have its own tentative song, tumbling tremulously over the smooth-worn ledges and cornices of granite and columns of ice.

"Forgive us, grandmother," Wolf Lance said, standing in the passageway just outside the chamber. "My own people shame me this night."

"They are afraid. Fear colors their words. It clouds their thoughts. They do not want to die."

"No one wants to die." Wolf Lance shuddered.

"Only the rocks last forever." The medicine woman had spoken her piece. She sat on her bedding and pulled aside the bearskin blanket to reassure herself that there were no more uninvited guests hidden in the folds.

Wolf Lance eased back into the passageway. He glanced over his shoulder at the larger chamber where the survivors of his village settled back into sleep. He walked instead toward the entrance of the cave. The air became noticeably cooler where the autumnal breezes wafted through the shimmering falls. Wolf Lance sidestepped the pool formed within the cavern and, hugging the smooth-worn walls, made his way past the curtain of water into the cool night. He spied a solitary figure standing at the edge of the pond, her back to the cave; she searched the shadow-shrouded valley, keeping a silent, faithful vigil beneath the silver moon.

Sparrow—

Wolf Lance hesitated, wondering if he should approach. His restlessness made him bold. The brave made as much noise as possible so as not to startle the young woman as he drew abreast of her.

"Cold Maker is near," she said. The blanket covered her head like a cowl. Indeed the air had a bite to it, hinting of things to come.

"Then there will be hard times," Wolf Lance said. "Men and horses leave tracks in the snow—tracks that might lead White Buffalo to us. The cave will not be so well hidden once the water begins to freeze on the cliff above."

Sparrow could tell he was working up to something. Better that he should speak his mind. They were friends. He had always stood by Lone Walker and had argued against his friend's expulsion from the village.

"What are you saying?" she asked. "Speak clear. I will listen with the ears of a friend."

"We cannot remain here much longer, hiding, waiting for one who may never . . ." Wolf Lance faltered as Sparrow gave him a sharp look. "Return," he finished.

"Lone Walker is not dead," Sparrow flatly stated.

"You are no shaman. How can you know?"

"Because my heart is full of love."

Wolf Lance sighed, aware she had bested him with an insurmountable argument, one women always seemed to use in the face of grim reality. Lone Walker was alive because Sparrow, in love, would not permit otherwise.

"Still, we must leave before the Hard-Faced Moon comes. You and the old woman can remain. Two can hide easier than thirty." Wolf Lance studied the dark ridges and spied what had earlier caught Sparrow's attention, the orange-red glare of the distant camp fire nestled among the trees just below the skyline. At first his own heart leapt excitedly at the sight; then he too realized what

Sparrow had already concluded. Lone Walker would have ridden in by the light of the moon. This was a Shoshoni camp fire.

"Tell the others," Sparrow said. "The children must remain in the cave."

"All of us, until our enemies have left the valley," Wolf Lance said. "We hide like whipped dogs. We do not even number enough to raid the village of Elkhorn Creek and free the women and children White Buffalo has captured."

Sparrow heard the pain in his voice. Wolf Lance was a brave man. Had he been present when the Shoshoni attacked the village, he probably would have died rather than flee. Now he hid from the very enemy who had destroyed his village, and each day he died a little because of it.

"I shall stay with Singing Woman. And when Lone Walker returns, we will find you," Sparrow told him.

Wolf Lance nodded. He was loath to abandon the young woman. Maybe they could all abide just a little longer. He might yet convince Sparrow to join them.

Suddenly the sky blazed with color. An unearthly green bathed the valley as a molten orb trailing fire streaked across the night sky. Every tree, every detail of the ridge behind them, shone with stark clarity. The waterfall, once a shimmering veil of quicksilver, for a few brief seconds radiated incandescent emerald light, transformed by a meteorite that arced across the sky.

It was gone.

Sparrow and Wolf Lance stared as darkness returned to the night sky. Momentarily blinded, they tried to focus on the moon and the stars and the valley around them and each other's features. Neither spoke. Words could not capture what each felt. One thing was certain. Sparrow recognized a warning when she saw it. As did Wolf Lance.

As did White Buffalo—for it was his camp fire on the ridge above the narrow valley. He stood transfixed as the meteorite ripped across the heavens. A dozen braves gathered round, rolled out their blankets, and uttered prayers to the All-Father, in whose presence they deemed to be.

Drum, the Shoshoni Dog Soldier, waited in White Buffalo's shadow and watched the shaman's features reflect the macabre green glow. Drum was not as unsettled as the others; he was too interested in White Buffalo's reaction to the strange and awesome event.

"Surely the Great One rides forth on his stallion of fire," Drum said, looking up at the shaman. Drum was neither strong nor quick, but he possessed a shrewd mind and had a keen eye for the future. He could envision a time when the Shoshoni of Elkhorn Creek swelled in number and could move out to the plains and drive their enemies from the land of the buffalo. With the shaman's magic they could not fail.

As the Shoshoni prospered, so would Drum rise in stature. Wealth, many fine horses, and comely wives would be his. Drum was the shaman's right arm and the Shoshoni braves feared him as they did Stone Bear, who stood at White Buffalo's left.

"Tell me what this means, shaman?" Drum said in a humble voice. He had never witnessed such a phenomenon. Even brash, outspoken Stone Bear stood in awe, leaning on his trade gun and waiting, ready for the worst. He searched the skies for another threat.

"A warning," White Buffalo muttered. "He's closer than I thought. But why does he not come?" The shaman hurried to the camp fire and gathered his rifle, powder horn, and shot pouch. He knew what had to be done. White Buffalo only hoped he wasn't too late. He called for his horse. A young Shoshoni brave scampered off to do his bidding.

"Finish the hunt," the shaman said to the smaller of the two, who had followed him from beneath the spruce.

"And what will you do?"

"I also will hunt," White Buffalo replied. "But for this prey I need no gun."

There is something about standing upon the Backbone of the World and being able to see across hundreds of

miles of craggy snow-swept mountains that overwhelms
even the most painful mourning. So it was with Morgan
Penmerry, who in the time of the Starting-to-Freeze Moon,
in what surely seemed the October of his life, stood at the
edge of a granite precipice on the eastern face of the
Continental Divide. He looked across a terrain of such
immensity, it dwarfed even the pain that had poisoned
his heart. It did not heal the hurt or drive it away, but
the chaotic splendor unfolding before him and the lonely high-country trails he had followed with Lone Walker
filled him with a sense of the Creator. If Julia had returned into the embrace of such a miracle, then all was
not lost, merely transformed. If she had become one with
the spirit behind such beauty, then indeed she must be
happy.

Lone Walker rose just before daybreak and, noting
Morgan's empty bedroll, looked around for the white man.
The Indian stirred the ashes of the camp fire and added
the dry twisted limbs from a pine tree whose stunted form
was one of many scattered along the serrated ridge. Leaving the comfort of the camp fire, the Blackfoot ventured
alone a few yards out from beneath the ledge where the
two men had camped. His moccasined feet crunched the
new-fallen snow that had dusted the pass during the night.
He paused, sensing another's presence. He turned and
spied Morgan Penmerry standing atop the overhang they
had used for shelter. Lone Walker wondered why the
white man had risen early—after all, he knew no medicine
songs.

The Blackfoot shrugged and scooped up a handful of
powdery snow and sprinkled it upon the wind, and as it
blew away beyond the edge of the cliff, a fleck of gold
appeared on the eastern horizon and Lone Walker began
to sing softly a medicine chant, accepting his part in the
drama of creation as the world began anew.

Morgan closed his eyes and listened to the soft voice
drifting on the wind and he listened to the wind itself. He
marveled at how one could hear it coming, like a locomo-
tive barreling across the mountain slopes and roaring

down valleys and glacial troughs. He could hear the wind
long before he felt it upon his face, before it tugged at his
greatcoat with unseen talons. Afterward, he could listen to
its wayward course as it rushed away, like a living sentient
creature, as alive as the mountain lion they'd spooked the
day before or the golden eagle circling overhead. And he
began to understand something of Lone Walker's belief in
an All-Father and the sacredness of things found in the
world around them, from the creatures of earth and air to
the very earth itself, the shallow mountain soil underfoot,
the granite cliffs, fire, rain, and, yes, the wind.

On a more practical level, being a practical man, Morgan
had developed a working knowledge of signing and the
Blackfoot language. Being alone with the young mystic
warrior for seven weeks had forced Morgan to listen and
learn quickly. He understood most of Lone Walker's prayer
chant and thought with a moment's wry introspection that
Lone Walker did more praying than any two Emile
Emersons. The notion brought another pang of memory. If
Lone Walker was any indication, it appeared the so-called
"heathens" were on mighty personal terms with the Almighty without the help of the white man's religion.

Morgan climbed down from the ledge and busied himself by the fire. He had brought down a mountain goat
only the day before, killed the animal with a single shot
from his flintlock. Until yesterday Lone Walker had brought
in all the game so far during their journey.

Morgan placed a couple of chunks of meat on the
makeshift spit and set the cuts over the flames. Lone
Walker's shadow fell across him as the Blackfoot returned
to the camp fire. The sun had cleared the horizon behind
him and hung between two distant peaks. The meat began
to sizzle, and blood dripped into the fire.

"How many more days until we reach your people?"
Morgan asked. Lone Walker was amused. His "people"
were Sparrow and the old medicine woman, the ghost of
the mountain. What if they were no longer by the falls?
What if the Shoshoni had captured them? Or worse,

White Buffalo himself? The shaman's magic might have found them out.

"When the sun is born three more times, we will be close," Lone Walker said.

Morgan's thoughts were filled with still another question. Once they reached their destination and Lone Walker was reunited with his woman, what then for the former sea captain? He had come along because finding a boat to captain was impossible and remaining at the mission was unthinkable.

Lone Walker read Morgan's expression. The expression on the white man's face was obvious in its pain.

"There was nothing you could do to save her," Lone Walker said.

"There is always something."

Morgan had replayed the scene on the hill over and over again in his mind: the flame-engulfed inn and Demetruis Vlad standing his ground, the guns in his hands spitting fire, the flash of powder smoke, the pirate's leering smile before Morgan brought him down, and Julia running toward him. *Protect her, oh, God, protect her!*

"I could have done something," he said.

"It was her time to die. Yours will come. And mine," said Lone Walker.

Morgan sliced a morsel of meat from the spit and plopped it in his mouth. He wiped the blade of his throwing knife on his shirt sleeve. Maybe the Indian was right. Better not to think. He changed the subject. "And when we reach the cave, what then?"

"I must prepare myself. I must find White Buffalo, my enemy, and kill him." This path had revealed itself to Lone Walker in a dream. Yet for all he had seen and done, the young Blackfoot dreaded the confrontation. White Buffalo's magic was strong for all the evil manner he had come by it. How could Lone Walker hope to prevail? Or any man, for that matter? Somehow, he resolved, he would do what must be done.

Morgan patted the rifle, the cutlass, and the brace of pistols he'd brought from Astoria. Whatever else happened, he had a debt to repay. Lone Walker, though a stranger, had risked his life to free Morgan from the cross.

"I shall stand with you," Morgan told him.

"There are many Shoshoni."

"I shall stand with you."

"And White Buffalo has stolen a sacred power. His magic is strong. It is said no man can destroy him."

"I shall stand with you," Morgan repeated.

"Why?" the Blackfoot asked, still puzzled.

"Because you are my friend." Morgan had spoken from the heart. The two men stared at each other with the flames between them, a fiery gulf between two cultures. Yet did not the fire warm them both, cook their food and nourish them both?

Lone Walker studied the darkly bearded, grief-worn features of Morgan Penmerry, whose gaze never wavered. The white man had come to Lone Walker in a dream and become part of the warrior's vision quest. They should have been enemies, yet the Above Ones had bound them together and set them upon the same trail.

But Morgan, not the All-Father, had made the choice to be here now, to make Lone Walker's war his war.

"Friend?" said the Blackfoot brave. He stood and clasped the forearm—wrist to wrist—of his companion, the white man, Morgan Penmerry. "Let it be so."

These days Moon Shadow felt as homeless as the mongrel pups that gathered round her lodge of a morning. Too old and ungainly to flee when the Shoshoni attacked the village, Lone Walker's aunt had remained behind and now endured captivity in the place she had once called home. Rather than killing her outright, the Shoshoni women had given Moon Shadow and many of the other Blackfoot women menial tasks to perform. Theirs was a life of slavery, from which they sought escape. With so many of the Shoshoni men out hunting, and more leaving with every passing of the moon, the time was ripe for the Blackfoot captives to make their bid for freedom.

Blind Weed was the most vocal of the captives. The

women looked to her to lead them. She was determined to seek out the surviving Scalpdancers and be reunited with them.

Escape, Moon Shadow thought with a sigh. She did not look forward to riding a horse. Surely she was too old and too fat. One the other hand, once her usefulness had ended and she was no longer able to work the fields or tan hides or make war shields for the warrior societies, she would be driven out to die alone in the mountains. Wasn't it better to be killed than to be enslaved? She knew Blind Weed's answer, but as for her own, she wished she had courage.

Moon Shadow broke pemmican cake into morsels and scattered it among the camp dogs, who made a mad dash to consume every last crumb.

"A foolish waste, Moon Shadow," Blind Weed said, returning from the creek. She carried a water bag over her shoulder, bringing living water to the lodge she now shared with the older woman. Blind Weed had yet to be taken for wife by any of the men. Her sharp tongue cut like a knife and no brave wished the life of trouble she would bring him. With her strong build, clubbing her into submission would not work. No, it was better to have the women of the camp put her to work. And if she caused mischief—kill her outright.

Blind Weed set the water bag upon a post just inside the tepee. The dogs had retreated a few paces at her arrival; now Moon Shadow's soothing voice restored their courage and they drew near to receive a morsel of food. Blind Weed watched her and had to smile.

"You feed the strays and open your lodge to those without a home," she said. Her own lodge had been burned and her people killed during the Shoshoni raid.

"It is a good way," Moon Shadow replied. The last pup tentatively approached, stretched forth its muzzle, its brown tail tucked between its legs; the animal came closer . . . trembling.

White Buffalo on his lathered mount scattered the animals as he brought his stallion to a savage halt before

Moon Shadow's tepee and alighted. The dust his horse had churned in its wake drifted across them. The pup, anxious for a share of the food, was too slow in making good its escape. White Buffalo's moccasined foot caught the animal on the side and dealt the camp dog a brutal kick. The pup landed ten feet away and scurried off.

For two hard days White Buffalo had pushed his horse, resting only when there was simply not enough light to see the trail. The stallion's sides heaved with every gasping breath; flecks of pink froth formed around its nostrils.

"Take my horse to water and then lead it to the meadow," White Buffalo snapped as he approached, his rifle cradled in his arms. The notched feather in his hair fluttered as he walked. His eyes were shaded by the sacred white buffalo headdress and added to the aura of menace that surrounded him like some invisible shroud.

"You have ridden this animal to its death," Blind Weed retorted.

White Buffalo reached in his pouch and removed a talisman he had fashioned from the rib of the sacred animal whose power he had stolen. The rib was painted with swirls of faded blood and one end had been sharpened into a point. A fragment of the buffalo's skin had been wrapped around the blunt end to serve as a grip. White Buffalo pointed the fetish at Blind Weed and began to chant in a voice barely audible to the young woman.

"*E-hoone-setse,*" the shaman said and he lowered the talisman to Blind Weed's chest.

Blind Weed shrank back from the relic, her eyes wide with horror. Her breathing suddenly became ragged; a sharp pain in her side caused her to wince. Her senses reeled as she struggled to fill her lungs with air. And all the while White Buffalo continued his chant, no louder than a whisper.

Moon Shadow acted on instinct to save the life of her friend. She pushed forward and with her great bulk shoved Blind Weed back toward the tanning racks and the winded stallion White Buffalo had ridden to the village.

"Foolish girl! Do as you are told!" Moon Shadow scolded,

breaking the shaman's concentration. Immediately Blind
Weed began to breathe properly and the stabbing pain in
her side lessened to a dull ache. She gathered the reins of
the stallion and hurriedly led the animal down to Elkhorn
Creek. She could not withstand the power of White
Buffalo, but she vowed she would escape or perish in the
attempt.

White Buffalo turned on the woman at his side. Moon
Shadow lowered her gaze and her shoulders sagged.

"You have come to my lodge, great shaman, but what
have I to share with you?" She spoke in the same tone of
voice she used to calm the wild dogs.

"Never stand between me and the sharp-tongued she-
wolf again," the shaman answered coldly, returning his
talisman to the pouch at his side. He raised his voice so
that the men and women in the surrounding tepees could
listen to his words and know fear. "Or I will curse you that
your entrails will burn as if you swallowed fire and you will
writhe upon the ground and beg for water and die with
only the taunts of the Shoshoni women for your death
chant."

Moon Shadow tried to make herself smaller, an impossible task for one so round and well padded. She did
manage to dodge aside as White Buffalo headed for her
tepee. The shaman ducked inside. Moon Shadow could
hear him rummaging among her possessions. She looked
around, helpless at the intrusion. There was no one to
help her. The Shoshoni did not care what happened to
her. The Blackfeet feared the wrath of their captors. Only
a madwoman would defy a man like White Buffalo.

Moon Shadow leaned forward and picked up a scraper, a
crescent-wedge stone honed sharp from months of use.
She continued to work on a deer hide stretched upon a
rack made from pine saplings lashed together with sinew.
White Buffalo emerged from the tepee carrying a worn-
out buckskin shirt. He held it up for Moon Shadow's
inspection.

"Tell me, old grandmother, is this the shirt of Lost
Eyes?"

"Lost Eyes is dead," Moon Shadow replied glumly. White Buffalo advanced on her, towering menacingly over his prisoner. Moon Shadow slowly nodded. What harm was there? She was saving her own life. "He wore it long ago," she answered.

White Buffalo grunted a reply and hurried off through the village with the shirt. The braves in camp cleared a path for the renegade who had betrayed the Scalpdancers and made war against his own people. Even the Shoshoni who frowned upon such misdeeds kept private their opinions and rarely voiced them, for the powers of the shaman were not to be denied.

Blue Cap sat on the ground just outside the tepee she shared with White Buffalo. Being young, it pleased her that she should be the wife of the most important and powerful man in the village.

She waited and watched as he climbed the hillside to where her tepee sat all alone among the pines.

"It is good you have returned early, my husband," she called out. White Buffalo failed to answer. He marched right on past the flirtatious and willing young woman he had taken for wife.

"Stay away from me," White Buffalo warned. "I will come to you when it's time." He spoke without looking at her, his words floating back to her as he entered the forest. Blue Cap settled into a sullen pout. She did not like being ignored. She was young and pretty and accustomed to being sought after, not set aside like a meal her husband was too busy to consume.

White Buffalo pressed on into the woods until he came to a clearing a dozen yards from his lodge. Here he had swept clean the ground. Here he had laid stones in a circle and piled dry kindling at the center. He shoved the mound of branches aside and removed his fetish, the sacred rib. He ripped a fragment from the buckskin shirt taken from Moon Shadow's tepee and placed the patch in the center of the circle. Then with the rib bone he drew four circles in the dirt around the piece of buckskin. With the pointed tip of bone he stabbed the patch four times.

Then he turned the rib on himself and jabbed the pointed end into his forearm until blood oozed from the wound. He allowed four drops of the blood to fall on the shirt. Then White Buffalo covered it over with branches and tree bark and lit the ceremonial pyre.

> "Death striker—
> Trickster spirit—
> My enemy is Lost Eyes.
> Stand before me,
> Hear my voice,
> Follow my words,
> For they have bound you.
> Death striker—
> Trickster spirit—
> My enemy comes."

So it was spoken. White Buffalo eased back on his heels and heard the crack of a twig along the path, and when he looked up, he saw Blue Cap gingerly approaching from the trail. Sacred smoke from the fire wafted toward the path, stirred by a passing breeze. The gray smoke caused her to cough and it momentarily blinded her. Still the young girl dared to approach.

White Buffalo had finished the ceremony and found himself both amused by the young girl's presence and angry that she had not obeyed him.

"I have news," she hurriedly told him, unable to keep her secret any longer. "Blind Weed and some of the other Blackfoot women and children are planning to escape. One night soon, they intend to steal horses and ride from the valley."

"And you with them?"

"You are my husband!" Blue Cap retorted, incensed by the mere suggestion of disloyalty. She came to within a foot of the ceremonial fire and stared in amazement as White Buffalo laughed.

"Good," he told her. Flames lapped at the air, masking

his expression. "I will let them go and send men to follow them. Perhaps these women will lead me to the other Scalpdancers. Perhaps even to the one I seek above all others. For I must kill him or he must kill me."

White Buffalo walked around the crackling branches. The pyre shattered and collapsed in on itself in a shower of orange sparks. The magic was done, the curse set in motion. And as sure as his victim's name was Lost Eyes, there was no escaping his fate.

20

His name was Red Owl and he was to watch over the horses this night—a lonely vigil on the hillside above Elkhorn Creek. He was young and in love with a winsome Shoshoni maiden whose father had many horses and many scalps taken in battle. Red Owl had little to offer for the daughter, but he dreamed that one day he might. It was a cold, rainy night and even the desire he felt failed to warm him as he huddled in the darkness at the base of a lodgepole pine.

Wrapped in his blanket with his head lowered against the rain, Red Owl never noticed the subtle shift of movement in the village as shadow shapes crept from silent tepees and made their way upslope, coalescing as they came on into a body of women and children numbering twenty in all. After four months, the Shoshoni had lowered their guard. By now it was reasonable to expect the Blackfeet prisoners had been assimilated into the tribe. Indeed, some had, but not all.

Red Owl stirred as a branch cracked nearby. His nod-

ding head came up; he straightened. Grabbing his flintlock, the young sentry scrambled to his feet and cocked
the weapon but covered the flash pan with the palm of his
hand. He squinted at the darkness surrounding him and
stepped back behind the pine for protection. He considered raising a cry of alarm or firing a warning shot—and
he would have but for the woman who emerged from the
blackness of the forest.

Blind Weed walked to within a few yards of the brave.
Her tall, muscular physique was hidden by a trade blanket. Her black hair was matted to her skull. She did not
seem to mind the autumn shower.

In fact, to Red Owl's amazement, she allowed the
blanket to fall to the ground and walked away from it,
naked and vulnerable, a feast for his hungry eyes. Rain
plastered her long hair to her bare shoulders. Rivulets of
water rushed between her rounded breasts and fell in
sumptuous cascades down her belly.

Red Owl lowered his gaze and licked his lips, and for
the life of him, he couldn't even remember the name of
the woman he had moments earlier been longing for. The
Shoshoni brave recognized Blind Weed as one of the
prisoners they had captured in the aftermath of the raid.
He wondered if all the Scalpdancers were prone to such
madness. However, he wasn't about to bring this one to
her senses.

Red Owl watched as the madwoman raised her hands to
the downpour and arched her back so that the water
spilled over her lithe form. The sentry lowered his gun.
Blind Weed seemed to notice him for the first time. She
appeared startled at first; then a wicked smile brightened
her features and she held out her arms to the keeper of
the horses. Rain or not, Red Owl was aroused. He leaned
his rifle against a tree and slipped off his powder horn and
shot pouch and motioned for the woman to come under
the canopy of branches. Blind Weed gingerly approached,
taking one step, hesitating, then another. He reached out
to her, his fingers trembling, his breath ragged from
anticipated pleasure. He never saw the hand that took up

his rifle, never heard the whisper of the barrel as Moon Shadow swung the weapon like a club. The rifle butt caught the warrior alongside his head. There came a sickening sound of crunched bone as he slumped against the pine, cupping his head in his hands. Blind Weed scampered up and yanked the rifle from Moon Shadow's grasp and, swinging it in a vicious arc, laid the rifle barrel across the wounded man's skull. He toppled like a felled timber.

A third woman stepped forward and handed Blind Weed a buckskin shift and leggings. Blind Weed gratefully pulled the clothes over her shivering limbs. She caught the woman by the arm and turned her benefactor about.

"You are Shoshoni," she said, suspecting treachery. "What is your name?"

"I am called Magpie Woman, sister of Broken Knife."

"Why are you among us?"

"I will not stay here. White Buffalo will destroy my people. He has stolen the power of the Sacred One. He is evil. I will go with you or go alone, but I will not remain." Magpie Woman was small but resolute, and the defiance in her voice lent credence to her words. The Blackfoot could not deny her.

"Come," Blind Weed said. She motioned to the women and children clustered back in the trees. At her command the younger women moved quickly along the hillside, finding mounts for all who intended to escape. The animals recognized the scent of the village on the women in their midst and allowed themselves to be led back into the trees. Half an hour later, everyone had a horse. It took Blind Weed and Magpie Woman to help Moon Shadow up on the back of a big-boned roan gelding.

Once firmly astride the animal, Moon Shadow swore she would never dismount until they were safe from the reach of the Shoshoni.

Blind Weed took the lead on a bay mare. She chose a path that followed the contour of the hill toward the entrance to the valley. The route was far more precipitous especially during a rainstorm, but they were less likely to alert the village of their passing if they stayed above the valley floor. They kept to the hill trail until the pass widened and the cluster of tepee around the creek was lost to the shadows of night. Only then did Blind Weed bring them down from the forested slopes. When they reached the valley floor, the fugitives urged their stolen ponies to a gallop, trusting the rain to muffle the sounds of their horses as they made their bid for freedom.

At a discreet distance two horsemen waited in a grove of aspens, their patience at last rewarded. For three nights White Buffalo had come to the grove, sensing the time was ripe for the captives to attempt their escape. He had never doubted Blind Weed's ability to lead the attempt or to secure the horses. He had seen her in a dream, riding a bald-faced bay mare. She held a rifle in her hand, and there was blood. She was a warrior woman worthy to lead the others. Yes, he had seen her then as he watched her now.

White Buffalo turned to the smaller man at his side.

"Drum, you will take your braves and follow them. See if this warrior woman leads you to others of her kind, perhaps even to my enemy, Lost Eyes." The shaman instructed in a deep and resonant voice; his eyes were but patches of black beneath his headdress. "Bring me word of his death and great will be your reward."

Drum, who had only just returned from a fruitless hunt, nodded, hiding his weariness. He longed to remain in the village, but he kept his wishes to himself. Even if they did not find the rest of the Scalpdancers, he and his companions might cut across some buffalo sign as they had once before, in the middle of the summer. Maybe this time the herd would not elude them.

"I will take only Crazy Dog Soldiers with me," Drum replied. He had no intention of following a bunch of Scalpdancers any longer than was necessary. He'd give them a day, maybe two, and then loose the Crazy Dogs on these thieving women and teach them the high price of Shoshoni horses!

* * *

Well to the north of the village, two days by horse over switchback trails and along twisting, scarred valleys, in the heart of Singing Woman Ridge, a white-haired woman stared at the ceiling of her cave chamber and listened to the muffled voices beyond the stone walls of the home that had become her prison. Her exile was self-imposed. Illness had robbed her of energy and nearly of breath. She rolled on her side as a coughing spell shattered the stillness and kept her from much-needed rest. When the moment had passed and the sound of her own voice faded, the coughing was taken up by others; some of the women and children in the larger chamber back in the cave suffered the same sickness. The coughing came in lengthy spasms that rattled deep in the chest and left the person weak. Singing Woman closed her eyes and tried to concentrate on what must be done. It was difficult, not only because of her illness—other thoughts and feelings warred within her heart and mind. Her feverish sleep had become filled with vibrant swirling images that formed to reveal fragments of the past and the future. *I am the wind's daughter. I am the fire's bride*.

She had seen White Buffalo standing strong and invincible upon the plain. He seemed lonely and remote. Darkness swirled about him, and where he tread, the buffalo grass turned yellow and died. There was another . . . She began to cough again, and her thin frame contracted violently. She closed her eyes and endured the attack. When it had ended, she gasped and lay back; opening her eyes, she looked up at Sparrow's worried face.

"Grandmother, I am here," Sparrow said in a gentle voice.

"Has the All-Father ridden across the sky again?" Three days had passed since the phenomenon. Singing Woman had interpreted the event as a harbinger of change. But whether for good or ill she would not say.

"Not while I watched. But Shoshoni camp fires no longer shine in the hills."

The hunting party had left the morning after the meteorite. The Shoshoni had ridden past the waterfall without noting the cave behind the falls where Wolf Lance, Black Fox, and the other men had watched their enemies and yearned to ride forth and do battle with the hunting party. But the Shoshoni outnumbered them, and the Scalpdancers could not afford the losses even if they destroyed the hunting party. So they had remained hidden, their spirits hungry for a revenge that lay beyond their grasp. Remaining in the cave had been the bitterest blow of all. However, Sparrow felt no such remorse. The cave had become a home to her, and Singing Woman, as dear to her as her own mother.

"Then it is safe to leave?" the old woman asked in a cracked voice.

"I will never leave you." Sparrow took the woman's hand in her own. The leathery flesh felt hot to the touch.

"Foolish one. Who else will bring us the red medicine to ease the suffering of your people? I have shown you the plant," Singing Woman chided gently.

"Yes, I know it. The plant that grows in the valley of the Stone Bear," Sparrow recalled. She scolded herself for not thinking of it earlier. Singing Woman seemed to read her thoughts.

"I did not think of it until a little while ago," the medicine woman said. "But you must be watchful, for the valley lies between us and Elkhorn Creek. Take Wolf Lance with you."

"No. Better to go alone," Sparrow told her. "It does not shame me to run to cover."

Singing Woman understood. It galled her to feel so weak when strength above all else was needed.

"He is near," she said softly, fearful of raising the girl's hopes too high.

Sparrow grew pale. She forced herself to take several deep breaths. "What . . . are you saying?"

"I have said it," Singing Woman rasped.

Sparrow thought of Wolf Lance and his intentions to take the Scalpdancers away from this place, beyond the reach of the Shoshoni. Might she be able to leave with her people—and with the man she loved by her side?

"Lone Walker does not return to you alone. He has changed. He will know what must be done."

Sparrow felt a sinking sensation in the pit of her stomach. She hated to hear any more and yet had to press the matter.

"What do you mean?" Singing Woman had begun to nod off to sleep. Sparrow nudged her awake. "Grandmother, hear me."

"He must kill White Buffalo."

Sparrow drew away from the fever-wracked old one. "No man can do such a thing."

"I can help him," Singing Woman told her, wheezing as she spoke. "There is much I know of the shaman."

"You are the spirit of the mountain. You are the old woman of the waterfall whose songs no longer frighten us away. What can you know of White Buffalo?"

Singing Woman cackled, her voice a rasping whisper. She closed her eyes. "He is my grandson."

Singing Woman began to snore. Sparrow was tempted to try and shake the white-haired one awake but at last took pity and allowed the woman her much-needed rest.

She stole from the chamber and entered the larger area of the cave that had become the Scalpdancers' temporary home. She walked over to where Yellow Stalk tried to calm her distraught infant. The baby had recently been taken ill, and worry lines etched the woman's features.

"The old one . . ." Yellow Stalk began.

"She burns with the same sickness." Sparrow noted that Yellow Stalk did not look too well herself.

Black Fox was standing close at hand. For the first time in months he had lost some of his arrogance and air of disapproval. He was worried for the life of his son. Nothing else mattered now.

"We need her," Black Fox grumbled. He'd come as close to pleading as pride would allow. He knew his sister had learned much of the healing arts from Singing Woman.

"I will leave at first light and gather the berries and leaves of the red medicine plant. Your little one will grow strong, and one day he will hunt at his father's side."

Sparrow glanced up at her brother and saw his expression of gratitude.

"Your horse should be fed and taken to water before you leave," Black Fox stated. He made his way through the torchlit chamber.

Wood smoke collected in a ghostly layer along the vaulted ceiling and lent an eerie quality to the stalactites protruding through the thick gray layer like enormous fangs. Black Fox slipped through the entrance to another part of the cave where the horses were brought for the night.

"He is grateful," Yellow Stalk said, watching her husband. She lifted Little Elk to her breast, but the infant refused to eat. It mewed halfheartedly, a pitiful sound.

> *"Pouokahyo,* do not cry.
> The hunter may hear.
> And take you home.
> *Pouokahyo,* do not cry."

Yellow Stalk sang her lullaby as Sparrow looked on enviously. Would the day ever come when she might cradle her own child to her breast, hold in her arms the son or daughter of Lone Walker?

Sparrow's pulse quickened, remembering the medicine woman's words. *"He is near."* But there was nothing she could do to bring him any sooner. If nothing else, she had learned patience lo these many months. And there was work to be done.

> *"Pouokahyo,* my little elk,
> Why do you cry?
> What do you fear?"

Morgan Penmerry stared up through the latticework of branches overhead. Here in this timeless garden towering fir, aspen, and ponderosa pine seemed to absorb all unnecessary sound, leaving only the chatter of ground squirrels and the cry of a hawk on the rushing wind. The previous night's storms had passed them by, leaving Lone Walker's campsite unscathed by rain or lightning. They had slept well in this aspen grove near a spring-fed pond. Distant thunder had lulled them to sleep. After the barren battlements of the Continental Divide, it was good to have made camp in a safe place.

Morgan sighed and raised himself up on one elbow and looked at Lone Walker, who was standing in the middle of the buffalo wallow cupping icy water over his naked torso. "I have seen much buffalo sign. It is good," Lone Walker said.

Morgan rubbed his eyes and glanced at the empty rum bottle near his bedroll. He remembered last night and how the Blackfoot had eagerly informed him that they were indeed near their destination, Singing Woman Ridge. Hell, that was reason enough for Morgan Penmerry to celebrate, so he had finished off his last bottle of rum. The rest of his life in this wilderness promised to be mighty dry, he glumly considered. His stomach growled and he glanced over at the camp fire, where a quartered rabbit was spitted above the flames.

He noticed a rawhide vessel in which Lone Walker had steeped a kind of tea by adding a handful of dark-green leaves and roots to water in a tin pot of Morgan's.

"My throat's as scratchy as the underside of a johnny boat," Morgan muttered.

The "tea" certainly smelled strong enough to clear the cobwebs from his head. He dipped a clay cup into the brew and tasted it. The liquid left him gasping as it burned a bitter passage down his gullet.

"What's this called?" he gasped.

"*Kha-ohk-tsi-me is-tse-hi*," Lone Walker replied.

"What does it mean?" Morgan asked, taking another mouthful.

"It-passes-from-a-skunk."

Morgan doubled over and spewed out the contents. "Good Christ!"

Lone Walker threw back his head and laughed. The white man made a funny spectacle indeed. The Blackfoot

emerged from the bitter-cold water and shook the moisture from his torso and moved with pantherlike quickness
into the grove, where he donned his garments of brushed
and beaded buckskin.

"I don't see what's so funny," Morgan said as the Blackfoot
continued to chuckle at his expense.

They were a study in contrasts, the broad-shouldered,
bearded Cornishman and his smaller, agile red-skinned
companion. The Scalpdancer took the clay cup from Morgan
and helped himself to his own concoction. He grimaced
and spat out the liquid and emptied the rest of it onto the
ground.

"This comes from the Spotted Horses people," Lone
Walker explained in a rueful voice. "They eat their dogs."

Morgan shook his head. "Well, by my oath, with enough
of that in his belly a man would take a bite out of
anything."

He picked up his cutlass and sawed a portion of rabbit
meat from the spit. He passed the cutlass to Lone Walker,
who seemed continually fascinated with the heavy-bladed
weapon. It was Morgan's last link to his former life, one he
wasn't quite ready to sever.

Lone Walker hefted the weapon. He had little use for
Morgan's other weapons. A flintlock rifle and pistol were
deadly enough, but in the time it took to reload them, the
Blackfoot could pepper an enemy with arrows from his
elkhorn bow. But the long knife, now this was a weapon.
He secretly coveted the blade, but he had nothing of
equal value to trade for it. Lone Walker stabbed the
weapon into the ground near the fire and tore a leg
quarter from the spit. He held up the meat and pointed to
it.

"Rabbit," Morgan said in English. "I hope," he added
under his breath.

"Rabbit." The Blackfoot nodded, repeating the words,
adding it to his growing English vocabulary.

They continued to eat as they had throughout the many
weeks on the trail. They sat facing each other across the
camp fire and trading words back and forth, using sign

language to help in the understanding. When they had finished, Lone Walker took one of the bones and drew in the dirt. He made a mark for the cave by the falls and another for the valley of the Elkhorn, then a third mark in between the two and slightly off to the side.

Lone Walker drew an indirect route that allowed for the condition of their horses, a pair of sturdy brown geldings given them by a grateful Reap McCorkle. Lone Walker's gray had served as a pack animal for part of the journey and was reasonably rested. It carried a relatively easy load: extra blankets, some provisions, and powder and shot for Morgan Penmerry.

"We shall reach the cave before the sun wakes again," the Blackfoot said.

"And what will you do?" Morgan asked.

A sheepish grin lit the Indian's features despite his best efforts to hide his feelings.

"I mean after that," Morgan said.

Lone Walker turned serious. He brushed his matted hair back from his forehead to reveal the furrow of scar tissue left by White Buffalo's bullet. "I will find the shaman."

"From the way you make him sound, it might take both of us." Morgan sheathed his cutlass. The scabbard hung from a broad leather belt draped across his chest.

"I must face him alone."

"Like hell," Morgan blurted out in English. He caught himself and continued in the dialect of the Blackfeet. "I will stand with you."

"It is not in my dream," Lone Walker retorted.

"So maybe it's in mine," Morgan said in English.

Lone Walker gave up trying to explain anything to the crazy white man. He wondered why he had ever let such a one accompany him back across the Backbone of the World. Yet the moment he lowered his eyes he knew the reason. Stretched out before him were two shadows upon the ground. They were bound together, two paths become one.

"Maybe we better get started," Morgan suggested, kicking

dirt into the fire and smothering the embers. A column of smoke spiraled up to collect in the branches. "Where do we ride?"

Lone Walker pointed to a glacier-scalloped jumble of boulders and broken cliffs rising to the south. "The Stone Bear—" The words died on his lips. Wearing a look of consternation, he inhaled and the stench of blood and gunsmoke filled his nostrils. There was anger and death in the valley. "We must go!" he blurted out. There was no time to explain.

21

The plant was the curlydock and it grew in patches throughout the narrow confines of the valley, its large, dark leaves upturned to the sunlight. Red medicine, the Blackfeet called the plant. Sparrow filled her beaver skin pouch with the brown heart-shaped seedlike fruit and young crisp leaves gathered from stalks as tall as herself. It was midafternoon and the autumn sun warmed her shoulders as she moved among the swaying stalks, her hands darting from plant to plant, harvesting what she needed. The dun pony she had ridden from the cave was hobbled close by. The mare contentedly cropped the buffalo grass growing amid the wildflowers.

Bees swarmed from plant to plant and cut lazy circles in the warmth of the afternoon. Lark buntings shooshed and dived and darted after insects. Mountain chickadees circled overhead, eyeing the human intruder with suspicion. They swooped low and, lacking the bravery of the buntings, avoided the young woman and soared upslope, returning to their nests among the lodgepole pines. Out on the floor of the narrow valley a family of prairie dogs rummaged in the earth and chased one another from burrow to burrow. Their antics brought a smile to Sparrow's face. But her reverie didn't last long.

A horse and rider suddenly appeared, riding hell-bent along the floor of the valley. Then several other horsemen galloped into view. Pursued and pursuer maintained a course that would bring them right below Sparrow. A rifle shot rang out. Sparrow hurried to her horse and forced the animal to lie on its side in the wildflower patch. The mare balked at first, but the young woman knew how to handle the animal and soon they were both concealed among the wildflowers.

The rider came on. Hoofbeats drummed the earth. Sparrow raised herself up. The fugitive was closer now; Sparrow could see it was a woman. Closer now and the rider turned her face to the sun. "Blind Weed!" Sparrow whispered the name of her friend. Shoshoni rifles fired a ragged volley at their quarry. Blind Weed leaned forward over the neck of her horse and for a single awful moment Sparrow thought her friend had been hit. But the Blackfoot woman was merely making as small a target as possible out of herself. A hundred yards became seventy, then fifty, and then Blind Weed was right below Sparrow. She leapt from her horse as the animal fell. Blood spurted from a mortal wound in the horse's neck.

Afoot now, Blind Weed had no chance at all. The Shoshoni, with Drum in the lead, knew it only too well and with war cries ringing out, charged forward. Sparrow acted on reflex. She cut loose the hobble and brought her mare upright and swung up onto the animal's back as the mare clambered to its feet. Sparrow pointed the dun toward the stranded young woman, who waited, her face to the enemy. Blind Weed gripped a trade knife in her fist. She was determined to sell her life as dearly as possible, preferring to die rather than reveal where she had left Moon Shadow and the others in order to lead the Crazy Dog soldiers on a merry chase.

"Blind Weed!" Sparrow called out.

The woman afoot spun around and stared in total disbelief at her rescuer. Sparrow reined in her mount alongside Blind Weed.

"Foolish girl, leave me. We can never escape with two of us together," Blind Weed gasped, shoving the dun away.

"I won't leave you," Sparrow shouted. Bullets plucked the air around her as the war party came on.

Drum was as surprised as anyone to see the second Blackfoot maiden rise up out of the tall grass. He checked the slope as best he could to see if there were any more surprises concealed among the flowers.

"Take them alive!" he shouted to his companions and reloaded his rifle at a gallop.

Sparrow fought her frightened mount and brought the horse under control as Blind Weed, unable to make her friend listen to reason, leapt up behind the younger woman. Sparrow whirled her mount and, whipping the poor beast about the neck and flanks, galloped off toward the opposite end of the valley.

Maybe if they could reach the north end... She glanced over her shoulder and bit her lower lip to keep from crying out in despair. The Shoshoni were slowly, inexorably gaining.

"We will never make it out of the valley alive." The bag of red medicine leaves slapped uselessly at her side, a taunting reminder that she would never return to Singing Woman Ridge. But it would not be for lack of trying.

She slapped the dun along the side of the neck and the animal quickened its stride yet again, carrying its double burden across the buffalo grass. She leaned low over the animal's neck until the mane lashed her features. Blind Weed suddenly tightened her embrace about the smaller woman's midriff.

"The Shoshoni have sprung their trap!" she shouted and pointed past Sparrow's shoulder to the opposite end of the valley, a narrow gap between the heavily wooded slopes.

Sparrow had hoped to reach the tall timber and lose

their pursuers in the emerald twilight of the pine forest. Now two horsemen had arrived to block their escape. With war party behind them and another two braves a hundred yards ahead Sparrow's hopes collapsed. She veered from the trail, headed for the hillside. But the incline was too steep for the mare's double burden. A few yards into the climb the horse lost its footing. Blind Weed dropped off as the animal faltered. Sparrow followed suit, leaping lightly to the ground. The mare recovered its balance and darted off in the opposite direction. Sparrow made a futile attempt to catch the horsehair reins, but the mare eluded her grasp with a toss of its head.

Blind Weed and Sparrow glanced at each other, the gravity of their situation impossible to ignore. Knife in hand, Sparrow turned to face her attackers. Blind Weed stood at her side.

"Moon Shadow and the others will have escaped," Blind Weed said, resigned to her fate. She looked toward the war party who were—surprisingly—drawn up in a line about sixty yards from the two women.

"What is this?"

The war party should have been swarming over the women on the hillside.

Sparrow was as surprised as her companion. Impossible, the Shoshoni party no longer appeared interested in the women. Sparrow shaded her eyes against the burning glare of the sun and studied the horsemen at the north end of the narrow valley. The wind in the buffalo grass seemed to whisper a name. She feared to listen, warned herself not to hear it, not to believe. But the wind that stirred the long grass and ruffled her hair would not be denied. It caressed her cheek as it rushed past, leaving only his name. And when she could deny it no longer, Sparrow surrendered to a hope that love had not let die.

"Lone Walker," she said.

"Sparrow." Lone Walker dropped the reins of the pack animal, the gray mare, and grabbed his powerful elkhorn bow from the back of it. His heart felt as if it were about to burst through his chest. He wanted to run to Sparrow and lose himself in the wonder of her embrace. Surely the Great One had guided him to this place that he might come to her aid.

"Your woman?" Morgan asked. Lone Walker nodded. Morgan exhaled. He'd seen enough of the inexplicable to accept without question their miraculous and timely arrival.

"Who are the others?" Morgan asked.

"Shoshoni," Lone Walker replied contemptuously. "They are no match for us."

Morgan counted six Shoshoni. "I admire your notion of fair odds," he said in English.

The Blackfoot mulled over the white man's remark, trying to comprehend Morgan's words. "What are you saying?" he asked.

"Nothing," Morgan said. "Only six Shoshoni. I wish there were ten." He gulped and tightened his grip on the reins, primed his long-barreled flintlock rifle. Ships he knew, back-alley fighting he knew, but this was something else. He nervously eyed the horse beneath him. Even after two months on the trail he could hardly call himself a proficient rider.

"Listen, maybe I better—" He never finished.

> "On this day,
> All-Father,
> Ride before me.
> Let the wolf be my courage,
> Let the hawk be my shield
> On this day."

Lone Walker finished his prayer. He ended with a blood-curdling war whoop and charged the war party.

"Oh, shit!" Morgan exclaimed as his mount of its own volition lunged forward at a gallop. Morgan clung to horseback for all he was worth and rode pell-mell into the fray.

Drum and his Crazy Dog Soldiers were taken aback by the sudden arrival of the two strangers and searched the hills for signs of a trap.

"Who are these two?" one of the braves muttered.

"Dead men," another said, brandishing a ten-foot lance.

Drum was not a man to back down from a fight. He called for the other braves to follow his lead. He could have saved his breath. These were Crazy Dogs. To them, any day was a good day to fight—and if need be, to die. Warriors with names like Bold Hawk and Little Sky and Snake Killer started forward as one; their war cries rent the stillness as they charged.

Lone Walker snatched a couple of arrows from his otter skin quiver and clamped them between his teeth, then notched another to his sinew bowstring. He allowed the gelding free rein, controlling the horse with the pressure of his legs. The animal wasn't as well trained as the gray, but it did have heart and could run with the wind. That was all Lone Walker required. The gelding had a steady, easy gait; its long-legged stride devoured the distance and soon brought him within range of Shoshoni rifles.

A coyote, spooked from its den in the tall grass, scurried out of harm's way. The sleek pelt became a rust-red blur of motion through the buffalo grass and wildflowers.

Lone Walker saw the guns of his enemies belch powder smoke and heard the crack of gunshots above the thundering hooves. He returned their fire, with arrows.

Morgan rode into battle Indian style. He dropped his reins and tightened his legs about the animal; he hefted his rifle, sighted, and fired. The weapon's recoil shoved him off balance. He kicked up his feet, pawed the air, and tumbled from the horse as a couple of slugs from the Shoshoni rifles fanned the space he had once occupied. Morgan hit hard, rolled, heard a loud crack, and waited for the first spasm of pain to tell him he had broken an arm or a leg. He crawled to one knee as a shadow flitted across him and a Shoshoni lunged at him with a spear.

Morgan scrambled out of the path of the chiseled blade

and grabbed for his cutlass. He drew the weapon and parried a spear thrust from the brave towering over him. Morgan lunged with the cutlass in what should have been a killing thrust except for the fact that the weapon was only half as long as it once had been. He stared up at the jagged end of the blade.

Christ, he'd broken the damn thing in his fall. The Shoshoni didn't give Morgan much time to dwell on the past. He kicked the white man and knocked the blade aside and rode off for a few paces, then whirled his horse with a savage tug on the reins and charged.

Morgan didn't have time to try for one of his pistols. The brave was on him in a second. This time Morgan was ready. He was a big man, so the Shoshoni brave had not expected such quickness in him. Morgan did the unexpected. He darted in front of the Indian's horse and waved and screamed and so startled the animal that it reared and tossed the brave in the dirt.

The warrior rolled to his feet. Dust caked his features; hate filled his eyes. He lunged with his spear. Morgan parried the thrust, leapt inside the reach of the spear, and drove home the jagged blade of the cutlass. The Shoshoni brave gasped, his expression contorted, and he sagged to the ground.

A horse pounded the earth behind Morgan. The white man spun about, pistol in hand, only to face a dead man bearing down on him. The Crazy Dog Soldier toppled from his horse and rolled across the trampled grass almost to the white man's boots. The broken shaft of an arrow protruded from a bloody patch in the center of his chest below his breastbone.

Drum was down and scrambling from his dying mount. Lone Walker counted coup on him, striking the brave's shoulder with the tip of the elkhorn bow. A Shoshoni, Little Sky, rammed home a powder charge down the barrel of his rifle and seated the charge and lead shot by slapping the butt of the trade gun on his thigh. He had circled his horse and came around behind Lone Walker, who was busy with another enemy.

The Crazy Dog Soldier called Snake Killer was priming his musket when a Blackfoot arrow struck him. A puff of dust rose from his buckskin shirt. He dropped his powder horn as a second arrow passed completely through his left side and thwacked into the buffalo grass just behind the man. Snake Killer slumped forward over the neck of his horse and slid to the ground.

Lone Walker heard his name shouted from the hillside. Sparrow was pointing behind him as she ran across the valley floor.

He swung about as Little Sky held his horse steady and leveled his rifle. This time he wouldn't miss. Lone Walker faced the man and reached for the last of his arrows. Too late, Little Sky would take his shot. Lone Walker tensed, ready to leap from horseback.

Sparrow would remember the next few moments of her life and recount the event for her people until it passed into history and became legend.

A red-tailed hawk plummeted out of the sky like a bolt of living fire, its four-foot wingspan passing inches from Little Sky's rifle barrel. Perhaps the hawk had been so intent on some prey hidden in the grass that it had ignored the man thing until the last possible second when it rocketed earthward for the kill.

In a flurry of brown and scarlet plumage and cruel talons the hawk reversed its course and swooped up toward the Shoshoni brave, just missing the startled man's face and blocking his shot. The hawk rose on powerful wings toward the safety of the distant trees. It would find another prey, but not the Shoshoni brave.

Little Sky steadied his mount. The Crazy Dog Soldier was just bringing his rifle to bear when Lone Walker's arrow pierced his groin. At the same instant a blast from one of Morgan Penmerry's pistols knocked the brave from his horse and left him dying in the grass. Morgan trotted forward, a second pistol cocked and primed in his hand.

The last of the Shoshoni braves on horseback fled for his

life and never looked back. He left only a trail of dust in his wake to mark his passing.

Drum managed to stagger to his feet. He spied his rifle lying a few yards away, over by his dead horse. He started toward it; then a shadow fell between him and the weapon. Blind Weed stood with her skinning knife in hand all but daring the brave to try for the rifle. Drum thought about it, then thought better. For one thing, Blind Weed was bigger than Drum. She was smiling and seemed eager for him to come within reach of her iron knife.

Lone Walker managed to salvage Drum's pride. He rode up leading a captured horse and dropped the reins in Drum's hand. The Shoshoni looked up into the eyes of his benefactor and felt the same sensation, the identical fears, he had experienced upon first coming face-to-face with White Buffalo. The Shoshoni had also seen the incident with the red-tailed hawk and how it had saved the life of the Blackfoot.

"Go. I give you your life," the Blackfoot said. Drum could not bear the man's dark stare, his eyes like chips of obsidian that never wavered. "Tell White Buffalo, Lost Eyes is no more. Say Lone Walker is coming to destroy him. Four mornings from now. I will come." Drum quickly mounted the horse, ignoring the fresh blood matting the animal's mane.

"I will tell him," Drum said. "White Buffalo will hang your hair from his belt." Turning his horse with a savage tug on the reins, he galloped toward the south end of Stone Bear pass, grateful to be alive.

Then Lone Walker turned his back on the field of battle. Sparrow came running to him. He reached down and gathered her into his arms. She wrapped her arms around his neck. He held her close. She knew him despite his wind-burned face and eyes that had grown wise and sad.

Blind Weed held back. She watched the white man, her expression registering suspicion. Morgan shifted his stance. In beholding the man and woman's embrace, Morgan could not help but relive another time and place, a woman

and a love he would never find again. He turned and
walked to his horse. His rifle lay out in the grass where he
had ignominiously fallen off his horse. The gelding cropped
the dry shoots, oblivious to its former rider.

"Avast, you pitch-for-brains." Morgan retrieved his rifle
and remounted. When he looked to the side, Lone Walker
had ridden up. Sparrow was behind him, her arms firmly
wrapped around his middle.

"Sparrow," Morgan said her name with a gentlemanly
bow. He spoke in her own language. "It is good to see
you."

"This is Mor-gan," Lone Walker said to his woman. "He
is my friend."

Sparrow said, "I have much to learn. You are welcome
at our fire."

"You honor me," Morgan replied.

They gathered the guns and the horses of their enemies
and within half an hour they were ready to depart. Sparrow had her red medicine. Blind Weed, somewhat in awe
of Lone Walker, led the way to where she had left Moon
Shadow and the other fugitives. All they left behind to
mark their passing were trampled wildflowers, the bodies
of the dead, and the shadow of a circling red-tailed
hawk.

On the following day Singing Woman awoke early, startled from sleep by a commotion outside the cave. She
knew in her heart that her dream had come to pass. Lone
Walker had returned from the edge of the world. She
wanted to rise to see him, but she was much too fragile.
Still she made the attempt, propping herself up against a
willow backrest and only then deciding she must wait for
the young spirit singer to find her. She could picture the
scene outside the cave, how those who had remained
faithful to Lone Walker received him with open arms
while the others held back and watched him with a
mixture of wariness and uncertainty. It would be that way
all his life.

Those Scalpdancers who were healthy enough gathered

outside around the falls when Lone Walker and Sparrow
arrived leading Blind Weed's party of fugitives. Moon
Shadow rode proudly at Lone Walker's side. She had
instantly recognized the changes in him; he had returned
from where the sun sleeps a man of power and vision.
Morgan Penmerry, on the other hand, kept a nervous
guard. Had he not been in Lone Walker's entourage, he
might have been killed outright, for white men were
considered intruders in the land of the Blackfoot. As long
as the white traders encroached no further than the land
of the Cheyenne to the south, they could be tolerated and
traded with. But this "Mor-gan" stood with Lone Walker
and therefore came under the protection of He Who Had
Been Lost Eyes.

Sparrow wasted no time, but hurried to the nearest
camp fire. She began the process of boiling water and
steeping the red medicine. Every now and then she
glanced toward the cave entrance, anxious over what
might happen when her brother appeared. Wolf Lance
walked forward out of the crowd and embraced his
friend.

"You have returned to us. It is good." Wolf Lance
glanced past his friend's shoulder at Morgan, who waited
uncomfortably a few paces back.

"You have always been as my brother," Lone Walker
said. "I would have you be his."

"Let it be so," Wolf Lance said.

Morgan sighed in relief and gently eased his finger off
the trigger of his rifle. He placed his hand across his heart
and held it palm open toward Wolf Lance in the traditional
greeting among the northern tribes. It showed he arrived
with an open hand as well as an open heart.

Another figure appeared in the mist of the falls, emerging from the cave entrance to see for himself the source of
all the excitement. Sparrow wasn't the only one to grow
tense at the arrival of her brother. It was common knowledge there was no love lost between Black Fox and Lone
Walker. Women and children paused in the midst of their
own reunions and moved away from the two men.

Lone Walker saw Sparrow's brother. His expression guarded, Lone Walker stepped around his friend and headed straight for the man in the mist. Black Fox, in turn, quickened his pace as he walked toward the man he had sworn to kill. They met away from the falls where lily pads grew near the water's edge.

Black Fox glanced around at all the newcomers; there was even a white man. Then he noticed Sparrow by the camp fire adding the stems and berries she had gathered to a water bag made from the stomach of a buffalo.

Lone Walker heard cries overhead and lifted his eyes to the sight of a flurry of Canadian geese, twenty by the count, lazily circling one another. Their calls echoed along the ridge as they flew in ever-tightening spirals. They were preparing to begin their southward migration. It was the way it had been, the way it always would be.

"I have sworn to take the life of Lost Eyes," Black Fox said. "I have sworn to dip my knife in his blood, to avenge the honor of my sister."

"A man must be careful what he swears," Lone Walker observed dryly. "Lost Eyes is dead."

"Your words tell me that. But my eyes see otherwise."

"Do they?" Lone Walker moved nearer.

Black Fox dropped his hand to his knife. Lone Walker's hand closed around his antagonist's wrist. Black Fox tried to overpower the smaller man and failed. Black Fox felt the trade knife slip from its scabbard. Then, despite all his efforts, the blade turned in the viselike grip until the iron tip pointed toward his own chest. He tried to wrench free as the naked blade drew inexorably near. The tip of the blade pierced his flesh and a droplet of blood spilled down Black Fox's naked belly.

"Kill me and you kill yourself," Lone Walker said in a voice no louder than a whisper. His burning gaze caused Black Fox to avert his eyes. Black Fox opened his hand and the knife dropped to the ground.

Lone Walker raised the arm in his grasp and pointed his opponent's hand toward the sky, where the airborne dance of the geese had re-formed itself into a giant "V" disappearing into the southern quadrant. They were poetry in flight, the power of the All-Father revealed for every man, woman, and child to see . . . if they would but lift their heads to look.

"Even these ones know enough to leave the past behind," Lone Walker said. He released the wrist. Black Fox studied the departing formation. His arm ached from the grip that had rendered him powerless. He retrieved his knife from the ground and returned it to the sheath. Even his vanity and stubborn pride could not deny what he had experienced and the wisdom in Lone Walker's words.

"I am the last of the Kit Fox Society," he said, eyes lowered.

"There will be others," Lone Walker told him. "Our village will grow again. There will be new life."

"Where?"

"In Ever Shadow," Lone Walker said, looking to the north, where beyond Singing Woman Ridge the land rose and plummeted in mazelike canyons, upthrust peaks, and verdant, glacier-carved valleys.

"Who will lead us?"

"I am the one."

"And I will follow," Black Fox said, leaving the past behind.

Lone Walker hesitated outside the torchlit entrance to the old woman's chamber. He could see her propped up against the willow backrest, the snow-white hair spilling like an avalanche across the bony plateaus of her shoulders. At first she seemed asleep or—worse to him—still and lifeless there in the dancing shadows.

"I have finished my vision quest, grandmother," he said gently, so as not to startle her. "My journey is ended."

"Foolish one, have you learned nothing?" an aged, almost disembodied voice spoke to him from the chamber. "The journey will never end. You are a shaman, but young—so young. Spirit singer, it is the way of things."

"A shaman?" Lone Walker gasped. "How can that be? Who will show me such a path?"

"The path is the circle. The circle is within you."

Lone Walker moved into the room and knelt by the medicine woman's side. Her eyes were wide open, but she seemed unable to focus on him. Singing Woman spoke to him though her attention was rooted on the shifting patterns on the stalactite ceiling. She could see a pack of green-eyed wolves in those dancing patterns. The beasts had turned on themselves with bared fang and claw, destroying one another while the old woman looked on in terror.

"What do you see?" Lone Walker asked and looked up toward the bristled ceiling of the chamber and studied the writhing shadows.

"He wants you dead," Singing Woman said. "You must face White Buffalo and kill him or he will surely kill you."

"Yes. From the first moment I stood at the edge of the world and saw the sleeping sun and the *Maiyun* dancing at the end of all days, I knew what I must do." Lone Walker stood by the old one's hide-covered bedding and leaned against the cold stone wall. "But White Buffalo's power is great. And he has many men, many guns. We are but a handful."

"No," Singing Woman said. "You must go alone."

"Do you send me to my death, old woman? I could take my woman and leave. There are other mountains, other valleys. We will find a place in Ever Shadow and live in peace."

"The good can never live in peace while evil walks the land." Singing Woman was weary and sick. She feared that time was running out for all of them. "Hear me. White Buffalo is my daughter's son. I took him when his mother and father died of the spotted sickness. I taught him. But he had no eyes. He could not see beyond seeing. He had no vision." She sighed and propped herself up on an elbow and drank a cup of water. "Where is Sparrow?"

"Making the red medicine," Lone Walker replied.

Her revelation had caught him by surprise. White Buffalo was the old woman's grandson; they were linked to each other by blood, yet she would see him dead! "White

Buffalo has told me how he killed the sacred *Iniskim* and took its power. He even offered to share his magic with me."

"But what was your answer?"

"That I would rather be blind than to have his stolen visions."

Singing Woman nodded. "From that moment on, White Buffalo surely plotted to kill you. By refusing him you revealed your own strength. One of you must die or your songs will die. They will no longer have life. Nor will any of us." The medicine woman pointed toward the rear of the chamber, where she had built a small ceremonial altar of limestone and chert and surrounded it with sage and bitterroot. A small fire burned in the center of the altar. A rawhide image of a man had been placed to the right of the fire and a clay figurine of a woman to the left. The woman symbolized the moon, and the man the morning star, while the fragrant little blaze served to represent the sun.

Behind the altar was an elkskin case. Singing Woman instructed Lone Walker to take it. The young Blackfoot obeyed her and unwrapped what turned out to be a seven-foot-tall Medicine Cane, a pine staff fringed with raven feathers. The crook was stained a dull red and wrapped with strips of white buffalo hide.

Lone Walker gasped at the sight of the sacred skin similar to the hide White Buffalo wore about his head and shoulders.

"The night White Buffalo returned and told me what he had done I waited until he fell asleep and then I cut a strip from the sacred skin and fled our people to live alone in these mountains."

Lone Walker had been but a child; the affairs of a medicine woman would have meant nothing to him. He could not even remember from that time. She was a Scalpdancer who had left her people only to have them come to her for sanctuary.

"This will be your weapon," said the woman on the pallet, rising up on her elbows, the oval of her face radiant with wisdom. "And your songs," she added. "And the *Maiyun* of the plains, if you have the courage to summon them."

She sighed and leaned against the backrest, exhausted from her speech. The Medicine Cane scraped the ceiling as Lone Walker eased back into the light to study the markings on the staff. But Singing Woman interrupted him.

"Bring the white man to me."

Morgan Penmerry's bulky frame filled the opening.

"I am no child to be led by the hand," he replied in her own tongue and irreverently entered the chamber. He glanced at his friend holding the Medicine Cane. "A few of the lads were appearing to take a liking to my scalp. Figured I best hunt up a friendly face." He peered out from under his black brows at the Blackfoot, as if trying to determine whether or not he'd found a friendly face. He returned his attention to the old woman.

"Why are you here?" she asked.

"Why not?" Morgan replied with a shrug. "A man has to be somewhere." He wrinkled his nose at the strong scent of sage mingling with the stench of illness.

Singing Woman managed a dry laugh and motioned him closer. "Give me your hand."

Morgan glanced in Lone Walker's direction. The young spirit singer nodded. Morgan knelt alongside the white-haired one and extended his hand. With a single fluid motion, surprisingly quick for her age, the woman of the mountain raked the palm of his hand with an eagle's talon she had hidden by her side.

"Dammit, you old witch," Morgan exclaimed as blood welled from his slashed palm. Before he could completely draw back from her, the woman repeated the gesture, this time summoning Lone Walker forward and using his right hand. Droplets of crimson oozed from his wound. She reached out and joined their hands together and placed the eagle's talon upon their clasped flesh.

"Now you are bound by blood as well as friendship. Your fates are two rivers becoming one." She removed the

talon and settled against the bulrush mat she used for a
bed. "Tell me, white man, what do you dream?"

"I dream of what is lost," Morgan replied. He could not
lie to this medicine woman.

"Now you will dream of that which is yet to be found,"
Lone Walker said. The words came unbidden to his mind,
full of truth and a strength he was only just discovering
within himself. It had taken Singing Woman to bring the
power out of him. *What will I do when I face White
Buffalo alone?*

22

Near sunset Morgan Penmerry left the cave and ventured into the meadow to bring in the horse he had ground-tethered to graze on the buffalo grass. Singing Woman Falls glowed golden in the last light of day as shadows swept down the bluffs. He wasn't alone upon the valley floor.

Even as he tended his horse, Morgan spied a couple walk their mounts from beneath the falls and slip away from the pool, angling toward the grove of aspens a couple hundred yards up the valley. They kept to the spreading darkness just below the bluffs, but Morgan recognized Lone Walker—and that meant the girl could only be Sparrow.

His thoughts slipped to the past and a tryst he had shared with the woman of his heart. He felt envy for the Blackfoot brave and pity for the path Lone Walker had chosen. For the path that had been chosen *for* him, Morgan mentally corrected. Even with all the Scalpdancers at his side, Lone Walker would find himself hopelessly outmanned and outgunned.

Maybe a single musket was no match for a well-strung bow, but an armed force was quite another matter. As far as Morgan was concerned, his friend didn't stand a chance.

He breathed deeply, inhaling the scent of pines and the faint odor of roasted elk that wafted through the narrow mouth of the cave. Women sung to their children and someone had begun to play a reed flute. Morgan looked back toward the cave and debated whether or not to join the families hidden behind the falls. No. He was a stranger lost in alien country a lifetime away from the pain of the past.

Tonight it seemed a lifetime wasn't enough.

Lone Walker and Sparrow entered the grove together. They found a small patch of clear ground and covered the leaves with a blanket and bearskin robe and shed their clothes. They loved each other first with a passion born of absence and longing, then again, taking time to explore, tease, and arouse.

When they had spent their passion, Lone Walker pulled his bearskin robe aside. The night had grown unusually warm and he lay with his love in his arms, his flesh glistening with sweat, and he watched the stars through the overhanging branches. He stroked her hair. She turned onto her side and nuzzled his neck.

"You know what I must do." He had not yet spoken to her of White Buffalo, but word had spread among the Scalpdancers, and she must have heard as she ministered the red medicine.

"A little bird has spoken to me," she said.

"And the bird had snow-white plumage," Lone Walker guessed. "And was very old."

"Perhaps."

"The others say if I go to face White Buffalo I will not return."

"They are not Lone Walker's woman," Sparrow said, a

note of contempt in her voice. As she sat upright, her hair spilled across her breasts. "You will return to me."

Lone Walker reached out and stroked her naked back. His loins stirred, and Sparrow whispered a secret name to him and lay on her side, her back to him, as he entered her. He pressed his face into Sparrow's dark hair. She smelled of wildflowers and passion. Lone Walker thought his heart would burst from loving her.

Darkness draped its purple cloak about them, and afterwards, they slept.

Lone Walker opened his eyes and waited until his vision adjusted to the night before moving. Then he worked his way out of Sparrow's embrace and stood naked in the moonlight. He listened, his breathing shallow. He waited, and heard once more the screech of a great horned owl, a harbinger of death. *Had it called him by name?* He heard the rush of wings and looked up. The predator, its wings outstretched, glided just above the treetops. Once, twice, three times, then four, it traced circles against the moonlit sky. Then the great horned owl dropped from the sky as if to attack the man below.

The Blackfoot ducked, attempting to protect his face. The owl rose on its strong wide wings, then dropped again. Lone Walker flinched as the bird swooped past his eyes and climbed the warm breeze back into the safety of the sky. It dived yet again from the branches of the aspens only to swerve aside from its attack. For the fourth time the bird repeated its actions, fanning the air as it skimmed past Lone Walker's head. The young brave's blood ran cold. Four times circling, four times an aborted attack—he understood now. Magic was at work against him. As the great horned owl began its final ascent, Lone Walker could have sworn he glimpsed two baleful green eyes staring at him from the predator's shrouded features.

"White Buffalo," Lone Walker whispered.

The owl soared above the aspen grove and vanished from sight without a single cry to mark its passing. In the creature's wake there was an eerie, oppressive stillness.

Lone Walker swallowed only with effort, and breathing itself became an act of concentration. He wanted to run from the clearing, to flee his unseen attacker, but he knew there was no escape—a curse was upon him.

The pressure in his chest was worse now, unendurable. He grew dizzy and struggled to fill his lungs but to no avail. The great horned owl had called him by name, diving out of the sky like . . . the hawk that had saved . . . Lone Walker's life the . . . day before. He collapsed to his knees; the world began to spin as he gasped for air. The owl . . . the hawk . . . White Buffalo's magic was killing him. The shaman had placed his curse and who could resist such power? None. Except, perhaps, a man who could summon a hawk, a man who had stood upon the edge of the world and been taught the sacred songs—a man who had returned from where the sun sleeps.

> "I place my foot upon the path of night.
> All-Father, lead me.
> I place my foot upon the path of morning.
> All-Father, strengthen me.
> I follow the circle and find death.
> I follow the circle and find life."

His voice was barely audible in the clearing. But it was loud enough to break the hold of White Buffalo's evil handiwork. With a force that almost knocked Lone Walker on his back, air rushed into his lungs. He got to his feet and stood with his face tilted upward, eyes closed. He breathed, just breathed the sweet clean air. When he could move without stumbling, he returned to Sparrow's side. She stirred, opened her eyes, and reached out to him.

"What is it?" she mumbled softly.

His only reply was to enfold her in his arms and in the silent passage of the hours, embrace life.

"White Buffalo must die," Lone Walker told the warriors arranged around the morning council fire.

Throughout the night the remnants of the Scalpdancers had argued what their next course of action should be. They talked of the change that had come over Lone Walker as well. He who had once been Lost Eyes and the object of derision had traveled beyond the Backbone of the World. His visions had led him to where the sun sleeps. He had laid claim to their respect. Those who had once harbored ill will toward him were ashamed, all the more so because he had forgiven them and called each man by name as would a brother.

To try to kill White Buffalo, this indeed was a mad quest. Yet, they were willing to ride at his side and die before the Shoshoni rifles. His fate would be theirs and he loved them for it. But Lone Walker refused the help each of them offered. His dreams had told him to go alone and that was the way of it. He would accept only two things—a promise from Wolf Lance to care for Sparrow if Lone Walker failed to return, and a magnificent roan stallion, a powerful mountain-bred animal that had been Black Fox's pride and joy.

And when the last of the braves acceded to his will, Lone Walker left them by the banks of the pond and once more entered the cave. He came to Singing Woman's chamber in time to see her double over in a coughing fit. Her body shook, her gaunt frame seemed about to fall apart, then the spasm subsided, and to his surprise the old woman looked up, saw him, and chuckled.

"Keep your worries, my young friend. Look to yourself. You have cause to be concerned. White Buffalo will try to kill you any way he can."

"He already has," Lone Walker replied. "Last night. But I am still here."

"White Buffalo's power is great, yet I think he begins to fear you. Doubt is like a spark in dry grass, soon it is out of control."

Lone Walker would control his own misgivings. He was anxious to be on his way. The more he lingered, the less he wanted to leave at all. She sensed this as well and was determined to be rid of him, though she had come to love him for his courage and to respect him for his vision.

"Who are you?" she said.

"I am Lone Walker."

"And what do you see?"

"What is beyond seeing."

"And what is in you?"

"Songs."

"And why do you sing?"

"So the world will not die."

Singing Woman sat upright. Her eyes held him bound. "I dreamed you. I saw you in the flames of my sacred fire. The wolf called you by name; the spirit of *Iniskim* spoke of your coming. Follow the herd; they will bring you to Elkhorn Creek." She waved a hand. "Go and find your fate." She sank against the backrest and would look at him no more.

Lone Walker did as the old woman commanded and hurried from the cave. Morgan Penmerry was waiting outside the falls, his rifle cradled in his arm. He fell into step alongside his companion. Lone Walker wore an unadorned buckskin shirt and deerskin breeches. His hair hung long and was unbraided. He carried no provisions, intending to fast on the way to Elkhorn Creek. The only weapon he carried, if it could be called that, was the Medicine Cane, with its raven feathers that fluttered with each step.

"I must go alone," he said to Morgan. The white man never broke stride.

"Now see here—" Morgan began.

Lone Walker raised a hand to silence his friend. The Blackfoot pointed to the other men of his tribe gathered along the bank of the pond. All eyes were on Lone Walker.

"I have told the Scalpdancers to shoot your horse if you try to follow. And then to shoot you if the first fails."

"You have a strange notion of friendship." Morgan glared at him.

"Maybe I am saving your life, Mor-gan." Lone Walker placed his fist over his heart, then brought his hand palm-open toward the white man. "I must walk this path alone. Farewell, my friend," he added in English.

Lone Walker gathered the reins of the stallion Black Fox had tethered near the creek. It pleased the young spirit singer to see how the Scalpdancers had left the cave and come out of hiding. Children were busily gathering stones to ring the cook fires. Preparations had begun for the trek into Ever Shadow, the country to the north. Lone Walker's presence had infused them with new life. He did not fully understand how or why—yet he too felt the difference. The journey had changed him and the journey had yet to end.

He looked for and found Sparrow. She was busy at her own campsite, heating stones to bring to boil the red-medicine tea. Her ministrations had already begun to bring relief to the ill. Fevers had broken. Yellow Stalk's infant was resting, allowing the mother to do the same. She appeared to treat his departure as a matter-of-fact event, as if he were merely leaving for the hunt.

Only once did she pause to meet his eyes. She masked her fears and smiled. Her courage became his courage. It enabled him to ride away.

Morgan gnawed a piece of jerked meat and meandered behind the falls and across the slippery jumble of rocks and tall yellow-green reeds, then followed a narrow little path out onto the opposite bank where Sparrow had built her fire. The flames unwound a fragrant banner of smoke that floated upward on the warm listless air. Morgan wondered why she had chosen a site apart from the rest of the Scalpdancers. When he saw the glistening trace of tears on her cheeks, he knew.

She watched him approach and turned away to tend the tea mixture she had brewed from the curlydocks. She added an armful of dried cornflowers to the flames and a handful of dried chokecherries to the mixture. She kept herself busy, hoping the white man would leave her in peace. Even if Lone Walker claimed him as friend, she was still shy and unused to such men. The white men were a mercurial race, friendly one moment, enemies the next.

Morgan shifted his big frame and cleared his throat, and when she still did not acknowledge him, he stepped around and placed himself between the woman and the medicine she brewed. Sparrow was in no mood to be trifled with. Lone Walker had just ridden off to do battle with an invincible foe. Now that she was alone, all her doubts sprang up, like wolves to a kill. Her eyes blazed with fury as she confronted Morgan.

"I shall need a parfleche of dried meat and a water bag," Morgan said. "You ought to be able to fetch them without attracting attention," he said, scratching his beard.

His instructions took her by surprise; then she noticed he wore his pistols in his belt, cradled his rifle in his arm. And out in the meadow his mouse-brown gelding, a hammerheaded steed with an ugly long-legged gait, was already saddled. Realization brightened her features. His teeth flashed in a smile. Her mistrust melted. She touched his hand, then hurried to do as he bid. So this Mor-gan was going to follow after all. But he was not born to these mountains. He was no tracker. The white man would need help, someone who could read a trail.

Sparrow knew just the person for the job.

Lone Walker momentarily skylined himself atop the ridge overlooking the valley and halted the stallion down within the shadows of the ponderosas and checked his back trail. Satisfied he wasn't being followed, Lone Walker dismounted and leaned the Medicine Cane against the nearest tree trunk. He'd spied a suspicious glint of metal beneath the water bag slung behind him.

Lone Walker lifted the folds of the pelts draped across the back of the roan and, shoving aside the buffalo gut he used for a water bag, the brave uncovered Morgan Penmerry's cutlass. The weapon's fourteen-inch blade remnant had been worked to a lethal point by Morgan, then secured in place by a strip of buckskin looped around the basket hilt. He'd wrapped the weapon in a swath of brushed buckskin, but the grip had worked free and sunlight reflecting off its brass hilt had caught the young brave's attention.

He untied the weapon, shook his head in disbelief, and started to toss the cutlass aside. No, that didn't seem the right thing to do. However, the Medicine Cane was the only weapon he'd need to face White Buffalo, at least so he'd been told by Singing Woman. He considered returning the cutlass to the Scalpdancers' camp and as quickly dismissed the notion. No, his feet were on the trail and White Buffalo was waiting at the end of it.

Lone Walker tucked the cutlass in his beaded belt. He took up the Medicine Cane and mounted the roan stallion. The animal descended the hillside at a breakneck pace, fighting Lone Walker all the way as it cut along a winding path worn into the hillside by elk and antelope. They startled a gray she-wolf and her cubs from their den and frightened a nesting falcon from its treetop perch.

It wasn't until they reached the valley floor that Lone Walker brought the willful stallion under control. But there was more here to occupy his attention than the skittish roan. The buffalo grass was trampled flat, and for at least a hundred yards across the meadow and leading off to the east, the bitterroot and tall amber-green stalks of grass had been churned into the earth by the passing of a large herd of bison.

"So *Iniskim* is to lead me after all," Lone Walker said aloud.

A large herd had passed sometime during the night. He knew that by the freshness of the droppings. How far ahead they were was anyone's guess. The way was clear and he hurried the roan onto the trail left by the passing herd.

White Buffalo chose a spot midway between the hills near the entrance to the pass, about a stone's throw from the cluster of underbrush where Elkhorn Creek petered out. He cleared the ground and gathered enough rocks to delineate a circle six feet in diameter. Once the circle was formed, he built a fire of grass and twigs and added crushed bitterroot, the leaves of sweet pine, pulverized dried mushrooms, and a fragment of his sacred robe. He continued to wear the buffalo headdress despite the warmth of the day.

When the fire had burned to ashes, the shaman scooped them onto a flat piece of bark and sprinkled the stone circle until he had dusted every rock with the magical substance.

He organized his weapons in the circle: a rifle, powder horn and shot, and a Green River tomahawk; the buffalo rib fetish he kept in a pouch dangling from his belt. By noon the shaman's preparations were nearly complete. White Buffalo returned to the blaze-faced stallion tethered by the brush back near the creek. He mounted and rode the animal four times around the circle of stone and then, reversing direction, repeated the ritual.

As he finished the ceremony, he noticed Drum and Stone Bear watching him from the hillside. They walked their horses toward him. The Shoshoni braves were reticent to approach. White Buffalo was no man to trifle with and once disturbed might fly into a rage and unleash his curse on them. They came to a halt a couple of horse lengths from the stone circle.

Blue Cap appeared at the edge of the thicket. She had returned with the two warriors at White Buffalo's direction.

"I remain here until this 'Lone Walker' comes," White Buffalo told them. "Tell your people to remain in the village. When I have finished, I will lead them out over the bones of my enemy."

Drum glanced aside at Stone Bear, his friend, and then replied, "The people will wait."

"Grieving for the dead who did not return with Drum," Stone Bear said, much to the smaller man's discomfort. Drum had endured much abuse since his shameful return, his failure made all the more reprehensible by the manner in which six Shoshoni Crazy Dog Soldiers had been killed or routed by two men, a white eyes and this Scalpdancer named Lone Walker.

"Wait if you must," Drum began. "But let me be the weapon you wield against this *Pikuni*."

"You have already tried once and failed," White Buffalo reminded him.

"I must face him," Drum said, desperation in his voice. White Buffalo could see some merit in using the Crazy Dog Soldier. Why not allow him the chance to redeem himself? And if he managed to kill the one called Lone Walker, then so much the better. Then again, the shaman had called a death curse down upon his enemy, so truly, by whatever name he chose to call himself, he was already dead.

"Go and bring me his scalp and your voice will be loudest at the council. You will walk the path of power with me," White Buffalo said. His eyes glittered and his words had a hypnotic effect on the two men.

"And if I bring his scalp?" Stone Bear interjected.

"Then Drum will sit in your shadow," White Buffalo told him.

"Let it be as you say," the larger of the two warriors said. Stone Bear ignored Drum's look of anger. This was more than a matter of honor. "We will ride together, my blood brother and I."

Before Drum could utter a protest, Stone Bear trotted off on his war-horse, his trade gun gripped in his strong right hand. He had never been beaten in a fight; he had never run from an enemy. Drum urged his own mount forward and White Buffalo watched the deadly companions ride abreast out of the valley of the Elkhorn.

Blue Cap started forward, but White Buffalo halted her. "Return to your lodge, little one. For I must be alone with my fate."

How proud he looked, yes, this man who had taken her to his blanket, how powerful and full of fierce energy; there were none like him.

"I will wait for you," she told him.

He alone was her light and shadow; he alone her people; there were no others. She skirted the thicket and galloped up the valley, retracing her route to the village.

She was young and her heart was full of secret passions.
She did not like being ordered about, however, and considered confronting the shaman. But that might not be
wise. So she held her tongue and did as she was told.
She'd charge through camp at a wild gallop, scattering
dogs and children and overturning tanning racks in her
wake. It made obedience much easier to take.

Alone again, White Buffalo added deadwood to the
embers of the fire. Flames lapped greedily at the fresh
fuel. He opened the pouch at his side and removed the
fetish he carried, and placed the buffalo rib on a small
stone altar near the fire. He sat cross-legged before the
altar and began to chant softly. Upon the blood of the
buffalo he had killed, the shaman summoned his powers
and called for the likes of the Coyote Trickster to confuse
his enemies and for the Death Striker to slay them.

He could not help but ponder this man called Lone
Walker who had once been Lost Eyes. How had he
received his vision? What had it been? White Buffalo
thought he had killed the young warrior. That was his first
mistake with Lone Walker. There would not be another.

White Buffalo remained by the fire the rest of the day
and all through the night. Come morning he drank his fill
from the creek and then hurried back to his power circle
with an armful of branches for the fire. Time meant
nothing. All the shaman's attention was centered inward,
where he walked in dreams of blood.

23

The buffalo herd, a thousand strong, moved from valley to valley, meadow to meadow, in autumn. Lone Walker felt a kinship with the beasts from his vantage point on the edge of the herd. They too measured the land, enduring an endless journey from life to death, a quest for sweet grass and fresh water. He saw calves keeping close to their mothers as they staggered through another day of heat.

Lone Walker was familiar with these hills. The nearest water would be Elkhorn Creek another two hours by horseback. It was already near sunset. The herd would pass another thirsty night if they halted at dusk. Not Lone Walker though. He touched his heels to the big stallion's sides and the animal galloped ahead of the herd. One battle-scarred bull with only one horn lifted its shaggy head and studied horse and rider. This bison was over eleven feet in length and stood as tall as a man at the shoulders. The beast snorted dust from its snout and bellowed a warning. Lone Walker raised the Medicine

Cane, its raven feathers streaming, and cried out to the herd and the one-horned monarch at the forefront.

"*Ha-ka-hai, Iniskim,* See, I ride with you. Today we are one. Why so slow? Has the shaman stolen all your power? We will see if he can keep it!"

Lone Walker's cry rang out over the meadow and the one-horned bull turned toward the solitary figure on the nut-brown stallion and shook its head and bellowed a challenge that reverberated through the hills. However, Lone Walker had not come to do battle with the beast but a man who had become as a beast, who would continue to work his evil among men. So he rode from the herd, and left it behind. There would be other hunts.

Darkness cloaked the hillside and obscured the two men hidden in a stand of juniper. They had wrapped the hooves of their horses with buckskin strips to muffle their descent toward the camp fire at the bottom of the hill.

"It is he. I was right," Drum whispered excitedly. He had been the first to sight the camp fire from the hilltop a half-hour's ride from the valley of the Elkhorn.

Stone Bear had followed the Crazy Dog Soldier downslope. He never let down his guard but remained wary of the enemy below and the companion at his side. They were blood brothers, true, and ordinarily he'd not interfere. But why should Drum alone be allowed to win White Buffalo's special honor? If there were power and prestige to be won, Stone Bear figured he deserved the same chances as his friend.

Drum eased past the branches of the saplings he had chosen to crouch behind. A flash of lightning caught his attention and he lifted his eyes to the western hills and glimpsed a second flicker of faint light. There was a storm on the way, perhaps Cold Maker had tired of these warm days and still nights and was coming to bring them to an end.

"We must hurry," Drum said, wiping his mouth on the sleeve of his elkskin shirt. He tightened the porcupine quill breastplate he wore and patted the barrel of the flintlock rifle he'd borrowed from another brave in camp. "He said four mornings. It must be Lone Walker."

"Perhaps." Stone Bear smelled of wood smoke and grease and he was fed up with waiting. "I shall see for myself." He swung up on his own mount.

"What are you doing?" Drum asked in alarm.

"I will not kill a man from hiding." Stone Bear grimaced, his voice thick with disapproval. "The Shoshoni are warriors, not rabbits."

Drum colored and his eyes narrowed in anger. He placed a hand upon his breastplate; its buckskin border was fringed with the scalps of his enemies.

"I fear no man," he hoarsely proclaimed and returned to horseback. "Least of all, you, my brother."

"Once this Lone Walker is dead, we shall see who wears his hair," Stone Bear sneered.

"He who first counts coup," Drum retorted and, slapping Stone Bear across the face with his quirt, rode out of the clearing and downslope at a breakneck pace.

Stone Bear's horse shied and almost threw him. He fought the animal and brought him under control. Blood seeped from a gash on his cheek. He uttered a feral growl and charged after his companion, bent on revenge.

Lone Walker chose a campsite at the foot of a hill near a fallen ponderosa that the natural forces were reclaiming. He noted the presence of a beehive in the bowels of the rotting trunk and promised himself a dollop of fresh honey, later, after . . . He left the thought unfinished.

He broke another couple of thick limbs from the tree trunk and tossed them on the camp fire. He wanted a good large blaze so as to attract the attention of the two who were following him. He had spotted Morgan and Sparrow his first day out. A dust plume from their horses had given them away. And once on a ridge he had watched from hiding as the couple rode into view, thinking themselves very clever as they trailed Lone Walker among the forested ridges and silent hills.

Perhaps the fire so obviously larger than one man needed would lure them into camp, the Blackfoot hoped

as he stood the Medicine Cane upright in the soft earth.
Lone Walker opened a parfleche and sprinkled the burning branches with sacred meal, then sat back on his heels
and watched the ruby-red coals pulse with life and tried to
will away the knot in the pit of his stomach. He glanced
down at the cutlass alongside him and that turned his
thoughts to the two who had followed him. They must go
no farther. He must tell them. If only they would see the
fire and understand. If only . . .

Lone Walker heard the approach of horses and breathed
a sigh of relief. He glanced at the faintly illuminated patch
of hillside and realized in the same moment that the
horses couldn't possibly belong to Sparrow and Morgan
unless they'd somehow ridden ahead of him and backtracked.

Lone Walker dived aside as a flintlock cracked and a ball
sliced the air where he'd been standing. He hit the
ground, rolled to his feet, and grabbed for the cutlass.

Drum charged into the firelight. He yelled his challenge and, using his rifle for a coup stick, stretched out as
he rode past and tried to strike Lone Walker's shoulder
and missed. The rifle barrel clanged against the cutlass
blade as Lone Walker parried the blow.

Drum flew past and disappeared into the darkness
beyond the circle of firelight. Lone Walker barely had
time to face a second threat. Stone Bear was only seconds
behind his blood brother and he was riding to the kill. His
war-horse bore down on the Blackfoot. Stone Bear dropped
the reins and raised his rifle.

Lone Walker stabbed the cutlass into the fire and skewered
a branch as thick as a man's arm and completely engulfed
in flames. With a quick flick of the wrist he flipped the
burning branch into the horse's face. The animal reared
and pitched the Shoshoni from horseback and bolted from
the branch that burned its flesh.

Stone Bear hit hard. His rifle discharged harmlessly
toward the sky. The Shoshoni leapt upright and drew his
iron-bladed tomahawk, scrambled toward Lone Walker.
The Blackfoot closed with the larger man—which was to
Stone Bear's liking. They grappled for a moment and the

Shoshoni tried to bring his greater strength to bear, hoping to force the Blackfoot to the ground and crush his skull with a single swipe of his tomahawk.

It was a good plan and would have worked except that Lone Walker was quicker and stronger than he appeared. His right hand twisted free of the Shoshoni's imprisoning grip. Stone Bear made a vain attempt to retrieve his hold. He failed and Lone Walker buried the cutlass blade in Stone Bear's belly. The Shoshoni gasped and fell backward, a look of astonishment on his face. The blade pulled free.

He landed on his back, staring up at the overcast sky. He smelled rain in the air and noted how the world was still, so still...

Blood dripped from the blade onto the chest of the dying man.

Lone Walker staggered back, sucking air into his lungs. A rifle blossomed fire and the Blackfoot spun around as pain seared his side and a ball plowed a nasty furrow through his flesh. He dropped to his hands and knees, and managed to remain conscious. Brandishing the cutlass, Lone Walker tried to stand. It took effort, but he made it.

Drum hurriedly loaded his rifle out beyond the glare of the fire. He cocked and primed the trade gun and then confidently walked his horse into the light. He noted with satisfaction Stone Bear's corpse.

Lone Walker clutched his left side. The gash was superficial, but the pain only fueled the Blackfoot's anger and renewed his strength. His muscles tightened and he prepared to hurl the cutlass at his foe.

"I have you, Blackfoot," Drum said, "Your hair shall—" His voice faded and his eyes widened as he looked past his intended victim. Lone Walker felt his own hackles rise and turned despite himself and saw materializing out of the black night on a blaze-faced stallion a figure of great and terrible proportion wrapped in the ghostly hide of the white buffalo.

The shaman fired his rifle. Lone Walker flinched, thinking he was the intended victim. Drum spun back into darkness. Blood exploded from his chest. His rifle went spinning through the air. It landed among the rocks and discharged into the dirt.

Lone Walker stood motionless, stunned by the actions of his enemy.

"You saved my life once. Have you forgotten?" White Buffalo said. "Now I have done the same for you."

He did not venture completely into the light, as if unable to sever his ties with darkness he must remain in shadow. The buffalo headdress he wore with its curved horns gave him the appearance of a demon. White Buffalo studied his opponent with renewed interest.

The young man's hair was already showing streaks of silver and the once young face was windburned and made wise with the gift of the spirit songs as if youth could not contain all he had seen.

"So you have found your eyes," White Buffalo remarked. "What do they see, 'Lone Walker'? What do your visions tell you? What power have you now? Perhaps your name is all there is."

"Before the sun rises, you will know," Lone Walker said.

White Buffalo respected a bold reply. He even sensed a kinship with the younger man. The shaman lifted his gaze and noticed the Medicine Cane thrust into the ground. He recognized it as a symbol of power, but what caught his attention was the portion of the cane wrapped in a grayish-white piece of buffalo hide. Alarm flickered behind his brooding expression. Something stirred in his memory, but the shaman couldn't dredge it up. Then he remembered. No, it could not possibly be. But his blood ran cold nonetheless.

White Buffalo cautiously walked his stallion around the campsite, always remaining on the fringe and never wholly venturing into the yellow-orange radius of firelight. Lone Walker turned on his heels, facing the shaman as he circled the clearing. Four times White Buffalo rode about the younger brave and chanted in a low voice, a chant for the dying.

Lone Walker watched and listened and at first was

afraid, for the shaman called upon Death Striker and demons of fire and darkness. Yet, the sound of distant thunder awakened in him the memory of the buffalo herd he had followed for a time. They were life to his people as were the storms that nourished the land, and the good earth itself.

Then the fear left him and he did not falter. And when White Buffalo had finished, Lone Walker found a man facing him. The shaman nodded.

"Let it be so," he said. "Your power is here. But the valley of the Elkhorn is mine." His voice rang out, reverberated among the hills. "Once, Lone Walker, we heard an owl call a name. Before the sun rises we will know at last whether it was yours or mine."

Was it a trick of the dancing flames or did the shaman's eyes seem to glow against the backdrop of night?

Lone Walker dropped the cutlass in the dirt and folded his arms across his chest. He met the shaman's malevolent stare with a look of pity.

"It is good for men to know the truth of things—of their visions and of their lives," he said.

But White Buffalo was gone, leaving Lone Walker to his own visions.

The sound of White Buffalo's stallion departing at a canter through the dry grass had barely faded when Morgan Penmerry and Sparrow galloped into camp. Their horses were lathered, they'd been ridden hard since the sound of gunfire. Morgan brandished his rifle, Sparrow held one of his pistols and from the serious expression on her face she was prepared to use it.

Morgan searched from side to side, expecting an attack at any moment from every direction. When none was forthcoming, not even a war whoop, he returned his attention to the two dead Shoshoni braves Lone Walker had dragged out of the clearing. Morgan dismounted to help the Blackfoot and as they tumbled the bodies into a nearby gully, Morgan couldn't help but mutter, "Let the dead bury the dead."

Lone Walker led the way back to the camp fire, where Sparrow had already prepared a poultice and elkskin bandage. She motioned for him to sit near the fire. He stripped off his shirt. Then the woman cleaned his wound and applied the poultice, a mixture of columbine root, fungus, spider web, and crushed juniper leaves.

"You followed against my will. Both of you..." Lone Walker looked over at Morgan, who averted his eyes and found the clouds that scudded across the face of the moon more to his liking.

"And if we had not, you would be bleeding to death," Sparrow told him. He raised his arms as she wrapped the elkskin bandage around his middle and handed him his shirt. "*Saaa-vaa*. Are you the only one who dreams?"

Lone Walker didn't know how to reply. Her words were like a web and he a struggling insect, caught and held at her mercy. Indeed, he was glad to see them both. Solitude had begun to weigh on him like a sodden buffalo robe.

"The Scalpdancers are poor horsemen indeed if they could not catch you," Lone Walker remarked, impressed that the couple had escaped the likes of Wolf Lance and Black Fox.

"They didn't have any horses," Morgan said. "Blind Weed spooked them as we rode away. She was shouting and waving a blanket like the devil himself was after her." He laughed again, recalling the sight. There had been so much commotion a child could have escaped the valley.

"Tell me, white man. Did your dreams bring you here?" Lone Walker asked.

Morgan shrugged. "Who brought me? Your woman."

Sparrow had proved an able tracker. Morgan alone would never have picked up Lone Walker's tracks beyond the other side of the buffalo herd.

"You understand what I'm saying," Morgan continued. "I may not see things like you, but I see what *is*. So here I am." Morgan hooked a thumb in his belt and with the other arm leaned upon his rifle. "Sometimes you have to back up your dreams with powder and shot."

"I do not understand any of this," Lone Walker said.

"Oh, hell, friend, who does?" Morgan said.

"Before the sun rises I must face White Buffalo. Alone."

"Go right ahead," Morgan replied. "But if you go under—then he will have to deal with me."

"And then me," Sparrow added.

"You have journeyed far to lose your life," Lone Walker cautioned Morgan.

"I lost my life weeks ago. Now, I'm trying to *find* it again." Morgan stalked past the fire and headed for the horses. A gusting breeze had begun to worry them. He ground-tethered each of the animals, a task he performed with a minimum of effort, for Lone Walker had been a splendid teacher.

The Blackfoot studied Morgan a moment longer, sensing the white man's hurt, his anger, and his power; then Sparrow touched his arm.

"What shall I do for you?" she asked.

"You have done it," Lone Walker said, his eyes full of love. He drew a reed flute from his belt and walked out of the firelight.

Sparrow wrapped a blanket around her shoulders and found a place by the fire. Morgan hunched down alongside her and warmed himself. There was a cold wind coming.

Lone Walker crushed the brittle grass as he circled the campsite. Rain had begun to wash the hills, but here only the wind blew while Lone Walker played upon the flute, sad, sweet, trilling notes that gave one pause.

"Mor-gan?" Sparrow said in halting English.

"Yes?" he answered.

"It is good you are here."

"Thanks."

"Your woman—she was brave?"

"Very brave."

"I shall try to be brave," Sparrow said.

"Yes."

"You are also my friend, Mor-gan."

The gunshot sounded like a broadside fired from an English frigate and wrenched Morgan from dreams of

Macao and cockfights and wild nights and a missionary's daughter. He jerked upright, and saw Lone Walker astride his brown stallion against a predawn sky. The north wind moaned and set the spirit singer's unbound hair streaming, and the raven feathers on the Medicine Cane fluttered as if charged with energy. The stallion's nostrils flared and it pawed the ground near the circle of embers that had been the fire. Lone Walker tossed Morgan his rifle, still warm from the blast.

Morgan Penmerry scrambled to his feet. How the devil had he fallen asleep? He checked the horizon. How long before sunup was anybody's guess. All he could see was a mass of angry clouds and he shivered. The wind was biting. He noticed that Sparrow had brought both their horses. He began to wonder if she had drugged his tea or Lone Walker had put a spell on the white man to lull him to sleep. Maybe there was something to these fetishes and dreams and songs after all.

"Take Sparrow to the hillside," Lone Walker commanded. "It is no longer safe here. Wait for me."

"Where are you going?" Morgan shouted.

Lone Walker pointed to a gap between two ridges a half-hour's ride from the camp—less if a man rode full out.

"White Buffalo is there," the Blackfoot said.

"He could have a dozen braves waiting for you."

"I will not be alone," Lone Walker replied. With a wave of his hand and a long last look at Sparrow—who showed no weakness though her heart was filled with worry—the warrior rode away, running with the wind, racing Cold Maker toward the mouth of the valley.

He had emptied himself of emotion and doubts. He allowed himself to be a vessel in which visions and dreams might reside. Lone Walker's flute had summoned the *Maiyun*. They spoke to him of his power; they revealed the secret of the Medicine Cane and warned him he might die. He heard their warning even now and still he rode on, because this was what must be done. The evil must end. If it cost his life, so be it.

* * *

The herd had passed a restless night ringed by storms and the flashes of lightning in the mountains to the west. The herd nervously huddled, a thousand strong, in the center of the plain. Calves bleated alongside anxious mothers while the young bulls pawed the ground as they eyed the passing storms.

Anything could have started them moving.

As it was, the one-horned bull, all two thousand pounds of muscle and bone, stood half-dozing at the forefront of the herd when a tumbleweed, caught up in the grip of the approaching front, came rolling toward the bison and leapt a ditch. The tumbleweed became airborne for a matter of seconds, long enough to slap the old bull upon the rump and dig its spiny brambles into the beast's scarred flesh. The startled animal brayed in terror, lunged forward, and charged across the amber plain.

And the herd, all thousand of them, moved as one, galvanized into an unstoppable force by the actions of a single bull. Panic spread and the frightened charge became a headlong stampede, crushing everything in its path.

White Buffalo waited within his circle of strength. He held the rib fetish in both hands and searched the entrance to the pass, a hundred yards ahead. The bleak gray light became tinged with cobalt-blue as the front barreled out of the northwest. He watched the speeding clouds transform themselves into demons and bluffs, buffalo and wraithlike warriors, jumbled battlements and winged maidens.

He waited and watched and, suddenly, White Buffalo was no longer alone. He returned his attention to the mouth of the valley and glimpsed a solitary horseman outlined against a slate-gray sky. Lone Walker entered the valley of the Elkhorn but not alone. Cold Maker came with him. The wind increased in intensity and filled the air with ghostly mourning.

The Blackfoot rode up and dismounted about twenty-

five feet from the shaman. He landed, catlike. White
Buffalo continued to sit back on his heels in the center of
his power circle.

"So you have come to die. Let it be so," White Buffalo
said and raised his talisman as he began to chant.

A savage blast of wind spooked Lone Walker's stallion
and the animal scampered off toward the hillside. Lone
Walker saw it as another manifestation of White Buffalo's
power.

He wouldn't need a horse to do what must be done but
to save his own life afterward. His courage momentarily
failed and when it did, a horrible kind of pressure began
building in Lone Walker's chest. He stared at the shaman's
fetish, could not tear his eyes away even though his
breathing became labored. The wind hurled its warning in
his ears. But he could not move.

"All-Father . . ." Lone Walker tried to pray, to call on his
songs. He was dying, and there was nothing he could do.
In vain, he worked his sluggish limbs and held the Medicine Cane out before him.

White Buffalo stood and the wind tugged at his sacred
white robe and his eyes burned beneath the buffalo headdress as he continued his chant with renewed intensity,
summoning Death Striker to destroy Lone Walker.

"You are a boy no longer. You are a man now," White
Buffalo called out, breaking the pattern of his chant. "But
men die. You must die. Do you think your feathered cane
can stand against my magic?"

White Buffalo was wrong. Even as he spoke, a north
wind parted the clouds and for a few moments the land
was bathed in the fresh golden light of a newly risen sun.

With the light came visions, the same spirits Lone
Walker had seen at the edge of the world. He turned
toward the dawn and saw the Ones Who Had Come
Before springing out of the sunrise, and he heard their
songs in his soul. He faced White Buffalo again.

"See the Medicine Cane!" he called out. "Know the
truth. It carries the same magic cut from your own robe!"
It took every ounce of strength, but Lone Walker managed

to lift the Medicine Cane, and the shaman once more beheld the hide fragment. He looked down at his own robe. He didn't understand how Lone Walker had come by it, but he believed.

"Foolish one. You seek to harm me with that? Then your own talisman is my power to command. Mine!"

Lone Walker shuddered and a violent gust almost tore the cane from his grasp. He was dying. And not even the songs would save him. He had lost . . .

"*Who are you?*" An old woman's voice spoke within his mind: Singing Woman.

"*Who are you?*"

"Lone Walker," the young man rasped.

"*What have you come to do?*"

"Destroy the shaman."

"*Then do it!*"

The songs of sunlight washed over him, through him, and gave him strength even as darkness closed in on the periphery of his vision.

"Here is your power!" Lone Walker roared out. The darkness retreated as he raised the cane above his head with both hands. His shoulder muscles bulged and the cane bowed, then snapped in half with a resounding crack.

The pressure in his chest suddenly subsided and he gulped in lungfuls of air. Thunder rumbled over the land and rose quickly to deafening proportion. The ground trembled underfoot.

As Lone Walker hurled the fragments of the shattered Medicine Cane to the ground, the source of the thunder revealed itself. In a swirl of dust and noise a thousand stampeding bison rounded a steep hill and charged headlong into the valley. The herd fanned out behind the frontrunning bulls.

White Buffalo wore a look of horror and spun on his heels to dash toward his own stallion, but the animal had pulled free of its ground stake and was already a quarter of a mile down the valley, the wooden pin bouncing along at the end of its reins.

White Buffalo turned back in anger. Afoot, they were in

the same trap. He tucked the talisman in his belt. Let
Lone Walker break the power of a rifle ball through his
heart! White Buffalo took up his rifle, cocked the weapon,
and snapped it to his shoulder. He squeezed the trigger.
The flint struck sparks. Nothing else happened. The shaman stared down at the rifle in his hands and realized with
sinking heart he had forgotten to reload from the night
before.

The oncoming herd blared and brayed like denizens of
hell.

Lone Walker, however, turned to face them; he would
meet his fate head on. "Come, *Iniskim*," he prayed softly.
"It is the hour of your vengeance. I have brought you for
this."

Lone Walker glanced toward the hills. No. He'd never
reach the trees in time, so he outstretched his arms to the
stampeding herd, and as the great beasts of the plains
closed the distance, he spied a horseman in their midst.
Lone Walker could scarcely believe his eyes.

Morgan Penmerry rode at the forefront of the stampede,
outdistancing the herd by mere yards. Leaning low over
the neck of his gelding, he reached for Lone Walker.

Closer. Closer. The ground shuddered underfoot. Morgan
didn't need to look back, he'd be the first to know if he lost
his race with death.

"Oh, God," he muttered and almost lost his balance.
He tightened his legs about the gelding's middle. They'd
only have one chance and this was it.

Closer still. His hand opened, reaching, and suddenly
closed around flesh and he pulled. Lone Walker timed his
motion and leapt. The gelding's forward momentum swung
Lone Walker up behind Morgan with a force that threatened
to dislodge them both. A few yards behind them, the
one-horned bull shook its shaggy head and bellowed.

Morgan righted himself and, tugging on the reins,
angled for the safety of the ridge. He wasn't certain they'd
make it.

White Buffalo tossed his rifle aside and drew the rib
talisman from his belt. He planted himself firmly in his

circle of strength. I am protected here, he thought, my magic is unbroken. The shaman began to chant as he held the talisman in both hands and raised it aloft, stretching to his full height. His powerful physique cloaked in sacred trappings seemed invincible right up to the moment the one-horned bull smashed him to the earth.

White Buffalo shrieked beneath the crushing hooves and tried to claw his way to safety as hundreds more bison trampled flesh and bone and sacred pelt into a single indistinguishable smear where once a man of power had stood.

24

Sparrow waited at the entrance to Elkhorn Valley. She had caught up the reins of the brown stallion but could not bring herself to enter in the aftermath of the herd. As the gusting breezes cleared the last of the dust from the pass, Lone Walker and Morgan emerged from the place of death and rode toward the woman.

The winds of change were blowing across the flattened grass, and the sunlight grew fragrant with the perfume of wildflowers, cedar, and pine. Sparrow huddled in her blanket and thought how good it was to be full of life and love in the turning of the seasons.

Neither man spoke. Their eyes were weary from what they had seen. Blood oozed from the gelding's flanks where a horn had hooked the animal as it brought the men to safety.

Sparrow would make a compress back at her makeshift camp among the quaking aspens. She led the men to her campsite. Lone Walker fell exhausted on the nearest unrolled blanket and Morgan didn't last much longer. But it was

Lone Walker who slept the day away and all of the night as well.

The following morning dawned clear and cool, and the land seemed a whole and beautiful place again. And true to his calling, Lone Walker stood upon the hillside overlooking the plain, washed by the colors of the risen sun, and he began to sing in thanksgiving for another day of life.

Morgan Penmerry knew no prayers, but he was bloody grateful to be alive, and so he let the feeling in his heart be a hosanna to the Almighty as he saddled the gelding. Sparrow watched him for a while, then she cautiously approached and placed her hand upon his shoulder. He patted it and swung a leg over the gelding's blanketed back, and pulled himself upright. He was still a little clumsy, but he'd learn.

Morgan walked the gelding out of the aspens and reined to a halt alongside Lone Walker, who paused in mid-chant, in a most uncharacteristic fashion.

"You are leaving, Mor-gan?"

"Yeah. Figure I better before you *dream* up some new trouble to get me into." Morgan eased back and appraised his friend. Their bond ran as deep as blood, maybe deeper.

Lone Walker's hair was braided now, and Sparrow had attached a raven feather to one of the braids and notched it accordingly, to indicate the young warrior was a shaman in his own right.

Lone Walker's features shone bright with new life, though his eyes were tinged with a subtle sadness that time would never completely erase.

It was the same with Morgan. They had both glimpsed a portion of the truth of things, how men are subject to a harsh and irrevocable justice.

"We have walked in a dream together. It has changed us," Lone Walker said. "Where will you go?"

Morgan shrugged and indicated the vast expanse below them with a sweep of his hand.

"You could journey with us. Walk the path with us, into Ever Shadow," Lone Walker said.

"That's your vision, my friend. Maybe I better find my own." Morgan pursed his lips and thought a moment. This good-bye was more difficult than he had imagined it would be. There was only one way to get through it. He started the surefooted gelding down the slope.

"Mor-gan," Lone Walker called after him. "My heart's glad you disobeyed me one last time and followed me into the valley."

Morgan Penmerry lifted his hand without looking back. Lone Walker suddenly remembered the broken-blade cutlass thrust in his beaded belt.

"Mor-gan! Your long knife—?"

Morgan waved again, never looking over his shoulder. He continued downhill until he reached the plain.

"Farewell, my friend," Lone Walker said softly. He raised his hands outward to the sky and sang to the sunlight and the cool autumn breezes off the mountains of Ever Shadow. He sang of the birth of new dreams and new journeys, of sacrifices and friendships. He sang of the Great Circle and the mystery that lies at its heart.

Morgan Penmerry rode directly into the sun until at last his shining silhouette lingered upon the horizon for a final moment before vanishing into the yellow day and the good wind.

> "All-Father,
> It is finished.
> In beauty, it is finished.
> Before me, behind me,
> Beneath my feet, may I
> Find peace.
> Let there be long life and breath—
> And let the end of one song
> Begin another."

TERRY C. JOHNSTON

Winner of the prestigious Western Writer's award, Terry C. Johnston brings you his award-winning saga of mountain men Josiah Paddock and Titus Bass who strive together to meet the challenges of the western wilderness in the 1830's.

The final volume in the trilogy begun with *Carry the Wind* and *Borderlords*, ONE-EYED DREAM is a rich, textured tale of an 1830's trapper and his protegé, told at the height of the American fur trade.

Following a harrowing pursuit by vengeful Arapaho warriors, mountain man Titus "Scratch" Bass and his apprentice Josiah Paddock must travel south to old Taos. But their journey is cut short when they learn they must return to St. Louis…and old enemies.

Look for these books wherever Bantam books are sold, or use this handy coupon for ordering:

DON'T MISS
THESE CURRENT
Bantam Bestsellers

THE
TOTALLY
BREAD
COOKBOOK

THE
TOTALLY
BREAD
COOKBOOK

By Helene Siegel & Karen Gillingham
Illustrated by Carolyn Vibbert

CELESTIAL ARTS
BERKELEY, CALIFORNIA

The Totally Bread Cookbook is produced
by becker&mayer!, Kirkland, Washington.
www.beckermayer.com

Printed in Singapore.

Cover design and illustration: Bob Greisen
Interior design: Susan Hernday
Typesetting: Sheila VanNortwick
Interior illustrations: Carolyn Vibbert

Library of Congress Catalog Card Number:
99-74550

ISBN 0-89087-897-8

Celestial Arts Publishing
P.O. Box 7123
Berkeley, CA 94707
Look for all 30 *Totally* books at your local store!

FOR GRANDPA PHILLIP

CONTENTS

INTRODUCTION

B aking bread at home is more about the voyage than the destination. It's about wearing comfortable clothes, letting a fine dusting of flour settle over your kitchen, and watching the eternal mystery of flour, yeast, and water move to its own rhythm.

The end result is always a gift. The crust may not be quite as crunchy as your favorite store-bought sourdough and the flavorings not as exotic as that artisanal baker down the road. Your homely loaf may be lop-sided and the crumb may be slightly uneven, but if it's homemade, the bread is bound to be loved. And so is the baker.

I know this because I fell in love with my husband when he presented me with a loaf of homemade white bread during our courtship.

I figured any man who stayed at home on a weekend baking bread for me had to be as solid and wholesome as the loaf he presented. Life, of course, turned out to be more complicated than that. But good bread remains a simple and constant pleasure.

In this little volume, most of the breads can be made by hand using mixing bowls and spoons. A few richer doughs call for a heavy-duty mixer, and special equipment may be needed to make such treats as doughnuts and holiday breads. But the focus is on tried-and-true, low-tech yeast breads for the home baker. No bread machines or time-intensive home-made starters are necessary to make tender, golden brioche, a rugged round country loaf, or a fine old-fashioned potato bread. All it takes is flour, water, yeast, and a pinch of this or that for flavor. The rest is magic—and some time in the kitchen.

How to Knead

Kneading by hand is an age-old tension releaser, second only to punching down the dough. To enjoy it fully, you need to work on a surface that is low enough to lean into without standing on your toes. A wooden board on top of a kitchen table is ideal. If you place a damp kitchen towel beneath it, the board will stay still.

The basic kneading method is to fold an outside edge toward you, push away with the heels of your hands, and make a quarter turn in a continuous motion. It's best to start with a lightly floured board (and hands, if necessary) and then add flour, a pinch at a time, as needed. Be patient: the dough will keep changing, and become more pliable, as you work it. A good way to learn is to observe an experienced baker and copy the movements until they come naturally. The typical dough needs about 8 minutes of kneading.

CLASSIC
YEAST
LOAVES

BASIC WHITE BREAD

Once you've tasted homemade white bread, you'll have a better understanding of why it became the symbol of all that is wholesome and good in American food. Nothing beats it for morning toast.

1 package dry yeast
¼ cup warm water
2 cups nonfat milk, warmed
3 tablespoons melted butter
2 teaspoons salt
2 tablespoons sugar
4 to 5 cups unbleached flour, or more

In a large bowl, stir yeast into water until dissolved. Stir in milk, butter, salt, and sugar.

Sprinkle 1 cup flour over mixture, and stir until evenly moistened. Add 3 more cups flour, 1 cup at a time, mixing thoroughly after each addition.

Turn out onto a board sprinkled with half of remaining flour. Knead until smooth and elastic, about 10 minutes, adding more flour as needed to prevent sticking. Transfer to an oiled bowl. Cover with plastic wrap and let rise until doubled, about 2 hours.

Punch down dough. Transfer to lightly floured surface, and knead several times. Divide in half and form each into a loaf. Place in two buttered loaf pans. Cover and let rise in a warm place until almost doubled, about 45 minutes.

Preheat oven to 375 degrees F.

Bake until tops are golden brown and bread sounds hollow when tapped, about 45 minutes. Turn out and cool on rack.

MAKES 2 LOAVES

POTATO BREAD

This crusty yellow loaf gets its extra moistness from a mashed potato in the dough. One cup of leftover mashed potatoes can be substituted.

1 baking potato, peeled and cut into chunks
1 cup 2% milk
3 tablespoons softened butter
1 teaspoon salt
1 tablespoon sugar
1 package dry yeast
⅓ cup warm water
5 cups bread flour
1 egg white beaten with 1 tablespoon water

Place the potato in a pot with enough water to cover. Boil until soft, 20 minutes. Drain, reserving cooking water, and mash the potato.

Scald milk and combine with ½ cup reserved cooking liquid. Place in bowl of electric mixer. Add potato, butter, salt, and sugar. Cool to room temperature.

Combine yeast and warm water, and set aside 10 minutes. When milk mixture has cooled, pour in yeast. Add flour, and knead with dough hook on low speed until smooth, about 8 minutes. Or knead by hand until smooth.

Transfer to a buttered bowl, cover with a towel, and set aside to rise about ½ hour. On a counter, punch down and briefly knead. Divide in half, shape into loaves, and transfer to two buttered loaf pans. Cover and let rise until doubled, about 45 minutes.

Preheat oven to 350 degrees F.

Brush the tops of the loaves with egg wash. Bake about 1 hour, until tops are golden and bread sounds hollow when tapped. Turn out and cool on rack.

MAKES 2 LOAVES

CRACKED WHEAT SUNFLOWER LOAF

For virtuous bakers—a whole grain loaf with sunflower seeds for added crunch and fiber.

  1 package dry yeast
  ¼ cup warm water
  1½ cups warm milk
  3 tablespoons melted butter
  2 tablespoons honey
  1 teaspoon salt
  2½ to 3 cups unbleached flour
  1¼ cups stone-ground whole wheat flour,
    or more
  ½ cup plain sunflower seeds, shelled

In a large bowl, stir yeast into water until dissolved. Stir in milk, 2 tablespoons butter, honey, and salt. Mix in unbleached flour, 1 cup at a time. Cover with a towel, and let stand until smooth, about 30 minutes.

Beat in 1 cup whole wheat flour and the sunflower seeds. Turn out dough onto surface sprinkled with ¼ cup of remaining whole wheat flour. Knead at least 10 minutes or until dough is smooth and elastic, adding more flour as needed to prevent sticking. Transfer to an oiled bowl. Cover with plastic wrap and let rise until doubled, about 1½ hours.

Punch down dough. Transfer to lightly floured surface, and knead several times. Form into loaf, and place in buttered loaf pan. Cover and let rise until almost doubled, about 45 minutes.

Preheat oven to 375 degrees F.

Brush top of loaf with remaining butter, and bake until top is deep golden and bread sounds hollow when tapped, about 45 minutes. Turn out of pan and cool on rack.

MAKES 1 LOAF

JEWISH RYE

The secret of this free-form rye's dark, rich color is the addition of cocoa and molasses. The sandwich bread of choice for deli-quality sandwiches.

2 packages dry yeast
1¾ cups warm water
1½ teaspoons salt
¼ cup molasses
¼ cup unsweetened cocoa powder
1½ cups rye flour
2½ cups unbleached flour, or more
2 tablespoons cornmeal

In a large bowl, stir yeast into water until dissolved. Add salt, molasses, cocoa powder, rye flour, and 1¼ cups unbleached flour. Beat until thoroughly blended. Beat in remaining unbleached flour. Turn out onto lightly floured surface, cover, and let rest 10 minutes.

Knead by hand about 10 minutes or until smooth and elastic, adding more unbleached flour as needed to prevent sticking. Transfer to an oiled bowl. Cover and let rise until doubled, about 1½ hours.

Punch down dough, and shape into round loaf. Sprinkle baking sheet with cornmeal, and top with loaf. Cover and let rise until almost doubled, about 1 hour.

Preheat oven to 350 degrees F.

With a sharp knife or razor blade, slash ½-inch-deep X into the top of the dough. Bake about 1 hour or until bread sounds hollow when tapped.

MAKES 1 LARGE LOAF

PUMPERNICKEL

Pumpernickel is rye bread with a twist.
It's made with darker, coarser rye grain and
contains fragrant caraway seeds.

2 packages dry yeast
½ cup warm water
2 cups warm milk
2 tablespoons dark molasses
2 tablespoons Postum
1 tablespoon caraway seeds
1½ teaspoons salt
3 to 3½ cups unbleached flour, or more
1 cup whole bran cereal
2½ cups dark rye flour
1 egg yolk beaten with 2 tablespoons water,
   for wash

In a large bowl, stir yeast into water until dissolved. Add milk, molasses, Postum, caraway, salt, and 2 cups unbleached flour, and combine thoroughly. Beat well. Beat in bran, remaining unbleached flour, and 2 cups rye flour. Turn out dough onto a surface sprinkled with half of the remaining rye flour.

Knead by hand, gradually adding remaining rye flour. Continue to knead until smooth and elastic, about 10 minutes. Transfer dough to an oiled bowl. Cover and let rise until doubled, about 1 hour.

Punch down dough, and knead several turns. Divide in half, shape each into oblong loaf, and place on uncoated baking sheet. Cover and let rise until puffy, about 30 minutes.

Preheat oven to 350 degrees F.

Brush tops of loaves with egg wash. Bake 30 minutes or until bread sounds hollow when tapped. Cool on rack.

MAKES 2 LOAVES

OATMEAL BRAN BREAD

For those who like their oatmeal toasted in the morning, here is a pretty oat loaf that is excellent for toast or sandwiches.

1 cup plus 2 tablespoons old-fashioned
   rolled oats
¾ cup plus 1 tablespoon oat bran
2 cups boiling water
1 package dry yeast
½ cup warm water
½ cup maple syrup
1½ teaspoons salt
2 tablespoons butter, melted
4½ to 5 cups unbleached flour
2 tablespoons milk, for wash

In the top of a double boiler, combine 1 cup oats and ¾ cup bran. Gradually stir in boiling water. Set over pan of simmering water and cover. Cook until water is absorbed, about 30 minutes. Transfer to a bowl and cool.

In a large bowl, stir yeast into warm water until dissolved. Stir in syrup, salt, and butter. Beat in about 4 cups flour. Turn out dough onto a surface dusted with half of remaining flour, and knead by hand until smooth and elastic, about 10 minutes, adding more flour as needed. Transfer to an oiled bowl. Cover and let rise until doubled, about 2 hours.

Coat two loaf pans with butter, then sprinkle each with 1 tablespoon remaining oat bran.

Punch down dough. Knead a few turns. Divide in half, shape into two loaves, and place in prepared pans. Cover and let rise until almost doubled, about 45 minutes.

Preheat oven to 400 degrees F.

Brush tops of loaves with milk and sprinkle with remaining oats. Bake 40 minutes or until bread sounds hollow when tapped. Turn out onto rack to cool.

MAKES 2 LOAVES

RUSTIC COUNTRY LOAF

This free-form round loaf develops a crackly brown crust similar to sourdough.

1 package dry yeast
2½ cups warm water
4 teaspoons salt
6 to 6½ cups unbleached flour, or more
2 tablespoons cornmeal
1 egg white beaten with 1 tablespoon water, for egg wash

In a large bowl, stir yeast into water until dissolved. Add salt and beat in 5 cups flour until well blended. Beat in 1½ to 2 cups more flour, until dough is manageable.

Turn dough out onto surface sprinkled with half of remaining flour and knead by hand 1 to 2 minutes. Let rest 10 minutes, then continue kneading until smooth and elastic, about 10 minutes, adding more flour as needed. Transfer to an oiled bowl. Cover with plastic wrap, and let rise until doubled, about 2 hours.

Punch down dough. Transfer to floured surface, and knead several times. Divide in half and form each into a round loaf. Place on a large baking sheet sprinkled with cornmeal. Using a mister, spray lightly with water. Cover loaves loosely with a clean towel, and let rise 45 minutes.

Preheat oven to 450 degrees F.

Use a sharp knife to cut large, ½-inch-deep X or three parallel lines in tops of loaves. Brush with egg wash.

Bake 15 minutes. Reduce oven temperature to 375 degrees F, lightly spray with water, and bake until tops are deep golden, about 30 minutes longer, spraying again halfway through. Transfer to rack to cool.

MAKES 2 LOAVES

ENGLISH MUFFIN TOASTING BREAD

Here is a great puffy white bread to have in your repertoire for special weekend breakfasts. With only one rising, it's a very quick yeast bread.

   butter for coating
   cornmeal for dusting
   5½ to 6 cups unbleached flour, or more
   2 packages dry yeast
   1 tablespoon sugar
   2 teaspoons salt
   ¼ teaspoon baking soda
   2 cups milk
   ½ cup water

Butter two loaf pans and dust with cornmeal.

In a large bowl, combine 3 cups flour, yeast, sugar, salt, and soda.

Combine milk and water in medium saucepan, and heat over a low flame until small bubbles form around edges. Add to dry ingredients, stirring until a stiff dough forms. Divide in half, shape into loaves, and place in prepared pans. Cover and let rise 45 minutes.

Preheat oven to 400 degrees F.

Bake 45 minutes or until tops are deep golden and bread sounds hollow when tapped. Turn out and cool on rack.

MAKES 2 LOAVES

"Bread is like dresses, hats, and shoes—in other words, essential!"
— *Emily Post*

A Short History of White Bread

Before automated sifters were invented circa 1800, wheat bran had to be separated by hand, making white wheat very expensive—a gourmet treat for the upper classes. By the turn of the next century, however, when white flour production was automated and everyone could afford it, white bread was embraced, in part because of its former elevated status. Now, at the turn of the millennium, roughhewn artisanal breads are in vogue, while white bread remains a hot seller.

WORLDLY
BREADS

BRIOCHE

Bakeshop-quality brioche is easy to make at home, with the help of a heavy-duty mixer. This rich, tender egg bread depends on lots of butter and blending for its delicate texture.

1 package dry yeast
¼ cup warm water
1 tablespoon sugar
4 eggs
1 teaspoon salt
2 cups unbleached flour
12 tablespoons (1½ sticks) butter, slightly
  softened
1 egg beaten with 1 tablespoon water

Stir together yeast, water, and sugar. Let stand 10 minutes.

In the bowl of an electric mixer, combine eggs, salt, yeast mixture, and flour. Beat with paddle at low speed about 2 minutes. Increase speed to medium, and mix about 5 minutes longer, until dough is stringy.

With machine running, add butter one tablespoon at a time, until dough is smooth, wet, and sticky. Transfer dough to a buttered bowl, cover with buttered plastic wrap, and let rise 1½ hours. Turn out, punch down, return to bowl, cover, and let rise in the refrigerator 12 hours or overnight.

On a generously floured board, turn out dough and with a dough scraper, divide into eight pieces. Gently and briefly knead each to form a smooth ball. Roll between your palms to form a cylinder and place each in a well-buttered muffin pan cup. Cover with plastic wrap, and let rise until doubled, about 1 to 1½ hours.

Preheat oven to 375 degrees F.

Gently brush tops of loaves with egg wash. Bake about 25 minutes, until tops are golden. Turn out, and cool on a rack.

MAKES 8 BRIOCHE

BAGUETTES

Purists might argue that these long, thin French loaves are best left to professionals, but when there's no bakery in the vicinity, grab your plant mister and give these a try.

1 package dry yeast
2 cups warm water
2 tablespoons melted butter
1½ tablespoons sugar
2 teaspoons salt
6 to 6½ cups unbleached flour, or more
1 egg white beaten with 1 tablespoon water,
    for egg wash

In a large bowl, dissolve yeast in water. Stir in butter, sugar, and salt. Beat in about 5 cups flour to form stiff dough. Turn out dough onto a surface sprinkled with half of remaining flour. Knead by hand until smooth and elastic, about 10 minutes, adding more flour as needed. Transfer to an oiled bowl.

Cover with plastic wrap, and let rise in a warm place until doubled, about 1½ hours.

Coat a large baking sheet with butter or spray.

Punch down dough, and divide into three pieces. Shape each into a long, thin loaf by rolling into a smooth log about 10 inches long. With your palms on the center of loaf, quickly roll back and forth, gently sliding hands from center to ends until about 15 inches long, or whatever your oven will accommodate.

Place loaves on a prepared baking sheet. Using a mister, spray lightly with water. Cover loaves loosely with a towel, and let rise until puffy, about 20 minutes.

Preheat oven to 375 degrees F.

Brush loaves with egg wash. Use a sharp knife to cut three ½-inch-deep diagonal slashes along each loaf. Bake 40 minutes or until loaves are deep golden, misting every 10 minutes. Cool on wire racks.

MAKES 3 BAGUETTES

CROISSANTS

These classic flaky French pastries are a good choice for a snowed-in winter weekend. Bring out your best jam and butter as an accompaniment.

1 package dry yeast
¼ cup warm water
¾ cup warm milk
4 teaspoons sugar
½ teaspoon salt
2½ to 3 cups unbleached flour, or more
2 sticks butter, room temperature
1 egg yolk beaten with 1 tablespoon milk

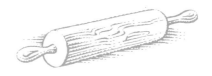

In a large bowl, dissolve yeast in water. Stir in milk, sugar, and salt. Beat in about 2 cups flour. Turn out dough onto surface dusted with ½ cup flour, and knead by hand until smooth and elastic, about 10 minutes, adding more flour as needed to prevent sticking. Shape into round. Transfer dough to an oiled bowl. Cover and let rise until doubled, about 2 hours.

Punch down dough, and knead a few times on floured surface. Roll dough out to ¼-inch-thick rectangle, about 14 x 10 inches. Place horizontally on counter. Cut butter into thick slices, and arrange evenly over center third of dough. Fold each side over butter to enclose, pressing ends to seal. Roll out dough again until rectangle is about ⅜-inch thick. (If butter becomes too soft, refrigerate briefly as needed.) Fold dough in thirds, roll, and fold again, dusting with flour as needed. Wrap in plastic and chill ½ hour.

Repeat rolling and folding twice, and chill ½ hour.

Roll dough into a ¼-inch-thick rectangle, about 24 x 7 inches. Cut into triangles about 6 inches at base and eight inches on two other sides. Starting from 6-inch side, roll up triangles, pinching the tips to seal and shaping into crescents. Reroll scraps, if necessary, and cut as above for eight croissants. Place about 1 inch apart on ungreased baking sheet. Cover and let rise in a warm place until doubled, about 2 hours.

Preheat oven to 375 degrees F.

Brush tops lightly with egg yolk mixture. Bake 25 minutes, or until deep golden brown. Serve warm.

MAKES 8 CROISSANTS

"I do like a bit of butter to my bread."
—A.A. Milne from Winnie the Pooh

CURRANT–WALNUT BAGUETTES

Serve thin slices of this chewy brown baguette at your next cheese tasting for an authentic French touch. A heavy-duty mixer really comes in handy with such a dense dough.

1 package dry yeast
1½ tablespoons honey
1¼ cups warm water
1¼ cups bread flour, or more
1¼ cups whole wheat flour, or more
1 teaspoon salt
¾ cup roughly chopped walnuts, toasted
½ cup currants
½ cup raisins
butter for coating bowl and baking sheet
1 egg, beaten, for glaze

Stir the yeast and honey in ¼ cup warm water, and let stand till foamy, 10 minutes.

In the bowl of an electric mixer, combine the flours, salt, and walnuts. Mix with a fork. While stirring at low speed with the paddle, pour in the water-yeast mixture. Add the remaining water, and slowly mix until the dough starts to hold a shape. Switch to the dough hook, and knead at low speed, adding the currants and raisins a handful at a time, until dough is smooth, about 6 minutes.

Transfer to a lightly floured board, and knead by hand about 3 minutes. Transfer the dough ball to a butter-coated bowl. Cover with a damp towel, and let rise until doubled, 1 to 1½ hours.

Punch down dough and turn out onto a lightly floured board. Divide in half. Roll out each part to a 6- x 15-inch sheet. Roll the sheets width-wise, pinching the ends and edges to seal. Transfer, seam-side down, to a buttered baking sheet. Cover with a damp towel, and let rise until doubled again, about 1 hour.

Preheat oven to 425 degrees F.

Brush the loaves with the beaten egg, and slash each a few times along the diagonal. Bake 30 to 40 minutes, until well browned. Cool on a rack.

MAKES 2 BAGUETTES

CHALLAH

This traditional braided Jewish egg bread is served at Sabbath meals all over the world. It also makes delicious sandwich bread and toast.

1½ cups warm water
3 tablespoons sugar
2 packages dry yeast
6 to 6½ cups all-purpose flour
2 teaspoons salt
⅓ cup vegetable shortening
3 eggs
cornmeal for sprinkling
1 egg yolk beaten with 1 tablespoon water,
    for glaze
poppy or sesame seeds, for sprinkling
    (optional)

In a liquid measuring cup, stir together ½ cup of the water, the sugar, and the yeast. Set aside to foam.

In the bowl of an electric mixer, place 4 cups of the flour, the salt, and shortening. Mix with paddle at low speed to form crumbly mixture. Add the eggs, the yeast mixture, 2 additional cups flour, and the remaining cup water. Mix to combine, then switch to the dough hook.

Knead at low speed, sprinkling in remaining flour until dough is smooth and elastic, 5 to 10 minutes. Remove and knead by hand on an unfloured counter for about 1 minute. Transfer to a butter-coated bowl, cover with plastic wrap, and let rise until doubled, 1 to 2 hours.

Punch down dough, divide in half, and lightly knead each into a ball. Let rest 10 minutes. Reserve one in the refrigerator, and divide the other into three equal pieces for braiding.

Roll each third into a 9-inch-long rope. Arrange the three ropes alongside each other on the counter, and pinch together the ends at the top to seal. Braid the ropes, pinching and tucking the ends together at the bottom and top. Repeat with second dough ball, and place both on a baking sheet sprinkled with cornmeal. Cover and let rest 45 minutes.

Preheat oven to 375 degrees F.

Brush loaves with egg wash, being careful not to touch the pan, and then sprinkle with seeds, if desired.

Bake about 45 minutes, until tops are golden and bread sounds hollow when tapped. Cool on racks.

MAKES 2 LOAVES

"Bread baking is not as exacting as other kinds of baking, yet the sense of satisfaction and pleasure is enough to make you a devoted bread baker for life."
—Marion Cunningham from
The Fannie Farmer Baking Book

PARMESAN BREAD

Strongly flavored Parmesan cheese makes a terrific bread to serve at a meal with other Italian flavors or a good vegetable soup.

1 cup warm water
1 package dry yeast
2 eggs
2 tablespoons olive oil
3½ cups unbleached flour
2 teaspoons salt
1 cup grated Parmesan cheese
1 egg white, beaten, for egg wash

Stir together the water and yeast. Let sit until foamy, 10 minutes.

In the bowl of an electric mixer, combine eggs, oil, and yeast-water mixture. Mix with paddle. Add flour, salt, and Parmesan, and slowly mix until combined. Switch to the dough hook and knead until smooth and elastic, about 5 minutes. Transfer to an oil-coated bowl, cover with a towel, and let sit until doubled, about 2 hours.

Punch down the dough, briefly knead, and divide in half. Shape each into a loaf and place in oil-coated loaf pans. Cover and let rise until doubled, about 1 hour.

Preheat oven to 425 degrees F.

Brush the loaves with egg wash and slash each with a sharp knife three times across the width of the loaf. Bake about 45 minutes, or until hollow when tapped. Cool on rack.

MAKES 2 LOAVES

NEW YORK BAGELS

This authentic chewy bagel recipe comes from retired Los Angeles baker Izzy Cohen.

2 cups cool water
3 tablespoons sugar
1½ tablespoons salt
2 tablespoons barley malt syrup (available at natural food stores)
7 cups bread flour, or more
1½ tablespoons dry milk
1½ tablespoons vital wheat gluten
5 teaspoons dry yeast
cornmeal for dusting

In the bowl of a heavy-duty electric mixer with dough hook, combine water, sugar, salt, and malt syrup. In a separate bowl, combine flour, dry milk, gluten, and dry yeast. Add to the liquid mixture all at once, and knead at low speed until dough clears the sides of the bowl. Continue kneading at low speed, until the dough is smooth, about 5 minutes. (If sticky, sprinkle in a bit more flour.)

Transfer to a board, cover with plastic wrap, and let rise 10 minutes. (Do not be concerned with a few wrinkles in the dough.)

With a dough blade or sharp knife, divide the dough into 16 pieces. On an unfloured board, knead each into a smooth ball. First flatten with the palm of your hand, and then pull the edges into the center, bearing down and pushing away with the heel of your hand with each quarter turn. Cover with a towel and let rest 5 minutes.

Have ready a cardboard sheet or wooden board lightly dusted with cornmeal. To make the holes, pick up each ball, and press a hole through the center with an index finger. Then push your other index finger through the opposing side, and pull and stretch the hole by running your fingers around each other, enlarging it to 1½ to 2 inches. Place on coated sheets, cover with a towel, and let rise 1½ hours, until not quite doubled.

Meanwhile, bring a large pot of water to a boil. Preheat oven to 425 degrees F and have ready two sheet pans lined with parchment paper. (If you have baking or pizza tiles, place on the baking rack.)

Being careful not to crowd the pot, drop in three or four bagels at a time. (They should immediately rise to the surface.) Boil about 20 seconds, dunking and turning with a spoon to moisten evenly. Immediately transfer with a slotted spoon to a large strainer, being careful not to stack, and shake off excess liquid. If adding toppings, dip drained bagels in bowls of seeds or spices. Transfer to a lined baking sheet.

Bake 15 to 20 minutes, turning once, until golden and crisp all over. Cool on racks and store.

MAKES 16 THREE-OUNCE BAGELS

ITALIAN PIZZA ROLLS

Use this dough to make six individual pizzas or hearty, rustic rolls. Use for sandwiches of fresh mozzarella, basil, and tomato, or as a substantial morning roll.

1½ cups warm water
1 package dry yeast
1 tablespoon sugar
3½ cups unbleached flour
½ cup semolina *or* cornmeal
1 tablespoon salt
3 tablespoons olive oil
olive oil for drizzling
coarse salt, cracked black pepper, fennel seed

Fill a measuring cup with ½ cup warm water. Stir in the yeast and sugar.

Combine flour, semolina or cornmeal, and salt in a large mixing bowl. Stir in olive oil. Stir in the yeast mixture, then slowly add remaining water until stiff and sticky.

Turn onto a lightly floured board, and knead until smooth, moist, and elastic, about 10 minutes. Transfer to an oiled bowl, cover with a damp towel, and let rise in a warm place until doubled, 1 to 2 hours.

Punch down and turn out onto a lightly floured board. Cut into six pieces for rolls. Gently knead each into ball.

Preheat oven to 425 degrees F with pizza stone in place.

Brush dough balls with olive oil and sprinkle with toppings. Place on pizza stone or uncoated baking sheet. Bake about 20 minutes, until golden and center sounds hollow when tapped with a finger. Cool slightly and serve.

MAKES 6 ROLLS

CORN TORTILLAS

Homemade tortillas take no time at all, and they are infinitely more satisfying than the store-bought kind.

> 1 cup Quaker Oats masa harina
> ½ cup warm water

Preheat a cast-iron skillet over high heat for 15 minutes.

Combine the masa and water in a mixing bowl, and mix with a wooden spoon. Press by hand to form a smooth dough ball. (Add more water if dry, more masa if too moist.) Divide into eight pieces and roll each in moistened palms to form small balls. Set aside, and cover with plastic wrap.

When skillet is hot, start pressing out tortillas one at a time. Line the bottom of the tortilla press with a plastic freezer bag. Place a slightly flattened dough ball on top. Cover the dough with another plastic bag, and press the handle down to flatten. Lift the cover, peel away the top bag, and flip the tortilla, dough-side down, onto the palm of your other hand. Peel off the plastic, and slap the tortilla onto the hot pan.

Cook about 20 seconds, until the edges begin to darken. Turn with a spatula and cook about 40 seconds longer, pressing with the spatula so the tortilla puffs slightly. Flip and cook 10 seconds longer. Stack on a towel and wrap to keep warm. To reheat, wrap in foil and warm 10 minutes in a 350-degrees-F oven.

MAKES 8 FOUR-INCH TORTILLAS

IRISH SODA BREAD

Eileen Wohl and her grandmother Mary Frances Regan Lynch contributed this wonderful Irish quickbread recipe. It is perfect served plain, wrapped in a napkin, hot from the oven, or sliced and toasted the next day with some melted butter.

1⅔ cups milk
½ stick butter, melted
1 egg, beaten
1 cup golden raisins
⅛ teaspoon vinegar
4 cups unbleached flour
¼ cup sugar
2 teaspoons baking powder
1 teaspoon baking soda
1 teaspoon salt
2 tablespoons caraway seeds
flour for dusting

Preheat oven to 375 degrees F. Grease a 9-inch round cake pan or cast-iron skillet.

In a large bowl, whisk together milk, butter, egg, raisins, and vinegar. In another bowl, combine remaining ingredients. Add dry mixture to liquid, and stir until evenly moistened. Knead on floured board about ten times.

Place dough in a prepared pan, and dust top with a handful of flour. Bake 50 minutes, until bread sounds hollow when tapped. Remove from pan, and cool on rack.

MAKES 1 LARGE LOAF

"The world is divided into two camps: those who can live happily on bread alone and those who also need vegetables, meat, and dairy products."
—*Jeffrey Steingarten from*
The Man Who Ate Everything

CHINESE STEAMED BUNS

Astound your guests at your next dim sum buffet with these dense, chewy little buns. Consider adding minced Chinese barbecued pork to the scallions for total bliss.

1 recipe "Basic White Bread" (see page 12)
1 tablespoon vegetable oil
2 teaspoons dark sesame oil
1 cup thinly sliced green onion
12 (3-inch) waxed paper squares

Prepare "Basic White Bread" according to directions through first rising. Punch down dough and divide in half.

On a floured surface, roll one piece of dough into an 18- x 9-inch rectangle. (Repeat instructions with second half or store in freezer.)

In a small skillet, heat the oils. Sauté green onion just until soft. Cool slightly, then spread over dough rectangle. Starting at the long side, roll dough up and pinch seam to seal. Cut into twelve equal slices, crosswise, and place each on a waxed paper square. Arrange in the top of a steamer or on a plate. Cover and let rise until puffy, about 45 minutes.

Bring about 1 inch of water to a simmer in the bottom of steamer or a pan large enough to hold plate. Set buns over simmering water, cover, and steam 25 minutes. Serve warm.

MAKES 12 BUNS

PAN DULCE

*For full enjoyment, serve these rich, smooth
sugar-coated egg buns with steaming cups of
café con leché and a selection of fresh juices at
your next Mexican brunch.*

  1 cup milk
  6 tablespoons butter
  1 package dry yeast
  ¾ teaspoon salt
  ½ cup sugar
  4½ to 5 cups unbleached flour
  2 eggs, lightly beaten
  Topping (see page 58)
  1 egg beaten with 2 tablespoons milk

In a saucepan, combine milk and butter.
Set over low heat and cook just until butter
is melted.

  In the large bowl of a heavy-duty electric
mixer, combine yeast, salt, sugar, and 2 cups

flour. Add warm milk mixture, and beat with paddle at medium speed, 2 minutes. Slowly stir in eggs and 1 cup additional flour. Beat on high for 2 minutes. Gradually beat in enough remaining flour to form stiff dough. Switch to dough hook and knead on medium until smooth and elastic, about 6 minutes, adding flour as needed to prevent sticking. Transfer dough to an oiled bowl. Cover and let rise until doubled, about 1½ hours.

Prepare Topping and set aside. Grease baking sheet.

Punch down dough, and knead several times. Divide dough into twelve pieces and shape each into 3-inch round, flat buns. Place on prepared baking sheet. Spread equal amounts of Topping over each bun, and press lightly into dough. Use a sharp blade to score tops ½-inch deep to create a grid of 1-inch squares. Loosely cover, and let rise until almost doubled, about 45 minutes.

Preheat oven to 400 degrees F.

Bake 15 to 20 minutes or until topping is pale golden. Transfer to a wire rack to cool.

MAKES 12 BUNS

TOPPING

1 stick butter
½ cup sugar
1 egg yolk
1 teaspoon vanilla
⅔ cup flour

In medium bowl, cream butter and sugar. Add egg yolk and vanilla and blend. Stir in flour, and mix well.

QUICK
BREADS

BANANA BREAD

Banana bread is a great way to get reluctant eaters to eat their bananas. This is a good one for the first-time bread baker with overripe bananas in the house.

2 cups unbleached flour
1 tablespoon baking powder
½ teaspoon salt
1 stick butter, softened
¾ cup brown sugar
2 eggs
1½ teaspoons vanilla
1½ cups mashed ripe bananas (about 3)
½ cup chopped walnuts, toasted
¼ cup semisweet chocolate chips

Preheat oven to 350 degrees F. Grease a loaf pan.

In a bowl, combine flour, baking powder, and salt.

In another bowl, cream butter and sugar until smooth and creamy. Beat in eggs one at a time. Add vanilla and mashed bananas, and beat until combined.

Stir dry ingredients into banana mixture just until flour disappears. Lightly stir in nuts and chocolate chips. Pour batter into pan, smoothing the top. Bake 50 to 60 minutes, until toothpick comes out clean. Cool on rack.

MAKES 1 LOAF

"Bread is an emotive substance. Shortage of it has traditionally been a sign of dangerous irritation among those prone to riot."
—Daily Telegraph, *1978*

SKILLET CORN BREAD

Here is the classic accompaniment to homemade chili or Southern fried chicken.

1 cup yellow cornmeal
1 cup flour
1 teaspoon baking powder
1½ teaspoons salt
½ stick butter, melted
2 eggs
1 cup milk
¾ cup grated cheddar cheese
½ cup corn kernels

Preheat oven to 425 degrees F. Coat a 9-inch cast-iron skillet with butter and place in oven.

Combine cornmeal, flour, baking powder, and salt in a large mixing bowl. Mix with fork.

In another bowl, whisk together melted butter, eggs, and milk. Add to dry ingredients and mix with wooden spoon. Stir in cheese and corn to combine.

Carefully remove the hot pan from oven.
Pour batter into the pan, swirling to coat evenly.
Bake about 25 minutes, until a toothpick
inserted in center comes out clean. Cut into
wedges to serve.

SERVES 8, MAKES 1 LOAF

"But it takes a lot of time. If you can find that, the
rest is easy. And if you cannot rightly find it, make
it, for there is no chiropractic treatment, no Yoga
exercise, no hour of meditation. . .that will leave you
emptier of bad thoughts than this homely ceremony
of baking bread."

—M.F.K. Fisher from How to Cook a Wolf

LEMON PECAN TEA BREAD

Substitute orange juice and zest (and a touch of Grand Marnier in place of the vanilla) if you prefer orange bread.

1 stick butter, softened
1 cup sugar
2 eggs, lightly beaten
1½ cups unbleached flour
½ teaspoon baking powder
½ teaspoon baking soda
½ teaspoon salt
½ teaspoon vanilla
2½ teaspoons grated lemon zest
½ cup plus 1 tablespoon lemon juice
¾ cup finely chopped pecans
¾ cup confectioners' sugar
pecan halves, for decorating

Preheat oven to 350 degrees F. Butter and flour a loaf pan.

Beat butter in a large mixing bowl until smooth. Gradually add sugar, beating until light. Beat in eggs.

In another bowl, mix together flour, baking powder, baking soda, and salt. Add half of flour mixture to butter mixture, and gently beat until blended.

Combine vanilla, 2 teaspoons lemon zest, and ½ cup juice. Beat half of liquid mixture into batter. Add remaining dry ingredients and liquid, and gently beat until smooth. Stir in chopped nuts.

Pour into prepared pan. Bake about 45 minutes or until a toothpick inserted in center comes out clean. Cool in the pan on a rack 10 minutes, then turn out bread and cool completely.

In small bowl, combine confectioners' sugar with remaining tablespoon lemon juice and ½ teaspoon zest. Stir until smooth. Pour over cooled loaf. Decorate top with pecan halves.

MAKES 1 LOAF

SPOON BREAD

Served as an accompaniment, this traditional deep-dish cornmeal casserole from the South is eaten with a spoon.

1½ cups cornmeal
1 teaspoon baking powder
1 teaspoon baking soda
1 teaspoon salt
2 eggs, lightly beaten
2½ cups buttermilk
2 tablespoons butter
¾ cup milk

Preheat oven to 450 degrees F.

In a large bowl, mix cornmeal, baking powder, baking soda, and salt. Stir in eggs and buttermilk. Place butter in 2-quart casserole and set in oven. When butter is melted, pour batter into casserole. Pour milk over top, but do not stir.

Bake 35 minutes or until top is deep golden brown. Let stand 10 minutes before serving.

SERVES 6

WHEAT CURRANT SCONES

If you haven't tried making scones before, you'll be pleasantly surprised at the ease with which these satisfying tea and breakfast treats can be tossed together.

1½ cups unbleached flour
1½ cups whole wheat flour
1 tablespoon baking powder
1 teaspoon baking soda
¼ cup sugar
¼ teaspoon salt
1 stick butter, cold and cut in 1¼-inch slices
1 cup currants or raisins
1 cup buttermilk
1 egg, beaten, for glaze

Preheat oven to 450 degrees F.

In a large bowl, combine white and wheat flours, baking powder, baking soda, sugar, and salt. Mix with a fork. Add cut-up butter, and blend with fingertips or pastry blender until butter is evenly dispersed and mixture resembles coarse meal. Add currants or raisins and buttermilk, and stir just until evenly moistened.

Turn out onto a floured board and gently knead until shaggy, dry dough forms. Cut in half, and pat each piece into a disk. The key is not to over handle the dough, which makes it tough. Lightly roll each into 6-inch circle. Transfer to an uncoated baking sheet and brush tops with beaten egg. Score each into six wedges. Bake 20 minutes, until tops are brown. Cool on racks and serve.

MAKES 12 SCONES

SWEET TREATS
AND
NOVELTIES

BUTTERMILK DOUGHNUTS

Now that doughnuts are in, why not go back to the source and fry up an old-fashioned batch for the family? All it takes is hot cocoa and coffee to round out the menu.

1 cup buttermilk
¾ cup sugar
½ teaspoon ground nutmeg
2 eggs
2 tablespoons melted butter
2½ to 3 cups self-rising flour
oil for deep-frying
2 tablespoons ground cinnamon

In a large bowl, combine buttermilk, ½ cup of the sugar, nutmeg, eggs, and butter. Beat in enough flour for dough to hold together. Let rest 10 minutes.

Turn dough out onto a floured board and knead 5 minutes. Roll out to a circle ½-inch thick. Cut out with floured 3-inch doughnut cutter, setting centers aside. Arrange doughnuts and centers on lightly floured baking sheet or board. Let rest 5 minutes.

Heat about 4 inches oil in a fryer or other deep pan to 375 degrees F. Fry doughnuts, a few at a time, 2 to 3 minutes, turning once. Fry centers separately about 1 minute. Drain on paper towels. Mix remaining sugar and cinnamon and sprinkle over hot doughnuts.

MAKES ABOUT 1 DOZEN DOUGHNUTS AND HOLES

PECAN STICKY BUNS

These brown sticky buns could definitely get you in trouble with the nutrition police.

> 1 recipe "Basic White Bread" (see page 12)
> 6 tablespoons melted butter
> 1 cup packed brown sugar
> 3 tablespoons light corn syrup
> 1 cup roughly chopped pecans
> 1 tablespoon ground cinnamon

Prepare "Basic White Bread" through the first rising. Punch down dough, divide in two, and freeze half for another use.

In 13- x 9-inch baking pan, combine ¼ cup melted butter, ⅔ cup brown sugar, and corn syrup. Spread evenly over pan bottom, then sprinkle evenly with pecans.

On a floured surface, roll dough into an 18- x 9-inch rectangle. Spread with remaining melted butter, and sprinkle evenly with remaining sugar and cinnamon. Starting on long side, roll up, pinching seam to seal. Cut crosswise into twelve slices. Arrange slices, cut-side down, in single layer in a prepared pan. Cover and let rise until almost doubled, about 1 hour.

Preheat oven to 375 degrees F.

Bake 25 minutes or until tops are well browned. Invert pan onto a large tray. Wait a few minutes, then lift pan, allowing syrup to flow over buns. Serve warm.

MAKES 12 BUNS

GIANT CINNAMON BUNS

Be warned when baking these gloriously oversized sugary buns. The scent of cinnamon buns baking in the oven has been known to play havoc with the male libido.

1 recipe "Basic White Bread" (see page 12)
¼ cup melted butter
1 cup sugar
2 tablespoons cinnamon
1 cup confectioners' sugar
¼ teaspoon vanilla
1 tablespoon milk or water

Prepare "Basic White Bread" through the first rising.

Grease 13- x 9-inch pan.

Punch down dough. On a floured surface, roll out dough to an 18- x 9-inch rectangle. Brush with melted butter. Mix sugar and cinnamon, and sprinkle evenly over butter. Starting at 9-inch side, roll dough up, pinching seam to seal. Cut crosswise into six equal slices. Arrange slices in single layer in a prepared pan. Cover and let rise in a warm place until almost doubled, about 1½ hours.

Preheat oven to 350 degrees F.

In a small bowl, mix confectioners' sugar, vanilla, and milk or water.

Bake buns 30 to 35 minutes or until deep golden. Turn out, transfer to wire rack, and drizzle with sugar mixture. Serve warm.

MAKES 6 LARGE BUNS

"The history of man from the beginning has been the history of his struggle for his daily bread."
—*Josue de Castro from* Waverly Root's Food

SOFT PRETZELS

These soft, crusty, salted pretzels are a terrific treat for a Halloween or Oktoberfest gathering.

1 package dry yeast
1½ cups warm water
4 teaspoons sugar
¾ teaspoon salt
3½ to 4 cups unbleached flour
3 tablespoons baking soda
coarse salt

In a large bowl, stir yeast into water until dissolved. Stir in 1 teaspoon sugar and salt.

Add 2 cups flour and beat until well blended. Stir in 1½ cups additional flour. Turn dough out onto a surface dusted with half of remaining flour. Knead by hand until smooth and elastic, about 10 minutes, adding more flour as needed. Transfer dough to an oiled bowl, cover with plastic wrap, and let rise until doubled, about 1½ hours.

Punch down dough and cut into twelve pieces. Roll each to form a 16-inch rope. Form each into a pretzel shape by first curving into a horseshoe shape with ends pointing toward you. Twist ends around each other, then lift them away from you and rest them on top of the horseshoe loop. Transfer to a floured board, cover, and let rise in a warm place for 30 minutes.

Line a large baking sheet with parchment paper. Preheat oven to 425 degrees F.

In 9-inch stainless steel or enameled skillet, bring to a simmer 1 quart of water with remaining sugar and baking soda. Slip three pretzels at a time into water and simmer 20 seconds. Using a skimmer or large slotted spatula, carefully turn pretzels over, and simmer 20 seconds longer. Carefully remove from water and place on a prepared baking sheet. Sprinkle with coarse salt to taste. Repeat with remaining pretzels, three at a time.

Bake pretzels in the center of the oven 15 minutes, or until well browned. Cool just until warm and serve, or cool completely and store in a plastic bag.

MAKES 12 PRETZELS

KAISER ROLLS

These flat, brown rolls topped with poppy seeds are perfect for sandwiches, or simply spread with butter for breakfast.

3½ to 4 cups unbleached flour
1 package dry yeast
1 tablespoon sugar
2 teaspoons salt
1 cup hot water
1 egg
1 egg white
1 tablespoon shortening, melted and cooled
poppy seeds for sprinkling

In a large bowl, combine 1 cup flour, yeast, sugar, and salt. Add hot water and beat to form a smooth batter. Beat in egg, egg white, and shortening. Gradually add enough remaining flour to form stiff dough.

Turn dough out onto a surface dusted with some of remaining flour. Knead ten minutes, or until smooth and elastic, adding more flour as needed. Transfer dough to an oiled bowl. Cover and let rise until doubled, about 1½ hours.

Punch down dough. Knead several times, then roll into 12-inch rope. Cut into ten equal pieces. With your cupped palm, shape each piece into smooth rounds. Let rest 5 minutes. With a rolling pin or your hand, flatten each roll to ¾-inch thickness. Dust lightly with flour. To shape, use a sharp knife or razor blade to make 5½-inch-deep curved cuts extending from the center of each roll.

Sprinkle baking sheet generously with poppy seeds, and arrange rolls facedown over seeds. Cover and let rise in a warm place until almost doubled, about 45 minutes.

Preheat oven to 400 degrees F.

Carefully turn rolls right-side up on a baking sheet. Place a pan of hot water under oven shelf. Bake rolls 20 to 25 minutes, until hollow-sounding when tapped. Transfer to wire rack to cool. Serve warm or cooled.

MAKES 10 ROLLS

"I am going to learn how to bake bread tomorrow. So you may imagine me with my sleeves rolled up, mixing flour, milk, saleratus, etc., with a deal of grace. I advise that if you don't know how to make the staff of life to learn with dispatch."
        —*Emily Dickinson*

HOT DOG AND BURGER BUNS

Once you've mastered the "Basic White Bread" recipe, homemade burger and hot dog buns are a wonderful option.

1 recipe "Basic White Bread" (see page 12)
flour, for dusting

Prepare "Basic White Bread" through first rising.

Punch down dough. Knead several turns. Divide into twelve equal pieces. Let rest 5 minutes.

For burger buns, form each piece of dough into a round by cupping in your palm and rolling dough on a lightly floured surface until smooth. Place smooth-side up on greased baking sheet, and flatten to 4-inch diameter with your hands or a rolling pin.

For hot dog buns, roll each piece into approximately 7-inch long cylinder. Place on a baking sheet, and flatten slightly with your hands or a rolling pin.

Cover and let rise until almost doubled, about 45 minutes.

Preheat oven to 350 degrees F.

Bake 20 minutes or until golden. Transfer to a wire rack to cool. Slice in half horizontally.

MAKES 12 BUNS

"Truly good white bread satisfies, I think, like no other loaf. It is the one thing we eat that has been wholly shaped to comfort human hunger."
　　　—John Thorne from Outlaw Cook

Cooling Down and Storing

To test bread for doneness, tap the top with your knuckles and listen for a hollow sound. Also look for golden brown tops and, if the pans are glass, well-browned sides and bottom. Bread should be cooled out of the pan to avoid sogginess. Just invert to remove, and rest the loaf on a rack until thoroughly cooled. Bread can be stored in a bag at room temperature, wrapped in foil for the freezer, or better yet, eaten immediately with room-temperature butter. Frozen bread can be reheated, out of its wrapper, in a 350-degrees-F oven for 20 to 30 minutes.

HOLIDAY
SPECIALS

GREEK EASTER BRAID

Place this beautiful round braid on a buffet table or use as a centerpiece for Easter Sunday brunch.

½ cup milk
½ stick butter
¼ cup sugar
½ teaspoon salt
2 to 2½ cups unbleached flour, or more
1 package dry yeast
2 eggs, lightly beaten
1 teaspoon vanilla
grated zest of 1 small lemon
6 hard-cooked eggs, dyed
1 egg yolk beaten with 1 tablespoon water

In a saucepan, combine milk, butter, sugar, and salt. Set over low heat and cook until butter melts. Remove from heat.

In the large bowl of an electric mixer, combine 1 cup flour with yeast. Add warm milk mixture, eggs, vanilla, and lemon zest. Use paddle to beat on low speed, scraping bowl, until evenly moistened. Turn up to high speed, and beat 3 minutes longer. By hand with a spoon, beat in enough remaining flour to make a stiff dough.

With the dough hook of an electric mixer, knead at medium speed until smooth and elastic, about 6 minutes, adding flour as needed. Transfer to an oiled bowl. Cover and let rise until doubled, about 1½ hours.

Grease a large baking sheet.

Punch down dough, and knead a few times. Flatten into disk, then roll out to 14- x 6-inch rectangle. Cut lengthwise into three equal strips. Stretch and roll each strip by hand into a 28-inch rope. Line ropes up, side by side, on prepared baking sheet and pinch tops together.

Loosely braid, then form into ring, pinching ends together to seal. Fit eggs between ropes at evenly spaced intervals. Cover and let rise until almost doubled, about 30 minutes. (Press eggs back into dough if necessary.)

Preheat oven to 350 degrees F.

Brush top of loaf evenly with egg wash, being careful not to brush eggs. Bake 25 to 30 minutes or until deep golden. Cool on rack.

MAKES 1 LOAF

"In order to become a baker, I'd have to stop looking for answers and just bake some bread, not four times a year as a special occasion, not even once a month."
—*Nancy Silverton from*
Breads from the La Brea Bakery

PANETTONE

Panettone, the citrus- and nut-studded holiday bread from Italy that is almost a cake, makes wonderful toast for weeks after Christmas.

1 egg
2 egg yolks
¾ cup sugar
1 stick butter, melted and cooled
grated zest of 1 lemon
1 teaspoon anise extract
1 teaspoon anise seed
¼ cup candied citron *or* orange peel
¼ cup golden raisins
¼ cup pine nuts
2½ cups unbleached flour
2 teaspoons baking powder
½ teaspoon salt
1 cup milk

In a large bowl, beat egg and egg yolks with sugar until thick. Beat in butter. Add lemon zest, anise extract and seed, citron or orange peel, raisins, and pine nuts, and beat.

In a separate large bowl, combine flour, baking powder, and salt. Add half of dry ingredients to egg mixture, and mix. Stir in half of milk. Add remaining dry ingredients, and combine. Blend in remaining milk.

Preheat oven to 350 degrees F.

Fold down 2¾-inch flap on top of a brown paper lunch bag. Coat inside of the bag with nonstick vegetable spray. Set on a baking sheet and pour in batter. Bake about 1½ hours or until deep golden brown and a toothpick inserted in the center comes out clean. Cool slightly on rack, tear off bag, and cut in tall wedges. Or leave bread in the bag, wrap in foil, and cool completely.

MAKES 1 LOAF

KULICH

This towering Russian Easter bread is enriched with plenty of eggs and a river of sugary frosting dripping down its sides.

½ cup milk
2 sticks butter, room temperature
3 cups unbleached flour
1 egg
1 package dry yeast
¼ cup warm water
1 cup sugar
½ teaspoon salt
8 egg yolks
2 teaspoons vanilla
grated peel of 1 lemon
½ cup finely chopped blanched almonds
½ cup raisins
½ cup confectioners' sugar

In a small saucepan, bring ¼ cup milk and 2 tablespoons butter to boil. All at once, add ¼ cup flour. Remove from heat, and beat with a wooden spoon until mixture pulls away from the sides of the pan. Add egg, and beat until blended. Set aside.

In a large bowl, dissolve yeast in warm water, stir in 1 teaspoon sugar, and let stand 5 minutes. Stir cooked mixture into yeast mixture. Cover and let stand in a warm place until foamy, about 30 minutes.

In a separate bowl, beat remaining butter with salt and remaining sugar. Beat in egg yolks and vanilla. Stir into yeast mixture. Beat in 2½ cups flour alternately with ¼ remaining cup milk.

Turn out dough onto a surface dusted with remaining flour. Sprinkle lemon peel, almonds, and raisins over dough, and knead by hand to incorporate. Knead 10 minutes longer, or until smooth and elastic. Transfer to an oiled bowl. Cover and let rise in a warm place until doubled, at least 2 hours.

Grease insides of two 46-ounce juice cans.

Punch down dough and knead a few turns. Divide in half and place each piece in a prepared can. Cover and let rise until dough is 1 inch from top, about 2 hours.

Preheat oven to 350 degrees F.

Bake on lowest oven rack 15 minutes, then reduce heat to 300 degrees F, and bake 45 minutes longer, or until a toothpick inserted in the centers comes out clean. Cool breads in cans on a wire rack 10 minutes. Then turn out and lay horizontally on rack to cool completely.

In a small bowl, blend confectioners' sugar with 1 tablespoon water. To serve breads, stand upright and pour glaze evenly over tops, allowing some glaze to drizzle down the sides.

MAKES 2 LOAVES

STOLLEN

This rich Christmas bread from Germany is packed with dried fruit, candied fruit, nuts, and a healthy dollop of sugar and spice.

| 1 package dry yeast
½ cup warm milk
⅓ cup sugar
½ stick butter, melted and cooled
1 egg, lightly beaten
½ teaspoon salt
½ teaspoon ground mace
¼ teaspoon ground cardamom
2 to 2½ cups unbleached flour, or more
½ cup finely chopped blanched almonds
½ cup golden raisins
½ cup mixed chopped candied fruit
grated zest of 1 lemon
2 tablespoons confectioners' sugar

In a large bowl, stir yeast into warm milk until dissolved. Stir in sugar, butter, egg, salt, mace, and cardamom. Beat in about half the flour until well blended, then gradually beat in additional flour until stiff dough forms. Turn out onto a surface dusted with some remaining flour, and sprinkle with almonds, raisins, candied fruit, and lemon zest.

Knead by hand about 10 minutes, or until smooth and elastic, adding more flour as needed to prevent sticking. Transfer to an oiled bowl. Cover and let rise until doubled, at least 2 hours.

Grease a large baking sheet.

Punch down dough and knead a few turns. Shape into roughly 10- x 4-inch oval. Fold lengthwise, leaving about one third of bottom bare. Place on the prepared baking sheet, cover, and let rise in a warm place until almost doubled, about 45 minutes.

Preheat oven to 350 degrees F.

Bake about 45 minutes or until deep golden. Transfer to a wire rack and dust with confectioners' sugar. Cool.

MAKES 1 LOAF

"And whatever happened to that delectable dish, milk toast? I used to have it for lunch when I was a child, and it was a comfort when I didn't feel too well. Lovely crisp, buttered toast with hot milk poured over it—a delicious meal indeed."

—James Beard from Beard on Bread